# Vanished

## Book One of The Gwen St. James Affair

### Nicole McKeon

Tower Room Publishing

Copyright © 2023 by Nicole McKeon

All rights reserved.

This is a work of fiction. Names, characters, businesses, places, events, locales, and incidents are either the products of the author's imagination or used in a fictitious manner. Any resemblance to actual persons, living or dead, or actual events is purely coincidental. No portion of this book may be reproduced in any form without written permission from the publisher or author, except as permitted by U.S. copyright law.

# Content Notice

## PG 13

This book contains mature themes and some material that may not be suitable for every reader.

- Swearing (very minimal)

- Violence and violence toward minors

- Death of a minor (off page)

- Kidnapping

- Parental Abandonment

- Suicide

- Drug use (minor)

# Note from the author

Hello reader!

I'm so excited to welcome you into the world of Gwen St. James and all the magical shenanigans of New London. I have never fallen in love with a character as much as I love Gwen, and this cast has such a special place in my heart, I just know you will love them, too.

The Gwen St. James Affair is comprised of 6 books, which are already written and will be released regularly, as well as two companion romance novels featuring characters from the books. Both of those novels are being written one chapter at a time on my website and released to my members, along with the accompanying audiobooks. Beware: those novels might have a slow burn but they are spicy ;)

If you want to learn more, check out nicoleyork.com/lounge-member-signup

If you'd like extra goodies but the Lounge is not for you, I send fun updates to my newsletter subscribers every Tuesday.

- reading recs

- deleted scenes

- advanced chapters of new books

- scenes of the week

- reveals and sneak peeks

- bookish art

- contests & giveaways

- discounts

- updates

If you would like to join, you can do so at https://nicoleyork.com/novel-newsletter-landing

Writing isn't worth doing if it cannot be shared with readers like you. You make my dreams of writing for a living possible. Thank you.

# *Dedication*

For Amy.
You'll always be the missing piece of my heart.
Love, Sissy.

# 1

# Back Alley Brawls

## SALLY

**New London, East End 1900**

Following the sound of screams into the dark, narrow alleys of New London's East Side was a good way to get robbed, killed, or both, but Sally could not help herself. She knew better; life on the street was a merciless teacher. But the piteous cries pulled at her as if an invisible string was tied round her heart, and someone was tugging on it.

She should have kept her head down and continued home, should have celebrated her first honest pay by spoiling herself and Sam with fresh bread. They could have gone to bed with full bellies for once.

Instead, she crept toward the cries echoing off the stone buildings along New Market Street with a small iron bar clutched in one hand for protection.

Damsels in distress were an irresistible lure to naïve do-gooders; something the children of New London's streets took advantage of whenever possible. Sally used the damsel con more than once when she and Sam were close to starving. But there were more dangerous things than half-wild urchins roaming the streets after dark.

Sally knew it, but she snuck into the alley, anyway.

It was dark and stank of rotten food and other less appealing things. She breathed through her mouth, slinking through the shadows like a wraith until she caught sight of the source of the screams. The moon wasn't full yet, but it was high enough to peek between the narrow buildings and illuminate a distressing scene.

Sally forgot about bread, about her brother, about the pennies in her pocket and making it home safely, and charged into the alley with furious ringing in her ears.

The girl was small, perhaps twelve years old, but she fought valiantly against the two men who were trying to gag and bind her. Her pale blonde hair shone even in the near blackness as she kicked and scratched her attackers. But it was a losing battle. They were thin, as were most who made their living on the streets, but the men were still twice her height and weight, and strong as old leather.

Sally was not strong enough to beat or stop them. She told herself to run, but the strange, irresistible pull made her step into the alley.

Against her better sense, she shouted, "Oi! Piss off and let her be!"

All three combatants stilled as the men turned hard, dark eyes toward her. "What've you got to say about it, eh? You want a beatin'?"

Sally dimly realized the danger she was in, but she also recognized the face of the victim. It was Virginia, the girl who folded sheets two stations down from Sally. She was small and frail, and seeing her at the mercy of those men made Sally too furious to flee. She knew how it felt to be attacked by bigger, stronger opponents, and no one ever stood up for her.

"If you don't let her go, I'll make you!" Sally shouted, raising the iron bar.

"Yeah?" one man said as he left the struggling girl to his partner. "Let's see you try it, then, skivvy. Maybe we'll give you some of what we got for ol' puss, here."

Sally had lived on the streets long enough to know that being defensive only meant you didn't get the chance to hit back, so she did not wait for the man to advance or take up a superior position. She charged him, swinging the pipe as she screamed every swear word her father had ever shouted. The man was so shocked by her onslaught that she connected a few times, gashing him across the cheek and backing him toward his partner. But he hadn't survived this long by being weak.

He caught her arm, snatched the pipe out of her hand, and slapped her hard enough to blur her vision and make her ears ring. Then he sunk his fist deep into her gut, driving the breath from her lungs and dropping her to the dirty cobbles.

"If you keep squallin', I'll crack your stupid skull on those paving stones and let the rats eat whatever comes out."

His speech was followed by a kick. Sally rolled with the impact to stop the kick from breaking any ribs—something else she learned on the receiving end of her father's anger—and ended up in a puddle on the lee side of a stack of crates.

"Don't break her, Harry," the other man said. "We can get two for the price of one."

Harry advanced, clutching the iron bar and wiping the blood off his cheek with the back of his hand. "Nah, I want fair play for this scar I'm going to 'ave. I'll split her face open real quick like, and then we'll be gone."

Sally had to get to her feet, ignore the dizziness and the burning pain in her stomach, and get up. A scar would be the least of her worries if Harry caught her, but all she managed was a wobbly scrabble backward and a few painful breaths. She was going to die, and she wouldn't even have saved Virginia.

And Sam would be alone and hungry.

A clear voice cut the stagnant air of the alley like the peal of church bells. "And the valkyrie descended upon them with thunder and great fury to separate the living from the glorious dead!"

A sharp crack lit the alley in green flame and filled it with smoke, followed by a bitter stench that swamped the mildew stink. A shadowy silhouette emerged from the dark, lit by the fire in its hands.

"And those who dare her wrath by falling in cowardice," the figure intoned, "forfeit Valhalla and find themselves in the dark and lonely halls of Hel."

"Witch!" Harry's companion shouted.

In the sickly light, Harry's expression changed from rage to terror. He dropped the iron bar and bolted toward his companion, shouting, "Run, Will!"

The green fire sputtered and died, leaving the alley dark and drowned in smoke, echoing with the cries of the stolen girl.

Sally couldn't stand without falling over, but she managed to lunge forward and wrap her fingers around the iron bar Harry left on the cobbles.

"I got a weapon," she said, but her voice was unsteady. "Don't come no closer!"

"Any closer," the voice corrected.

Sally blinked back a wave of dizziness. "What?"

"Any closer, not 'no closer.' That is a double negative, my girl, and while I enjoy talking nonsense as much as the next woman, I much prefer to save it for afternoon tea. A dark alley at night is no place for nonsense."

None of that made sense to Sally, but the smoke was dissipating as she peered through the darkness, using the crates to steady herself. If it was a witch, she didn't want to be on the ground with no options.

One moment a dark figure stood wreathed in smoke, and the next a lady in a walking dress emerged with an umbrella in her hand and a strangely shaped hat perched atop her head. Or were there two ladies?

"Poor darling, you are a sight, aren't you? Are you hurt badly?"

Despite the sharp bolts of pain throbbing behind her eyes, Sally said, "I'm fine, thanks."

"Don't you lie prettily?" The lady said as she stepped over the alley garbage the way one might step over a tree root on a country path. "Your lip is bleeding and you've the beginning of what will be a beautiful black eye. In fact"—she leaned toward Sally and split again into two people—"you may have a concussion."

Sally tried to focus through the dark and the pounding in her head, but the world tilted. She caught her balance on the crate so she didn't tip off the side of it.

"Oops," the lady said, catching Sally before she toppled over. "There, there, my dear. Come along, let's get you cleaned up."

Sally meant to object, but everything spun around the way it did when she and Sam raised their arms, looked at the sky, and spun like tops until they couldn't stand up anymore.

The lady kept talking but Sally was floating and tilting and spinning like her father after a trip to the pub. She tried to say something about Virginia, felt the breeze on her face, heard the clop of horse's hooves.

Someone shook her.

Everything went quiet and dark.

The scent of beeswax, lavender, tea, and something bitter pulled Sally from the dark. Those were not the smells of home. The soft blanket, the crackling fire, and the musical humming were also alien. Where was the traffic, the stomping of the upstairs neighbor, and her scratchy wool blanket? She opened her eyes, then squeezed them shut against the headache pulsing in time with her heartbeat. A single glimpse of the room proved she was not in her cot by the little coal stove.

"I cannot see why you needed to bring her here, in any case," a woman's voice said in a low thrum that reminded Sally of buzzing bees.

"Because no one else would care for her as skillfully as you, Mrs. Chapman."

A snort. "You merely like to vex me, my lady. As if I don't have enough to do here trying to keep you out of trouble."

"And a wonderful job you do of it, too. Now, where is that book?"

"Which book, my lady?" That was a man's voice, calm and collected.

"The book on dwarven artifice, what was it called? By Hardfist the Elder?"

"I believe you shelved it next to A Treatise on Elven Literature in the Seventeenth Century, my lady."

"So I did, well played Mr. Yates. Where would I be without you?"

Sally used the moment of silence to clear her throat.

"Are you coming round, my girl?" a feminine voice said.

Hands at Sally's shoulders helped raise her and prop pillows at her back. She opened her eyes a slit to see the same strange hat worn by the woman in the alley, the one who made green fire in her hands.

Sally clutched the blanket to her chest and whispered, "Are you a witch?"

Brown eyes crinkled in a smile. "Indeed, not."

The woman turned her face so the steady light of the dwarven lamps illuminated her features. She was younger than Sally would have guessed, somewhere in her late twenties. She wasn't particularly pretty but had an engaging expression, clear skin a bit darker than Sally's own, and big brown eyes surrounded by thick lashes.

"Would I look like this if I were a witch? Do you see any warts, any wrinkles? Wait, don't answer. I do not think I want to hear what you may say. Rest assured, my dear, I am no witch."

"Then, how did you make the fire?"

"Why chemistry, of course. In fact—" She turned toward a butler standing with his hands clasped in front of him. "Mr. Yates, will you remind me to lessen the sugar in that recipe by a quarter? The fire was everything I'd hoped for but resulted in far too much smoke. No! Wait. The smoke might come in quite handy in the right circumstances. I shall simply do both."

"Very good, my lady. However, was it wise to test such a recipe whilst in danger?"

The lady snorted. Actually snorted. Sally had dipped her fingers into the pockets of many wealthy people and she'd never heard a lady make such a noise.

"Danger, Yates? Indeed, not. I had my umbrella, after all, should worse have come to worst."

Sally closed her eyes again and pressed the heels of both hands against her temples. She was in the home of a lady. Had been rescued by a lady who made fire in her hands but was not a witch. And Sam was home by himself, likely wondering where his sister was. She needed to get out of there.

"Mrs. Chapman," the lady said, "do you happen to have the tea ready? I believe our guest is still suffering the effects of her run-in with the seedier side of New London."

Mrs. Chapman, who looked like a vulture in a dress, gestured at the tea service she was preparing with the flick of a bony wrist. "It would have been finished much sooner if you would give me leave to pluck that pest of yours so he could not fly up and get into my spices and herbs. A few cut feathers is exactly what the beast needs."

An amused croak came from the far side of the room. An enormous raven was perched on top of one of the many bookshelves. It turned its black head, tilted one eye at the thin woman, and said in a masculine voice, "He's a pretty bird."

The older woman pointed at him like a witch laying down a curse. "I will have you one day, Aristotle. See if I don't."

"While we wait for that titanic clash," the lady said, "perhaps the tea?"

Mrs. Chapman's dark brows lowered over her beaklike nose in a scowl that said she'd rather be doing anything but serving tea so late at night, but she carried the tray to the small side table near Sally and the lady. The older woman did not want her here. She did not belong in a place like this. Around people like these. *Women who don't know their place come to grief*, her mother had always said.

"Do you take sugar and cream?" the lady asked.

"Ah... I've never... that is, if you don't mind, my lady, I'm most grateful for all you've done, but I'd be happy to see myself home."

The lady dismissed Sally's offer with a flick of her fingers. "Indeed, I do mind. A rescuer has got some rights, after all. And I'd like to ask you a few questions before you go. But first." She scooped a couple of spoonfuls of sugar into a delicate little cup and stirred it while pouring cream. How could someone make simple motions look so graceful?

There was no way to refuse the tea without insulting the woman, so Sally took the cup. The porcelain was thin and warm in her hands, with flowers painted in blue all around the outside. She'd never held anything so lovely. Even so, she waited until the lady had taken a sip of her own tea, poured from the same pot, before she drank. It was sweet and rich, with a hint of bitterness and something else that went straight to her head.

"Just a bit of brandy," the lady said. "To help the medicine go down."

"Medicine?"

"Our Mrs. Chapman is gifted with healing herbs. I'd wager she'll have your headache in hand in no time."

"What you call gifted, I call hard-earned skill," Mrs. Chapman groused.

"Quite so. Very well then, my dear. May I ask your name?"

Before she thought better of hiding her identity, Sally found herself saying, "Sally, my lady."

The woman smiled and Sally smiled back, but she did not trust this strange, well-bred lady who showed up in dark alleys to rescue poor girls. But there was such kindness and good nature in her eyes. It was impossible not to at least begin to like her. Or was that the brandy?

"I'm glad to have met you, Sally. My name is Gwenevere St. James, but you may call me Gwen."

"Oh, I can't do that, my lady."

"Of course, you can. I've heard proof of your tongue and teeth functioning quite well. In fact, I plan to use some of your curses the next time I need to take someone down a peg."

Sally blushed. It was one thing to swear at a cutthroat trying to kidnap a helpless girl, and quite another to scream them in front of a lady.

"Where did you learn such words? They were some of the most impressive imprecations I've ever heard."

"My father worked on the docks."

"Ah," Lady Gwen said with a smile. "That profession certainly does introduce one to the more colorful side of language."

"Yes, ma'am."

"And how is your head, now?"

"A bit better."

"I'm glad to hear it. Are you hungry? Would you like a sandwich before we begin?"

At the word sandwich, the raven leaped from the bookcase and sailed down to the edge of the chaise behind Sally's head. She jerked out of the way, making a spike of pain shoot through her ribcage, and glared at the bird. He hopped to the edge of the cushion nearest the tea and stared at the small sandwiches with a bead-black eye.

"Sandwich," he croaked.

Lady Gwen made a clucking sound and shooed the bird backward, but the raven side-stepped her hand and pushed forward to nuzzle Sally's cheek with his beak. She froze, not wanting to startle him, not with his sharp beak so close to her ear. He tilted his head as if examining her, then looked at Lady Gwen and said, "Feed us, woman."

She chuckled and reached for the plate. "Aristotle, how rude. Allow the guest to choose a sandwich before you shove your feathered face in, and do stop being so bossy. Mrs. Chapman, do we happen to have any marmalade?"

"How you can eat marmalade on everything will never cease to amaze," Mrs. Chapman said, pulling a small jar from her apron pocket. "You will make yourself sick with it, one day, mark me."

Aristotle cawed and hopped back and forth impatiently. Lady Gwen chose a sandwich, offered the tray to Sally, then allowed the bird to pluck his meal neatly from the pile. Once he had secured his prize, the bird flew off to enjoy the meal on the head of a carved bust sitting near the window.

The sandwich was as good as the tea had been, and Sally wondered if a few bruises were not a worthy price to pay to be warm and well-fed.

After they'd eaten, Lady Gwen surreptitiously dipped her finger into the little pot and stuck it in her mouth as she set the tea things aside. "Do you feel able to answer some questions for me?"

The ease Sally had begun to feel toward the pleasant woman with the kind brown eyes stuttered as suspicion clawed back into her mind. She glanced from the staid Mr. Yates by the door to Mrs. Chapman, who loomed over them like a vulture looking for something, or someone, to consume. As warm and comfortable as she was, Sally wasn't safe. No matter how nice these people seemed, they would be quick to turn on her if she gave them a reason. That's what wealthy people did. So she'd be careful and make herself useful until she could escape.

"As best as I can, ma'am."

"That is all anyone can hope to do. Your insight may help us sort out this affair."

"Sort out, ma'am?"

"Indeed."

"What's to sort out? It was just a kidnapping."

Lady Gwen rolled her eyes. "And what is the world coming to when we can dismiss abduction so easily? No, that's not a question you can answer, my dear. What I mean is this: there was more happening in the alley than a couple of street toughs looking to earn a few dollars or... well, never mind about that. There were several strange things you may not have noticed that I would very much like answers to. Can you tell me how you came to be in the alley after you left the laundry?"

"I—how did you know I worked at the laundry? My lady," she added the honorific when she recovered from her surprise.

"I can smell the solvents on you, there are leftover soap flakes caked to your shoe, and your hands have new blisters in places that suggest working a dolly. You appear to be of an age to enter service, so it seemed a logical conclusion."

Sally considered her hands. The new blisters on her palms stared back at her like pairs of red-rimmed eyes. Her own powers of observation weren't lacking. Sally knew where people kept their valuables, who was worth stealing from, and who was too suspicious or dangerous to risk an encounter with. She could tell someone's profession by their clothes and the way they moved. She earned those skills over four years of scratching out a living on the street, but she'd never suspected someone in the upper class might use the same tricks on her. If that were the case, Lady Gwen might be able to tell if Sally lied. So, she recounted her experience honestly, from the time she left the laundry late and tired with a few pennies in her pocket, to the time she lost consciousness.

"When you entered the alley," Lady Gwen said, "did you notice anything on the ground or the walls?"

"Only the rubbish and the water."

"And the man who attacked you, was anything strange about him?"

Sally frowned. He'd been of average height, thin but strong, and he'd stunk of body odor and stale tobacco. But the same was true of a thousand men. "No, ma'am."

Lady Gwen stood and pulled her hat from her head, revealing thick brown curls the color of bitter chocolate. "So, you entered the alley upon hearing the cries of the poor girl we could not save?"

"Virginia," Sally put in, sadly.

"Virginia? You knew her?"

"Only that she began work a few days before me, and her name was Virginia. She was quiet."

"Was that the reason you put yourself in such danger, because you were friends?"

Sally blushed. "I only know of her from work. But I knew I should have left well enough alone. I've seen more than one robbery use a damsel in distress to lure people in." She didn't say she'd taken part in those robberies. Best to leave that part out of her tale.

"But when I heard her cry it felt like something was pulling me forward and I couldn't stop myself, though I knew better."

"Have you ever felt such a sensation before?"

"Sensation?"

"The pull you felt to help, the one you couldn't stop."

"No, ma'am." Her instincts for self-preservation were stronger than that. Usually.

"Can you fetch me the book we spoke of, Mr. Yates?"

Mr. Yates crossed the room to the bookcase on silent feet. He had the kind of broad shoulders and soft belly that could either be nice to hug, or dangerous in a fight. It was hard to tell beneath his uniform. Though his face was calm and pleasant, his indifferent eyes missed nothing, and he moved like the kind of man Sally would avoid on the street.

"Thank you for telling me your tale, Sally. I believe, if I can follow the clues left me, we might be able to save the girl. Or, at the very least, track down who kidnapped her and stop them."

Sally's stomach sank into her shoes. "We?"

Lady Gwen turned to her with bright eyes as Mr. Yates handed over the large tome. When she smiled, a dimple appeared in her right cheek, just below the small mole high on her cheekbone.

"You're coming to work for me, of course. Aristotle likes you and he is an excellent judge of character."

"Work for you, my lady?"

"Of course. Unless you'd rather stay in the laundry."

Sally clenched her fists, and the blisters on her palms stung.

# 2
# Meet Lady St. James
## GWEN

Convincing young Miss Dawes to stay the night rather than venture back to the flat she shared with her brother took the better part of an hour and all my considerable powers of persuasion. In the end, it wasn't my charm that stopped her from disappearing into the night, but her inability to stand without collapsing.

She had shrugged off my offer to send James out with the buggy to fetch the boy and proclaimed she would go, let her brother know she was safe, and return in the morning for her first day of work. But as soon as she tried to stand, the strength went right out of her legs. Mrs. Chapman and I hauled the girl back onto the sofa and waited for the medicine to kick in. As she fell asleep, she muttered to herself about Samuel, how she needed to protect him, and how he would never trust a stranger who appeared at their door without her. And rightly so.

I did not like the idea of the boy staying alone in their one-room flat, but from the sound of it, the Dawes siblings had been forced to grow up quickly. We had little choice but to trust the twelve-year-old to have the good sense to keep himself safely indoors at night. Morning would be soon enough to risk allowing Sally back on the street after she'd nearly been beaten to death.

If my suspicions were right, she'd also been touched by magic, which would only make her more vulnerable to the same spell if she encountered it again, and I had no intention of allowing her to fall prey to the monsters who abducted the girl I could not save.

Every time I closed my eyes, I saw Virginia's young face in the sickly glow of my fire, red and streaked with tears, drawn into lines of desperate panic. Her hair was the same honey-gold color Lia's had been, and the sight of it had nearly stopped my heart with memories. But the children were in danger, and I did not have time to get lost in the past. I hadn't even time for a plan.

One might think confronting two strange men in an alley at night with no plan was a bad idea. And it was. They would think so, too. That a lady should be abroad on her own so late, and without a chaperone, would never have crossed their minds, which put the element of surprise at my disposal. I had also been in the very end stages of experimentation on how to light smoke grenades without a source of fire and happened to have one in my coat pocket. And, of course, my umbrella. A lady can never be too prepared.

"Do you truly mean to hire the girl?"

I blinked, pulled myself from my reverie, and focused on my housekeeper. "Forgive me, Mrs. Chapman, what did you say?"

"Getting lost in your thoughts and talking to yourself again, I see."

"A girl needs clever conversation every once in a while, my dear lady. Keeps the mind sharp."

She scowled at my prim tone, if not my meaning, and repeated, "Do you truly mean to hire this street child? She's had no training, and she smells like... well, something it wouldn't be polite to name."

She stood over the sleeping girl, glaring down with her arms folded, looking for all the world like a malevolent beanpole with her black skirt and blouse buttoned up to her chin. Amused affection washed over me, but I treated the question with the serious answer it deserved.

"There is more to that girl than meets the eye, Mrs. Chapman, I would swear to it. I cannot allow her back onto the streets. She is trying to support herself and her brother on the wages of a laundress. There is no future in that."

"These children are not your responsibility. An orphanage is the best place for them. If you let the girl live and work here, sure as sunrise I'll wake up one morning and the silverware will be gone."

I rolled my eyes. As if I could not afford to replace the silverware. "She fought a grown man to save someone in danger. I'll not let such bravery and selflessness be wasted in a laundry."

"Growing up on the streets will have given the girl all sorts of dangerous habits, and you will be the one to suffer from them, mark me."

"Indeed, she has grown up with dangerous habits, and they kept her alive long enough for me to find her. If she were a gentle, proper thing, she'd be dead."

Mrs. Chapman frowned down at the blonde head on the pillow. "And how did you stumble upon this young scamp? She cannot have been in any part of the city safe for you."

I lay The Theory and Practice of Artificery in my lap so that when I raised an eyebrow, I could accompany the gesture with the dramatic thump of the heavy book closing. One should always indulge in melodrama if one can. "Pray, Mrs. Chapman" thump—"what part of the city is safe for me?"

Her lips thinned until they disappeared. She knew better. No part of the city was truly safe for me, even if a footman trailed behind, but I did not want her to dwell on the fact that I had outgrown her ability to protect me, so I said, "If you want to know, I was on my way back from the milliners when I heard the girl scream, 'Go to the devil you poxy-faced, bootlicking arsewipe,' in the most glorious tones of pubescent fury I've ever had the pleasure of encountering."

Mrs. Chapman's grey eyes bulged nearly out of her head and her cheeks went up in flames. I had the distinct pleasure of watching her cover her lips with her fingers as she regarded the girl. Purposefully offending Mrs. Chapman's delicate sensibilities was a pleasure I only allowed myself on rare occasions, though I seemed to do so by accident with nearly every breath since I was six years old. If Sally had been awake, the housekeeper would have scolded me soundly for repeating such language. As she considered the girl, however, her expression slowly changed to something like respect.

"Well," she said, turning away to clean the forgotten tea service, "the hat maker is at least a marginally respectful establishment, though I cannot fathom why you should be there at such a late hour."

That reminder smothered my amusement. How easily the dear woman forgot who I was. "I would not harm Mr. Bywater's income by being seen in his shop during the day. When I need to visit, we coordinate late hours and I pay him well for his time."

Her nostrils flared as she hefted the tea tray, but that was the only sign she was offended on my behalf. The older woman may browbeat and scold me, but Abigail Chapman never could bring herself to see me as anything other than a lady, despite my most valiant efforts to prove otherwise. And even after being promoted to Head Housekeeper, she could not leave behind her early role as my nursemaid. Dear soul.

"You had best put those books away and get cleaned up before bed," she ordered on her way out the door.

We would both pretend I'd listen, and we both knew I would still be up for hours. My mind was too full of everything I had seen. This kidnapping had been no common affair. Ordinary criminals did not employ magical symbols. Such symbols required years of study to produce properly and there were dangerous consequences should one fail to draw every line perfectly. That made the knowledge rare and expensive, so I needed to capture as much of the memory as possible before it eluded me.

As soon as Mrs. Chapman's footfalls disappeared down the hallway, I hurried to the desk for pen and paper and began sketching what I had seen. I put myself back in the alley, smelled the urine and mildew and rot, felt the burn of the gunpowder as pressure from my fingers ignited the fuse of the smoke grenade, heard Virginia's cries, and felt the chill of the night air on my cheeks. The vision came back clear, still strong and sharp, so I drew as quickly as I could.

The fire had nearly blinded me in the dark (I did need to lessen the sugar and decrease the gunpowder in that recipe), but in the brief time before the flames died, I'd seen several noteworthy things. First, there had been a symbol scrawled on the ground in the center of the alley beneath the second man and the struggling girl. Second, several circular markings had been inked on the left wrist of the man who beat Sally, which had been exposed while his arm was raised to strike her. They were like dwarven runes, though not as angular.

When I was done, a relatively clean sketch lay before me showing the layout of the alley, the stacks of wooden crates and barrels waiting to be cleaned and reused, the puddles, and the positions of the combatants, as well as what they wore. I set the preliminary sketch aside and copied the symbols I had seen onto a fresh sheet of paper. They were not perfect, but they gave me a place to begin.

"Good evening, Mr. Yates," I said as I copied out the last of the runes. "You're up late."

The butler entered the study and approached the desk on silent feet. "Yes, ma'am."

He stopped next to me and peered down at my drawings with characteristic thoughtfulness, asking after a moment of study, "You believe magic may be at play?"

I pointed at the symbol I'd just finished transcribing from my sketch. "This was drawn in blue chalk on the cobblestones in the center of the alley. It was partly worn away—I assume by the struggle but perhaps also by passing feet—so this is all I saw. The outer circle contains and constrains the magic, defines and gives it shape. I recognize a few of the symbols from my studies abroad, standard marks of protection and power. Those within the inner circle, however, appear dwarven, though not a perfect representation of the runes I've studied. Those are mixed with symbols I recollect clearly from the diary of Millicent Edevane, which is not a grimoire, so please do not tattle to Mrs. Chapman that I have read it."

"Tattle?"

"Oh, I know your propensity for carrying tales, Mr. Yates. You cannot fool me."

"Your secrets are safe with me, madame."

I gave him a small smile.

"So what of these symbols?"

I tried to regain my previous train of thought. "It is quite beyond me to see how the symbols are related, and I can only decipher a few of the runes. Dwarves are notoriously secretive with knowledge of artificery, but I believe this symbol"—I tapped a square with a line through it and three dots on the right side—"denotes the following rune will contain a command, and this one"—I tapped another symbol just beneath the square—"is like the rune engraved on street lamps allowing the filaments inside to draw and store energy from the sun."

"A command to gather? To draw something?"

"So it would seem. Miss Dawes admitted she felt a compulsion to answer the cries of the victim."

"She may have merely wanted to help."

I eyed the butler. He stood there like a solemn bear, with his dark eyes placid in his swarthy face and his hands held loosely in front of his belly. Despite being a man of few words, Mr. Yates was no fool, which meant he was playing devil's advocate for my sake. I rarely had someone to share my thoughts with, so I took full advantage of the opportunity.

"Very well. What can we deduce from the circumstances of a fourteen-year-old girl from the Eastside with better manners and diction than the rest of her class? Who is caring for herself and her younger brother, but has blisters on her hands instead of calluses to denote a history of hard work? Any other girl her age would have long ago entered service and have the calluses associated with her position. With such soft hands, while living in a flat instead of an orphanage, Miss Dawes can only have been thieving, and doing it well. And thieves who make stupid decisions end up dead. Investigating cries in a dark alley at night is, most certainly, a stupid decision. Without the symbol to draw her, I doubt very much if our new maid would have answered those cries."

"But you answered them."

"Mr. Yates, I never would have suspected such cruel humor lurked in your soul. Stupid? Me? How dare you suggest such a thing."

The ghost of a smile touched his eyes.

I considered my friend. Yes, I realized it was bad form to befriend one's staff, but I had made a career out of transgressing the gentler rules of society and both Mr. Yates and Mrs. Chapman were uncommonly good people. Not to befriend them would have been foolishness, and I remain convinced that arrogance is the capital mistake of my class. And, to tell the truth, I do not have so many friends I can afford to snub those closest to me.

"Very well," I admitted, "you are right. But I was prepared, and all's well that ends well."

"Might I ask a question?"

"Please."

"Is there any chance someone else drew the symbol and your kidnappers were merely in the wrong place at the right time?"

I narrowed my eyes and ran through the information I'd gathered. Despite New London being an incredibly cosmopolitan city, with humans, elves, and dwarves all cohabiting in something resembling peace, magic remained a taboo subject, even for the rare people who believed it was real. And given the difficulty of obtaining such information, let alone the skill to use it, the chance of someone like Harry the Kidnapper stumbling across useful magic on his own was incredibly slim.

I said, "If it were not for the unique circumstances, I would certainly suspect someone with more time and wealth. Magical knowledge does not come cheap and using it isn't easy. Still, given what I saw, I believe it was the criminals. The drawing was in chalk, and already half worn away by the time I appeared on the scene. There were still puddles in the alley from the midday rain, so it's unlikely to have been drawn any earlier than this evening. Otherwise, the weather would have washed it away."

"What next, then, my lady?"

I took a moment to consider. If Sally was drawn, as I suspected, by the symbols within the circle on the ground, then likely the other girl was, as well. I didn't have enough evidence to tell whether the spell had been focused on young, light-haired girls or if the girls who appeared merely happened to be the first two victims within range. Since I had felt no such compulsion, I was inclined to think the spell must have been more specific. And the symbols were certainly magical even though they were not common, and practicing witches had been outlawed in New London for more than a hundred years.

More than that, why would someone go to all the work of drawing the symbols to lure in young women when run-of-the-mill kidnappings were not uncommon? The only way to answer those questions would be to learn what the symbols meant.

"I must find an artificer willing to share delicate information with me," I said with a sigh of resignation.

"I do not envy you that task."

"Then I suppose I had better not ask you to do it. Really, Mr. Yates, I was counting on you. You are such a disappointment to me."

"Can you bear it, my lady?"

"If I must."

"How will you get them to talk?"

Good question. "I shall think of something. Even the most stubborn lock has a key, does it not? In the meantime, I'd better notify Scotland Yard."

If Mr. Yates were the type to snort or roll his eyes, he would have. My previous entanglements with Scotland Yard had not been fruitful.

He said, "Then you have my best wishes twice over, ma'am. Can I do anything for you?"

Can you save the girl I abandoned to the dark? "No, Mr. Yates, thank you. You may retire."

He bowed and left me chewing my lip. There was no way to know what those men wanted with the girl. But I may still find her if I could patch together the clues left at the scene of the crime and decipher the symbols on the ground. I refused to leave another girl lost with no one to find her.

Unbidden, a vision of Lia's face as I'd last seen it floated to the front of my memory and crowded out the puzzle I was trying to solve. Her blue eyes were amused, the curl of her lip mocking, her golden hair a halo beneath the crown of flowers we'd woven that afternoon. The hole in my chest felt endless, a hungry void growing to devour everything I had learned to love. I didn't want to remember her or relive the worst day of my life.

I yanked a small key from the hidden pocket in my skirt, unlocked the lowest drawer of the desk, and pulled a bottle of laudanum from the compartment. A quick, small sip would do. I let my eyes close, ignoring the bitter burn, and waited for the euphoric rush. When it hit, the vision of Lia disappeared. The bottle was heavy in my hand. Another sip would be so easy to take, would stave off any other memories...

I dropped the bottle into the drawer, locked it, and pocketed the key. Virginia deserved a lucid mind on her side, which was the only thing I had to offer.

Tomorrow I would return to the alley to examine the symbols in the light of day, fetch young Samuel if he could be fetched, notify Scotland Yard of the kidnapping, and find an artificer willing to share closely guarded trade secrets and cultural history with a human.

"I shall take your best wishes, Mr. Yates," I murmured as I closed my eyes and let my head fall back on my shoulders. "I shall certainly need them."

"He's a pretty bird," Aristotle said as he peered at me from his favorite perch atop the bookshelf.

"Indeed, he is. It appears to be just you and me, pretty bird. How shall we spend our evening?"

The raven left his perch and sailed down to land on my shoulder and pick at my hair with delicate clicks of his beak.

"Want to help me save a lost girl?"

He tilted his head at me, making the lamplight shimmer like oil on the feathers of his neck. "Save the girl."

"Shh. Don't wake our sleeper. Of course, Mrs. Chapman put enough medicine in her tea to keep the girl asleep for several hours more, so I doubt even your cawing could wake her."

"Cawing?" He sounded terribly offended.

I laughed and stroked his back. "Please forgive me. Your voice is lovely. Now" —I hefted the book and cleared a spot for it on the desk— "shall we get to work?"

# 3

## *An Unexpected Guest*

## GWEN

It was after three in the morning when I finally hauled myself up the stairs. Mrs. Chapman left electric lamps burning, and I thumbed them down as I passed, letting the stair and hallway behind me fall into darkness. Charlotte, the upstairs girl Mrs. Chapman hired after my return, was sleeping in a chair by my door. Her cap had fallen to the side, and her black curls peeked out beneath the brim.

Poor girl, I should have remembered she would be there, waiting to help me undress. I put a hand on her shoulder.

"Charlotte? Wake up, my girl. Take yourself to bed. And sleep as long as you need in the morning."

Her eyes popped open. "My lady! I'm so sorry, here." She stood and fixed her cap. "May I help you prepare for bed?"

"No, Charlotte. Get yourself to sleep. Do you need a candle?"

She narrowed her eyes at me just long enough to be certain I didn't need her, then said, "No, ma'am, thank you."

Then she was gone.

Despite my efforts to corrupt the girl with science and other shenanigans, Charlotte had remained thoroughly disengaged and professional. She was rarely seen, seldom heard, and she was the joy of Mrs. Chapman's life. The girl was highly recommended and knew nothing of my history other than I was an heiress and daughter of the Duke of Wainwright, so she hadn't bothered to look for more respectable employment elsewhere. That made her the catch of the year, as far as my housekeeper was concerned.

I opened the door and began peeling myself out of the walking dress I'd chosen for my evening errand, using the plackets and clever stitchery hiding the buttons and laces along the front and sides of the outfit. I didn't want to be unfashionable, but I did want to alter my clothing on my own, without relying on a second pair of hands, as more fashionable dresses were designed to do. After all, only the wealthy could afford consistent help buttoning up the back of an expensive dress.

What utter rubbish. Aside from a display of wealth, who wanted to rely on another pair of hands to do something as fundamental as dressing? In my travels, I had seen and worn clothing infinitely more manageable than popular fashions in Europe and found the ability to dress and undress myself desirable on more than one memorable occasion.

Only elven dressmakers had the skill to create hidden plackets unnoticeable to the untrained eye, and since no one but I required such feats of tailoring, they charged accordingly. Mama nearly had a heart attack when I ordered the first dress and wrote me a strongly worded letter about thrift and extravagance. But even she could not argue that the dresses were unsuitable. The faux buttons on the back maintained the appearance of wealthy propriety while retaining the flexibility of changing at will. Spending my late and estranged father's money made it a compromise I was more than happy to accept.

I tossed the garments on the chair and turned toward the bed. A mostly naked man slept on my bed with both arms flung across the pillows. Moonlight filtering through the windows showed acres of exposed flesh and shined on the empty cup and bottle of wine on the side table.

"Dammit," I muttered to myself, but smiled, anyway. Ashley or Andrew—I could not remember which because I had been more than a little intoxicated at the time—had been pleasant enough company last night. But he was supposed to have left while I was out on my errand and Mrs. Chapman was busy planning the menu with our chef, Monsieur.

Apparently, the wine and comfortable bed were more tempting than whatever responsibilities he might have had today. It was a good thing for all of us that I had a very strict rule about who entered my room and when. If poor Charlotte walked in to tidy things in the morning and discovered my guest in a revealing state of deshabille, she would be ruined, and Mrs. Chapman would never forgive me for running off her favorite maid. So, I crossed the room to confront my guest.

"Wake up," I said, patting his cheek. "I would like my bed back for the night, if you don't mind."

He mumbled something in his sleep, rolled toward me, wrapped both arms about my chest, and pulled me into the bed. I barely restrained a surprised squeal. Ashley–if that was his name–wasn't a large man, but he was strong enough, and he pulled me down to bury his face against my neck, mumbling something made unintelligible by sleep or wine or both.

Had I not been so tired, another romp might have been worthwhile, though I will admit the hands roaming along my back felt rather nice. But I was tired, and he should not be here, so I used my hands and elbows to lever myself out of his grasp and stare down with exasperation.

"Fate has already smiled upon you once, dear boy, and she is a fickle mistress. Do not push your luck."

"You make no sense, darling," he slurred. "But it is charming. Come here."

Clopping hooves and carriage wheels echoed up from the street outside, loud enough to stop whatever reply I had been about to make. The fool had left a window open. I pressed my hand over the man's mouth as a deep sense of foreboding blossomed in my chest.

The vehicle stopped.

I held my breath.

Mrs. Chapman's rapid but uneven footfalls sounded in the hallway. Double damn. I grabbed my ardent guest by the wrist and dragged him off the bed. He hit the ground with a loud thump and an "Oof."

"Be quiet," I hissed, just before the housekeeper knocked.

I took a breath to steady myself, feigned a yawn, and said, "Yes, Mrs. Chapman?"

The door opened and the hallway light shone on the fuzzy mess of hair Mrs. Chapman had gathered into a hasty bun. Her eyes were wide with panic, but she paused and said, "Are you well, My lady? I heard–"

"Fell out of bed," I interrupted, ignoring the fingers wrapped possessively around my calf. "No need for concern."

Mrs. Chapman clasped her long, bony fingers in front of herself and said, "Oh, but there is, I'm afraid. It's the Duchess. She's here."

Of course, she was. I'd known it from the moment I heard the carriage stop. Who else would arrive unannounced at this time of night? Well, I had enjoyed several months of freedom before she realized I was in town, and all good things must end.

But endings were the last thing on my guest's mind, because his hand began a slow slide toward my thigh. I clamped my knees together, trapping the wandering limb, and tried not to let panic show on my face. If Mrs. Chapman realized there was a man in my bed, the scandal would make her expire on the spot, and her screams would bring the entire house–and Mama–down upon me. Whatever freedom I had left would be stripped away as neatly as the peel from an apple.

"Very good, Mrs. Chapman," I said in an impressively calm voice. "Thank you for letting me know. Please tell Mama I am sleeping and not to disturb me. And do keep her out of the study, if you can."

Mrs. Chapman looked affronted. "I will not try to stop Her Grace from using any room in the house she chooses."

"Would you like to explain to Her Grace why a young orphan girl from the East End is sleeping in the study, then?"

Her expression told me she would rather swallow a swarm of bees, so I gave her a winsome smile, tried not to wiggle as my guest made an effort to free his hand, and said, "Thank you, Mrs. Chapman, that will be all."

She gave me a disapproving glare before hurrying away to ready the Ducal suite for Mama. As formidable as Mrs. Chapman was, no one pitted themselves against Her Grace the Duchess of Wainwright. Not even I could resist her. While my father had been off living whatever life seemed best to him that did not include us, my mother ran the estate, raised her daughters, presided over disagreements in the parish, and—in effect—ran the entire countryside around Wainwright Manor with an iron fist coated in a velvet glove.

She had even bullied the queen once when she stayed at Wainwright during her trip north to Scotland. My mother was a truly frightening human, more so because she dominated people with grace and charm, rather than outright threats. And she had seen fit to come to town and manage my life. As soon as I returned home from abroad, I knew this would happen, eventually. But I had hoped to have a few months to prepare myself before relinquishing the hard-won control of my life.

Mrs. Chapman's footsteps disappeared down the hall and I released the wayward hand to search for its owner's clothing. Ashely/Andrew sat up and gave me a blurry-eyed smile probably meant to be charming.

"Get up, you lout. We've got to get you out of here before anyone sees you."

It took several minutes to wrestle the man into his clothing and herd him out of my room. Walking him to the servant's stairs unseen was easy enough, with the rest of the household trying to prepare for Mama, but guiding him down the stairs was an entirely different matter. The servant's stairs were cramped and dark compared to the grand staircase. Ashley/Andrew bounced off the walls several times, careening into me and nearly dragging us both down. The servants' entrance was also in the basement, meaning I had to survive three flights of treacherous stairs while guiding a mostly drunk man who kept trying to grab me in inconvenient places.

Finally, we reached the bottom stair. I stopped, planting one hand on his chest to keep him still long enough to listen for movement in the basement. It was mostly quiet, but–

The basement door opened, and Mr. Yates stood there, already in his suit, his face impassive. A click echoed down the staircase, followed by the upstairs door shutting and the sound of hurrying feet mixed with low, panicked voices.

"Her Grace prefers honey," Mrs. Chapman said from above, "not sugar in her tea."

She was probably speaking to Charlotte as they headed for the kitchen. That meant, within moments, fully half of the household staff would know I had snuck a man into my bed. They wouldn't know about the men before him, but I was an unmarried woman, and to them, one was as good as twenty.

I turned the full force of my panicked eyes on Mr. Yates and braced myself for a proper scolding. Being a pariah in the eyes of the public was a worthy price to pay if it meant living a life I chose, but I refused to suffer that fate in my own home. Not in the eyes of these people. And Mrs. Chapman was nearing the first-floor landing.

Mr. Yates sighed, pulled open the basement door, and motioned us through with a tilt of his head before climbing the stairs to intercept the housekeeper and her minion. I ushered my guest down the hall past the butler's pantry and wine cellar, and to the door of the servants' entrance. He tried to kiss me goodbye, but I pushed him none-too-gently into the chill October night.

"It was fun while it lasted," I whispered, "but do kindly forget you ever met me, sir."

Ashley/Andrew was apparently not the type to hold grudges, and he gave me a good-natured wave and disappeared into the night, only wobbling once or twice. I ghosted back down the hall, climbed the stairs at full speed, and slid into the chilly sheets while gritting my teeth.

If Mama had not seen fit to show up at such a godforsaken hour, I might have had a warm bed and a warm body to share it with. Of course, everything would change, now, not merely my nightly escapades. She would expect the behavior of the heiress to Wainright to be beyond reproach. Eccentricity was allowable, but impropriety and, in her eyes, low morality, were not; which would include searching the East End for magical kidnappers.

I could live without male company, but I refused to give up on the girl. I would employ every sneaky trick I'd spent six years learning to solve this mystery while my mother shared the townhouse and received callers and generally held court. I was certain to get dragged through dinner parties and trips to the opera where other aristocrats would whisper snide remarks about me just loud enough to overhear. And I would have to do it all while ferreting out who taught magic to common thugs, rescuing poor Virginia, and retrieving Sally's recalcitrant little brother.

Not to mention convincing Scotland Yard that I had witnessed a magical kidnapping.

Lovely.

Then again, I thought as I pulled the covers up to my chin, what was life without a bit of a challenge?

# 4
## Concerning Little Brothers

### SALLY

Sally woke with a gasp and her stomach lurched as she fell off the couch. The blanket had somehow tangled round her legs, and she fought to free herself. Where on earth was she? Flashes of the night, of blonde hair, and a shadow spewing green smoke and fire, came back to her. Of course. She'd stumbled upon a kidnapping last night, gotten herself into a fight, and now... she was in Lady Gwen's study.

She'd slept warm and comfortable in the extravagant home, but Sam was probably cold and scared. And Virginia was gone, lost to the night.

She didn't want to think of Virginia, now. She wanted to calm her stomach and recover from the shock of waking up in a strange place. Sally resumed her seat on the chaise and pulled the warm blanket back into place. Her headache was mostly gone, and her ribs only ached when she moved quickly. She'd been incredibly, ridiculously lucky. By all rights, she should have been bleeding in an alley. She closed her eyes and said a quick prayer for Virginia... and that Sam was smart enough to stay home and not go looking for her.

She wanted to go home last night, but when she tried to stand, a wave of dizziness buckled her knees. The idea of Sam by himself, wondering if she'd left him as their father had, or if she was dead, like their mother, made her eyes well with tears.

The open window drapes revealed dawn was still half an hour away. If she left now, she could sneak back to the Narrows before anyone knew she was gone. It was the smart move, the safe move. And pocketing a few trinkets to pawn at the nearest fence was easy, enough.

Sally scanned the room. Last night the headache and questions had distracted her, and then the tea laced with brandy, so she had no attention to spare for her surroundings. But it was much easier to focus now that she was recovered, and since pink light just touched the horizon, no one was likely to bother her for a while.

The study was large, with a high ceiling, and a bank of windows along one wall that let in the weak morning light. Bookshelves lined the opposite wall, filled with so many tomes it made her dizzy. How much knowledge was stored in this room alone? She'd never learned to read, but if she had, she would have devoured every book. There was no use in bemoaning her fate, she reminded herself. Street urchins didn't need to learn to read, just to work.

The raven sat on his perch with his head turned toward his back, beak tucked beneath a wing in sleep. Sally didn't want to wake him—who knew what he might say if he caught her stealing from his mistress—so she eased off the chaise and crept around the room, inspecting every strange and wonderful object.

It was like a wizard's tower, full of magic. There were curious devices, papers with cryptic symbols that didn't look like letters, and scrolls sealed with wax. There were glasses filled with liquid and curved into fantastical shapes, scales with colored powder on their brass plates, and other mysterious gadgets.

Even the bookshelves held artifacts; a mask carved of some dark wood stared out at the room from beneath long braids of straw hair, and exotic lamps, jars, carvings, and sculptures sat scattered between books. And the desk was full of just as many wonders, little brass and gold instruments whose functions were a mystery. She picked up something that looked vaguely like a pocket watch but was the size of her palm. It had layers of carvings that moved independently of one another so, depending on which way one turned the dial, the little numbers and arrows pointed to different lines carved beneath.

Lady St. James claimed she wasn't a witch, but this room certainly seemed like a place where magic was brewed. True, the Lady seemed to be in the prime of youth without a wart or boil or crooked limb in sight, so she was clearly not a witch. She was, however, a fascinating woman.

For a moment Sally wished she could truly work here instead of the laundry. The poor pay wasn't enough compensation for the heat and humid air and chemicals and burns. The older women who worked there had bent backs that caused them constant pain. They had scars on their forearms and red, sweaty faces. She had been willing to accept such a fate for honest pay. But now a new world opened up before her. Entering service in a home like this had been so far beyond her comprehension it hadn't even been a dream, but it would change everything.

It would give Sam a chance at an honest life that wouldn't end with him in prison or knifed in some rotten alley.

Sam. He would never come here. What happened to their father had taught them both a lesson about how having too much money put greed in people's hearts, greed that made them do terrible, selfish things. Better to choose a few small trinkets to keep them fed and disappear into the misty streets.

She picked up the little gold device and turned the dial, watching the carvings shift. The way they moved, so smoothly and in perfect circles, was almost hypnotic. She could watch the carvings shift forever.

The doorknob clicked, and Sally's heart stopped. What were they doing up so early? She leaped back to the chaise just as the door opened and a maid walked in carrying a silver tray and an armful of black and white fabric.

The girl had a head of curly, dark hair beneath her white cap and she was enviously well-fed with healthy, rosy cheeks.

"You must be Sally," she said as she set the tray down on the end table. "I'm Charlotte, the upstairs maid. This breakfast is for you, but get yourself cleaned up and changed into your uniform before you eat it. Mrs. Chapman said you're to be ready to go when her Ladyship comes downstairs."

Sally's fingers tightened on the fabric of the blanket for a moment before she took the offered bundle. If she wore the uniform of a maid, it would be much harder to go unnoticed in the Narrows. But Charlotte stood there with her bright eyes and smile, as if she had nothing better to do than watch Sally change.

Fine. She'd play along until the other girl went back to her duties. "Where should I change?"

Charlotte showed Sally the downstairs bathroom, which had a flushing toilet that reordered Sally's entire notion of taking care of the necessities of life, and when Sally reentered the study, she wore the same simple black dress, white frilly apron, and cap Charlotte wore. The clothing may have been simple, but it was the finest thing Sally had ever worn. She ran her hands over the tight weave of the fabric, amazed at the quality.

That is until Charlotte told her to break her fast. The other girl should have attended to the rest of her morning chores, but she simply watched as Sally sat down to toast with butter and jam, porridge sweetened with sugar and milk, and strong tea. She felt guilty for indulging when Sam would have nothing for breakfast this morning, so she wrapped half the toast in a napkin and put it in the front pocket of her apron when Charlotte wasn't looking.

"Thank you," she told the other girl. "But you don't have to stay. I'm fine."

"It's no trouble," Charlotte said amiably. "I'm to wait with you until Her Ladyship collects you. She didn't want you to feel alone, this being such a large townhouse."

"How nice," Sally said through gritted teeth.

There was nothing for it. She was stuck here until Lady Gwen came downstairs. So, she stood and ambled around the room, letting herself get lost in the wonders collected from all over the world. Before long Sally found herself at the desk again, examining the little circular device and spinning the dial on the front as if it were fate and she the arbiter of the future.

"That," a voice said, "is an astrolabe. Fascinating, isn't it?"

Sally spun, nearly dropping the little device. Lady St. James stood in the doorway in a splendid walking skirt and jacket, her dark hair twisted into a neat bun.

Sally's face heated at being caught handling the mistress's things. She put the astro-whatever-it-was back on the desk as carefully as possible and said, "Yes, my lady."

The woman walked into the room, thanked Charlotte—who curtsied and hurried away—and said, "Astrolabes were the principal means of navigation for hundreds of years, though they've fallen out of use in favor of the sextant. A shame, because they're much prettier. Particularly this one. It is Islamic. See the beauty of the script?"

"Yes, my lady."

"Found this on a haunted ship in the Mediterranean, and the captain gave it to me."

"Haunted?"

"Don't look so surprised. It was rather a nice ship, and if I had died as its captain I think I would have had a hard time giving it up, too." She picked up the pretty little tool and turned it over in her hands. "Not wondering how much an antique like this would fetch at a pawnbroker, are we?"

Sally Dawes may have been an accomplished thief out of necessity, but she would never be a good liar. Her cheeks went up in flames, but she managed a, "No, ma'am."

Lady Gwen smiled. She'd seen Sally blush with those clever eyes of hers, but she said softly, "I didn't think so, but that will put Mrs. Chapman's mind at ease. Won't it, Mrs. Chapman?"

On cue, the housekeeper trundled into the room with a scowl. "I expect so, though Miss Dawes will do better to prove her worth with work and not words."

Lady Gwen knew. She had looked into Sally's face and knew exactly what she'd been thinking, and she hadn't said a thing about it. Sally wasn't sure whether to be reassured or warier, but something unexpected burned in her chest, something she hadn't felt since her mother died, and she found herself straightening her shoulders and saying proudly, in the sort of speech her mother had used, "I will, ma'am. I am not insensible to the honor my lady does me by taking me on for such a position. I would not dishonor or betray her trust."

When the words were out, Sally realized how much she wanted them to be true. It was a stupid desire, one she shouldn't listen to, but it was there. And knowing that she had not forgotten all of her mother's lessons in proper speech made her feel a bit braver. Mrs. Chapman looked both surprised and taken aback by her speech, but Lady St. James only clapped her gloved hands.

"Bravo, my dear, bravo. You've won this round, but Mrs. Chapman is a worthy opponent, so don't let it go to your head. Have you eaten?"

Sally nodded.

"Very well then, let's be off before... before something arises to detain us."

They hurried from the room under Mrs. Chapman's smoldering gaze, with Sally close on Lady St. James's heels just in case the housekeeper wanted to exact revenge for being surprised.

When the driver held out a hand to help her up into the carriage, Sally hesitated for only a moment. Never in her life had any man taken pains to help her with anything. He gave her a small, encouraging smile, and steadied her as she climbed in.

Lady St. James sat opposite her, looking at Sally with curious brown eyes. "Is Sally Dawes your full name?"

*Don't say it, Sally. Keep your mouth shut.*

"My full name is Sarah Elizabeth Dawes."

"Do you mind if I call you Sally?"

"Of course not, my lady."

"Very good. And you must call me Gwen. I'd prefer not to choke on formality when we're alone."

Sally's mouth popped open, and she shook her head. Refer to a member of the gentry by her given name alone? "Oh, I couldn't do that, my lady."

"Charlotte said the same thing. I swear, the premier job of English propriety seems to be complicating everything. Will calling me Lady Gwen offend your manners?"

She considered it. "No, Lady Gwen."

"Good!" Lady Gwen smiled, showing dimples that made her face girlish and engaging. "That's one hurdle taken. For the next, we must make a closer inspection of the alley before we pick up your brother. I do not know how many clues may be left but I don't want to lose the chance to learn what we can."

They bumped along in silence as the intimidating townhomes gave way to fashionable homes, and then to shops and other official buildings. Sally's chance for escape was passing, just like the scenery.

The alley was on the border between the retail district and the East End, and seemed significantly less threatening by daylight than it had in the dark. The shops, bakeries, boutiques, and cookhouses were being replaced by warehouses and factories, so the cramped space was filled with wooden crates and barrels for shipping and storing goods. There was only a moderate amount of refuse, and even this unattractive space was cleaner than Sally's neighborhood. She followed Lady Gwen from the carriage and considered disappearing into the crowd as the driver left to circle the block, but Lady Gwen gestured her forward.

Before they entered the alley, Lady Gwen stopped and asked, "Do you feel anything now? Anything like the pull you said you felt last night?"

Sally's brows furrowed and her eyes went distant, as if she were looking inward. She still wasn't sure she hadn't imagined the desire she felt to enter the alley last night. She closed her eyes to shut out the sights and clenched her fists as she concentrated on separating her desires from any compulsions she might have felt.

"I'm not sure," she said finally. "I would rather walk into this alley than any other. It feels like I might find something in there if I do. Something important."

When she opened her eyes, she found she had taken several steps forward without realizing it. She looked down at her feet as if they'd betrayed her, then back at Lady Gwen, whose head tilted to one side, like a cat.

"Interesting," she said. "Let us continue."

There, near the center of the alley, were the remains of the circle Lady Gwen had seen and Sally had missed entirely. Many of the marks had been scuffed, leaving blurry traces of chalk, but most of the symbols remained clear. Lady Gwen pulled her hat off, reached inside, and took out the small notepad with a pen attached. Sally's eyes bulged but she couldn't convince herself of what she'd seen. How had a notebook and pen been hiding in that hat? Lady Gwen began recording the symbols alongside copies of the ones she already had, then bent down to trace a finger through the edge of the outside circle.

"The chalk is rough, lumpy, low in pigment, and heavy in clay. Cheap," she said to herself. "Whoever drew it had to trace their marks several times to make the lines clear and unbroken. And look, there is a pitted hole in the center of the circle. What is this around the pit, rock dust? Most likely. They used a string as a compass to draw the circle."

Lady Gwen stood and unfocused her eyes, as if she could take in everything at once. "What do you see, Sally? Does anything about the alley stand out to you?"

Sally frowned and let her eyes roam over the space. There was an obscure symbol, a bit of Thieves' Cant scratched into a door telling homeless children they might get scraps of food within. Someone had stacked a few of the boxes for temporary shelter. But she saw nothing suspicious.

If she stayed with Lady Gwen, would she be able to help the other girl? To learn these tricks that let the woman see what other people did not? Not if she couldn't make herself useful.

She sighed in disappointment. "No, ma'am."

"Very well. Don't fret, my dear. We will find her, we simply need to chase the clues we've already found. Let's be off."

They headed back out to the sidewalk to wait near the turnabout used for carriages. A stream of foot traffic, tradesmen, factory workers, and the occasional well-to-do patrons streamed around them.

Sally had to ask, "Did you find anything that will help find Virginia, Lady Gwen?"

The woman tucked the notebook away, replaced her hat, and said, "That will depend upon what other information we can scrounge up today. Few people in town believe magic exists, let alone know how to use it, which should narrow our pool of suspects, but I cannot say how far."

Sally bit her lip and nodded. She'd hoped to hear assurances, a promise that her guilt would be eased if they found and rescued the young woman... but Lady Gwen said nothing more.

"Isn't that Lady St. James?" The delicate feminine voice floated over the noise of the crowd. "The rumor mill claimed she was in town but I did not believe a word of it."

"Neither did I, but who else would wear such a hat? So small and terribly out of fashion," another replied.

"And to be out with no escort but a maid? I can think of no one else so brazen."

"I believe it is her. Can we cross the street?"

"Where would we wait for the carriage? This is the only turnabout for blocks."

Lady Gwen's face paled. She clenched her hands and tried not to look at the two women approaching the turnabout. Other people on the street had also caught on to the uncomfortable happenings and sent speculative glances toward her lady from the corners of their eyes as they passed.

Sally looked back and forth between the overdressed women and Lady Gwen, angry and wishing it was acceptable for her to call those women out for being the rude, brazen gossips they were. But she was part of the very lowest rung of society and would only embarrass her mistress. Sally realized, suddenly, that she wouldn't embarrass this woman for all the world, as much as she wished she could embarrass the others.

Lady Gwen had saved her and was trying to take Sally's broken little family under her wing. The only thing Sally could do was give her a brave smile. Her mistress drew herself up, the color returned to her face, and she raised her chin. The air of controlled intelligence she wore like a mantle reasserted itself, and she smiled back.

"Take no heed, my dear," she said airily. "When animals want attention, they flaunt their feathers and make loud noises. But some noises, such as horses breaking wind and barking dogs, are not worth listening to."

Shocked silence replaced the women's muttered insults, followed by muffled laughter from the passersby. Sally had to turn her back to hide the satisfied grin spread across her face. The carriage pulled up to the stop, and as they climbed in, Lady Gwen glanced back over her shoulder at the women, whose faces had gone the color of summer strawberries, and smiled.

Once they were safely inside, Lady Gwen said, "Why did you let me say such terrible things, Sally? It was the absolute height of rudeness."

But an unrepentant grin made her eyes sparkle, so Sally swallowed her nervousness and said, "I wish I would have said it."

They spent the next half an hour in silence as they neared the East End and Sally struggled with what to do. She wanted to jump out of the coach and flee, but the daydreams of being safe, and fed, and wearing warm clothes filled her heart with longing.

The buildings became more worn, lining the thinning street like bent old men in tattered cloaks. Street traffic changed, with the vehicles becoming rougher, the people thinner, and less well dressed, and the air fetid.

Sally clasped her hands, fidgeted with her nails, shuffled her feet, sent wary glances out the window, and changed her posture a dozen times. Allowing Lady Gwen to bring her home, to the grimy reality that raised her, made Sally want to run and hide. Who would want a maid who grew out of the East End mud working and living in their clean, expensive home?

"Sally," Lady Gwen said.

Sally clenched her hands and forced her eyes to meet Lady Gwen's. She saw only sympathy and determination there.

"I have lived in tents and slept beneath the stars," Lady Gwen said, softly. "I've gone months without a proper bath and relieved myself in holes in the ground. Never be ashamed of the home that has sheltered and kept you safe. You have nothing to be ashamed of. Do you hear me?"

Tears sprung to Sally's eyes. She was ashamed. She was ashamed of the times she'd hidden while her father beat her mother, ashamed of the mud and filth, of the money she'd stolen and the times she was so hungry she'd considered standing on the street corner with her skirts raised. She was ashamed of Sam's thin face, and the coarseness of her manners. She was especially ashamed that she had considered stealing from such a kind woman. If Sally could have run, she would have.

"Look at me, my dear," Lady Gwen said. The warmth in her voice forced Sally to look at her. "I did not choose to be born to a wealthy family, just as you did not choose your parents or the home you were born into. I've done nothing to earn the clothing I wear, or the food in my belly. But you earned your way. You've kept yourself safe and alive, and your brother with you. And you've done it all while maintaining your selflessness. Do you know how rare that is? You have more reason to be proud of yourself than I shall ever have, and I will not allow you to feel bad for it. Do you hear me?"

Sally swallowed as warmth grew in her chest. She knew at that moment she would work for the lady and do her best to deserve a place in her home. Fear still gnawed on her backbone, but she heard herself say, "Yes, Lady Gwen."

When she turned back to the window, her shoulders were straight and her chin high.

The air grew close and thick with the pervasive smell of body odor, excrement, and mildew as they neared the tenements. The buildings that hadn't collapsed looked as if a stiff breeze would topple them, and the dirty-faced citizens glared at the carriage from the safety of doorways and alleys with angry mistrust on their gaunt faces. It was the atmosphere of Sally's childhood: claustrophobic, desperate hunger mixed with a stubborn determination to survive.

Sally knew every patched hole and crooked street. As they neared the end of the Narrows, a series of broken-down buildings stacked ramshackle atop one another, she knocked on the wood behind her head and the carriage pulled to a stop.

"Would you like me to accompany you?"

Sally bit her lip but shook her head. "He'd never come out."

She hopped down into the mud and slogged toward her building before Lady Gwen could say anything else.

The courtyard in front of the three-story structure was still soggy from yesterday's rain, and Sally jumped from dry spot to dry spot, trying to save her new shoes and stockings from the muck. The building glowered down at her with broken eyes and a gaping mouth, letting in the cool morning air through every scar and crack. She pushed through the creaky door and stomped the mud off her shoes.

"Sally Dawes, what on earth are you doing back so late?" a querulous voice demanded. Sally turned to the old woman sitting on the wooden stairs, her body a shapeless lump beneath layers of blankets and tattered scarves. "Shouldn't you be at the laundry?"

"Good morning Mrs. Copperfield. See my new dress? I've just entered service at a fancy house on Grosvenor Square."

The old woman peered at her through rheumy eyes. "Have you now? That is something, isn't it."

"It is. Have you seen Sam?"

"Not since he come home last night."

Sally edged around her and climbed the stairs. She felt a twinge of guilt, wishing she'd stuffed more food into her pockets, but she only said, "Thank you, Mrs. Copperfield."

The old woman grunted as Sally passed her and climbed the stairs to the second floor, avoiding the missing plank and the weak spot in the handrail. Sally stopped at the third door on the right, tested the handle, and sighed in relief. It was locked tight.

"Sammy? It's me, let me in."

Nothing.

"Sam, I'm sorry. I didn't come home last night because I had a concrush—" She couldn't remember the word Mrs. Chapman had used, so she settled for, "I got hit in the head and I couldn't walk. Please let me in."

For a few dreadful moments, no sound filtered through the door. Sally had just determined to break her way in when the double thump of feet hitting the creaky floorboards told her Sam had jumped down from his favorite spot on the windowsill. A moment later the door opened and her little brother stood there, dirty light brown hair mussed and his eyes shadowed above cheeks that were too hollow.

She pulled the napkin-wrapped toast from her pocket and held it out to him. As soon as he realized what she held, Sam snatched the cold toast and turned back into the flat. By the time Sally pushed the wooden bar into place, the toast was gone and Sam was sucking his fingers.

"I thought you left me," he said around his thumb.

The words stopped in her throat for a painful moment, then she took two steps forward and threw her arms around him. He pressed his face into her uniform and the hot sting of his tears bled through her dress and onto her skin.

"I'd never leave you, stupid," she said lightly, but her voice quavered. "Who else would put up with you, anyway?"

He didn't respond, so she simply held him until he pulled away and stuffed his hands in his pockets. "So? Where'd you steal it?"

"This?" She plucked at the front of her uniform. "I didn't. That's what I came to tell you. I got hit in the head last night and a lady took me home to tend to it."

"A lady?" He scoffed.

"I promise. Her name is Lady Gwen, and she's the strangest person I've ever met. But she offered me a position in her house on Grosvenor Square, and you too. We start today."

Sam balled his hands into fists that stood out against the threadbare fabric of his trousers and glared at her from the corners of his eyes. "I can't work for some rich lady when it was them what made us poor. I won't."

"Sam—"

"And I don't know how you can. Can't you just go back to the laundry?"

"And have a bent back and burned-up hands and never live anywhere but this broken-down old flat?"

"I don't want to live somewhere else."

Sally looked at the bare, utilitarian furniture. A leather strap nailed to the underside of the table was the only thing stopping the boards from separating. They shared one blanket between the two of them, and neither had a change of clothes. All of her childhood, she saw this small, sad place as inevitable. But just one night in the townhome proved an entirely different world existed. Perhaps she would never be a member of that world, but even living on the edge of it would be better than this.

But when Sam looked at these four walls and their meager possessions, he saw the only home he'd ever known, and whatever few happy memories they fought to make.

She put her hands on her brother's shoulders and waited for him to look into her face. "He's not coming back, Sammy."

Sam jerked out of her grasp and yelled, "How do you know? You don't! How's he supposed to find us if we're all the way across town? And what's he going to think if he finds us working for the same people what broke him? That we betrayed him, that's what!"

"Sammy—"

"No!"

She bit her lips together. Until that moment, Sally had not realized how deeply she wanted the new life dangling in front of her. "We have a chance to live in a fine home, and wear clean clothes, have full bellies, and earn money. Our money, Sam."

"I earn money," he countered with a scowl.

"You steal money. It's not the same thing."

"It buys bread."

"Sometimes. But it's never safe. If you got killed or packed away, I would never know! I don't want to lose you."

His hard expression softened but his mouth was still pressed into a thin line; he didn't want to give up on their father. But Sally knew better. She had given up on him long before he'd abandoned them. He wasn't coming back, and there was no use waiting in squalor when a better life stood before them with open arms.

"I will not live this way anymore. I'm tired of fighting for every scrap and always wondering if you'll come home. We have a chance for a better life than this... and I'm going to take it."

Sam's throat worked as he swallowed. His eyes darted around the room they'd grown up in, absorbing all the memories that had been laughed, sweated, cried, and bled into every fiber of the place.

When she took his hand, he didn't resist. She hoped she could lead him into their new life as easily as she led him from the broken leftovers of their old one.

# 5

## Scotland Yard

### GWEN

It is a truth universally acknowledged that food—sweet food, in particular—is the most effective way to soften a young boy's heart. Even a boy as defiant and intractable as Samuel Dawes. At least, I hoped it was true, because if it were not, he may not be waiting for us in the carriage when Sally and I finished our business at Scotland Yard.

We'd stopped by a bakery on the way, and young Mr. Dawes now had in his possession a paper sack full of sweet and savory things to keep him busy while we talked to the inspector. I hoped the bag, as a goodwill offering, would keep Sally's brother busy and safe as we pushed open the green doors and entered the headquarters of the New London Police.

After telling the receptionist I wished to report a kidnapping, she escorted us to a small office, instructed us to wait for Inspector Hardwicke, and abandoned us. His desk was worn and ink-stained, sporting several stacks of paper in danger of toppling. A brown jacket was slung across the back of the padded wooden chair. The leather was cracked and worn in several places.

In less than a quarter of an hour, I had cataloged nearly everything in the room and concluded that all the evidence pointed toward Inspector Hardwicke being a very diligent but bland fellow. I imagined a short, sturdy man with a comfortable belly and a walrus mustache.

"How can you guess what he'll look like?" Sally asked, wide-eyed after I'd explained my guess.

"Well, I cannot, in truth. But judging by the state of his chair he spends a great deal of time seated and shifting his weight, which would appear to be considerable, given the wear on the cushion. The room is orderly and smacks of attention to detail, but there is not a shred of personality about the place. In addition, the stacks of paper suggest a heavy workload. So, I've begun concocting a picture in my mind of what our inspector will look like."

Measured, purposeful footfalls echoed in the hall outside the office, and I gave Sally a conspiratorial grin. "Let us see how well I've done."

The doorknob turned, the door opened, and Inspector Hardwicke stepped inside and squashed my carefully constructed imaginings. Sally bit her lips together to stop herself from smiling, and I cleared my throat. At least I had gotten the weight bit right, though not quite how I'd imagined it.

Inspector Hardwicke didn't sit at his desk so much as descend upon it. The chair protested beneath his weight as he settled himself, then appraised us with dark, disinterested eyes that had seen hundreds of Gwens and Sallys. But when he focused on Sally's face and noticed the glorious black eye she sported, the disinterested mask broke. There was genuine concern in his voice when he asked, "Are you well, miss? Do you require medical attention?"

A blush lit up beneath her freckles and the girl said, "No, sir. Lady Gwen took care of me."

He looked at her for a moment longer, as if studying her face would reveal the source of the black eye, then the disinterested mask returned and he looked at me. "You've come to report a kidnapping?"

I took a moment to collect myself and manage my emotions. I had been looking forward to a short, portly, middle-aged Hardwicke, and the man sitting before me was a strapping, solidly handsome, and solemn-eyed Hardwicke with a jaw strong enough to crack granite.

I cleared my throat. "Indeed, we have, Inspector."

He nodded and pulled a notepad and pen from a drawer. "Very well, let us begin with your names, please."

"My companion is Sarah Elizabeth Dawes," I said. His pen began scratching across the paper. "And I am Lady Gwenevere St. James."

The scratching stopped, and the inspector raised his brown eyes hesitantly to meet mine, as if he'd rather not be looking me in the eye but couldn't help himself. "Gwenevere St. James?"

"Yes, it is an uncommon name, I know. Spelled phonetically, instead of in the Welsh way."

His pen resumed scratching, and I said in an aside to Sally, "My mother thought her daughters should have names that served as constant reminders of what happens when a woman attaches herself to the wrong man."

Sally choked back a surprised laugh, but the inspector didn't take the bait.

"You were witness to this kidnapping?" he asked.

"Yes, we both were."

"Why don't we begin with Miss Dawes, then. When did this kidnapping take place?"

Sally detailed everything she remembered, with the iron-jawed inspector asking for clarification, repetition of details, and descriptions of the kidnappers. He must've only been in his thirties, but he asked keen, pointed questions that spoke of intelligence and years of experience.

"Harry was the man who hit me," Sally said, "and he had a face like a rat. A long nose and small eyes. He was bald and thin but strong."

"Did he have any distinguishing marks on his face? A scar, a birthmark, anything of note?"

"Not that I saw, sir. It was dark, but I did hit him in the face with an iron bar, so he has a gash on his cheek now."

He continued taking notes but with a bit of a smile on his face. "What about the other man?"

"I think Harry said his name was Will."

"And what did he look like?"

"I didn't get a good look at him, except he wasn't much taller than me. I remember his voice, though. It sounded like a grave, all hollow and dead."

"His clothing?"

"Dark trousers and coat."

He pushed Sally for another half an hour, and I worried about Sam, alone in the carriage. I hoped he'd eaten enough to make himself drowsy, for there was nothing more dangerous than a bored young man... at least, according to Mama. James was there, of course, but I doubted he would chase the boy down the street if he ran. I imagined Sam dodging between pedestrians and disappearing into the crush of bodies.

"Lady St. James?"

I blinked. "Forgive me, Inspector."

"I understand why Miss Dawes was out late in the city. Why were you?"

It was one thing to answer that question for Mrs. Chapman, who knew me. It was another thing to admit to a stranger my reputation alone could damage a whole business. I clamped down on the instinct to twist my hands and said, "I arranged a commission for a new hat with the milliner on Barkley Street."

"So late?"

"Is that germane to the conversation, sir?"

"You tell me."

A slow breath kept me calm enough to say, "Please feel free to verify my claim with Mr. Bywater, the hatter."

He considered my face, silent, for long enough to make the eye contact uncomfortable, then said, "Will you tell me your experience of the kidnapping, please."

It wasn't even a question. But I could be polite, so I told my side of the tale. When I mentioned my smoke grenade, the pen stopped scratching again.

"Explain this device to me."

"It is a combination of saltpeter, sugar, and colored wax. When a fuse is inserted and the spark reaches the mixture, it burns, emitting colored smoke. I wanted a solution that would allow me to light the device without carrying matches, so I altered a technique used in China by which gunpowder is mixed with—"

He held up a hand. "When you say grenade, you are not referring to an explosion?"

"Heavens no. I would hardly traipse about the city with an explosive device."

The way he raised his brow said he doubted my assertion, but he motioned me to continue. When I began describing the markings on Harry's wrist, he stopped me again.

"Are you certain these were not simple tattoos?"

"I would not stake my life on it, but tattooing runes or magical symbols on one's arms would be foolishness of the wildest degree, even if one could find a tattooist willing to perform the art."

"And why is that?"

"Because artificery is a highly skilled art that kills unskilled practitioners. Because combining runes in the wrong way can have dangerous consequences, for both the artist and the customer. The dwarves guard their secrets closely, and any tattooist who practiced the art would not practice it for long. Were you perhaps in town when the lamp factory exploded? That was due to an apprentice who missed a single line in the rune to store energy."

He narrowed his eyes at me. "You mentioned magical symbols."

"Yes, on Harry's arm, and on the ground." I pulled the sketches out of my bag and handed them to the inspector. "I returned to the site this morning to verify my initial impression."

I explained the purpose of the symbols and circles, my observations about the chalk, the meaning of the symbols I recognized, and my supposition about their usage. Inspector Hardwicke pushed back in his chair, folded his hands, and regarded me as if I were an exotic animal he had heard about but was seeing for the first time, his thick brows beetling above his eyes.

"Gwenevere St. James," he said, slowly, rolling my name around in his mouth like he was testing a fine vintage. I might have enjoyed hearing my name spoken in such a way by a handsome man, but I'd heard that particular tone of voice more times than I cared to remember, and every defense mechanism I'd cultivated over the years sprung to action.

My face grew hot, and my voice cold. "Yes?"

He tilted his head. "You are telling me you believe someone in the city is using magic to lure victims to specific locations where they can be abducted."

I raised my chin. "I believe someone has used magic for a purpose related to kidnapping at least once."

He steepled his fingers. "Have you come to Scotland Yard before with allegations of illegal magic usage, lady?"

I gritted my teeth but kept my voice relaxed. "Only when magic was clearly used."

"And you are an expert in such matters?"

"I am as close to an expert as you are likely to find, sir."

"Are you, indeed?"

"I am, indeed."

"Why would someone take such a dangerous risk, as you say, when ordinary kidnappings happen without such preparations?"

"Are you calling me a liar, sir?"

"It seems a rather far-fetched and unnecessary bit of subterfuge, you must admit."

"Must I? No, my worldview is not so small, Inspector. If you have no interest in pursuing this case, then you have wasted more than an hour of my day and I would rather be on my way than have my honesty questioned."

"I am not questioning your honesty but your beliefs."

"No, you are interrogating me when your time would be better spent looking into the matter."

"Exactly what do you think I have been doing, madame, if not looking into the matter?"

We glared at each other across the table, nostrils flared, breathing hard though not a single word had been uttered in a raised voice. And that was the benefit of English manners. You could fight with someone very, very nicely.

"Magic," he said the word as if it tasted bitter.

Sally fidgeted next to me, her eyes darting between the inspector and myself as if one of us might leap the desk and pummel the other. I was sorely tempted. The idea of clawing the suspicion off his handsome face was nearly unbearable. I hadn't spent years of study and practical application to have my theories thrown back in my face by someone who could not tell a rune from an alchemical symbol. The creak of his chair was loud in the silence.

Inspector Hardwicke stood, pushing back his chair with his legs, and leaned forward to rest his hands on the overworked desk. His voice was soft but firm as he said, "I will not pretend to believe in magic, Lady St.James, but I will tell you this: this is the third kidnapping reported in the last three days. One per night. All of them young women. No report but yours has included anything out of the ordinary as far as kidnappings go, and you are the only person to report a kidnapping who has also reported"—he stopped, dug into a drawer for several seconds, then produced a paper and read—"a fae related disappearance in the past."

Bile rose in the back of my throat. Would I never outrun my past?

"So you will please forgive me," he continued, "if I am hesitant to take your magical expertise at your word or to base my investigations on something I cannot track. Thank you for bringing this to our attention. I will do my best to find the missing girls, you have my word."

A dismissal. I gathered the pieces of my dignity, rolled myself in the psychological armor I'd built after years of being dismissed, and pulled on the mantle of the daughter of the Duke of Wainwright. I'd never cared much for the title, but being raised in the top tier of English aristocracy had its benefits. When I spoke my voice was cool, collected, and precise.

"Best of luck with your inspections, Mr. Hardwicke. I do hope your shortsightedness does not hinder them. Good day."

I turned and floated out of the room with Sally following behind me, pale-faced, leaving Inspector Hardwicke with his cast-iron jaw clenched and nothing left to say.

Once we were outside, I let my frustration fly.

"May you grow boils on your arse every time you sit," I swore as I stomped about the sidewalk, thinking up the most dreadful imprecations I could manage and muttering them under my breath. I could curse his mother or his offspring. Impotence would also work.

"Son of a rotten, poxy, bowlegged—"

"My lady," Sally said, her voice high and a bit panicked.

I turned. Inspector Hardwicke stood behind me, his eyes wide, brows raised, holding my sketches in one hand. I absolutely did not notice the way the sun made his dark blonde hair glow or the way the jacket strained to contain his shoulders. He was a non-believer, a closed-minded, judgmental beast and he could take a flying leap off a tall building and I would tell him so.

"Ah, Inspector," I said breathlessly instead, in the kind of pleasant, detached voice that would have made Mama proud. "I didn't expect to see you again so soon. What can I do for you?"

He hesitated, looking as if he'd like to turn and run. Good.

"Um… Lady St. James. I just wanted to return your sketches."

"They are only copies, Inspector. Please keep them."

He looked from the papers to me, then back at the papers. His expression said he wasn't sure they wouldn't burst into fire in his hands. Not a total unbeliever, then.

"Have no fear, sir, the sketch is not the same as a spell, in the same way a blueprint is not the same as a building."

"Very well." He bowed slightly, turned to go, then stopped, hesitated, and turned back to me. "If I have questions about your testimony, may I have leave to call upon you at home?"

"Of course."

"Good day, then, Lady St. James."

I returned the bow with an, "Inspector."

Sally and I watched the man walk back into the building, then Sally said, "There is James, ma'am."

"Indeed. Let us get you and Samuel home. If he's still in the carriage."

Luckily for us, he was. The boy had gorged himself, leaving sticky streaks on his cheeks, but the sweets didn't improve his disposition. He still glared at me with suspicious eyes, but he hadn't yet grown into his features and his snub nose and round cheeks made the expression amusing rather than intimidating.

"Perhaps, when all of this has been solved, we might do something fun," I suggested, watching Sam's expression from the corner of my eye. "What would you say to visiting the zoo? I believe the Unicorn has finally birthed a foal. They say it is the first born in captivity."

Sally's face lit up and a glimmer of interest sparked in Sam's eyes, but as soon as he saw me looking, he folded his arms over his chest and scowled out the window. A tough nut to crack, that one. Better in the meantime, perhaps, to give him space and allow him to get used to his new environment.

"What do we do now, my lady?" Sally asked.

"I think we'd better stop by the laundry before we go back to the house. I want to speak to your former employer about Virginia. They may know something about the girl that will help us."

Sally nodded and chewed her lower lip.

The laundry was a squat, two-story building of grey stone with large windows and a perpetual cap of wispy steam. Acrid solvents tainted the air, and I swallowed convulsively a few times before I could breathe properly. If I judged rightly, the alley was perhaps a five-minute walk from this building. Close enough.

The children clambered down from the carriage, Sam refusing to be left inside again, and followed me through the doors. We were engulfed in hot, moist air that clung to my cheeks and made the curls at the nape of my neck droop.

"Pardon me, ma'am," I said to a passing woman pushing a trolly full of folded white fabric. "Can you tell me where your supervisor is?"

She pointed a red finger toward a bank of offices in the back of the room, and we wound our way past vats of hot water and folding stations. I tried not to look at the women turning cranks, folding sheets, and trying to keep their damp hair out of their eyes. They were working hard enough without someone gawking.

The door opened, and I found myself staring into the florid face of a man who looked like he'd been dipped in oil. His hair was slicked back, cheeks coated with a fine sheen of sweat, and his small eyes were hostile as he looked over my shoulder at Sally.

"What do you want? Eh? Wait, I know you, girl. Why ain't you at work?"

"Sally has agreed to come to work for me," I told the man. "Mr…?"

"Cardiff," he said reluctantly, "and you are?"

"Lady St. James Wainwright. I've come to ask you about a girl who worked here named Virginia. She's been kidnapped, and we are trying to find her family."

"Lady, a lot of girls work here and I don't know their names. I got a lot to manage and no time to keep track of a single girl."

"It was the blonde girl," Sally offered. "Who started last week."

"Oh, her. Yeah, skinny little thing. Don't know nothing about her people but she worked with Maisy. Ask her on your way out."

Then he spun and slammed the door of his office.

"Amiable fellow," I muttered. "Sally, do you know who Maisie is?"

Sally led us toward the front of the bay where a woman in a clean, white uniform was writing on a clipboard. "Mrs. Maisie," Sally said, "this is Lady Gw—ah, Lady St. James."

The woman, who reminded me forcibly of Mrs. Chapman with her storklike limbs, stopped writing and said to Sally, "I expected you to be at work this morning, girl. But here you are, all got up in a maid's uniform. Good for you." Then she turned to me and gave a quick, neat curtsy. "Lady St. James. How can I help you?"

"I'm looking for information about a girl who worked here named Virginia. She was kidnapped last night, and I'm trying to find her family."

The woman's face fell, and she shook her head. "Well, I hate to hear it. Our girls just aren't safe, and so many of them only trying to help their families. But Virginia didn't have a family. The orphanage on Andrews Street sent her over as she was too old to stay and they needed more open beds."

"Does the orphanage send over many girls?"

"We do get our fair share," she said, pointing to the line of working women with her pencil. "Poor things. But the laundry pays enough to put food in their bellies and it's better than the other options they have, what with no one to look after them."

"At what age does the orphanage send them?"

She scratched her cheek with the back of her pencil. "Right around twelve years, I'd say. They allow the girls to stay at the orphanage until they get their first pay. We have a few beds here, but most of the women without families rent a flat together."

"And Virginia was still staying at the orphanage?"

"Far as I know."

I pressed for more information but there wasn't much. Virginia had been on her way back to the orphanage when they kidnapped her. It was only luck that Sally happened by at the same time and that I'd heard Sally's screams and come to investigate.

I thanked Maisie for her help and escorted the children out. Sally was pale, her lips pressed together, and she clutched her brother's hand so hard her knuckles were white.

"I'll drop you and Sam off at home," I told her, "and you can have something to eat and get some rest. Mrs. Chapman will take you both in hand to start training tomorrow."

"You're not coming in with us, ma'am?"

I thought of Mama at home, of how quickly she'd begin questioning and bullying, and said, "Not just yet. I should still like to find an artificer who can help me translate some of these runes before I return for afternoon tea."

"Tea?" Sam asked.

"And cakes. Mrs. Chapman will see to it," I told him.

"We don't have to serve no one, do we?"

"Not at all. You agreed to run errands for me, and that will be your position. Mrs. Chapman or Mr. Yates may have additional tasks for you when you aren't busy, but none of those will involve serving food or drink."

He looked only slightly mollified but was silent for the rest of the trip back. I would need to visit the orphanage at some point. But first, I needed to find out why two common criminals had used a complex magic circle and where they'd learned it. That meant finding out what the runes and other symbols were designed to do.

I thought my way through the artificers I was acquainted with, trying to decipher which would be the most likely to share trade secrets. Mr. Flintspark was a very well-regarded artificer, and I had commissioned several impressive little gadgets from him, but he was easily the most guarded dwarf I knew. He would not even allow me to watch as he engraved the timepiece I now wore at my hip.

Horace Delver was a doctor of medicine and penned several controversial books, all of which I owned. He was easily the most communicative but also shunned by his folk for sharing things they did not believe should be shared with outsiders. What artificery common people knew was all written by Mr. Delver. The other dwarves looked at his books like the first falling pebbles of an imminent rockslide. If he answered my request, it could sequester him further, or cause fall-out from his peers, who already expected him to betray them.

There was one other option, but I was loath to consider it. I'd left England without warning the last time, and while my departure had hurt my mother, she had known it was coming. But I had never told Delilah, only written to her once I was on the continent, and she never responded.

We'd made several inventions together, some that were still used in factories to keep workers safe from the monstrous machines powering English dominance in technology, but it wasn't our profits or our partnership that kept us together. It was our friendship, one based on being outsiders doing things we shouldn't have been doing because neither of us wanted to obey rules that squashed our potential.

I suspected I had hurt her badly, and to reappear now with a request, when I had not tried to mend what I had broken would be cruel and selfish. And yet, she was likely the best chance I had to save the girl I had failed. All I had to do was walk in and… throw myself at her feet, I supposed.

The carriage bumped up to the front of the townhouse, and the footman opened the door to let Sam and Sally climb out.

"Find Mrs. Chapman," I reminded them, "and stay far away from Her Grace if you can. She will have all kinds of tedious questions and it's better for all of us if I answer them."

They looked at one another, uncertainty pinching their faces, so I added, "Don't worry, my dears, Mrs. Chapman may run the house with an iron fist but she is a kind-hearted woman. She will make certain you're taken care of."

Sally straightened her shoulders and dragged her brother off into the house. As soon as she opened the door, the duchess stepped onto the landing with Mr. Yates at her shoulder. She was elegance itself, just as I remembered her. Her golden hair was untouched by grey. Her skin sported more lines at the corner of her eyes, but she was as radiantly beautiful as ever.

More than her beauty, there was a gravitas to Mama that was impossible to ignore. It was something in her carriage, in the way she held herself that told everyone around her, here is a person to revere. I wanted to leap from the carriage, to run into her arms to be petted and coddled, to give all my problems to her knowing she'd right every wrong.

So, I spun and pounded on the side of the carriage.

"Let's be off, James!" I called, and waved out the window as we pulled away, "I'll be back for tea, Mama!" Before she could order us to stop. She watched the carriage drive away and her expression didn't change, but disapproval radiated off her like heat from a stove.

I would have to answer for that.

Leaning back against the cushions, I unbuttoned my jacket and let out a long breath. There would be time enough to confront—or be confronted by—Mama when I got home, and I had more answers about the kidnapping to make the row we were sure to have worth the yelling.

In the meantime, I needed to speak to Delilah Irons, and pray she didn't crush me before I got through the front door.

# 6

# The Iron Rose

## GWEN

Late afternoon sunlight slanted down through the buildings, casting jagged shadows across the workshops and factories of the industrial district. Everything had been painted in shades of grey, with water stains and rust dripping from windows and smokestacks, and the air smelled of metal, smoke, and grease. Even the pall of coal fires contributed to the unremitting grey, hanging low over this part of the city like an unwashed blanket. One never would have guessed such amazing things were happening behind the closed doors of these lifeless buildings.

Delilah's workshop was smack in the center of Artificer's Row, part of the Guild of Dwarven Artificers which were at the heart of the industrial revolution. Here, colored smoke belching from chimneys and windows flashed with blue or green light.

I had been down this avenue so many times it felt like coming home, but a few new things caught my eye. Leaflets hung on the announcement boards of several buildings, and notices plastered every inch of open brick advertising the League for Equal Representation.

Voices echoed off the buildings, growing louder and clearer as we neared Delilah's workshop. I hung half out the window to listen as a rally came into view. It was being held in the courtyard between two warehouses, announced by signs reading, "Combined League for Equal Representation." Perhaps fifty protestors, dwarves, elves, and humans, gathered round a dwarven man who stood on the box as he called down to the crowd, "They claim we are equal citizens with equal rights but how many dwarves sit in Parliament? How many Elves hold hereditary titles? Can we be equal when we do not materially contribute to governing our own country? One or two Dwarves and Elves in the whole of Parliament are a mere token, and cannot speak for us all!"

A round of "hear-hear," went up from the crowd, and the speaker continued, "It is the craftsmanship of the Dwarves that propels this country forward. It is the art of the Elves that elevates our empire. Earning money is not enough. The guilds are not enough! For there to be true equality we must take part in the making and enforcing of the laws we live by, no matter what the cost. Our future depends upon it!"

The crowd disappeared behind the buildings but the chant of "equal representation" followed us until we reached Delilah's workshop. Since there was little traffic, James pulled to a halt outside the building and waited while I plucked up the nerve to enter the door next to the sign reading, "Iron Rose Industries" with a hammer and flowering awl beneath. I remembered when she'd designed the sign hoping it would hang outside her shop someday, a true guild-sanctioned business. A little spear of pride shot through me on her behalf. She had truly done it.

But I couldn't stand out here all day.

I gripped my umbrella for courage and pushed into the building.

The front reception area boasted a dented desk with a metal top, and two wooden chairs, but opened into the rest of the workshop. Worktables and benches were interspersed with more specialized equipment for heating and shaping metal, like mammoth stoves and coal-powered hammers. There were also forges, anvils, and areas dedicated to more delicate work, which was Delilah's specialty. While much of the workshop was in some level of disarray, the artificery station was clean, organized, and full of precision instruments for carving, engraving, etching, and embossing.

"Hello?" I said into the emptiness. My voice came out so weak the sound of hammering swallowed it. So I cleared my throat and tried again. "Delilah? Are you here? It's me, Gwen."

The hammering stopped, and my heart nearly followed suit. For a long moment, there was no sound or movement and I had a serious battle with myself about the benefits of running versus hiding and which would be more likely to keep me alive.

A head of dark, curly hair appeared around the corner of a stove, followed by thick brows and black eyes in a face devoid of emotion. Delilah. She looked at me for a long moment without moving, then stood, set down her tools, wiped her hands on the apron she wore, and stalked to the front of the shop.

Watching her approach was like waiting for Hephaestus to strike, which made perfect sense because my entire body was as hot as if it had just been pulled from the forge. But she was as cold as ice and advanced with the implacable speed of a glacier; one that would crush whatever was stupid enough to get in its way. And here I was, being unutterably stupid.

"Hello, Delilah. How are you?"

She stopped behind the dented table, rested her broad, capable hands on the surface, and tilted her head like a bird of prey. I supposed that made me the prey.

"I..." I began, then paused, realizing I had woefully under-prepared myself for this moment, and swallowed past the thickness in my throat. "I'm sorry I left."

That cracked her reserve, and incredulity followed by outrage twisted her features. She said in a voice more intimidating because it was soft, "You're sorry."

I couldn't stop my eyes from darting around the room as I nodded. It was the best I could manage because the rest of my body locked up in anticipation. Then, Delilah did the scariest thing I could imagine. She started laughing.

I didn't know what to do with my hands, so I clutched my umbrella– the umbrella she made me–as she held her stomach and laughed till tears rolled down her round, tanned cheeks.

"You're sorry," she sputtered between bouts of laughter, "you left? You're sorry you left. By the blessed hammer." She wiped tears from her eyes. "You're sorry."

The humor disappeared from her face as her eyes kindled with rage. She picked up a paperweight and threw it at me. This was what my instincts had been preparing me for. I jerked to the side as the little metal cube whizzed by my head and bounced off the wall behind me.

"Oh, did that almost take your head off?" she shouted. "Oh dear, I'm sorry."

Another object whistled past, too fast to track, and I avoided it only by instinct as I backed away. "Yes. I'm sorry, D."

"You're sorry!" she screamed, grabbing any object within reach and hurling them at me as she railed, "As if that were enough, you absolute, world-class, slagging idiot!"

I ducked behind a pillar as a tiny hammer embedded itself in the wall where my face had been. "She's got good aim," I muttered, peeking 'round the other side of the pillar. She'd retreated into the workshop to look for more projectiles.

"I am sorry, dammit!" I shouted. "I should have told you but—" Something heavy hit the pillar and I ducked as bits of dust dropped from the ceiling. "I was ashamed."

"I don't want to hear your stupid bloody excuses." Something else hit the pillar, which was developing a substantial crack. "You left me here without a partner to finish a project I'd sunk two years' profits into!"

I leaped across the open space and slid behind the cover of the heavy desk, panting. Tools sailed through the air over my head and crashed to the ground inches away. I tucked my feet up beneath me so they wouldn't get smashed by flying shop tools and opened the umbrella above my head.

"Gods, D, I just wanted to escape. I was ashamed and angry and I just couldn't stay here anymore, not with every pair of eyes knowing and judging, and"—I bounced the back of my head off the desk to jar the words loose—"I couldn't face you and I'm sorry. I should have told you everything but I couldn't even face it myself. If I didn't get away from here... I don't know what I would have done."

I dropped my head. I could easily have ruined Delilah's career when I left. The project was initially my design, an idea for protecting pedestrians from getting struck by vehicles on crowded streets. I left with my knowledge of physics and mathematics, with my intentions for the project, and Delilah had to make do on her own. It could have destroyed her prospects for beginning a business that would set her up as a guild member in her own right, rather than being stuck as an apprentice to another member. It was an act of cowardice.

A pair of heavy work boots appeared to my right, as well as the head of a large mallet. "I'm not mad at you for leaving, you great sparking fool. I'm mad because you didn't trust me enough to talk to me. You didn't even give me the respect of explaining why you had to go, you just disappeared two weeks before the guild trials and left me with a half-finished project while you ran away and hid."

"You don't understand."

She snorted. "What, you think the whole town didn't hear about your fiancé breaking off the engagement after you destroyed the sitting room in his family's house? I understand you were embarrassed, but that's not a good enough reason to leave your partner without an explanation before the biggest exam of her life."

It was so much more, so much worse. Of course, everyone had accepted his side of the story, that we'd disagreed, I'd broken some vases and a table in anger, and he called off the engagement because of my unstable nature. No one had blamed him. I was already considered a wild eccentric, and there was no point in trying to convince anyone of the truth now, especially not Delilah.

I tilted the umbrella to the side and looked up at her face, where sweat and tears mixed on her cheeks. "You still made it into the guild, didn't you?"

"Of course I did. No thanks to you."

I smiled one of those sad, apologetic smiles because it was all I could muster.

Delilah slid down across from me to sit cross-legged on the floor and peered into my face. "I don't care why you came back, or what you want, but if you don't want me to crush your head with this mallet, you'd better swear to me you'll tell me nothing but the truth from here on out."

"Of course, I—"

She held up her hand. "No, Gwen. I mean swear it."

The blood left my face. "If you'll just let me explain why I—"

"I don't want to hear it. It wouldn't be a good enough excuse, anyway. You left me without a word. You left me. I don't keep people in my life who hurt me, so either swear it"—she held the head of the sledge toward me—"or get the hell out of my shop."

I looked down at the dull metal and my hand went cold. Dwarves believe metal has a memory. Most people don't believe in magic, and they often overlooked the everyday type of magic that accompanies things like promises. But an oath, and one taken on metal, is more than a simple, everyday kind of magic. To the Dwarves, it's a binding tie that is broken only with death, because the metal remembers. To break the oath is, in short, to ask to be killed by the metal you've betrayed.

I could get up, brush the dirt off my skirts, and leave Delilah sitting in her shop. I could find another dwarf to ask about artificery and hope they'd tell me their secrets. But she had been a friend to me when no one else bothered, and I had left her. She deserved more from me than that. And so did the missing girl.

"Do you have a knife?" I asked.

Delilah pulled a pocket knife out of her leather apron and handed it to me. I flicked the knife open, pricked my third finger, and squeezed the tip till a generous drop of blood balanced on top. The heavy head of the sledgehammer stared at me as I imagined the weight crashing into my skull, then smeared the blood across the face of the sledge before I could think better of making the oath. "I promise to tell you only the truth."

Delilah looked at me for a long time, as if she were waiting for the truth to come pouring out my ears. Finally, she nodded and offered me her hand.

"You nearly took my head off," I grumbled as she pulled me to my feet.

"You're still alive, stop whining. I wasn't really trying to hit you."

"Accidents do happen."

"Not in my shop." She pushed past me, took her place at the opposite side of the table, and folded her arms over her chest. "So, Lady St. James," she said, her voice offensively civil, "what can I help you with, today?"

"You, Miss Delilah, are a brat."

She grinned, a real grin that made her eyes sparkle. "So I am. Well? Why are you bothering me?"

I fished in my pocket for the sketches and laid them out on the table before her.

"I happened upon a kidnapping last night. Two human men and two human girls. This symbol"—I pointed to the circle—"was chalked on the ground. And this one"—I pointed to the script I'd seen on Harry's wrist—"was inked on the skin of one of the kidnapper's forearms."

As Delilah examined the symbols, her face slowly drained of color. "This," she whispered, "is either blasphemy, or it will change artificery forever."

"Sally, the girl I rescued, told me she felt pulled toward the alley this was chalked in. Here are the runes for Command and Attract, but the others I'm familiar with look as if they've been changed. I can't make sense of them, or why common criminals would know how to use them. They're not standard artificery, are they?"

"No, they are most definitely not," she muttered under her breath as she scoured the sketches.

"Is there anything you can tell me?"

She ignored me for several minutes more and I let her work. Delilah was single-minded about schematics, and she could decipher almost anything given the time.

"What I cannot understand," she said, "is how any of this could even work. The circle and non-runic symbols should interfere with the runic sentences. See here"—she pointed to the marks between runes, the common ones for power and control I'd recognized—"these two runes must be connected to function, but they're separated by nonsense. By all rights, the runes within this inner circle should not function at all."

"To tell the truth, the only proof I have this symbol worked is the word of my new maid. But it seems more likely than two girls of about the same age being kidnapped at the same time on the same night."

"Oh, I have no doubt it did something, but what exactly?"

"I suspect the symbol draws in likely victims. Here." I pointed to the same runes I'd shown Mr. Yates.

"It's a possibility," she mused, then turned the paper ninety degrees and tilted her head. "But there is a larger problem. There are runes in use here that are not runes. What I mean is, they resemble runes I'm familiar with, but they've been altered. The flow is smoother, the shape off by just enough that energy should not have flowed properly."

I remembered telling Inspector Hardwicke that artificers had blown themselves up in the past, and shivered. "Shouldn't this have caused catastrophic problems?"

"It should have, but it clearly did not. These here"—she pointed to the set of marks spaced evenly around the outer circle—"they are magical?"

"I recognize several from my studies, yes."

She shook her head and dropped the paper on the desk, then rubbed a hand across her mouth. "Runes should not work with magic. Either this was brilliant artistry or it was only partly functional."

"Is there any way you can tell?"

Delilah took a deep breath. "The only way to be certain what it was intended to do is to recreate it."

My jaw slackened. "That's out of the question, D. It's not safe."

Hands on her hips, she glared up at me. "Nothing I do here is safe, Lady St. James."

"Using my rank as a weapon so soon? You haven't lost your sharp edges."

"I'll slap you with whatever is at my disposal if it helps you see straight. Listen to me. This"—she jerked a thumb at my sketches—"should not exist. If you had brought this to any other craftsman, they would have burned it before your eyes. It's an abomination to the craft. Runes are not magic. They channel natural forces, like a water wheel channels the power of the river and turns it to grinding grain, only runes channel forces we cannot get ahold of by any other means, like light. But Magic is the bending of forces, taking the energy and bringing it into your own body to bend it to your will, making it come back out as something else. That's why witches have warped bodies. Humans were not built to wield magic, and your bodies can only hold so much. But If someone were able to combine the two of those arts, magic and artifice, if they could harness natural power and magical power, it could be..."

"Catastrophic."

We both looked at my rendering of the circle, imagining what someone could do—or be—with such power.

"I wasn't able to capture everything. Even if we reproduce what I've remembered perfectly, we may not get the results that would lead us to whoever made it."

"There isn't enough information here to be certain, but there's too much to ignore, and not trying to understand it would be foolish."

I didn't want to agree with her. It would be worse than playing with fire, it would be playing with fire and water and wind and earth, sunlight and shadow, all at the same time. It would be trying to wrangle unimaginable energies. But a young girl's life was at stake. And if someone already had this skill, the only way we could learn how to protect people against it was to understand how it worked.

"I agree, as much as I hate to say it. I don't like it."

Delilah picked up the papers and headed back into the shop, saying over her shoulder, "You don't have to like it. Just help me make it."

"Today?"

"Of course not today. I'll need to study the diagrams and retrieve a few books to make sure I create the circle properly. Still have your books on the occult?"

"Naturally."

"Come back with them tomorrow morning. That should be soon enough to make the circle. You can make certain I get it right. And don't forget to bring your pocketbook."

I smirked.

"And the girl," she added.

I didn't need to ask why. Sally would be the only one who could verify whether what we created matched what she felt the night of the kidnapping. But I added, "I won't put her in danger again without her permission. If she agrees, I'll bring her."

She gave me a mocking bow. "Until tomorrow then, my lady."

When I stepped out of the building, sunlight barely peeked across the tops of the buildings. The familiar streets took on a more sinister air as shadows crept out of the corners and alleys, and my driver was nowhere to be seen.

James had moved the carriage, likely parking somewhere off the street. I'd have to make a circuit of the building, then. As I set off, I was equal measures tired and hungry. The adrenaline of nearly becoming a pincushion in Delilah's shop had burned away, leaving me feeling spent. But I had experienced the feeling more than once before and I would live. At least until tea.

I was going to have to face Mama. That would be almost as bad as facing Delilah had been, and I didn't want to think about how close I'd come to telling Delilah everything about my escape from England. I would rather not relive the story, particularly with Mama.

The faint clatter of horse hooves floated toward me. James had circled the building but, if I could judge from the sound of the echoes, he was coming back round from the other direction. I stopped and took stock of where I was: halfway round, so I'd better head back. I had no patience for waiting, not with my stomach making itself known after not eating all day.

As I rounded the corner back toward the front of the building, I nearly collided with a dwarven man and jerked to a stumbling halt so I didn't plow him over. Not that I could have. At five feet tall, the fellow was more powerfully built than most human men were at six. His shoulders and arms were heavy with ropey muscle, his chest broad beneath a wiry beard.

"Forgive me, sir," I said, righting myself. "I wasn't paying attention."

He looked me up and down and said in a growling voice, "You can't afford not to pay attention in a city like this. Especially not as the sun sets. There's a lot of bad things could happen to a young lady."

I tightened my grip on my umbrella. "Then I am glad I ran into an upstanding gentleman like yourself."

"That's a foolish thing to say. You don't know me or what I'm capable of. And if I were a bad sort, with no one else around"—he raised his hands—"you'd be at my mercy."

I refrained from informing him that one of us would certainly be in danger and it would not be me, because the carriage bumped around the far corner in time to make my point moot. "Your warning is well taken, sir."

He stepped to the side as James pulled the carriage to a stop.

"Take better care of your safety. The city is changing, lady." He turned away and walked into the growing shadows. "Things won't be as safe as they once were."

Though it was nearing tea time, with the autumn sun setting early, I asked James to stop by the orphanage on Andrews Street. I was pushing how much I could get done in one day, but I could not stop thinking about Virginia's tangled hair and tear-streaked face. Where was she now? Time felt as if it were running through my fingers like sand, and pictures of what two men might do to a helpless young girl—in fact, three girls, if the kidnappings were connected—made me nauseous.

I lay against the wall of the carriage, closed my eyes, and tried to breathe slowly in through my nose and out through my teeth until the nausea subsided. I imagined a calming scene, saw the trees dance in a summer breeze, heard the birdsong, and felt the cool earth beneath my feet.

Images of a white dress flashed across my memory; of flower crowns and Lia's wild hair and the branches we'd used as royal scepters while we laughed and made believe another world for ourselves. I could still see the dirty soles of her bare feet as she ran, calling back over her shoulder, *"Catch me up, Gigi! You'll never have the strength to dance all night with the faeries if you can't keep up!"*

The carriage rattled to a stop and James called, "Here we are, my lady."

I jerked upright, banished the memory, and climbed out for my last stop of the day.

There were many orphanages in New London, several of them founded and sponsored by wealthy benefactors whose charity gave the children a safe place in a dangerous world. The buildings were neat in an institutionalized way, and the children were at least well cared for, if not cared about. The Andrew's Home for Destitute Children was not such a place.

It was an austere brown brick building with small windows that loomed four stories above a dirty courtyard. The children outside played listlessly, their grungy smocks hanging loose on thin frames. I gritted my teeth and strode inside.

The foyer was large, with a high ceiling, bare wood floors, and dozens of rows of plain, empty tables and wood benches. A woman in a dark, serviceable wool dress stepped in front of me before I could go any farther and said, "How can I help you?"

"I've some questions about one of your children. A girl of twelve or so named Virginia."

The woman froze, her face locked into dismay for a heartbeat, then she mastered herself and said, "You'll want to speak to the matron, then. This way please."

We climbed the stairs and passed several open bays lined with two rows of iron bed frames and bare mattresses, and ended at an office with frosted glass windows. The woman knocked and said, "Matron? A lady is here to speak to you about Virginia Smith."

Smith. A perfunctory last name often given to children who had none.

After a moment of silence, a husky voice called, "See her in, Mary."

The matron of Andrews Home for Destitute Children sat behind a large, carved wooden desk. Small eyes stared back at me from a round face, her hair pulled back into a severe bun at the nape of her neck. A silver brooch with an ivory cameo was pinned below the collar of her black ruffled silk blouse, and her hands were folded on the table in front of her.

"Please come in," she said and gestured to the chair across from the desk. "I am Mrs. Edwards, the matron of Andrews Home."

The woman had a self-important expression that made me feel sorry for the children under her care. Her inferiority complex was as obvious in her neatly starched blouse and carefully manicured fingernails as it was in the smug smile masquerading as welcome.

"Lady St. James Wainwright," I said, pulling out the full title, and sat. Some people could only be dealt with from a place of power, and I had a feeling the Matron was one of them.

"How may I help you, my lady?"

"I am looking for any information you have about an orphan who boarded here. A twelve-year-old girl with blonde hair named Virginia. She recently began work at the laundry."

"I am sorry," she said in a voice that told me she wasn't sorry in the least, "but we do not give out the personal information of our children. It is for their safety, you understand."

"Most commendable. However, someone kidnapped the girl last night. Scotland Yard has already been notified. She is not the first child to go missing in so many days."

Mrs. Edward's face crumpled into something resembling sadness, as if the expression were unfamiliar and she had to remember what humans looked like when they were unhappy. "I am sorry to hear it. Virginia was a good, quiet girl, and a hard worker."

"Can you tell me anything about her?"

"I cannot."

"It may help me find the girl before serious harm is done."

She leaned forward and eyed me with false concern. "Forgive me, my lady, but what can you do for the poor girl that Scotland Yard cannot? If they have been informed, perhaps it is best to leave the matter in their hands and focus on… other more suitable entertainment."

I bit back what I wanted to say and made a heroic effort to maintain my composure. "I saw the kidnapping, Mrs. Edwards, which has engendered a sense of responsibility for the girl. And I have resources Scotland Yard does not. I would like to do what I can to help her."

The pretense of interest melted off the woman's face, replaced by disdain. "I see. Another do-gooder descended from Olympus to help the unfortunate wretches? How kind of you, my *lady*." She made the word sound like an insult. "But the children do not need the patronage of another guilt-ridden aristocrat who does not know what life is truly like for them. Leave the children to those who understand them, those of us who are here for them every day, and go back to your tea parties."

I masked my anger behind years of training at my mother's hands, put on the mantle of the future Duchess of Wainwright, and stood to my full height with color burning in my cheeks.

"Indeed, no one knows what the children need quite as you do, do they, Mrs. Edwards? They certainly do not need warm blankets on their beds, or wool socks for the winter, do they?"

She glowered at me, but I continued, "The children need to learn responsibility, to be of use in society, and work for their keep, is that right? Just like you have worked hard enough to earn the stunning brooch at your throat, and that fine silk blouse. After all, it is the finer things that make life worthwhile, is it not?"

Mrs. Edwards turned a sickly green color and her hand twitched as if she wanted to cover the brooch but controlled herself and said in a trembling voice, "I have as much right to fine things as anyone, including you."

"Of course you do. Unless you own them at the expense of the people it is your job to care for."

I dropped all pretense at civility and leaned down toward the woman, letting every bit of frustration show in my eyes and my voice.

"Tomorrow I am going to have blankets and socks sent to the orphanage. When I visit a month from now, I expect to see them on every bed in the building. And when I ask my lawyers to investigate the relationships Andrews Orphanage has with local businesses, I also expect to see that no money has changed hands that does not contribute directly to the funding of the welfare of these children you care for so passionately. Or, Mrs. Edwards," my voice dropped to a whisper, "I will come down upon your head with the entire weight of the Duchy at my back. Do you understand me?"

The woman clenched her hands, gave me a jerky nod (which was supremely gratifying,) and said in a weak voice, "Yes, my lady."

I smiled, showing her my teeth, and said, "If you remember anything I should know about Virginia Smith, please do not hesitate to let me know."

I left her sitting at her desk, slack-faced, and stormed out of the building ready to do battle with my mother.

After all... it was time for tea.

# 7

# *Afternoon Tea*

## GWEN

I entered the drawing room at precisely five o'clock, having fashionably girded my loins for battle. Every piece of armor I could muster, from a tea gown frothing with lace and ruffles to a perfectly styled updo, was strapped in place to deflect whatever arrows Mama would sling at me. I looked at the perfect picture of a proper lady and hoped that would blunt the edge of her tongue.

She stood by the table waiting, hands folded primly in front of her, and when her eyes lit upon me they did a quick inspection, head to foot. Then she hurried toward me with her arms open.

"My darling girl," she said in the low, sonorous voice that worked on everyone around her like magic. She held me tight, and I closed my eyes to enjoy the embrace, knowing these were merely the first tentative probes before battle began but not wanting to give up the warmth of her arms. I had traveled all over the world, had dangerous adventures, loved, lost, and learned long-hidden secrets under teachers so old they had stopped counting their ages. Despite all of that, I would never understand the magic of how every woman, no matter how old, becomes a little girl again in her mother's arms.

"Hello, Mama."

She held me for a moment longer, then pulled back and cupped my face in both hands. "You look beautiful, dear. And tan. It's not the fashion, of course, but I must admit it suits your coloring, especially in that blue dress. Come and sit with me."

She alighted on the couch and patted the cushion next to her. When I sat she took my hands and let herself look at me for a few moments. Lia had been fair and golden, with blue eyes like Mama, but I had dark hair and brown eyes. If it were not for our noses, we would have looked nothing alike.

"You are the very picture of health," she said. "I assume your travels suited you?"

"Very much."

"And which country was your favorite?"

"India was indescribable."

"Didn't I tell you it would be? It is the most incredible country. Did you visit Varanasi?"

"Of course."

"And how did you find it?"

"Inspiring."

"There is not a more magical place in the world. And the voyage home, was your lodging suitable?"

"Why are we doing this?"

Mama paused and tilted her head. "Whatever do you mean, my darling? I want to hear about your trip."

"I wrote you weekly. Surely you've not forgotten."

She put one hand on her chest. "Surely you cannot blame me for wanting to hear about the journey from your own lips?"

"Mama—"

"After all, I have not seen my child or heard her voice in better than five years. A bit of inquiry is only natural."

"I'm sorry I did not visit Wainwright first."

"No, you are sorry I showed up on your doorstep."

"Well, that too."

She pursed her lips at me, so I turned the tables to give her a taste of her own proverbial medicine. "How does everyone fare at Wainwright?"

"Winter was hard, but the herds are still healthy and the income this year should be substantial. We've turned twenty acres to market gardening, which already looks promising." She droned on about land usage and tenants as if the subject were the most interesting thing in the world, but she was actually reminding me I was no match for her in this game. My eyes began glazing over when Mama stopped and said, "Have we done with this, Gwen?"

"I don't know what you're talking about."

"Playing stupid does not suit you, dear."

"And here I thought it was my best color."

She blew a long breath through her nose and picked up her teacup, turning away from me to take a sip. I bit my lip. "I am sorry, Mama," I offered. This conversation was going exactly as I expected and it made me unhappier than I thought it would. "I behaved badly. I should have come home, but it was May and…"

A profound sadness filled her eyes. She set down the teacup and took my hands. This time it was not a perfunctory gesture. Her fingers tightened on mine and I did not miss the slight trembling. "I miss her, too, Gigi."

*Gigi.* The pet name Lia had always used for me.

She searched my face, sympathy and determination in her eyes. "You must let this wound heal, my darling. No"—she held up a hand to silence me—"listen to me. I did not stop you when you left. I understood you needed to find your own path and build yourself into a person who could withstand the difficulties you've encountered. But some healing can only happen by confronting those things, and until you do, the wounds will fester."

I looked away and shifted in my seat. I didn't want to have this conversation. "I've been perfectly well, Mama."

"Except for ignoring your closest relationships? Of hiding from society?"

"Society pushed me out."

"You didn't give them much of a choice in the matter."

"Nor do I intend to. What interest do I have in cultivating a society of closed-minded prudes?"

"Gwenevere," she sighed and closed her eyes. "How can I convince you not to be so short-sighted?"

"Short-sighted? Me?"

She let go of my hands and stood, taking a few steps away while she collected herself. "Do you not understand the great benefit you can derive from your peers? They are placed at the highest levels of society and—"

"And they use that power like a battering ram to destroy anyone who doesn't suit their ideals, and keep the lower classes in their place. It's a broken system, Mama. Why would I want to be one of the people who perpetrate it?"

She looked at me as if I were young and foolish, her dark eyes sad. "Let me ask you a question. If I want to bring down a castle, what is the most effective way to attack it? By hurling boulders at the walls? Or from the inside?"

"Are you suggesting I topple the aristocracy?"

"I'm suggesting the power is on the inside, not the outside."

I clenched my hands together and closed my eyes. She wasn't wrong. Mama moved through almost every stratum of society with equal ease, and if she wanted to accomplish something that required help, she had merely to ask. No one wanted to say no to the Dowager Duchess, and even if they didn't respect her title, they respected the connections she had formed. There wasn't a circle of society where Mama wasn't welcomed. I could not say the same.

"Do you truly want me to be like those people, Mama? To speak out both sides of my mouth while I smile behind my hand? To give up every hobby I love in favor of pointless accomplishments in needlepoint?"

The Duchess snorted. "Exactly who do you think I am, Gwenevere? How many aristocratic women do you know who fully run estates, manage charities, attend rallies, and fund suffragettes? I am hardly a shining example of ideal propriety."

Indeed, she was a paragon no one else lived up to, least of all me.

"I do not want you to be anyone other than who you are," she continued. "But I do want you to have the protection of connections and valuable acquaintance."

"I do."

Mama clenched her fists in her dress, took a deep breath, then released it slowly through her nose. "Enough," she said, finally. "I don't want the first day I have spent with my daughter in five years to be wasted in an argument."

I paused. Had I just... won? I'd never come out on top of a disagreement with Mama. When I imagined finally carrying the day during a confrontation with my formidable mother, I expected to feel satisfied. Instead, I felt like a little hole had been punched in my gut and the appetite I'd cultivated all day withered away.

"Well," she said, "tell me about your new maid and her little brother. How did these new hires come about? Mrs. Chapman escorted them out before I had a chance to see them."

I wasn't certain Mama truly wanted to hear this story. It would only cement her opinion of me as being unable to properly control my life. "I found her in the retail district trying to help another young woman in need. Her selflessness endeared her to me, of course, and she had just taken a position in a laundry with a young brother to support. With only Mrs. Chapman, Mr. Yates, and Charlotte here, it made sense to bring her on."

"Indeed, it appears Mrs. Chapman could use the help. I do hope she isn't a trouble for Charlotte to train."

"I can't imagine she will be. Sally Dawes is a clever girl and has already proved her loyalty."

"Dawes?"

"Mmm."

Her delicately arched brows drew together. "I feel as if I should know that name."

"It's not an uncommon name. In any case, the girl is uncommon and I believe she will suit very well here."

Mama smiled. "I am glad to hear it. The poor girl must have been hard put to care for herself and her brother. He was, what, around ten years old?"

"Twelve, but small for his age."

"That one will be trouble," she said, touching her nose.

I laughed. "I had the same suspicion. But he should only be carrying letters so hopefully, he cannot get himself into too many scrapes."

She touched my cheek fondly. "I am glad your heart is still soft, my darling. That is a quality in you I would not see changed for the world. So." Suddenly, the warm motherly look was gone and the Dowager Duchess was standing in the room. "I have arranged a dinner for Thursday night. And I think I would like to plan a ball, since I am rarely in town."

"Mama, the house is not fitted up for a dinner, much less a ball. I have only been living in a small way."

She waved one elegant hand as if that were nothing. "I have already sent to Wainwright for help. They will like to spend a while in town."

So, she had planned this. "I have important matters to address, I don't have time to spare for social engagements."

"Pish," she said, before taking a delicate bite of a scone. "You must eat, just like anyone. Dinner will be no inconvenience."

"But a ball—"

"Is only one evening, Gwenevere. Don't be so dramatic. What can be so important it keeps you from spending an evening with your mama?"

"Only my dignity," I huffed. "No one will attend a ball if I am present, and those who do are certain to attend only to gawk and carry tales."

"That, my dear, is arrogant. People have better things to do than gossip about you. Besides, no one will turn down an invitation from your mama. They are scared of me," she said with a conspiratorial wink.

A suspicion crept up the back of my neck. My dear, elegant, clever mother was planning a trap. I thought I had won our argument, but I should have known there would be a backup plan. "And just who are you inviting to this ball?"

"Merely a few acquaintances and old friends."

I glared at her. "Do any of those acquaintances happen to be eligible bachelors?"

"Of course, darling. How can I get the mamas to bring their daughters if there are not a few beaus around?" She said it as if it were the most natural expectation in the world but I knew better. The scheming woman was trying to set me up. Very well. Two could play this game. I would find the most hideous, unfashionable dress imaginable, and... no. I would never embarrass her that way. She saw her victory in my slumped shoulders and her eyes lit up with mirth.

The look of speculation in her eyes told me I'd better cut off her line of thought before she got any ideas into her head. We both knew that if I were to die without having children the title would revert to the crown until it was handed off to some bloke for doing good service to king and country, or until some younger prince came along and needed an income.

My father had blathered on about it as my duty often enough that it was burned into my memory. Being one of the rare women who would inherit title as well as landed property made my father very nervous for the future of the estate. Mama had held out hope for a love match, but I had seen the state of their unhappy relationship firsthand, and my own experience told me marriage would be a bad idea.

"I pray you do not intend any of those eligible gentlemen for me, for I have no intention of marrying, and I shall do my best to scare off anyone who cares to persuade me otherwise. I can be very scary, Mama, so be forewarned."

"I shall take it under advisement, dear. Now, why don't you have a scone? Monsieur has outdone himself and I have heard your stomach growl on more than three separate occasions since you entered the drawing room."

I opened my mouth to argue, but Mama said, "I will have my way in this, Gwen, so please keep your mouth shut unless you are filling it with a scone."

I should have known I was nowhere near wily enough to beat the woman at these games. Of course, the question now became how to continue tracking down clues while the dowager was scheduling social engagements and trying to arrange my future.

I should tell her. She would most certainly try to talk me out of it and tell me that Scotland Yard and the indubitable Inspector

Hardwicke would have the issue well in hand. But I was the one who failed Virginia. And Lia. She was my responsibility, and I would contribute everything in my power to finding her and the other girls.

Besides, the inspector didn't believe magic was involved, so he was unlikely to pursue the leads I had given him. That left this side of the investigation up to me.

But there was nothing to be done till tomorrow when I would attempt a bit of dangerous magic with Delilah and perhaps get myself blown up, so I took the only advice I was willing to accept from Mama.

Mr. Yates entered the room just as I bit into a cherry scone. It was light, slightly sweet, and crumbled in my mouth. It was delicious, and for some reason that made resentment bubble up in my chest.

Mr. Yates carried a silver tray with several sealed letters atop and set it on the table near Mama. "Your Grace," he said, "the replies have begun to arrive."

"Thank you, Mr. Yates. You see, Gwen," she said as she plucked one of the letters from the small pile with a self-congratulatory smirk, "our guests are already looking forward to dancing the night away."

Mr. Yates raised a brow at me, and I rolled my eyes. Mama plucked another letter from the stack and I stuffed the rest of the scone in my mouth and chewed noisily. Yates concealed a smile but Mama only said, "Mind your manners, darling. You sound like a hound cleaning itself."

"What an engaging mental picture, Mama. How delicate of you."

"Gwen?"

"Yes?"

"Shut up."

"Yes, Mama."

"Oh," she said a moment later. "This letter is addressed to you."

I took the proffered letter, and the hairs on my arms stood on end. It was warm. Not warm as if from body heat but warm as if it had been sitting in the sun for hours. Mama did not seem to have noticed, so I looked at the inscription. My name had been penned across the front in flowing script, but on the other side, there was a small mark above the wax seal. A triquetra. I didn't have my sketches on me, but I would swear the symbol was one of the marks from the chalk circle.

The hairs on my arms competed to discover which could stand the tallest. It may not be safe to open this letter here, in the drawing room near Mr. Yates and Mama. The likelihood of magic erupting from it was slim, but with witches having been exiled from New London a century ago, magic was difficult and dangerous to study. I had only scratched the surface in my scholastic pursuits so I couldn't accurately predict what would happen.

"If you'll excuse me, Mama, I will see you at dinner."

"Very well, darling. Will you invite the children? I'd like to meet them."

Mrs. Chapman would wring her hands at that request. Mama had never stood much on ceremony with family dinners. We often shared a table with the closest members of our household staff, a practice that would shock the gentry into a riot if they knew of it, but in the country, we hadn't felt the need to ignore people who were part of our everyday lives for the sake of propriety. At least, not when Father was gone traveling, or whatever he did not involving us. If there was anyone to blame for my rebellious streak, it was certainly Mama.

I told her I would, then turned to flee the drawing room. Aristotle left his perch and sailed down to land on my shoulder as I escaped and hurried up the stairs with the hot letter in my hands. When I reached my room, the bird hopped off my shoulder and landed on my writing desk, where I laid the letter and took a step back to examine it.

It appeared as bland as any letter. White paper, black ink, with deckled edges instead of clean-cut sides, and a dollop of red wax to seal it. The triquetra stared back at me. While it was a common enough design used in decoration from Germany, Scandinavia, and the Isles, I had never seen one included in a letter.

"What do you think, Aristotle? Is that magic?"

The bird eyed the letter, then pecked the edge with his beak, flipped the paper, and shook his head. "Magic," he repeated.

"I thought so, too."

I opened the drawer and pulled out a piece of chalk and a letter opener. With the chalk I drew a small circle around myself on the rug, tracing it several times to be sure it was solid. Then I took out a bit of salt and circled the letter. A little protection wouldn't hurt. Circles generally function for protection whether the user was magically inclined or not, which was a boon for me. If a spell did leap out of the paper, the salt circle should contain it and my circle should protect me from anything left over. A bit of protection was better than none.

The letter opener was a single piece of cast iron shaped like Excalibur with an opal in the hilt. I hoped the iron would nullify any active magic, but I supposed I would find out. I took a deep breath and slid the blade beneath the wax seal. As soon as the iron had traced across the paper, the heat drained out of the letter and it sat cold on my desk. That certainly meant something, but what? Did the magic change because of the iron, or because of the broken seal? The letter lay on the desk, looking completely innocuous.

"I don't want to open this," I told Aristotle.

He tilted his head, considered the letter, and began picking at it, making little clicking noises as he pried the paper open, then stepped on it with both feet, smearing the salt.

"Well, that was very helpful. You deserve a treat, don't you?"

But then I had to push him off the paper because he began picking and tearing at the corner. "Enough of that, good sir. Shall we see what it says? Will you protect me?"

Aristotle flew up on top of my head and gripped my scalp with surprisingly strong toes. I looked up at him, he down at me, and then we bent over the letter.

It was written in dark ink with the same flowing script as my name on the front. It read, "42 Tromwell Lane, Thursday, 11 am."

"That was anticlimactic," I said, breaking the circle with the toe of my shoe. Someone wanted me to be at this address two days from now. Two more days. What would happen to the girl in the meantime? Was she still alive? The uncertainty sat in the pit of my stomach like a rock.

Aristotle hopped back down onto the desk and plucked the paper again, playing with it and flipping it until it landed face down, revealing my name and a triquetra symbol inside a closed circle. The symbol looked like a rough triangle made of three half-circles joined at the tips, resembling a knot. It had several potential meanings but almost all of them centered on the power of the number 3: earth, sea, and sky; maiden, mother, and crone; life, death, and rebirth.

It was a common enough symbol it could not be tied to the kidnappings without a doubt. But the chance that I would receive a cryptic note the day after a kidnapping featuring the same symbol used as part of a complex magic circle, and it have nothing to do with the former, was too close for coincidence to explain it away.

I stalked around the room thinking, trying to tie the clues together as late October rain pelted my window, but I simply didn't have enough information.

"He's a pretty bird," Aristotle said helpfully. "Want a treat?"

I carried my assistant downstairs and to the kitchen, where Monsieur—who did not appreciate being addressed by his given name—was ordering his minions about the kitchen. I managed to secure a generous piece of raw meat for Aristotle, who gobbled his treat down greedily, and went in search of Mrs. Chapman.

I found her in the linen closet, handing towels to Charlotte who was passing them off to Sally.

"Good evening, Mrs. Chapman. I see we are getting our new friends integrated."

"As best we can," she said after shutting the cupboard. "However, that Samuel is going to be a problem, my lady, you mark me."

Sally frowned but said nothing as Charlotte led her away up the back stairs.

"If anyone can handle him, Mrs. Chapman, I am certain it is you. And to that end, Mama would like to have the children at dinner, can you make certain they're prepared?"

Her face pinched in lines of resignation. "Of course I can, though I can't think what they'd offer for company."

She stalked off, muttering under her breath, and I retreated to the study with Aristotle to hide in books until my presence was required. I made a note to myself to complete the purchase of wool blankets and socks, contact my lawyer Mr. Morris about investigating potential fraud in the running of the orphanage, and find out about the other companies contracted with Andrews.

Workhouses had been outlawed twenty years ago thanks to a push from the Women's Reformation League, but many orphanages still formed relationships with local businesses so children could earn a living when they grew too old to care for. Those relationships were never supposed to be financial, however, to protect the children from the same abuses workhouses had perpetrated.

But I was certain Matron Edwards had been pocketing her share of the wages of the children she'd farmed out to industry. Someone who was willing to take money from the hands of children and sell off supplies they needed might also be willing to profit in other ways. Would she have sold out her own charges to kidnappers for the right price? Even if she did, that wouldn't explain why they wanted the girls in the first place, and why they'd used magic to draw them in.

I paced from the bookshelf to the windows, Aristotle watching me with his dark head tilted to the side.

"I wish you could help," I told him. "It would be nice to have someone intelligent to talk to about all of this."

He croaked and began cleaning his feathers. Fine. I would figure this out on my own. I'd have to wait till tomorrow to learn more about the magic circle, but in the meantime, I asked myself whether there was anyone else who profited from kidnapping children. The answer was depressing: too many to count.

Too many people were willing to take advantage of the most innocent members of society for their own gain. I stopped at the window and leaned against the sill, looking out into the darkness. Fog wrapped everything in a silver mist, making pools of light beneath the street lamps. It was incredibly peaceful, save for the man standing beneath the lamp across from my window. He was a dark silhouette, absolutely still, and his eyes shone with a lurid green glow that lit up a familiar face.

Harry the Kidnapper.

I turned and ran from the room, flew down the stairs past a shocked Mr. Yates, and jerked open the front door.

There was no one there.

# 8

## Runes and Magic

### SALLY

"I'm not gonna wear it."

Sally looked down at her brother, standing there in his new uniform with his chin thrust out and his fists clenched at his sides. "What's wrong with it? It's clean and warm and nicer than anything you've ever worn."

"I look like a prig."

His jacket had a row of shiny buttons up the front and his trousers ended in wool stockings and sturdy leather shoes. Sally thought he looked rather sharp, though his hair evaded all attempts at being contained or styled. Tousled would have been a kind word to describe it. And he still had a smudge of jam on his cheek from breakfast.

But Sam wasn't interested in looking respectable so she couldn't appeal to his pride. Last night at dinner, though, she'd noticed something that might convince him.

"I don't know," she said thoughtfully. "I think you look nice. Though it doesn't matter what I think, as long as Her Grace approves."

Sam dropped his eyes and considered. When he bit his lips together, she knew she had him. He'd taken an immediate shine to the Duchess, who asked him questions and listened intently and looked impressed when he described some of his more daring adventures. It didn't hurt that Her Grace was also beautiful.

Their mother died when he was only eight years old, so Sammy didn't have many memories of her. The Duchess must have looked like a fairy godmother. She still couldn't believe they had eaten a meal with a real, live duchess. She had been so nervous she'd nearly slopped soup into her lap, but the woman had been so kind it was easy to forget she was one of the most powerful peers of the realm. Sam had certainly forgotten.

He tugged at the sleeves and scuffed the bottom of his shoe on the carpet. "They pinch," he complained, but it was half-hearted.

"I have to leave with Lady Gwen, but you'll behave yourself and listen to Mr. Yates, won't you?"

He brushed her hand aside as she tried to smooth his hair and said, "I'm not a baby, Sally, leave off."

She grabbed his face and kissed his cheek while he struggled against her grip, then left him in the hall and hurried toward the sitting room. As she passed the study, she heard voices and slowed her pace.

"I found her asleep on her books again last night." It was Mrs. Chapman's voice.

"I don't think she's ever really given up." That was Mr. Yates.

Mrs. Chapman sighed, her voice was sad. "I wish she would. I'm tired of seeing her with circles beneath her eyes, up all night with no friends, no husband. She will do herself damage if she continues to believe in this nonsense."

"Perhaps. But maybe knowing so much gives her some comfort, some sense of control."

There was a thump of books being stacked and Mrs. Chapman's voice again. "I still say it would be better if she kept her nose firmly in reality. A husband and children would fill that hole and then some."

Sally blushed at overhearing so much and walked faster, thankful for the carpet that silenced her footsteps. They must have been talking about Lady Gwen and private matters she had no right to overhear.

Lady Gwen was not in the study yet, but Aristotle was. The bird perched by the window and watched the passing traffic with a gimlet eye.

"What are you looking at?" she asked the bird.

The raven peered at her over his shoulder, then turned his attention back to the street, shuffling to and fro along the sill as he eyed the carriages and people. She approached the bird and tentatively stroked the feathers on his back; they were soft. He didn't notice.

To see him sitting on a windowsill staring at the outside world was profoundly sad and caught at something deep within her chest. She knew what it was to watch the passing of a world you could not be a part of.

"I bet you'd like to get out and fly, wouldn't you?"

He clacked his beak against the window and hopped from side to side.

"We can take him with us today," Lady Gwen said.

Sally turned as her mistress entered the room carrying a sturdy umbrella and wearing a blouse, vest, and jacket with a smart little tie, a walking skirt, and a pair of high boots.

She tried not to remember the overheard conversation and asked, "Is that safe for him? Won't he fly away?"

"He can if he wishes. Aristotle isn't my pet, he is my friend. He's free to come and go as he pleases; he simply pleases to stay here most of the time. He has a mind of his own. Of course, I would miss him terribly if he ever decided to leave us."

Aristotle let out a throaty caw, jumped off the windowsill, and landed on the curved handle of Lady Gwen's umbrella. It was too small for his feet but he hung on.

"Do you have a scarf, Sally?"

Sally dug the knitted scarf from the large pocket of the jacket Mrs. Chapman had given her and wrapped it round her neck. How Mrs. Chapman had found winter clothing for she and Sam so quickly was a mystery, but one Sally was grateful for.

"And you've breakfasted?"

"Yes, my lady."

"Very good, then." She clutched her umbrella in both hands and said with a twinkle in her eye, "Shall we try performing a bit of magic without blowing ourselves up?"

Sally swallowed, then said, "Yes, ma'am," satisfied that her voice didn't sound in the least scared.

As soon as they stepped out of doors, Aristotle launched himself from Lady Gwen's umbrella and took off into the sky. He completed a circuit of the park, then glided down to land on the corner of the coach where he spread his wings, pumped them a few times, and croaked happily.

James slapped the reins, and the coach jostled off down the street.

"My lady," Sally began, twisting the ends of her scarf between her fingers, "might I ask what you hope to learn today? How will knowing more about the circle help us find Virginia?"

"I'm glad you asked. I need to think aloud a bit to settle my mind before we begin." She laid her umbrella in the corner and pulled off her gloves. "Heaven knows we will not have time for a break once Delilah begins. Where to start? Ah, I have it. Throughout history, there have only been two peoples capable of wielding magic: humans, and faeries."

"Faeries? I thought they were just make-believe."

Lady Gwen gave her a wry smile. "Fairies are, if you mean small creatures with dragonfly wings and pointy ears, which, of course, are nothing like the pixies you might see in the garden. The Fae, the Fair Folk, are only considered make-believe because we humans like to equate ancient history with myth. Do you know why this city is called New London?"

Sally blushed. She had never been to school, and didn't want to admit her lack of education, but she had no answer to give, so she only shook her head.

"A city has stood on this spot along the river Thames for many thousands of years. The first London was inhabited by all the races together and from all over the world. Fae, humans, elves, and dwarves all lived within its walls. It was a grand city full of extraordinary buildings designed by elves and built by dwarves. There were great markets, festivals, bathhouses, and a marriage of magic and technology that kept everyone safe, fed, and content. All the peoples lived in harmony."

Sally tried to imagine New London as it would have been. It certainly seemed something out of a fairy story.

"At that time," Lady Gwen continued, "only the fae were capable of magic, and some of the more powerful faeries began to believe that their magic set them above mortals. They tried to subjugate us, so humans, elves, and dwarves banded together, and went to war."

Sally gulped.

"Some faeries did not want war, or to destroy the mortal races, so they taught humans to use magic. It took many years and many deaths, but the fae were eventually defeated. Unfortunately, the defeat was catastrophic. So many elves and dwarves died that they retreated to hidden places to recover."

"Like the mountains and tunnels!" Sally said, remembering the fairy tales her mother told of dwarves living in caverns, and elves in woodland fortresses.

"Exactly. They stayed hidden for so long that humans believed them extinct. We lost the technology of the dwarves and the advanced art and literature of the elves. And thus"—she spread her hands—"the dark ages. Several of the world's great cities were destroyed or damaged beyond recognition."

"That's why we have New London? They rebuilt it after the old one was destroyed?"

"Indeed."

"What happened to the fae, then?"

"Schools tell children that faeries were merely stories invented to explain a great plague that killed so many people it sent the world into a dark age. That is how they account for the massive loss of life, technology, and art. But it was war, not a plague. The survivors decided to separate mortals and immortals, so, they combined human and faerie magic to create the Sunset Lands: a separate realm for the fae to dwell in peace."

"I don't understand. Why don't we learn this?"

Lady Gwen slumped against the backrest and raised her hands in a helpless gesture. "Because humans have been in charge since they banished the fae, and we do not like to admit that there was once a stronger race."

"Why not?"

"Because it casts doubt on our belief that we should be in charge. No one with power wants their authority questioned."

"That's stupid. Why were we in charge in the first place, if elves had music and art and dwarves had artifice and all that?"

"There were simply more of us left. We reproduce faster than elves or dwarves, though they live much longer. An average human woman is fertile once per month and carries a babe for about ten months, where elven babies require almost two years in the womb, and dwarven women are only fertile once per year."

Sally bit her lip and furrowed her brow as she worked that out. "There were more humans, and elves and dwarves went into hiding, so we just... took everything?"

"That sums it up. The other races rejoined society a bit at a time, but by then, humans had already begun making the same mistake the fae made."

Sally's nose squinched up. "What do you mean?"

"The faeries believed themselves superior, and they nearly broke the world to prove it. If we do not recognize that same fault in ourselves, we will do the same. Luckily there are some brave people willing to prove otherwise."

Sally sat back and began picking at her skirt. Until now, she had believed that humans, elves, and dwarves had always lived side-by-side, and everything else was a fairytale.

"So we want to know who learned to do this magic, since the faeries are gone and there aren't any witches here. Because whoever learned it knows things no one else does."

"Exactly. And to find out who learned this magic and how, we must first discover what it does. I have studied dozens of grimoires, though"—she narrowed her eyes at Sally—"don't tell Mrs. Chapman that. She goes absolutely wild at any mention of witches and I rather like my ears as they are."

Sally smiled at the thought of Mrs. Chapman shouting her lady's ears off. "I promise."

"I have never seen markings that match the ones inside the circle. They resemble runes, and some are so close I can even decipher them, but others are alien. If it is magic, it is some form with which I am unfamiliar."

"Wait," Sally said, "how can we test it if none of us are witches?"

"That is the experiment. Harry and his companion were not witches, either. And artificery does not require magic to function, so if someone has discovered a way to combine artifice and magic…"

It took a moment for the realization to settle in, but when it did, Sally gasped. "Anyone could use it," she said. "For whatever they wanted. For anything."

Lady Gwen looked grim. "Witchcraft is incredibly hard to track or regulate. Dwarves are very careful with their knowledge of artificery, and there are laws about who can learn and practice it. There are tests and permits and so on, and runes must be inscribed, which makes them easy to see and track. An artificer must also leave their mark on any piece of artifice that is sold or given. But magic can be done in secret and leave no trace."

An entire, unknown world of danger unfolded itself in Sally's mind. The streets outside the carriage window suddenly looked a bit more ominous.

"So, my dear girl," Lady Gwen said, "we must learn what the circle does, and find out if that will help us understand why someone would use it. Who benefits from creating such magic? Knowing the answer may be our best chance of finding Virginia."

Sally nodded and bit her lip, thinking for the first time that Virginia was not the only person in danger. She was silent for the rest of the trip to Artificer's Row, chewing her lips and imagining what a world with unchecked magic would look like. A terrible, wonderful, very tempting idea crept into the back of her mind and made a home for itself there… What if she learned magic? Could she make it so Sam was always safe, always well-fed? Get herself a husband and a little cottage of her own? Make it so no other child had to see their mother die while their father drank himself into a drunken stupor? Magic like that wasn't so bad, was it?

"Ah," Lady Gwen said. "Here we are. A word of advice: do exactly what Delilah tells you to do, exactly how and when she tells you. Her temper is likely more dangerous than the runes."

Then she winked at Sally and climbed out of the coach.

---

Delilah Irons was at least four inches shorter than Sally, with a mop of dark curls and a face like a flower. Her round cheeks were red beneath tanned skin, her small nose pert, and her lips curved into a charming cupid's bow. But that was where any appearance of softness ended. The dwarven woman had forearms corded with strength, broad shoulders, capable hands, and a commanding, no-nonsense manner that Sally obeyed immediately.

As soon as they entered the workshop she said, "It's about time. Is this the girl? Good. Gwen, come and have a look at this."

And the two of them were off, pouring over what Delilah called schematics or something like that. Sally had only gotten a glimpse of white markings on blue paper before they'd laid the sheet on a huge worktable and crowded around it.

She placed herself on a bench between the table and an oven, so the warmth would keep the autumn chill at bay as she listened to them discuss their plans. During the ride, Sally had determined to learn as much as possible. About everything. She'd known that illiteracy was a weakness, but she'd never realized how much she didn't know, and what that lack of knowledge might cost her.

Lady Gwen knew just about everything, and her house was full of books. So Sally would pay attention, even if what they said made no sense, and she'd also teach herself to read. She never wanted to be at a disadvantage again.

"I took your drawings and cleaned them up," Delilah said, "and then replaced the incomplete runes with the ones they were most likely derived from. It looks to me as if the runes they used are old, perhaps archaic versions of the ones we've got now, or modified by some art I haven't learned. The angle of some of the lines—they're just not as clean and efficient as current runes."

"I didn't realize runes have evolved," Lady Gwen said.

"Well, don't tell anyone you heard it from me. Anyway, most of the runes are either legible or they have some close counterparts. Of course, I can't be certain, but from a purely runic standpoint, what we've got here"—Delilah pointed to the outer ring of symbols—"is a command for the circle to be energized by drawing on natural forces instead of magic. I have to assume once the circle has contained the power, it will also activate the magical symbols. Can that even be done?"

"I have never heard of such a thing."

"What have you learned about the symbols?"

Lady Gwen hunched over the paper, turning it this way and that, studying the markings. "I've been pouring over my research and I've only been able to decipher a few of them. Here is a triquetra, which has several meanings depending on who has written it, but the power of the number three is constant. And this symbol here is associated with purity, spring, and new growth. This one doesn't have a direct translation but is likened to desire. As for the rest... I have only conjecture."

"I don't suppose you know of any witches we can ask?"

Lady Gwen huffed. "Witches are even more secretive than dwarves. The grimoires I have are the most expensive books in my library and I don't like to talk about what it cost me to obtain them. In any case, I would not share this information with a witch."

Delilah ran her hands through her hair, then gestured to an empty spot on the workshop floor. "Then we'd better get started."

"I—" Sally began, then bit her lip. She didn't mean to interfere or interrupt but she'd begun speaking before she realized it.

Delilah put her hands on her hips. "Yes? Spit it out, girl."

"I was just wondering... why can you draw the runes on the paper and they don't work, but when you draw them on the ground they do?"

"Oh, that." Delilah waved her question away. "Runes must be written in sentences to capture and direct natural forces. Think of it like building a house. You've got a front door for people to enter the house. That's the first rune. Then different rooms in the house where people can do different things. When we write runic sentences, we build a back door, a place where the leftover energy can get out. But it has to be small enough so the energy we've captured can do its job before it leaves the house. When drawing schematics, we make the front door very, very small, and the back door very, very big."

"So nothing stays in the house," Sally said.

"It's a very simplified description," Lady Gwen complained.

"It's all we've got time for and more than she should know, anyway."

The blood drained from Sally's face. Had she just learned something that would put her in danger?

But Lady Gwen said, "Don't worry, dear girl. Delilah would never tell you anything you shouldn't know. She's merely being careful."

Sally breathed a sigh of relief. She wanted to learn, to know more, but she was already nervous enough about what they were doing.

"Stop chatting and get your chalk, my lady," the smaller woman ordered as she hustled Lady Gwen to the bare spot on the floor. Sally liked the way Delilah said *my lady*. It sounded like a pet name, and not a title, and made it clear their relationship was on even footing. And Lady Gwen never behaved as if she were a noblewoman and the artificer merely a common person. Delilah was someone to be respected. Which Sally supposed was especially smart when dealing with a person who directed invisible natural forces with a pencil.

The two women set up the schematic on a drawing board angled so they could both see it and drew a wide circle. Delilah tied the chalk to a piece of twine and Lady Gwen held the end of the string in the center of the circle while the other woman walked the chalk around at the taut end of the twine. The resulting circle was perfect, and the soft chalk made a solid, unbroken line.

They repeated the same process for a smaller circle at the center of the larger one. Then Delilah picked up three large aprons and handed them out. Sally almost dropped the apron, it was so heavy. There were metal plates sewn into the lining, runes stitched along the inside, and the leather covered her from neck to knees. A pair of helmets followed with similar protective precautions. Then Lady Gwen stepped out of the circle, and Delilah began drawing the magic symbols.

"Make this one a little more angular," Lady Gwen said, and Delilah altered the angle of her arm. They watched in silence as the symbols took up space on the floor, one by one, until Lady Gwen said, "Stop!"

Everyone froze, Sally with her fingers pressed to her chin, and Delilah with the chalk halfway through a complex symbol. She didn't move.

"When you make the tail," Lady Gwen said, "don't let the end of the tail touch the circle."

A bead of sweat dripped down Delilah's cheek. She nodded once, a small, curt movement, then finished the tail of the symbol. When she was done, they all breathed a sigh of relief.

"Good," Delilah said. "That's the spell in place. Now, to energize it. Check everything before I begin."

Lady Gwen circled the spell, comparing the symbols to the ones she'd drawn, and matching them against an old, leather-bound book she'd pulled from her carpetbag. Once she was certain everything was in good order, she told Delilah to continue.

The artificer began drawing runes with smooth, practiced motions, never a movement wasted. It was like watching a dance.

"Let us stand back a bit," Lady Gwen urged, and the two of them took shelter behind a low cement wall that reached mid-chest on the two of them, but would have come to Delilah's chin.

The dwarven woman reached the last rune, paused, and said, "If this blows up in my face, Gwen, you know what to do."

Lady Gwen swallowed audibly but said, "I do. And it won't. You're the most capable artificer in the city."

Delilah smiled, showing her teeth, but another drop of sweat trickled down to dangle from the tip of her nose. "You're damn right I am."

Lady Gwen put a reassuring hand on Sally's shoulder, but she barely felt it through the thick leather and metal. Delilah took a slow breath, and then she chalked the mark into the last space near the outside the circle. When the runes were done, Sally felt the change in the air as invisible forces gathered and activated the spell. It felt like wind rushing past her, swirling around the circle, and then the runes lit up with a flash of pale blue light just after Delilah leaped to safety behind a nearby table.

Sally blinked, but everything in the room had gone soft and fuzzy and slightly dark. Everything but the circle. It didn't glow, but it seemed to be the only thing sharp and clear; the only safe place in the room. The lines within the circle were elegant and inviting, and they called to her with the promise of warmth and safety.

She remembered the feel of her mother's arms, soft and safe and capable. No matter whether she'd scraped her shin or had her feelings hurt by some bully, there was safety in her mother's arms. Next to that memory, the rest of the world was dark and so cold. She couldn't stay here alone. It wasn't safe. Only the circle held the safety she desired. Only within its walls could she finally lay down the fear, the worry, the stomach-gnawing anxiety of never knowing if she would make it to the next week, the next day.

Then strong arms were around her, dragging her away from the warm glow of safety. She cried out, fighting against the arms, against the cold, kicking and scratching, and pushing herself toward sanctuary with all the strength in her body. If they forced her to stay in the dark, she'd die. She'd rather die than give up the promise of finally being safe and loved.

"Sally!" a voice shouted.

"Sit on her," another voice ordered; cold, cruel voices that would drag her back down into the abyss.

"Break the damn spell!" the first voice called.

And the world rocked on its axis, collapsing and then expanding as light and color flooded back. She was on the ground just outside the circle, a heavy weight on the small of her back, her fingers raw and sore from scrabbling at the stone floor. Tears ran down her cheeks and she realized suddenly why Virginia had been crying.

It wasn't because some horrid strangers were kidnapping her. She was not afraid for her life. It was because the promise of unconditional love, safety, and warmth—the promise of a mother—had been snatched away. In that moment, Sally lost her mother all over again, and the pain was as fresh as if she had just watched the light leave her eyes, heavy enough to crush all the air out of her lungs so that the only sound she made was a weak, broken sob.

# 9

# *Runaway*

## GWEN

I sat with Sally's head in my lap for a long time, stroking her hair as she cried. The circle needed to be tested if we were going to save Virginia and the other girls, and maybe keep the rest of the world safe from this magic. But knowing we hurt Sally so deeply in the process wrenched my stomach.

Whatever we had expected the circle to do, it certainly hadn't been a mad frenzy.

Both Delilah and I felt the energy enter the circle, but that was normal. Anyone would notice a strong wind or a hot ray of sunshine. But something else had happened to Sally, something she wasn't capable of sharing with us, yet.

Her expression had gone distant, then a hunger so deep it was painful to witness entered her eyes. I knew such hunger, had felt it bore a hole in my soul I still hadn't been able to mend. I'd only learned to live with it.

We had stopped Sally before she entered the circle; a careful test was one thing, but allowing the girl to be drawn into the magic was quite another. When she realized she could not enter, Sally lashed out with the ferocity of a cornered animal. We were all lucky the girl was relatively weak and didn't know how to fight properly. Yet.

Delilah hadn't said a word after she'd scuffed the capstone rune with the toe of her boot, breaking the flow of energy and nearly knocking herself off her feet. She'd simply gathered her pen and notebook and begun writing.

"My lady," Sally sniffed.

I reached down to take her by the shoulders and gathered the girl up into my arms. She hesitated, then wrapped her slender arms around my waist and buried her face in my apron, squeezing tightly. I held her, feeling again the fear that stopped my heart when she'd begun screaming and fighting us as we tried to keep her out of the circle.

"I'm so sorry. You never should have been subjected to that. I should have found another way."

She pulled back and wiped her eyes with the heels of her hands. "No," she said, her voice stronger. "No, it's okay. I understand what happened to Virginia, and maybe the other girls. The circle drew me, but not like what I felt the night they took her."

She was right. If Virginia reacted anything like Sally had, they would have destroyed the spell while trying to subdue her, which accounted for the scuff marks and Sally's weaker reaction to the leftover energy.

"The circle, the spell, it promised her... home. It felt like mum was calling me, like a warm fire and biscuits and hot chocolate. It felt like everything I ever wanted."

I swallowed. "Sally, how old were you when your mother died?"

"Ten."

Virginia was an orphan. Had the other children also been orphans or had the circle called to something else in them, something they had in common we didn't know about?

"Will you be okay?" I asked. "There are biscuits, sausages, and cheese in my bag if you'd like something to eat."

She shook her head, and the blonde hairs that had escaped her bun during the struggle floated back and forth. "I don't think I could eat right now. But I'll be okay."

I touched her cheek, then joined Delilah at the table.

"Alright," I said, pushing loose hair out of my face. "What do we know?"

"Did you feel the magic?"

"No," I said. "Did you?"

She blew a hair off her forehead. "No. Nothing."

"Then whatever we have in common with Sally can be crossed off the list. She said the magic broadcast her deepest desire for home and safety. She specifically mentioned her mother, who died when she was ten years old. Virginia was an orphan, so either the spell only calls to orphans or there's some connection between the girls we haven't discovered yet."

"They were of a similar age?"

"Yes, a couple of years apart."

Delilah chewed on her lip. "Did you notice anything else about the magic?"

"It wasn't glamour, evocation, or any other type of magic I've heard of. From what I know of these types of spells, they must target a specific individual with some type of focus; hair or blood or a personal possession."

"That's what I suspected. Damn." Delilah's voice was low, concerned.

I glanced at Sally over my shoulder, who sat leaning against the cement wall with her arms locked around her knees, and lowered my voice. "The runes are affecting the manifestation of the magic, aren't they?"

"Yes," she growled. "That is not supposed to happen. And the altered runes should cause all kinds of energy leakage, but they're not."

"So either someone knows much deeper magic than we've heard of, or they've altered magic and artificery as we know it."

"I would say so."

"Which means we aren't dealing with a hedge witch or some fool who happened across the skill by accident. Only someone who understood both magic and artificery deeply could have mixed the two this way with such precision."

"Someone who is very, very slagging dangerous," she said as she tossed the pencil back onto the table. It rolled across the surface and bumped to a stop against my grimoire.

That was the bad news. The good news was the level of knowledge this skill required would limit the suspect pool significantly. It would have to be someone with both time, money, and the contacts required to learn both crafts. They would need access to both the knowledge of dwarves and witches, a safe place to learn and practice the craft, and quite a bit of money.

Humans and elves may both have enough money, space, and time, but dwarves were notoriously protective of artificery. I was well-informed for a human, and my knowledge did not even scratch the surface of basic artifice.

"Delilah," I said carefully, looking at her from the corner of my eye. "Is it in the least bit possible this new... Well, I don't know what to call it. This new rune magic, I suppose, results from dwarven study?"

Her face glowed with angry heat and her dark eyes looked like burning coals. For a moment, I wanted to leap the table and hide. Then she closed her eyes and sighed. "I want to say no, and take you apart for suggesting it. I know what you're thinking. And you're right. As much as I'd like to believe artificers would protect the sanctity of the craft..." she pounded a fist on the table, making the pencil jump. "I cannot guarantee it's not."

"Okay," I said. "An accomplished artificer would have access to the knowledge, the money, and space to practice. So we must at least consider that. What are the chances of a human coming into enough knowledge of artificery to make these kinds of changes safely?"

"Low. Very low... but not zero. Money can buy many things it shouldn't be able to buy. And there are other reasons someone might sell their knowledge."

I thought of the signs I'd seen plastered to the sides of buildings in Artificer's Row, of the rally of elves and dwarves, of meeting and the dwarven man who'd warned me not to be out too late. I didn't want to bring up the possibility of political dissension to Delilah yet, but there was always the chance that secrets were being sold for political gain. What I couldn't guess was why young orphans might be involved. What was the motivation?

"Who has the most to gain from such knowledge," I mused. "And what benefit is there in using it to kidnap orphans?"

Delilah ran a chalk-smeared hand through her hair, leaving white streaks in the dark curls. She glanced at Sally, then at me, and finally at the circle on the floor.

"I suppose you've seen the signs," she said as if reading my mind.

"Rather well done, aren't they? Not quite visual masterpieces but—"

"Don't try to lighten the mood," she growled, but there was less darkness in her eyes. "This is something to take seriously, Gwen. And it's not only the dwarves. The elves are making moves, as well."

At least she had broached the subject, so I felt safe saying, "You mean to say this might be politically motivated."

"Well, it seems strange this rune magic has popped up now, as dissension is being made public. And I'd like to—dammit I want to say no dwarf would sell out our people but there is much at stake."

I eyed Delilah, realizing why she was hesitant and so careful with her words. "And you agree," I said.

She darted a glance at me but said, "Yeah, I do. I hope you know I would never... but yes. I do."

I put a hand on her shoulder and waited until she made eye contact. "So do I. Already added my name to the roster."

Her shoulders slumped and some of the tension drained from her muscles. "I thought you might."

I turned and leaned against the table, folded my arms over my stomach, and ran through the other possible suspects. "Witches are unlikely," I guessed, "because they are outlawed in New London, and there is less for them to gain. They are already only barely tolerated in the country, and if girls began going missing, they would stand to lose too much. But they can't be ruled out."

"I agree."

"Elves don't traffic in magic of any kind," I said. "Their bodies are too delicate to channel it, though I suppose this form would be safer for them. In fact, it may give them a power base they would not have access to, otherwise. But I've never heard of any elf who even studied artificery."

Delilah's mouth twisted into an amused sneer. "No, they think the study is too base. It is either art for them or nothing. Though how they can not see the art in what we create is beyond me. Self-righteous little prigs."

Ah, the age-old fight between artists and craftsmen. Of course, not all dwarves entered the Artificer's Guild, and not all elves entered the Artisan's Guild, but the guilds were the main source of political power for their people, so everyone, even the doctors, lawyers, and innkeepers, supported them.

"That leaves humans and dwarves as suspects for creating the magic, with dwarves having an edge. And if it was a dwarf selling secrets or creating new artifice for political gain, there would have to be a human on the buying end."

"Indeed there would."

"Then," I turned to her, "what do you say to splitting the difference? You create a list of potential dwarves who might have the knowledge, skill, and money. I'll try to find out which humans might be in the market. Likely someone serving in parliament."

Delilah walked away from the table and began cleaning, sweeping up the chalk with brisk, almost angry motions.

"What is it?" I asked.

She jerked her jaw toward the corner of the room and said, "Can you hand me the scooper?"

I returned with the triangular device in hand and knelt while she brushed the remaining chalk into the bin. She waited silently while I emptied the dust, and didn't speak until I'd returned and positioned myself in front of her.

"I don't want to be involved in this, Gwen."

That was certainly not what I had hoped to hear. "There are lives at stake."

"I knew you'd say that," she growled, and stuffed her hands in her pockets. "But what about my life? What about everything I've sacrificed to build? Wherever this magic came from, the repercussions will not be small. If I poke my nose into this affair, I may have it burned off. I'm already walking the knife's-edge as a female artificer. There are damn few of us and we've fought hard to create a place for ourselves. I don't know if I'm willing to risk it all."

I remembered Virginia's face and Sally's bravery. Someone had to stand up for these girls. "I'm not asking you to investigate or risk yourself, just to create a list of people who have the right set of circumstances to gain this knowledge. I'll do the investigating, and deal with the trouble if any crops up. But, Delilah..." I waited for her to meet my eyes, but she didn't, so I plowed ahead. "You know how dangerous this knowledge could be. Once it's out, we cannot take it back. And we can't protect ourselves if we don't understand it."

She chewed her cheek, took a deep breath, and said, "I'll get you the list. And I'll keep studying. But that's all I can promise. I won't stick my neck out." She glanced at Sally, who had fallen asleep with her head pillowed on her arms, her blonde hair spilling out of her cap and onto the floor. She looked ridiculously young and vulnerable. Then Delilah wiped her hand down her face and turned away. "Not for her, and not even for you. There's too much to lose. And it's not just me, anymore. There's Fleur to consider, now. If I make a nuisance of myself—well, I won't endanger her."

Disappointment made my mouth taste sour, but I swallowed it back. "Fleur?"

Delilah's jaw clenched, but she nodded once.

"Does she make you happy?"

"She does."

I worked up the energy for a smile of congratulations. "Then I wish you well, my friend. When might I expect your list?"

"You'll have it by tomorrow night. But Gwen... don't come back here. Not for a few days, anyway. I want to wait for the smoke to blow over. You still have the umbrella I made you?"

"I do."

"Good. Keep it with you. And stay safe."

There was nothing else to say. She'd helped me get this far, despite the risk, and would help me still, just not as far as I'd hoped.

I gathered my valise, woke Sally, and bundled both of us into the carriage, knowing that I would be alone from here on out.

Sally leaned against the door as the city passed by, while I thought about how much more dangerous the situation had become. I'd dealt with danger before, but the risk had always been mine, alone. If the dwarves were selling unique magical secrets, the entire city would be in danger. The knowledge would eventually spread to the world because no politician would waste time buying power he couldn't use.

Magic accessible to anyone, that was channeled by runes instead of a body, would change everything, and not for the better. It couldn't be tracked or regulated, and if there was no physical cost associated to make people hesitate, chances were they'd use magic for nefarious or irresponsible purposes simply because they could. And if targeting people without some kind of focus was possible, no one would be safe.

I needed to know who was in the market for secrets and also had enough political power to grant the elves and dwarves the concessions they desired. Suddenly, the ball Mama planned didn't sound like such a bad idea. The duchess had a powerful circle of friends, and there was bound to be gossip. It would be much easier for me to speak to people trapped in a room with me than if I tried to make appointments or track them down in the city. And none of them would risk offending the duchess by ignoring her daughter. Which meant I would have to wear my most fashionable, flattering gown and be persuasive and charming. I could be charming.

*I could.*

"Oh!" Sally gasped as the coach pulled to a stop outside the townhouse. "The inspector is here, outside the house!"

"Bloody, everlasting, rotten hell," I growled. Charming, indeed.

"What do I do?" Sally whispered.

"Nothing. Nothing at all. Just head inside and go find Mrs. Chapman. She'll set you in order. I, however"—I gripped my umbrella like a weapon—"must stay calm and collected. Cool. Proper." I gritted my teeth. "Charming."

I followed Sally down and tried to hide my amusement as she completely ignored the inspector's attempt at a civil greeting. His puzzled expression was most gratifying, and it took me a moment to school my features into polite disinterest. He turned to me, took off his hat, and gave a creditable bow.

"My lady," he said.

I responded with a slight curtsy. Was the man wearing the same suit and jacket he'd worn yesterday? "Inspector. What a pleasure to see you again. What can I do for you?"

"You told me I might call upon you at home if I had questions about the kidnapping you saw."

"So I did. What are your questions?"

He glanced at the door, then at me. "Do you think we might discuss this indoors?"

And explain to Mama why I'm entertaining a police officer? No, thank you. "It's so nice out here, with the fall breeze," I said, waving my hand at the biting air and hoping he didn't realize my nose was turning red from the chill.

"If you'll forgive me, my lady, you're shivering."

The man was paying attention, damn him. "Only with anticipation, I assure you."

He raised one blonde brow. Maybe that hadn't been the cleverest thing to say.

"If we can just go inside," he began, but Sally appeared at the door, her face panicked as she shouted, "Lady Gwen, it's Sam! He's gone!"

My stomach dropped. "What?"

Mrs. Chapman pushed through to the front, her thin face pale. "Indeed, my lady, the boy is missing. Mr. Yates left him polishing boots in the upstairs hall and when he came back... Samuel was gone."

I turned to James and held up a hand to stop him pulling the coach away.

"Sally," I said. "Will Samuel have gone home?"

She bit her lips together, eyes worried, and considered for a moment. She didn't want to tell me, didn't want him to get in trouble, but there wasn't a better option.

She nodded. "He probably has. I don't know where else he would have gone, otherwise."

"If you'll excuse me, Inspector," I said, turning toward the coach. "I have a twelve-year-old to fetch. Hopefully before afternoon tea."

Sally came running, but I stopped her with a hand. "No, my dear. Samuel cannot hide behind your skirts, and you cannot protect him. He must take responsibility. I will fetch him."

"But he—"

"We will find him, miss," Inspector Hardwicke said. "I promise you."

"We?" I demanded, gaping.

"I am an officer of the law," he said, "and I still have questions for you, lady."

I ground my teeth, thinking of the long ride from Grosvenor Square to the East End, then remembered Mama inside the house and my cowardice rose to ruin everything. It would be highly improper, but I'd never cared much for propriety, especially not where important matters were concerned, like missing children and an angry mother.

I swallowed back a reply and said, "He's right, Sally. We'll find Samuel and bring him home. Trust me."

She bit her lip and wrung her hands but gave a hesitant nod. Before anyone else could interrupt, I turned and leaped into the carriage, ignoring the inspector's outstretched hand. He followed me in and we were off. Again. I was beginning to feel as if half my life was spent behind coach walls.

It wasn't until we were in the coach, with the doors closed, that the intrepid inspector realized the impropriety of our situation. He fidgeted with his hat and glanced at the door with longing in his eyes.

"I can have James slow if you'd like to leap out," I offered. "I won't even tell anyone. Just be sure to roll when you hit the ground."

"I was only thinking—"

"Please, Inspector, give me some credit. Your face is as easy to read as a book."

He glowered. At least he tried to glower. The man had too honest and kind a face to be truly intimidating. But my amused response only ruffled his feathers more, so I raised both my hands and said, "Please, Inspector, I am sorry. You mustn't take me too seriously, I cannot resist the chance to tease. We are here now so it is too late to turn back, and the carriage is closed so your honor will not be impugned."

"I am more concerned with your honor, madame," he said in a tone heavy with disapproval.

I did laugh, then. "My honor cannot be salvaged, sir. Pray, do not concern yourself with it. I know I never do."

The slack surprise on his face was delightful. "What a thing to say. If you do not care for what others may assume about your behavior, I certainly do. Stop the carriage and I will get out."

"And break your promise to Sally?"

He paused in the act of leaning out the window.

"Inspector, believe me, the truth of my actions is far beyond what anyone is likely to assume. Their gossip cannot hurt me. They may think what they like from the comfort of their drawing rooms and gossip behind their hands while we try to help those who need it."

It took him an uncomfortable moment to decide whether I was joking, then to reassume his mantle of professional detachment. Seeing the uncomfortable man disappear behind the mask of the competent inspector was a bit of a disappointment, but I bore it with aplomb.

"Very well, Lady St. James. Allow me to be frank."

I tried not to say it. I really did try. But Inspector Hardwicke had awoken my humor, and my natural response to stressful situations was to diminish them through laughter, so I found myself saying, "I will allow you to be Frank if you allow me to be Esmerelda. I have always loved that name. There is such romance to it, don't you think?"

His glower was much more impressive the second time. But he ignored me, which was probably for the best, and said, "They kidnapped another child last night. A young boy of approximately thirteen years."

My humor dried up, cracked, and turned into dust. "I am sorry to hear it. Did he have a family?"

"He did not. Why do you ask?"

"Because Sally and Virginia are both orphans."

He nodded gravely. "This seems to be a common thread amongst the victims. More than that, when I investigated the scene, I found the remnants of this." He held up my sketch of the magic circle. "A butcher tossed out a bucket of used water and washed most of it away, but what was left of the markings matched these symbols."

"And you did not find these at the scenes of the other two kidnappings?"

"No. Those were reported as missing persons, so there was no scene to investigate."

"Yet you classify them as kidnappings?"

"Both girls were employed, one as a maid and the other as an apprentice seamstress. Their employers spoke highly of them, and we have not recovered their bodies."

"A fair assumption, then. And may I ask who reported last night's kidnapping?"

The Inspector leaned forward, pulling his coat tight across his shoulders, and leveled a pair of serious brown eyes at me. His lashes were ridiculously, unfairly long. "I will answer your question if you answer one of mine."

I narrowed my eyes at him. Why the sudden hesitance when he'd shared the other information freely so far? "Very well."

"An artificer saw the kidnapping while returning home late from work. Witnesses have confirmed that he was at his workshop finishing a commission for a client. Are you associated with any witches in New London?"

He threw out the question before I processed his answer. Why did he mention witnesses? Did he just subtly accuse me of not having any corroboration for my alibi and then directly accuse me of witchcraft? "Am I what? No, of course not. There are no witches in New London."

"Then how do you know about this circle and what it means?"

"I have made a study of the occult. I've purchased many rare books at great expense, even traveled to the continent and Africa to obtain them."

"Why?"

I shrugged. "Why not. It is an interesting study."

"And how many other people in New London possess knowledge like yours?"

I paused as the implication of what he was asking plowed me over. It was a moment before I demanded, "Are you implying that I am behind these kidnappings?"

"Are you?"

I controlled my rising temper. "Why would I report a kidnapping and give you sketches of the evidence and then commit similar crimes leaving the same evidence behind? What kind of fool would do such a thing?"

"The kind who wishes to remove themselves from suspicion by cooperating with the police."

"I doubt anything I say could remove your suspicion."

"How about answering my question honestly? Are you connected to these kidnappings?"

I sighed. "No, Inspector. I am not."

"And yet, an orphan boy of the same age as the missing children has run from your house and you are on your way to retrieve him. You also, by your admission, care nothing for your honor."

"What would I have to gain by kidnapping children?"

"I was hoping you would tell me."

I crossed my arms, then said with exasperated disbelief, "Have you been reading Doyle?"

His expression didn't change, but a slow flush crept up his neck.

"Oh, for the love of all things—Inspector, please do not rely on fiction to guide your investigations."

"How I run my investigation is none of your concern, lady. Your concern should be convincing me not to implicate you in this affair."

I drew myself up and glared across the aisle. "You are potentially the most suspicious and irritating man I have ever had the misfortune to encounter, and believe me, sir, the list is long. Yes, I have given Sally and her brother a safe place to live and work. I could not, in all good conscience, leave them in the slums with no one to care for them when I can help. But the boy, Sam, hasn't run from my home because I kidnapped him, he ran back to the only home he has ever known because he refuses to believe his father is gone."

He looked at me down the length of his long, straight nose. "I assume you will not interfere if I question the boy when we return him to his sister?"

He said, return him to his sister, not, return him to your home. "Of course not. You may ask the boy anything you like."

"Good."

"Fine."

We glared at one another until the coach pulled to a stop. I ignored his attempt to help me down—as if I would accept any of his help now—and landed on the broken cobblestones with a jarring thump. The courtyard before us was as I remembered: ankle-deep in mud. I began casting about, reading the prints in the mud. I noticed several interesting things, and after a minute or so I said, "Ah, he has been this way. Shall we?"

"How do you know where he's gone? Missing his father does not guarantee he entered this building. It is a long walk, he may not even be here by now."

"If you insist on disbelieving everything I say, this trip is going to be even more uncomfortable than it already is." I bent and pointed at a muddy footprint. "Do you see this boot print? See the X in the center? I suspected Sam would have a hard time staying put considering he's had only himself and his sister to answer to for four years. I wanted to be able to find him, so I asked my butler,

Mr. Yates, to carve this x into the sole of his boots. What? Is that grudging respect in your eyes, Inspector Hardwicke?"

He snorted, sidled past me, and tracked the boot prints into the ramshackle building.

This was going to be fun. I sighed and followed him.

# 10
# Brass Knuckles
## GWEN

The muddy boot prints were easy to follow, and Sam did not even bother to raise his head when Inspector Hardwicke and I entered the dilapidated little flat. He sat on the bare mattress atop the only bed in the small room, hunched over a worn pocket knife he turned over and over, looking dreadfully out of place in his new uniform.

Guilt and shame welled up, leaving me sick. How could we be an empire of such wealth and yet still allow families and children to live in deprivation? I had been gone for too long and allowed myself to be blind to what was around me. But I would never forget the sight of Sam, so small, as he sat grieving the only life he had ever known.

"I forgot my pocket knife," he said.

"Was it a gift?"

He nodded.

I sat down next to him on the bed, hesitated for a moment, and then put my hand on his back. He didn't acknowledge me, but I plowed ahead, anyway. "I would have had James bring you back if you'd asked to retrieve it."

He squirmed out from under my touch and stood on the opposite side of the bed. Earning this boy's trust was going to take time, but I wanted to make one more offer. "I am glad we found you, Sam. I wanted to take out an advertisement in the paper. Someone will let this flat soon, and your father should know where you are when he comes back. Will you help me write it, so I know what to say?"

The boy bit his lip and looked around the room, likely imagining someone new in the home he'd always thought of as his own.

Finally, he said, "Yeah. Okay." Then he looked up and his expression changed to wary suspicion and he demanded, "Who's this?"

"Samuel Dawes," I said, "this is Inspector Hardwicke. He's helping me find your sister's friend, Virginia."

Samuel didn't believe a word of it. His lean little body tensed like a striking snake, and his eyes began darting around the room, looking for escape routes.

"Hullo, Sam," the inspector said in a friendlier voice than I had yet heard from him. "I'm Tony. The lady is right, I'm looking for the kids who've gone missing. I've heard you're a smart one and you know more about the streets than most. I thought I could use your help."

Sam's eyes flickered back and forth between the two of us as he clenched the pocket knife in a white-knuckled fist.

"Plus," Tony added, "your sister is worried about you. She's been frantic. Hasn't even eaten lunch, her stomach is so sick."

Clever to add in the bit about Sally. If anything would pull on the boy's heartstrings, it was his sister. Sam chewed his cheek for a moment, but then his ego got the better of him and he asked the inspector, "What do you want to know?"

"Shall we talk about it on the way?" I asked. "I'm hungry."

Tony gave Sam a conspiratorial look. "Girls are so finicky, aren't they?"

Sam snorted and said, "Tell me about it."

I left the room ahead of them and stomped down the stairs, making as much noise as possible and clutching my umbrella in my left hand. If I did not exit the building far enough in front of my companions, the situation may get messy.

The inspector would have happily taken the risk if I did not miss my guess about his character, but he would more than likely scare my prey off and cause us to miss a valuable opportunity. I would have to be the bait, so I took a deep breath, pushed the door open, and stepped into the sunlight.

A brass-knuckled fist flew at my head from the left of the doorway.

I ducked beneath the blow and spun, gripping my umbrella in both hands, one at the front and one at the end. The point of my makeshift weapon took the man square in the solar plexus with all the force of my spin. It did not break the skin, but it sank deep, forcing the breath from my attacker's body. He doubled over with a grunt and I stepped outside his range to pull the short blade from the shaft of the umbrella and point it at his midsection.

Runes covered the blade, making the metal light and strong, and years of training helped me wield it with absolute precision. At least my father had done one thing right.

"Do not move, sir," I told the man, and cut a button from his jacket with the tip of my rapier, "or I will carve you up the middle like a yule goose."

My assailant stumbled back and struggled to pull in a breath as Inspector Hardwicke leaped from the doorway with a snub-nosed pistol in his hand. And pointed the weapon right at me.

"Drop your weapon, Lady St. James."

"Inspector, are you pointing a gun at me for defending myself from a common criminal? He took a swing at me from cover, wearing brass knuckles. Have a look for yourself."

The inspector bent and presumably saw the illegal weapon on my assailant's hand because he grudgingly turned his pistol on the gasping man.

I sheathed the blade, returning my umbrella to its previously harmless appearance, and said, "This gentleman's name is Harry. And if you look at his right wrist, you'll see blue ink symbols drawn there in a band that circles his arm."

"Drop the knuckles," the inspector ordered. "Raise your hands."

Harry appeared to have regained his breath because he wheezed, "Go to 'ell."

"Well, that's hardly polite," I said.

"You can come out, Sam, I need your help," Inspector Hardwicke called, but the boy had already been watching from the door, his eyes wide.

"What do I do?" he asked.

"Run and find me the first bobbies you can, and bring them back here."

Sam hopped down from the doorway and took off at a dead run.

The inspector turned back to Harry and repeated, "Drop the brass knuckles." This time, his voice was cold and dangerous.

"Make me," Harry spat.

That was a mistake. Inspector Hardwicke stepped forward and, with a quick twist of his shoulder, brought the butt of the gun down on Harry's head. The man stumbled, fell backward, and landed on his arse in the mud.

The inspector stripped the knuckles from Harry's limp hand and hauled the man bodily to his feet before dragging him onto the cleaner cobbles near the coach. James had hopped down from the driver's seat and hovered protectively over my shoulder with a coach gun held low in both hands.

"Stay close to me, my lady," he said as the inspector searched the criminal, finally exposing his right wrist. The markings were there, inked in blue.

"May I?" I asked.

Inspector Hardwicke looked up at me over his shoulder, considered his options, then nodded and scooted to the side, making room for me to squat next to him. But he never took his suspicious gaze off me and stayed within reach.

The marks on Harry's wrist were certainly ink but not tattoos, and written in a different hand than the circle had been. These symbols were precise and clean and purposeful, with nary a smudge, and several of the symbols were familiar. But they were not runes, which would make them much harder to read.

Magic symbols, unfortunately, were not universal. Some practitioners reused common symbols, particularly those created by whoever taught them. There were rites, rituals, and potions learned or passed down from teacher to acolyte. But, eventually, all witches created symbols of their own, both to make their spells more powerful and to protect them from theft. Their intention when creating the symbol gave it meaning and power.

This was why grimoires were so important; they were not only a record but a dictionary. The only way to know which practitioner used which symbols was to be told, or to read her grimoire.

"Who wrote this spell on you?" I demanded, hoping he would still be dizzy enough to answer without thinking.

But Harry had regained enough consciousness to jerk his hand away from me and scoot into a sitting position. He glared at me through slitted eyes. "I ain't telling you nothing."

I learned then I had been wrong about the inspector. He certainly could be intimidating when he chose. He leveled a cold, calculating look at the man and said, "If you don't answer questions, there isn't much reason to keep you around, is there?"

Harry paled but didn't answer.

"Are the children still alive?" Inspector Hardwicke asked.

Harry didn't answer.

The inspector pressed the barrel of his gun against Harry's forehead. Sweat broke out on Harry's upper lip, but he nodded.

"Where are they?"

Harry shook his head.

Inspector Hardwicke thumbed back the hammer with a dangerous click. "Where. Are. They."

Harry's defiance melted, and his face twisted with desperation. "I can't tell you."

"What can you tell me?"

"Nothing."

The inspector pushed Harry over backward and knelt on the man's chest, pinning him with one knee, then he looked at me.

"Lady St. James, you have some martial skill."

"A bit," I hedged.

"Ever broken a finger?"

"Oh, is that all? Of course I have, more than once. Shall I give it a go?"

"One at a time, if you please, until he answers the question."

Following the inspector's lead, I knelt on Harry's arm and took his pinky firmly in my right hand. His palms were sweaty, his hand shaking.

"I can't," Harry squeaked, twisting his body to pull his arm from my grasp. Hardwicke nodded at me with a wink, so I put pressure on the pinky finger.

"No, no, no, don't! I can't tell you!" His voice had risen three octaves, and as I twisted further and the pain set in, Harry became truly desperate.

"I can't," he grunted, his face turning red. "Don't, please, I can't!"

Harry's body spasmed, and a sudden suspicion had me climbing off the man and pulling the inspector with me.

"Get off—" he began, but I squeezed his arm and said, "No, Inspector, look at him."

Harry's body jerked and twitched, his heels drumming on the ground as his arms flailed and twisted.

"Is he having a fit?"

"In a way. I think he may be under compulsion. Look at his eyes."

Blood vessels had burst in the sclera, turning the whites of Harry's eyes red. His nose bled, and a trickle leaked from his ears. Then his body rose off the ground by a full foot, hovering in the air as several cracking sounds punctuated the grunts of pain before he flopped back to the ground, completely still. We stood for a moment in shocked silence, and I don't mind admitting little tendrils of fear had curled up my legs to weaken my knees.

"What in the gory hell was that?" the inspector demanded.

I knelt near Harry's outstretched arm and peeled back his sleeve to feel for vital signs. He was breathing, though raggedly, and his heart beating thudded furiously against my fingertips. Three of the marks on his wrist had blackened, sinking into his skin like a brand and making the air smell like burnt flesh.

"He's still alive. God's breath," I muttered.

"Explain, Lady St. James." The inspector's voice was flat as he eyed me with thin-lipped suspicion. I had to tread carefully.

"Did you notice that when you asked him to answer your questions he said, 'I can't,' and not, 'I won't,'?"

"I did."

"Well, those marks on his wrist are magic. I don't recognize all of them, but those"—I pointed to the blackened marks—"began burning him when we pressured him to answer us. Either he fought the compulsion, or the spell was strong enough to damage him if he revealed things he shouldn't have. I've read about such spells but they are understandably rare. Few people would willingly submit to being controlled with such a spell, and the markings are very precise. A compulsion spell would never work if drawn on an unwilling victim unless someone drugged them."

"What do you mean by compulsion?"

I stood and brushed the dirt off the front of my dress. "Someone has given this man orders, and the spell on his wrist punishes him if he does not follow them. There is likely more, but I will need to research it."

Should I tell him Harry had been outside my home? Icy dread slid down my spine at the memory of green eyes in the dark. Had he been the only spy watching us, or were there others?

Inspector Hardwicke stood over Harry's limp body, watching the man's chest rise and fall with weak, staggered breaths, his eyes hard. "He did not start convulsing until you touched him."

"I could say the same about you," I scoffed.

"I know nothing of magic."

"And knowing is not the same as using. Are there any marks of magic on me, Inspector? Any green scars or unnatural deformities? Branches growing from my scalp instead of hair? No?"

"For all I know that is merely a rumor started to obfuscate the truth. Perhaps witches have none of those things and use the rumor as a cover."

"God's breath, you are a suspicious one. You would not say so if you'd ever met a witch. I have. They all appear decades older than their years and often have novel damages associated with the power of the magic they channel. No one does magic like this"—I gestured to Harry's body—"and gets away with it without visible damage."

He was silent for a long moment as he considered Harry, and then me. "I have no way to know whether you speak the truth. And the only way to verify your information is to leave the city and track down someone styling themselves a witch. Which would take me too far away from this investigation."

I rolled my eyes and folded my arms, then said dramatically, "You see what a diabolical villain I am? How Machiavellian? However do I weave such intricate and unexpected webs?"

He scowled at me, and I feigned wide-eyed innocence. The man could certainly arrest me on suspicion, but I refused to let doubt show on my face because it would only make me look even more guilty in his eyes.

"This is not a laughing matter, lady."

"No, Inspector, it is not. But you are focusing your investigative skills in the wrong place. I have told you the truth at every turn, even when it has made me appear guilty. I do not know what else I can do to convince you I am only trying to help."

He turned his gaze back to Harry's body and rubbed his hands on the front of his jacket as if wiping away some contamination. "You told me the kidnappers were using magic. I did not believe you. But this... I just watched a man's body break, while no one touched him, as he floated a foot off the ground. I cannot deny the truth of that. Magic does... does exist. And the best way you can prove your innocence is to continue to tell me the truth."

"All the while you shall continue to suspect me," I said.

"I shall suspect everyone until I have these children safe." He stared at the beaten man, his blonde brows drawn low over his eyes. "You knew he was there, didn't you? Outside the building."

"Yes, I did."

"How?"

"Why should I tell you? You will only disbelieve me."

He glowered, and I sighed. "The same way I knew where Samuel was: boot prints in the mud. Harry wears a size nine shoe. I had seen the size of the scuff marks that ruined the magical circle when Virginia was being kidnapped, and the resulting prints on the cobblestones. Size nine and flat-footed. When I searched for Samuel's prints, I saw the relatively recent print of a flat, size nine shoe."

"How do you know it was recent?"

"Because the print was still wet, even at the edges where footprints dry out the fastest."

"I'm here!" We both looked up as Sam's voice echoed off the buildings. A moment later, the boy appeared, pounding down the street as fast as his little legs could pump, with two blue-uniformed bobbies huffing behind him. They caught the boy, one by each arm, and hauled him up off his feet. He flailed and kicked, arching his body like a landed fish and shouting, "Let me go! He told me to get you, I told you! Let go!"

"Release the boy," the inspector ordered. The men turned toward us, their faces red and sweaty as they tried to dodge Sam's flying limbs. Upon seeing the inspector, they dropped Sam, and watched with red faces as the boy bolted for us, skidding to a stop on the other side of the coach behind James. The officer in front, a long-faced man with sallow skin and wiry hair, looked from Harry's body to Inspector Hardwicke with wide eyes.

"Ah, Inspector," he said. "We thought the boy was just causing trouble. Glad to see the little chap was telling the truth. Who's this on the ground, then?"

"Harry the Kidnapper," I said.

The inspector gave me a dirty look that said *if you don't mind*, and then explained everything, as I mentally sorted through information. Harry had been marked by a compulsion spell, and he had also learned enough about magic and runes to reproduce a complex and unique spell on his own. That meant he had access to someone with a great deal of knowledge, power, or both.

He said the children were still alive, but I wasn't sure how much of that to believe. Without knowing what the rest of the compulsion spell said, I wouldn't know if it had compelled him to lie, to avoid answering questions, or any number of other possibilities.

I took off my hat, pulled the notebook and pen out of it, and began sketching the marks. Once I knew what each of these symbols meant as part of a whole, I would have a better idea of what the spell compelled him to do, and what it stopped him from doing. That may be a critical clue in figuring out who was behind the kidnapping. And if I knew what the spell wanted him to do, I might also be able to puzzle out what it was protecting.

And Mama's ball was tomorrow, which meant I had little time. I wanted to gather as much information as possible before I started asking questions.

"Bring him to the holding cell and fetch a doctor," Inspector Hardwicke told his two subordinates. "Get him medical attention and hold him till I return."

"Wait," I looked up from my unfinished sketch. "I have more questions for this man."

"You've no jurisdiction to ask them," the Inspector pointed out coolly.

The bobbies hefted the body, and the lead constable asked, "Are you not coming back with us, sir?"

"No," he said. "I'm going to accompany Lady St. James and her footman safely home. Then I shall return."

"Very good," the constable said.

They bundled the limp body into a carrying position, but they would have a long, uncomfortable walk before they found a cab.

"Why not use my carriage, gentlemen? The man appears to be in a delicate condition, and time may be of the essence."

They looked at the inspector for approval, and James frowned at me. "The inspector will attend to our safety," I told James, while the man in question grudgingly told his subordinates to follow my suggestion. They loaded the body into the coach and left us standing on the dirty cobbles of the Narrows.

I took a deep breath, looked at my companions, and smiled. "A brisk walk sounds lovely. I've spent entirely too much time in coaches. Sam, will you lead the way?"

The boy positively glowed with excitement. He'd seen a fight, a gun, and a nearly dead man, been chased by the police, and now got to lead two adults through territory he knew better than they did. His smile was both confident and mischievous. "Alright, then. Let's go, m'lady."

He led us back out of the Narrows and into East End traffic, weaving through the crowd like a fish in a stream. Passing pedestrians gave me a speculative look, noticed Inspector Hardwicke at my side, and found something else to look at. People parted for us as soon as they saw him coming. Which made me wonder if they saw something in his face that I did not.

"Why, Inspector," I said. "You are quite as good as a guard dog. I should like you to accompany me on all my errands to keep me out of trouble."

He looked me up and down most inappropriately, and replied, "I don't think the Queen herself could keep you out of trouble with a hundred guards and a royal edict."

"I do not go looking for trouble, sir. It finds me while I am minding my own business."

He snorted.

A hackney appeared through breaks in traffic, parked near the corner. The hired cabs were rarer here, but proof that where there was money to be made, an enterprising person would create a vocation.

"Here we are," I said, stepping up to the hack and reaching for the handle.

"No, my lady!" Sam jumped up and wrapped his hands around my wrist, pulling me away.

"Samuel, what on earth?"

"You can't use that cab," he said, his face red.

"And why not. It appears perfectly serviceable."

"Didn't you see the handkerchief hanging out the window?"

I glanced back at the coach. "Yes. And?"

Sam said, in tones of great exasperation, "It means there's a tart inside, waiting for her next John."

"A what?"

Sam realized what he had just said aloud, and blushed scarlet as he looked around, then whispered, "A–a tart."

"Wonderful, Samuel, now I'm hungry. Is there a bakery nearby, do you think? A tart sounds like just the snack to perk me up."

Sam's face went green and Inspector Hardwicke said, "He means a working girl, Lady St. James."

I rolled my eyes. "Yes, Inspector, I know what he meant but, by all means, continue to ruin the fun. I cannot even tease the boy in peace. Sam, let us go on. We'll find another cab soon, I am certain."

The boy looked relieved, then said, "Can we still stop by a bakery? All the running made me hungry."

I laughed. I couldn't help it. "Of course, we can. Now, onward, brave leader."

We started walking again, and when Sam had outstripped us by a couple of paces, Inspector Hardwicke leaned toward me and said, in a low voice, "You should not tease the boy about such things."

"In heaven's name why not?"

"It's not proper for him to be talking about ladies of the night, much less for you to be joking about it."

"Please, enlighten me. What subjects should amuse me? What pleasures am I allowed, oh arbiter of morality?"

He scowled at me. I smiled back. "Samuel," I said, "let us hurry and get the inspector here back to his Ivory Tower. I do believe we've soiled his honor with our base conversation."

Samuel grinned. Inspector Hardwicke did not.

It wasn't long before we found a cab that was not otherwise engaged and set off toward home. The inspector kept shooting me troubled glances, but I ignored him and stared doggedly out the window. Sam ignored the both of us and focused on the apple tart we procured before finding the coach, which lasted just long enough for us to pull up outside the house. The wind had picked up, tearing the last of the leaves from the trees and hurling them down the street while howling with glee.

Sam hopped down and bolted for the house without waiting. I stood to exit, but Inspector Hardwicke blocked the door with his arm.

When I glared at him, he only responded by clenching his jaw.

"Excuse me, Inspector. I have had a long day and I would like to rest before dinner."

"Not until I am certain you've understood me, lady."

He leaned forward, close enough for his body heat to warm the space between us, and said in an icy voice, "I do not understand how you are tangled in this affair, but I don't believe you've told me everything. And if you are not working with the kidnapper, you are involved in some other way. I will find out how, and the kidnapper will be brought to justice. So I suggest you tread carefully because I will be watching you."

I wanted to slap the man. How far would I have to go to prove to this suspicious idiot that I was only trying to help? I refused to admit that, in his position, I would also find my actions and involvement questionable. That wasn't the point. He was not only coming to the absolute wrong conclusions, he was intruding on my personal space and irritating me when I was already tired. So I played the one card guaranteed to make him back away.

I leaned in close, close enough to feel his breath on my face, and said in a husky voice, "You'll be watching me, will you? Personally? Intimately? Should I wear something special for you, Tony? A bit of lace, maybe?"

He only hesitated for a moment before jerking back against the wall like he'd been burned, hitting his head on the wood panel. Oh, the delicious impropriety.

I let my voice return to normal and glared at the shocked man for all I was worth. "Do not threaten me again, sir. I have only the best of intentions where this case is concerned. I am also your best source of information unless you'd like to leave town and track down a witch to see if she will cooperate."

I climbed down from the carriage and looked back into the dark interior. If I didn't want the inspector tailing me around New London, I had better smooth the situation over. "I promise to share with you every piece of information I learn. I want these children safe. Please do not waste time. We don't know how much is left."

He scowled at me, red-faced, and pounded on the side of the hack. The driver flicked the reins, and the inspector said, as the coach pulled away, "Don't make any mistakes, Lady St. James. Or I will arrest you, personally."

The hired coach pulled around the square and disappeared into traffic, leaving me standing on the street with a dirty skirt, and the inspector's warning ringing in my ears.

Even worse, I didn't have much time to get ready for the dinner Mama was holding.

Damn.

# 11

# *Dinner and Discussions*

## GWEN

The drawing room was already filled with people when I arrived. It had taken longer than anticipated to clean myself up and have Charlotte arrange my hair. I preferred the simple bun I twisted up myself, but for an occasion such as this, simplicity would not do. The bigger and more elaborate the hair, the better. Luckily for me, I had enough hair not to require hair rats or forms to achieve fashionable volume, but I paid for it in broken brush handles and arms tired from holding so much weight above my head.

Instead of my floundering, Charlotte created a hairstyle with loose braids piled atop my head and curls framing my face at the temples, then used an ivory and pearl comb to hold everything in place. My blue silk dress exposed a wide expanse of décolletage, but my ensemble was positively tame compared with several women, and even some men, in the room.

There was an abundance of feathers and ribbons, silks and velvets, as all the wealthy visitors paraded for one another like mating birds, festooned in so much wealth it would have bought every flat in the Narrows three times over. And the ball tomorrow night would be worse. This was merely a prelude. I steeled myself and entered the fray, prepared to make myself agreeable while learning as much as possible about the state of politics. Which would not be easy.

These were Mama's friends and acquaintances, so they would be bound by friendship and the rules of polite society not to ignore me, but that did not mean they would be in a hurry to give up information, either.

Aristotle found a place for himself atop the fireplace mantle in the drawing room. When he spotted me, he sailed across the room, causing several guests to gasp and retreat. He landed on my bare shoulder, gripping delicately with his feet, and making me the subject of several shocked stares. "Thank you very much for that unwanted attention, you show off."

He tucked his head under my chin, hiding his head, then turning it as if eyeing my lack of jewelry. "What need do I have for adornment when I have you, my friend," I said fondly, and rubbed a gloved finger down his chest. Aristotle made a purring noise and clicked his beak together.

Mama joined us a moment later, giving the raven a look of exasperated amusement. "I told him he could stay in the drawing room if he didn't cause a scene, and here he is, disobeying my orders almost immediately."

"Aristotle does not take orders," I told her primly.

"Clearly not. Come, let us see if he can behave himself while I introduce you to a few of our guests. Some you will already know, of course, and others you will not remember. You were so small when they met you."

She dragged me over to a group of guests chatting by the fireplace, who turned to the approaching duchess with indulgent smiles.

"You must excuse my interruption," Mama said, "but you can hardly blame a woman for wanting to show off a beautiful daughter. All mamas must be indulged in this, as I'm sure you'll agree, Lady Weatherby. I hear Miss Weatherby has taken the season by storm."

The older woman was perhaps somewhere in her mid-sixties, with a sagging jawline and dark brown skin that caught the light and made her glow. The remains of a luminous beauty were still there in the lines of her face, which were drawn up and into a fan at the corners of her eyes when she smiled. "You know just how to flatter a woman, Your Grace," she said. "It is true, Gloriana has been quite the success, and we cannot dote upon her enough. But this cannot be young Gwenevere. The last time I saw you, miss, you were running wild with your hair hanging down your back and full of wildflowers. And here we have a young woman ready to take the world by the toes."

I laughed. Her smile was so genuine it was impossible not to feel flattered just by her attention. I responded to her compliment with a small curtsy. "Lady Weatherby, you are too kind. I regret that I have not met your Gloriana in town. I remember her as a cherub-faced girl, and now she is all grown up!"

"Nearly so," Lady Weatherby said, "but I am certain she would be pleased to see you. Shall I tell her you are receiving calls?"

I wanted to say no, I was trying to track down kidnappers and didn't have time to renew old acquaintances with a girl who was only a toddler the last time I'd seen her, but instead I said, "I would be very pleased if you did."

"Of course, I do not want to leave our other guests without proper introductions," Mama cut in smoothly. "Lord Kensington, Lady Marx, may I present my daughter Gwenevere, the future Duchess of Wainwright?"

And that is how the evening progressed. I was introduced to lords and ladies and honorable gentlemen, several of whom were, in fact, young and unmarried. Lord Kensington was Lady Weatherby's nephew by her sister, and was a solidly handsome fellow who gave me wary but interested sidelong glances. Mama never let me stay in one group for too long, but ushered me around to be certain I had met and renewed every acquaintance. We exchanged polite banalities, commented on the weather and the state of the roads, and by the time I was free to mingle on my own, I was ready to tear my hair out if it would save me from small talk.

Aristotle hadn't left my shoulder, and most of the guests had done a commendable job of ignoring him—propriety, you remember—except the Marquise of Rutledge, a stolid-looking sportsman with deeply tanned skin and a bulbous red nose who said, "I say. That's quite a specimen. Where did you find it?"

He spoke as if all the muscles round his mouth had gone limp and he had to push the words out past his flapping lips and mustache.

"Oh, he found me, sir. He followed me home from a ride on the estate one day, and has been with me ever since."

His question emboldened the other members of our party, and one young woman, who had been sending speculative glances toward handsome Lord Kensington, asked, "But doesn't the beast make a dreadful mess?"

I had been about to explain that Aristotle was both not a beast and extraordinarily clean—aside from the little trinkets he liked to steal and hide—when Aristotle spoke up for himself. He turned to the girl, tilted his head, and said, "You stink."

Her face went up in flames, but the rest of the party only laughed and tried to get him to say other things. When Aristotle decided he'd had enough of their company, and flew around the room to amuse himself by pestering the other visitors. I couldn't let that go on for long, because he was certain to annoy one of Mama's guests, so I excused myself and tracked him down.

I found my errant companion perched on the shoulder of an elegant, pale-skinned woman of middle years who sat alone by the fireplace. Mama had not introduced us, but Aristotle paved the way for the introduction so I approached and said, "I do hope my feathered friend here is not bothering you?"

She looked up at me with a charming smile and said, "Not at all. In fact, I was just contemplating how I might smuggle him out with me." Her voice was low and warm and husky, the kind of voice you wanted to hear reading on winter evenings by the fire.

I held out my hand and said, "I'm pleased to hear he has not been making a pest of himself, but I'd wager you want to return him within hours. He is too smart for his own good. I am Gwenevere, Lady St. James."

She took it, and I was struck by the way my white gloves and her black ones made such a striking contrast against one another. "And I am Cassandra, Lady Monmouth. It is a pleasure to meet you and your avian friend. May I ask his name?"

The bird in question was busy exploring his new friend, climbing from one shoulder to the other, up and down her arms, and finally, picking delicate curls from her elaborate coiffure. She made no move to shoo him.

"His name is Aristotle."

She smiled, but the expression was almost sad. "A carrion bird as a philosopher is exactly the thing to excite my sense of irony."

Aristotle flew away and resumed his perch on the hearth, watching the rest of the party with haughty disdain.

"I wish I could take credit for naming him," I said, "but he managed to get into the library one day, and I found him picking through a volume of Aristotle's Collected Works that had been left on the table."

"And does he speak?"

"When he chooses to. I'm afraid he's already insulted one young woman tonight."

The corner of her mouth curled up into a smile. "Good for him. Young women are too much fawned over, in my experience. Each of them fancies themselves the belle of the ball, which sets them up for disappointment when the next and prettiest girl appears. And she always appears."

I tilted my head, taking in her lovely bone structure and grey eyes. "Something tells me you have firsthand knowledge?"

She gestured to the seat across from hers, and I joined her by the fire. The conversation at dinner parties was, by general agreement, constrained to polite topics unlikely to ruffle any feathers and ensure everyone had a pleasant, if dull, evening. Lady Monmouth apparently didn't suffer from that affliction, and I found myself intrigued. I would happily sit by anyone who would save me from an evening of small talk.

She folded her hands in her lap, but the gesture didn't have the sense of elegant propriety Mama would have conveyed if she did the same. Lady Monmouth folded her hands as if she enjoyed the feeling of the satin gloves on her skin. There was an inherent sensuality in her movements that was fascinating.

"You guess correctly. My family taught me to treat my appearance as the value I contributed to the world. To be pretty and amiable was everything, because those would catch me a husband. And of course, every girl wants to catch the best husband on the market, and then flaunt him before the other girls who are still unengaged." A little twinkle of malice entered her eyes. "We are cruel creatures, are we not?"

"We certainly can be," I said, thinking of my own debut season.

"But there is no ring on your finger, Lady St. James. And you must be, what? Twenty-two?"

"Twenty-five, and you are correct. I have no intention of marrying."

She smiled. "Clever girl, particularly in your position. What inducement can an intelligent woman of means have to marry and sacrifice her freedom? Better to die a spinster who is free than a wife who spent the best part of her life as a servant to a man who cannot match her. It is a cruelty of nature and politics that we are the weaker sex."

"Indeed, I have never understood the term. We bring life into the world, and I cannot think of any task requiring greater strength."

Lady Monmouth's eyes took on a faraway look and her expression softened even as the lines around her mouth deepened. "You are correct, of course. And that is one aspect of womanhood I do not regret, though I may rage against the rest."

"I cannot pretend to desire motherhood," I said, quietly enough not to be overheard by more delicate ears, "I am far too selfish a creature. There is too much I want to do and see and learn. And the idea of carrying and birthing a child does not appeal. But your sentiment agrees with my observations of nature. Witness the strength and power of a mother bear, yet protecting her young also puts her in grave danger."

She leaned forward and the light of the fireplace was reflected in her grey eyes. "I am glad to have met you, Lady St. James. It is refreshing to have so frank a conversation, for once. I do hope we can be friends."

The little ember of recognition, of the meeting of a kindred spirit, kindled to light in my chest. "I should like that very much, Lady Monmouth."

"Then you must call me Cassandra, at least"—she looked over her shoulder—"when we aren't in such stodgy company," and gave me a wink.

"Good evening, ladies." It was the Marquise of Rutledge, who stood with both hands on his belly and his double chin resting comfortably on his chest. "I overheard you mention bear, Lady St. James."

"Indeed, sir, though the mention was in reference to motherhood, and not hunting."

"Ah yes, motherhood, a very proper and noble occupation. I cannot think of a happier woman than one with a babe to care for. Gives her life meaning, doesn't it? I'm sure you ladies must agree."

Cassandra raised an eyebrow at me in a challenge. Would I maintain my convictions even when faced with opposition? She didn't know me well enough, yet.

"I am sure, Lord Rutledge, that for those women who desire children, there can be no greater joy."

He waved a sturdy hand. "But of course all women desire children. I am sure I cannot think of a woman who doesn't."

"Well, now you have the pleasure of knowing one. I am content with my lot as it is and can see no good reason to change it."

A mischievous little smile curled Cassandra's lips as Lord Rutledge's already florid cheeks turned an unexpected color of red. "I have never heard of such a thing," he stammered, making his mustache wobble angrily. "A young woman not want children? It is absurd. You only think so because you are yet unmarried. No woman can fail to find joy in her duty once she is well and properly married."

I felt it happening, felt my sense of injustice rising, and found I had no strength to clamp it down. I did not want to cause problems tonight, or to embarrass Mama. But my voice came out of my mouth without my willing it to, sounding as sugary sweet as splinters of rock candy.

"It may surprise you, my lord, to hear some women have aspirations that do not include children or marriage, but I am, in fact, one of those women. And I find I do not like being told what I ought to desire, or what my natural and proper place is, by a man who can neither empathize nor understand what faces a woman as a natural consequence of her daily life."

Lord Rutledge inflated to twice his normal size with a deep breath certainly meant to prepare him for an epic reprimand, but Mr. Yates entered the room and announced dinner. The guests began gathering in pairs, and the butler approached with a small silver tray bearing a note and held it toward Lady Monmouth. She thanked him, broke the seal, and her face went pale.

"I am so sorry." She stood and tucked the note into her glove. "But I have been called away by an urgent affair. You will make my excuses to your lovely mother?"

"Indeed I will. I hope all will be well."

She smiled one of those quick, sad smiles of gratitude, then hurried off. By the time I thought to look for Lord Rutledge, he was already holding the arm of his dinner companion and queuing up to leave the drawing room. That exchange would come back to haunt me, I felt certain of it, but I found Lord Kensington approaching so I didn't have much time to think on it.

"My lady," he said, holding out an arm, "it appears we have been matched for dinner. May I?"

Lord Kensington was an appealing fellow, with light brown skin, a sturdy jaw, and eyes like warm honey, but I seriously doubted he would be interested in the only kind of relationship I would allow myself, especially if my mother had invited him. Chances were he had all the virtues she'd hope for in a son-in-law, which meant inviting him to become my paramour would be insulting... and probably find its way back to Mama.

She would contend that my travels had ruined me, but in reality, my exposure to other ways of life had opened my eyes to the reality that living a good life did not necessarily mean living one controlled by English notions of propriety and morality. Besides, it had been made painfully clear to me that if any man ever desired to marry me, it would be for my fortune and my title and not for myself.

So, I took the handsome young lord's arm and contented myself with smiling and enjoying his company. Hopefully, I would be charming enough to wheedle information out of him without his realizing it.

---

The dining room was decorated with the raiments of autumn and looked like a veritable harvest festival. Pumpkins sat in the corner and colorful gourds on the table, with garlands of dried leaves and berries draped over the doorways. A cornucopia lay in the middle of the table with fruit spilling out between the candles. Mama could have used lamps, but she said candles were better for intimacy. It was a hard observation to argue with. The dwarven lamps produced a steady, bright light that felt like daylight, not suitable to the soft, semi-private conversation of a dinner party, so the candelabra were spaced evenly across the table, making the room glow with a pleasant warmth. We were seated and the servants Mama had brought down from Wainwright began carrying out the food.

I saw a few I knew, and we exchanged smiles of recognition across the table. But I had to turn my attention to my dinner companion if I was ever going to find out more about what was happening in politics and deduce whether there was someone willing to champion the cause of equal representation in return for powerful secret magic.

"Pray, Lord Kensington," I turned to the gentleman, "will you stay in town for the winter season?"

"I had not intended to, but the company is so lively this year, I find myself hesitant to return to the country."

I smiled at that delicate little compliment and continued my forward push. "Surely it cannot be only society keeping you in town. There is so much to capture one's attention. I know many gentlemen who become absolute hedonists when they are not doing their duties in the House of Lords."

He bowed at my sally. "Indeed there are many pleasures to be had. I have been to the opera twice already, and cannot wait to go again. I confess, my companions have had to drag me away from Covent Garden, there is so much to see and do."

"And buy?"

He laughed. "Always."

"And how do you find your duties in the House of Lords? A hardship, or a pleasure?"

We took a moment to accept our bowls of soup, and I hoped I had softened him up enough that the question would appear to be genuine interest rather than leading the conversation. It was a trick Mama had used on my father when he was home and she needed to get things done. I had always watched her maneuver the conversation with awe. Father would look at her as the adoring wife doing her duty, never realizing she was playing him like a fiddle. I didn't want to manipulate the man but politics was not considered a proper topic of conversation for women, so I convinced myself manipulation was better than nothing.

"I understand why many would regard the duty as drudgery when there is so much to entertain otherwise," he said, "but I find the experience enlightening. It is like playing a game of chess with several wily opponents."

We took a moment to sip our soup, and I formulated my next question. "And there must be so many varied topics as to maintain your interest. There is the suffrage movement and city expansion. It must be endlessly intriguing. I have heard that The League for Equal Representation is seeking to bring grievances to the House of Commons, which will no doubt fall into your lap at some point, as well, so you will never be bored."

He blinked at me. Had I pushed too far? "Lady Gwen," he said, "you are uncommonly well-informed. Indeed, I have heard such rumblings as well. Their cause is gathering steam, and it seems certain there is support in the commons, though several lords have already spoken against the movement."

I breathed a silent sigh of relief and decided to push my luck a bit further after I encouraged him to keep talking. A bit of flattery never stopped up a tongue. "You are so well acquainted with the issue, I am sure you must see the situation clearly. I wonder whether they will take up the issue if the Commons passes any legislation with equal rights in mind."

He sighed. "I am certain they will. Most of the members are relatively ambivalent, but of course, there are extreme elements for and against."

"And they are surely the most vocal members."

He chuckled. "You do not miss the mark, lady. Though"—he dropped his voice—"the negative faction is much more vocal than those who wish to address the issue. The supporters work mostly behind the curtain. I believe they know there is not much open support, so they wish to fortify their position and garner public sympathy before introducing legislation in the Commons."

He was giving me everything I wanted, I just had to push him a bit more and find out who these silent supporters were. Unfortunately, my other dinner neighbor, the bilious Lord Rutledge, overheard enough to decide to poke his wiry mustache into our conversation. I would have to have words with Mama about sitting me next to the man.

"What's all this about politics," he said, "you trying to bore your partner to death, Kensington? Is that any way to talk to a pretty girl? Have some sense, man."

Lord Kensington's lips thinned and my chance for more information disappeared as he clammed up.

"We were not talking about politics, per se, Lord Rutledge," I said, trying to salvage my interrupted conversation, "so much as we were talking about social justice."

His voice raised in volume as he said, "Eh? Social Justice? What poppycock. What does such a term even mean?"

His voice was loud enough to capture the attention of several guests, their expressions either interested or irritated. I needed to smooth this over. "Why, I believe you tease me, my lord. I know you are engaged in social justice yourself, for you support many charities, do you not?"

It took a moment for him to decide whether to pursue his outrage or respond to my flattering question. Naturally, he fell for the flattery. "You are, indeed, correct, lady. I even support an orphanage on the east side, somewhere on Andrews Street. Has a most honorable record of helping young people find work when they're old enough to earn an income. Has a wonderful headmistress who is devoted to the poor children. Many of them have been through such troubles as would turn your hair white. Why, I heard one poor boy—"

"What a topic for conversation," Mama chided from the head of the table. "Lord Rutledge, where are your manners?"

She said the last in such a way, with a charming smile and a twinkle in her eye, that it nearly sounded like flirting. Lord Rutledge flushed and made some breathy mumbling sounds before he said, "You know how talk of such things riles this old goat, Your Grace. I simply care too much for the children. I know you'll forgive me."

"Of course, I could never stay mad at you, my lord, you are far too charming. Though I see I've monopolized your attention from your dining partner most unfairly. Lady Anesta, you must forgive me, too."

Lady Anesta, a fine-boned older woman with hair the color of cinnamon, had a tinkling, merry laugh that made everyone at the table smile. "I was droning on about my herb garden, I'm afraid, so you have, in fact, saved Lord Rutledge from a most boring conversation. But I will endeavor to find a more interesting topic. You have my thanks, Your Grace."

Mama waited till the guests turned back to their soup before giving me a wink. The woman was a magician. I, however, was clearly a bungler of the worst sort. In an endeavor to regain some lost ground, I took a few swallows of my now cold soup and said to Lord Kensington, "I apologize if I introduced an uncomfortable topic. I just find such matters of intellect so intriguing, I cannot help but ask."

He looked at me from the corner of his eye and said, "Not at all, lady," and that was nearly the last thing of substance he said to me all night. Oh, he commented on the flavor of the fish, on his plans for the Harvest Feast of Samhain, and on what opera he planned to attend next, but every time I tried to turn the conversation to more pertinent subjects, he withdrew. Damn Lord Rutledge to lice in his armpits and arms too short to scratch them. I wondered if he knew just how unsuitable the devoted headmistress really was.

The rest of the long evening was relegated to small talk and polite banalities while we finished dinner, gathered in the drawing room for cards, and I ground my teeth waiting for the last of our guests to leave. If I wasn't going to get any more information than the fact that there were several secretive supporters of whatever legislation may be introduced in the House of Commons, then I'd rather be in the study trying to track down the symbols used in the compulsion spell on Harry's wrist.

Mama cornered me at the end of the night, after we had said goodbye to the last guest, and said, "Thank you very much for behaving yourself tonight. At least, mostly behaving."

"Only for you, Mama."

"Did you meet anyone of note? I saw you in several conversations."

"I did, in fact. I took an immediate liking to Lady Monmouth. It was a shame she left early."

Some of the excitement left Mama's eyes. She was clearly expecting me to mention a man's name, but she rallied and said, "It was a shame, and I had to change the seating arrangement to account for her loss. Poor woman."

"Why poor?"

"Her daughter has been gravely ill, and she may have taken a turn for the worse. The physicians are not certain what is causing her sickness, so of course they do not know how to treat it. And everything they have tried so far has failed. I was surprised she attended at all, but of course, she must want some reprieve from the constant stress."

"I can only imagine. I hope her daughter recovers."

"So do I, my darling"—she touched my cheek—"but unfortunately there is nothing we can do to help, and dwelling on her misfortune will only make us unhappy."

That was true, and yet pain dug a deep well of sorrow for my new friend, and for Virginia, and everyone who didn't deserve to suffer but was suffering, anyway.

"So," Mama said, changing the subject. "Tell me, how did you like Lord Kensington? I found him a most amiable and responsible young man. He appears to have a good head on his shoulders."

"Oh he was. He also has delicate sensibilities. One wrong look from Lord Rutledge sent him hiding in a hole for the rest of the night. Nice try, Mama, but I cannot respect a character so easily swayed."

"I suppose it is a good thing, then, that so many other eligible gentlemen will be at the ball tomorrow night."

I rolled my eyes and beckoned Aristotle, who flew down and landed on my shoulder, then turned to head to the study. As I departed, I said, "And I shall take great pleasure in scaring them away."

Once we were in the safety of the study, I sank into my armchair and let the raven perch on the headrest, which was worn with his claw marks. By all rights, I should have been sleeping. After all, tomorrow morning I had an appointment with... someone. Someone who used magic to enchant a letter. A letter marked with the same symbol used in a circle responsible for the kidnapping of at least four children. I should be sleeping.

Instead, I pulled the grimoire into my lap and searched for hints to unravel the compulsion spell. A mere ten pages later there was a commotion at the stairs. I abandoned my book and went to investigate. Mr. Yates and Mrs. Chapman had been directing the cleanup, and they were both there escorting a pale-faced James into the kitchen where they sat him down. Mrs. Chapman began searching for tea things, and Mr. Yates knelt in front of the shocked driver.

"What is it, man?"

James swallowed, trying to calm himself, but his hands shook and the whites of his eyes showed. He tried to talk a few times but no words came out. Mrs. Chapman handed him a glass of tea with a generous helping of brandy in it, and he drank the whole cup in a quick swallow. What could have scared a solid man like James so much that he still shook with fear?

Mr. Yates placed a hand on his shoulder. "Alright, man? What's happened?"

"I was returning from driving Lord Kensington home," he whispered, clutching both hands together, "and there was no hurry so I thought we'd cross through Hyde Park. We were on the bridge when I heard a scream from the shore. It sounded like a woman, so I parked and hurried to investigate. There were a pair of lovers there, but they were staring at the water holding one another in fear. By the time I got to the water's edge, I saw what made the woman scream."

He dropped his head and sobbed. "It was a girl's body," he said through the tears. "She floated there with her chest cut open and blood all over in the water. I couldn't just leave her there, so I—" he choked, wiped his nose on his sleeve, and said, "I fished her out while the other two went to find help."

I forced myself to swallow, to sound calm, but my heart thudded as if I'd just run a race. "James, the girl. Did she have blonde hair?"

When he looked up at me, his eyes were red-ringed with tears. "No, ma'am. Brown. It was all tangled round her poor face." And then he broke into sobs again.

It wasn't Virginia. *It was not Virginia.* But it may have been one of the other girls Inspector Hardwicke had mentioned.

"Mrs. Chapman," I said, "will you give James something to help him sleep?"

"Course I will," she said, her dark eyes soft.

"Mr. Yates," I whispered, taking the Butler aside, "are the children safe in their rooms?"

"They are, my lady. Mrs. Chapman checked on them not an hour ago."

"Good. Take care of James, will you? We will want to call for Doctor Laghari in the morning. And be certain the doors and windows are locked tight, tonight."

"Always, ma'am."

I climbed the stairs in a daze with Aristotle on my shoulder. The killing had begun and I was already too late.

# 12

# *The Triumphant Sisterhood*

## GWEN

Aristotle refused to be left behind.

I spent my morning regretting the late night, dodging Mama as she tried to rope me into breakfast, and packing my carpet bag with things I thought might come in handy on my errands, like salt, my iron letter opener, a bundle of herbs that included agrimony, basil, and cayenne, and various other assorted tools. I even wore my amber necklace for psychic protection.

And every step of the way Aristotle was there, picking at my supplies or trying to hitch a ride on my head, dislodging every pin I needed to keep my hair in place so the ridiculous wide-brimmed hat would not fall off. I tried to leave him in the study after stuffing a book into my bag. He followed me out.

But I didn't have time to entertain him. I needed to prepare to protect myself, because last night's news had clarified the seriousness of our situation. If I was going to stop any more deaths, I needed to act fast. And if the kidnappers had access to uncommon magic, I must act while protecting myself. Passive methods, like herbs and talismans, should keep me safe enough from simple magic. But if they targeted me with more dangerous, novel magic?

How did one prepare for unpredictable magic? With educated guesses, and luck. But for mundane threats I needed something a little more direct.

I was drawing my umbrella from the stand by the door when Aristotle came flapping down the hallway. I tried to bribe him with a piece of the roast Monsieur was preparing for supper, but he would have none of it.

"I am about to walk into a place I have never heard of to confront people I do not know about things I don't understand. You cannot come with me," I tried to explain to the bird.

He climbed atop my hat, spread his wings, and started croaking. Loudly. When I tried to pry him off he avoided my hands and shouted, "Help! Murder! Attack! Help!"

"Oh, for heaven's sake," I huffed. "No need to be so bloody dramatic. Fine. You may come with me. But if you cause any problems, I will let Mrs. Chapman pluck you and use your feathers for a pillow. You hear me, bird? See if I don't."

"He's a pretty bird."

"He is an irritating bird."

Aristotle crowed happily and maneuvered down to my shoulder, where he rode until we climbed into the coach. Harold was taking over for James temporarily, and I brought another footman along for safety's sake. When I stepped out of the coach I would have to rely on myself. And Aristotle, apparently, who had hopped onto the windowsill and watched the world pass by with avian curiosity.

I slid to the window and peered out alongside him. There, as expected, was Inspector Hardwicke on the back of a bland horse. He had been serious yesterday when he threatened me with surveillance, which would complicate my errand, but must be accounted for. It was a good thing I had a stop to make before driving to the mysterious address on Tromwell Lane.

We pulled to a stop outside the milliner, and I took a deep breath before exiting the carriage. I hoped the enormous hat would disguise me enough that no one would recognize me walking into Mr. Bywater's shop, but if he already had customers and someone recognized me... I would just have to pay him extra.

"Behave yourself," I warned the bird, and pushed through the door.

Percival Bywater was, as far as I was concerned, the most talented milliner in New London. His shop was open and clean, with rows of stylish hats displayed in the large windows and on shelves lining the walls. Beneath the hats were ribbons, feathers, buttons, flowers, tulle, and other decorations sorted into neat piles or bunches or jars. There were even a few taxidermy animals and birds for the more extreme fashion elements.

At the end of the room, a long wooden counter separated the customer area from Percy's workstation. Luckily there was no one in the store. I hoped it was too early for the fashionable set to be out and about.

Percy looked up from where he was attaching ostrich feathers to a wide-brimmed hat. His face lit up with pleasure and he came to the counter. Percy had a delicate bone structure, eyes canted up a bit at the corners, and beautifully pointed ears. Elves possessed an elegance of form and movement, no matter what size their bodies, but Percy was as slender as a sapling.

I blurted, "I am sorry for visiting during normal business hours, but it is something of an emergency."

He crossed his arms, pursed his lips, and said in an airy tenor, "I never said you should do otherwise. That is your silly rule, not mine. I am happy to see you at any time."

He only said so because he did not realize how quickly his business would sink if the fashionable set saw me here. No one wanted to buy a hat from the same shop as a social outcast.

"I do appreciate the sentiment, my friend," I said, taking his hands in mine. "I would not endanger your business if I had another option."

I explained the circumstances as quickly as possible, and Percy's cornflower blue eyes grew progressively wider. By the time I finished, he said, "Then I am most glad you've come! And of course I will help you. But first"—he pulled a heavy piece of driftwood from the floor behind the counter with surprising ease—"let us set up the perch for my favorite guest."

Aristotle left my shoulder and lighted on the curving branch, giving it a satisfying squeeze with his claws. There was a small jar of dried berries behind the counter as well, and Percy spread a few before the happy raven, who began plucking them delicately off the table.

"Now that Aristotle is taken care of, let's have a look at your commission."

He disappeared into the back and returned with an absolute piece of art. The wool hat would fit against my head snugly and keep the winter cold at bay, allowing me to put my hair up low on the back of my head, instead of piled on top. It was shaped like a men's trilby, with a short brim turned up in the back and down in the front. But instead of a pinched crown, the top of the hat was rounded to fit against the head, and lifted into a curly little tail in the back, like a vine growing from a flower.

The shape was organic, like an acorn cap, only much more elegant. It was the color of late summer grass, dark green fading to light green near the top, with a thin hat band and a bunch of flowers along one side. And I was in love with it.

"Percy this a masterpiece," I breathed as he set the hat in my hands. "Does it—"

"Of course it does. Exactly who do you think I am? Give it a wave."

I hesitated a moment. I didn't want to change the hat; it was so beautiful. But Percy's craftsmanship was just shy of real magic so… I held the hat by the back brim and gave it a forceful shake. The interior of the hat blossomed outward like a blooming flower, and what I held instead of a small, elegant hat, was a red jacket woven of delicate wool and a fine metal filament I commissioned from an extraordinary artificer in Egypt.

He created a steel alloy drawn finer than any wire, which allowed it to be felted and fulled into the wool. The chaotic nature of felting meant there was no predictable pattern in the material, such as there would be in a woven fabric, making it harder to pierce so long as the filament was dense enough. He had also engraved delicate runes along the length of the wire that would redirect force. It cost more than any purchase I had ever made.

In essence, the elegant little red jacket was a coat of chain-mail.

I slid my arms through the sleeves and pulled the coat on. "Well?"

Percy walked around me with the fingers of one hand on his lips, his elbow held in the opposite hand, considering the fit. He stopped in front of me and said, "It's rumpled."

I ran my hands down the front of the coat, amazed that the texture should be so soft, and purred, "Don't you dare criticize my lovely coat. Hat. Hoat?"

"And don't you dare call my creation any such monstrous name."

"I suppose we'll have to scrap the whole project then," I said dramatically.

"I should tweak the design, make the folds tighter so they don't rumple while they're tucked up inside the hat."

"If you do, you cannot do it today. I need the hat-coat."

"Well, you cannot wear it about like that. The jacket looks as if you've slept in it."

"I shall only wear it at need and I promise not to tell anyone it is your design until you are perfectly happy with the results. Fair?"

He frowned at me, but finally gave in and said, "If you must, you must. But please be careful with it. It is a prototype, after all, and genius must be respected."

"You mean revered?"

"That, too."

"Do you have the rest of the filament?"

"Under lock and key."

"Good. I bought the entire supply and paid an embarrassing amount of money for it. If something untoward does happen to this beauty"—I ran my hands over the fabric again—"I want to be certain you can create another."

He gave me a speculative look from the corner of his eye, one brow raised. "Of course I can. But it will cost you."

"I'll make it worth your time, my friend. Will you show me how to put it back?"

There were a few complicated twists and tucks involved, but the result was the same beautiful little hat that I immediately abandoned my wide-brimmed hat for. We pulled down my hair and Percy helped me pin a sleek chignon low on my head so the hat would fit properly.

I couldn't take it with me, so I set my wide-brimmed hat on his counter, and my notebook fell out to bounce across the surface. It fell open to the sketch of the circle I'd described to Percy. He glanced at the sketch, froze, his dark skin growing ashen as he stared.

"Gwen," he began, and the words sounded as if he had to force them out, "is this the circle you spoke of?"

"Yes. Percy, are you okay? Why are your hands shaking?"

He looked at his hands as if surprised to find them on the end of his arms, then clenched them together so tightly his knuckles turned pale. "I just..." He swallowed and looked away. "That symbol makes everything you said feel more real. It... it scares me."

I held his hands in mine for a moment. Percy was a gentle soul, and if all this was frightening to me, with the knowledge I'd earned over the years, it must be even worse for him. When his hands stopped shaking, I stepped back and struck several ridiculous poses to lighten the mood.

"How do I look?"

He swallowed and gave me a sickly smile. "I do believe you may convince the rest of the aristocracy to abandon wide brims and gaudy decorations."

We shared a glance, then burst into laughter, and the tension fell away. The day the aristocracy abandoned gaudy flash for simple elegance would never come. Where fashion was concerned, more was always more.

"Well, If everything is in order, I had better go. I would like time to reconnoiter the building before I go inside."

"Good idea." He took the wide-brimmed hat and placed it on a mannequin head in his work area while I tucked my notepad into my carpet bag.

"Follow me, then."

I turned to call Aristotle and found him with his beak in a jar, busily stealing shiny little buttons.

"You rotten little thief," I scolded as I slipped my arm beneath his feet. "Are you trying to get us kicked out of my favorite hat shop? I'll never forgive you."

Aristotle ignored my reprimand with haughty disdain and took up his perch on my shoulder. Percy led us out the back and through a side passage connecting several shops in the row. We emerged on a street a block away.

"That ought to throw the good inspector off," he said with a mischievous gleam in his eyes. Indeed, the inspector was nowhere to be seen.

"One can only hope. Now I must be off and hope the inspector does not know the secrets of these old buildings."

Percy kissed my hand and disappeared into the shop. Armed with my new and wonderful hat, I set off to meet Harold at our prearranged rendezvous, hoping I would not need to use my new purchase for anything other than fashion. I did not know what to expect from the mysterious letter writer, but safe was always better than sorry.

Harold had parked in a lot set aside for the coaches of shoppers, and within ten minutes I was inside and headed toward Tromwell Lane. I dropped the bundle of protective herbs in the pocket of my walking skirt and double checked my umbrella.

The coach pulled to a stop outside a three story baroque building made of large blocks of white stone. Decorative columns flanked an ornate wooden door, and the edifice boasted dozens of street-facing windows, but they were all dark and empty. No telling what was inside. I climbed out with my umbrella in one hand and the carpetbag in the other, and told Harold, "If I do not leave this building, through this door, in fifteen minutes, come and fetch me."

"Yes, my lady."

He frowned in concern, but I gave him what I hoped was a reassuring smile, pulled the letter of invitation from my pocket, and entered the building with my head high. The foyer was two stories high, cavernous, and empty. I would need to make myself known. My footsteps echoed off the marble as I strode to the center of the entrance and tapped the end of my umbrella against the floor with a crack.

The sound was loud enough that if anyone had been in the room, they would have stopped and stared. Seconds after the noise faded, a woman appeared at the top of the staircase opposite the doors I'd entered through. She wore a simple, sleek, dark day dress and stood with her hands folded in front of her.

"Lady St. James," she said. "Welcome. Please, follow me."

A pale woman in a dark dress, alone at the top of a staircase? That was a fittingly ominous sign. I took a breath to steady my nerves, gripped my umbrella tightly, and climbed the stairs. She stood waiting for me like a statue; her face impassive.

When I reached the top, she simply turned and walked away. I followed, but held my umbrella at the ready. The emptiness was disconcerting, particularly considering the size and location of the building, in a relatively busy part of town.

We entered a long hall with doors opening up on either side. The young woman stopped at the fifth door in, knocked three times in measured beats, then opened it.

"Ah, Patricia. Thank you for escorting our guest," a cultured female voice said. The voice told me that, before I ever saw the woman, she was from the very upper crust of nobility. Perfectly modulated, cleanly annunciated, her diction would have set her apart anywhere.

Patricia stepped aside after we entered and left me standing just inside the doorway, looking into a room appointed in large pieces of mahogany furniture so dark they were nearly black. The cushions were all of burgundy velvet, and ornate scrollwork carvings surrounded the giant fireplace.

Several women sat or stood around the room in different positions, but each of them watched me with interested expressions. A woman sat by the fireplace in an overstuffed armchair, and soon as I saw her, I knew she had spoken. Her skin was a rich amber with olive undertones that glowed next to the black curls spilling over her shoulder, highlighting a long, elegant neck and proud jaw. She appraised me with dark eyes and offered a gentle welcoming smile as she stood.

"Lady St. James, welcome. I appreciate you answering our request on such short notice. Pray, sit, and let us speak awhile. May I offer you or your friend any refreshment?"

Perhaps it was the perfect control or expert poise making her seem inhuman, but I did not want to eat or accept anything from this woman. "No, thank you."

"Very well. Patricia, you may go."

Patricia bobbed a curtsy and left. I forced myself to acknowledge the other five women in the room and cross the thick Persian rug to take a seat across from the ring leader. My umbrella and carpet bag stayed by my feet for easy access. Aristotle hopped from my shoulder to the back of the chair, and paced behind me as he assessed the room.

I got directly to the point. "You appear to know quite a bit about me, madame. Might I have your name?"

She smiled, showing a row of perfectly white, straight teeth. "No, you may not. At least, not yet. Madame will do, for now, thank you."

"I am here at your behest, the least you can do is give me your name. Otherwise I see no reason to continue the interview."

She steepled long, elegant fingers just below her chin and tilted her head, her dark eyes unreadable as she studied my face. Her gaze dropped lower, stopped, and she said, "What a lovely amber necklace. The piece looks extraordinarily clear."

I didn't bother to answer. This woman was used to being in a position of power, and if I let her dictate the terms of this conversation, I would come out on the losing end. And, somehow, I knew losing my footing with this woman was not safe.

"That is a lovely bird."

"Thank you."

"How long have you had him?"

"Quite a long time."

Her mouth curled in a polite little smile that hid something, but I couldn't guess what. "How nice for you. May I ask you a question?"

"You may," I said, unable to keep the annoyance from my voice, "but I will not promise you an answer. And if I choose to answer, I expect one in return. But I will answer no questions until I know who I am talking to."

Amusement curled one side of her generous mouth. "Very well. You may call me Madame Matilda. And I have it on good authority you are currently pursuing information about a series of kidnappings. Are you?"

My heart skipped a beat. It wasn't exactly a secret, but I hadn't attempted to bandy the information about, either. The woman made me nervous, but I did not have a good reason not to tell her.

"I am. Why did you invite me here?"

She leaned against the armrest and folded her hands, considering me. "Because we would like to help."

"Why?"

She raised a finger. "Ah, but it is now my turn to ask a question. How did you discover the kidnappings?"

So, we were to continue the exchange of question and answer, then. I needed to be careful how I answered, and what questions I asked. "I stumbled upon a kidnapping in progress. How did you discover I was investigating the matter?"

"I have informants in the city who pay attention to strange happenings."

"Kidnappings are hardly strange."

"But kidnappings involving magic are."

I wanted to ask how she knew magic was involved in the kidnappings, but that would give away too much information, and it was her turn. Belief in magic was rare in New London, with all its science and technology. In the country, people recognized the magic inherent in the world because they lived with it every day.

Superstition existed of course, but folk wisdom also kept people safe, though the average person may not be able to tell the difference between the two. As an obvious city dweller and member of the aristocracy, how did she know about magic?

Her skin was smooth as the marble floor; she bore no strange colored scars or novel markings, and her long, elegant limbs were unbent, so she was clearly not a witch. She knew about magic from some other avenue. I needed to tread carefully.

She recognized my hesitation and smiled. "What do you know of the victims?"

This was safer, as it was plastered in the morning post. "They are all young, all orphans, and were kidnapped at night. Why do you want to help?"

"Is not the motivation to protect children reason enough?"

"That wasn't an answer."

She looked over her shoulder at the silent women. Not one of them so much as shifted their weight while we spoke.

After a moment, she said, "The women in this room are members of the Triumphant Sisterhood, dedicated to protecting New London. We secretly fund charities, sponsor legislation designed to benefit the working class, and help organize the Women's Suffrage movement. We are part of families, however, who would frown upon our endeavors, and so we keep our identities secret."

I held my breath for a moment as I realized these women had just added themselves to my list of suspects. They secretly sponsored legislation, which could easily include the grievances the dwarves and elves intended to bring before the House of Commons. But it wasn't my turn to ask a question, and she didn't appear to want to wait for a response.

She said, slowly, "From what part of the city have these children gone missing?"

Virginia was taken from the industrial district near the east side, but I knew nothing about the other children, and I told her so.

"Interesting," she said. "I would assume such information to be vital."

I refused to bite my lip, let my eyes wander, or show any other sign I hadn't thought of that. She was right. Knowing where the children had gone missing from would give me more information about the victims and potentially about the kidnapper's habits. If I knew what the victims had in common, I might be able to predict the next kidnapping.

Inspector Hardwicke already had Harry in custody, but I was willing to bet the compulsion spell would not allow him to answer questions even after he awoke from the beating the spell had given him.

It looked as if I must endure another meeting with Hardwicke. In fact... "Why come to me instead of Scotland Yard?"

"If we are to help while maintaining our anonymity, you are the proper person to contact. You know what it is like to be scorned by your peers for engaging in activity they deem inappropriate for your sex and station."

My stomach dropped. She knew far more about me than I expected. And she was right. What I was doing, and what these women were supposedly doing, was considered men's business. A woman may contribute to charity, or take in a ward, or sponsor an orphan, but she certainly did not engage in politics. And suffrage was absolutely taboo if one wanted to maintain social acceptability.

I leaned forward and took a moment to lock eyes with every woman in the room, memorizing as many of their facial features as possible.

Finally, I said to Madame Matilda, "How do you propose to help me find the girls and stop the kidnappers?"

She held up a crystal necklace, and smiled.

# 13
# A Turn for the Worse
## GWEN

Sunlight made me squint as I left the building on Tromwell Lane. My mind raced with everything I learned, creating theories and plans, only to stop dead when I saw Inspector Hardwicke standing in front of my carriage. Harold scowled at him from the driver's seat, and I scowled at him from the top of the stairs. That man found me, despite my subterfuge. Double and triple damn.

Of course, I could never let him see my frustration, so I plastered a bright smile on my face and breezed down the steps to say, "Why Inspector Hardwicke, what a surprise."

My voice, however, did not sound bright. It sounded irritated and sarcastic. Quadruple damn.

His expression was impassive but his jaw was already thrust forward as if prepared for a fight. "Somehow, Lady St. James, I doubt you're surprised at all. I have a few questions for you."

"And I'd be happy to answer them, but I have errands today and little time to spare."

When I reached for the door of the coach, he placed a hand flat on the wood, keeping it shut.

"This is not a request, lady. You'll answer my questions, and you'll do it in my office, or I will arrest you for obstruction."

"Help!" Aristotle cried from my shoulder. "Murder! Attack!"

The inspector growled in frustration, and the sound surprised me enough that I took a moment to examine his face. There were dark smudges beneath his eyes and a couple of days' worth of beard growth on his cheeks, which looked gaunt, as if his skin was stretched too tightly across his cheekbones.

My irritation faded away, and so did my desire to nettle the man. "You haven't slept in days, have you?"

He shook his head like it was too heavy for his shoulders. "I have not. I'm tired and I have no wish to fight with you."

Sympathy would not let me do anything else, not with those haunted eyes staring back at me, so I said with a sigh, "Shall I meet you there?"

---

As we headed for Scotland Yard, I wondered if I had just walked myself into being arrested and, if not, what the inspector wanted with me. If I were to be arrested, I wanted to keep Aristotle safe, so I left him in the coach, much to his chagrin. He screamed at me as I shut him in and walked into Scotland Yard.

My heart beat harder with every step toward the inspector's office. He was seated when I opened the door, draining a cup of coffee while surrounded by a mess of papers and open maps.

"I have made it no secret that I do not trust you," he said as I sat. "Every instinct I have tells me you are hiding something. You sneak about the city at night, spend time in abandoned buildings, behave inappropriately—"

"You say the nicest things," I inserted dryly.

He continued without noticing. "And your footman discovered the"—he swallowed—"the mutilated body of one of the kidnapped girls. You also warned me of magic, a subject you happen to study, leaving you as the only person I can consult on this case. Coincidence occurs far too often around you for it to be coincidental. That, alone, is suspicious. But you also have information I cannot get anywhere else, so I find myself in a difficult position."

"Try wearing a corset," I suggested. "*That* is a difficult position."

He scowled, and I felt a flush of guilt.

"I apologize. I'm not certain why I cannot help myself but something about you just... begs to be teased. Have you ever considered not being so stuffy?"

He didn't answer.

I added, more seriously, "I also joke when I'm nervous. It is one of the few effective coping mechanisms I possess. The rest... Well, in any case, I realize what my involvement must look like to you, but I cannot state more clearly: my only desire is to find these children before harm comes to anyone else."

He leaned forward, the light from his single window haloing him in a golden glow, and held out his hand, then gave a pointed glance at my own. With no little hesitance, and expecting a pair of handcuffs, I placed my hand in his. His palm was broad and calloused. It was also very warm. His fingertips rested against the inside of my wrist.

He looked deeply into my eyes and said, in an earnest voice low enough to expose a bit of a growl, "Can you swear it to me?"

His brown eyes had flecks of gold around the iris. They were exhausted, but resolute. I tried to allow the truth of my words to ring in my voice. He was trying to protect the children, too, and that deserved my honesty.

"I swear it. I only want to stop the kidnappings and find the children."

"And you know nothing about the kidnappings?"

"Nothing but what I've told you."

"And you know no witches in the city?"

"None."

He stared for the space of several heartbeats, then let go and sat back, running both hands through his hair and making the ends stand up like quills on a hedgehog.

I looked down at my hand and raised a questioning brow.

His lips thinned, but he said, "I was measuring your heartbeat and watching your pupils. When the average person lies, their heart beats faster, they perspire, and their pupils dilate. Your heart slowed down, your skin is dry, and your pupils remained the same size. It is not a perfect science, but I will take whatever small reassurances I can get. Please do not assume this means I will set aside my suspicions entirely. If I have any reason to believe you are involved in this affair, I will arrest you immediately."

"Of course, you will," I said sourly. "Why trust things like common sense and rock-solid alibis? And now that we've established I cannot be trusted entirely, why don't you ask me your questions so I can be on my way."

"Nothing would make me happier."

He seemed to expect a rebuttal, so we stared at one another across the desk for a few heartbeats. I let my eyes slowly cross. He gave a sharp, irritated exhale and demanded, "Can you take anything seriously?"

"I'm simply trying to amuse myself while I wait for you to ask me questions. You know, the questions you threatened me with arrest if I didn't agree to answer."

It was his turn to look ashamed. "Forgive me. I am under a great deal of stress. How about this," he said. "Let us agree to start over." He held out his hand. "I am Inspector Tony Hardwicke."

I hesitated long enough to clarify that I did not accept this new beginning without at least some consideration, then took his offered hand. "I am Gwen, Lady St. James."

"Pleased."

"A pleasure."

That must have been enough, because the Inspector dropped all pretense and got down to business. "You are aware one of the victims was murdered."

My voice came out in a whisper. "Yes."

"Now another child is missing. We do not know if the boy was kidnapped or only ran away, but they reported the absence this morning when he did not show up for roll call before breakfast."

"Roll call? Did an orphanage report the absence?"

"Yes."

I remembered what Madame Matilda said, and my experience with the headmistress, and asked, "From where did these children go missing?"

He eyed me for a moment, then pulled a map off the floor and pressed it flat on the desk. There were five little red Xs drawn at various points on the map. I studied them, then fished a pencil from the rubbish strewn across his office and circled the groupings.

"Here," I said, pointing with the pencil, "is the orphanage on Andrews Street. If this map is accurate, all of the kidnappings have happened within an hour's walk of the orphanage."

Tony looked at the map, his eyes running back and forth as if he were doing calculations in his head, then took the pencil from me and drew a few quick lines, and said, "You are correct."

"The orphanage is also within walking distance of the industrial district and Artificer's Row. And all of the children are orphans, children without families to fight for them."

"How do you know they're all orphans?"

"Are they not?"

"I can confirm only three. There was no identification for the other two kidnappings."

"And the others were identified because someone witnessed the kidnapping?"

"Yes."

I heard my molars grind together before realizing I had clenched my teeth. "We need to have a conversation with the headmistress of Andrews Orphanage. I have a feeling the other two children were beneath her care, as well."

His eyes hardened.

"In addition," I began, then stopped because I was about to share dangerous information. But, despite how I might feel about the inspector, he was committed to helping the children, so I forced myself to continue. "My tests suggest the kidnapping spell draws children who are hungry for home and safety. It lures them with the promise of what they've lost. Whoever created that magic is actively manipulating children they expect will not be missed."

The pencil snapped. Tony looked at the pieces in his hand as if surprised to find them there. "Who might be capable of creating such a spell?"

Here was more dangerous information. But lives were at stake. "The spell appears to be using both traditional human magic, and altered artificery. I have never seen such a thing."

"You believe the dwarves may be involved?"

Heaven help me. "I cannot rule it out."

"And you have been investigating this link?"

"I have."

"And you will share this information with me when you have it?"

I swallowed. As more people became aware of this new magic, it had a greater chance of spreading, which was terribly dangerous. But how many young lives would be lost if we did not stop the kidnappers because of my fear?

The deep, hungry pit opened before me once more, the pit that swallowed me after we lost Lia. I would have burned the world down to bring my sister home, had searched the world for a way to do it... but no one was searching for these children.

No one but us.

So I said, "I will."

There was a long pause while he processed the information, likely comparing it against what he already knew. Then he raised his eyes. "If you are correct, then yes. I think a conversation with the headmistress is in order. Thank you for telling me."

"It is my pleasure," I said, and that time I meant it. "Do you need anything else from me?"

He took a deep breath and said, "Follow me."

We left the office and trudged down several halls until turning into a wing labeled 'Infirmary.' Tony chose a door and led me through it. There, on a bed in the center of the small room, was Harry. I gasped, then turned away for a moment to compose myself. When my ears stopped ringing and the knots in my stomach loosened, I turned back, this time prepared.

Splotchy bruises and the spidery marks of broken blood vessels covered Harry's face. His features were difficult to distinguish through the swelling, and his eyes looked like overripe plums stuffed into too small sockets. The repercussions of the spell had truly beaten his body. It was hard not to feel sorry for the man. A human face should not look that way. At least, it was difficult until I remembered what he had done to the children.

"Has he not woken?" I asked.

"Not once. The nurses have had to use a tube to get water into him. Is this the result of the compulsion spell you mentioned?"

I nodded.

"If we were to wash the spell off, would he wake? I have instructed the nurses not to touch it."

"I am glad of that. It is not uncommon for traps to be woven into spells such as this one. After all, why go about the trouble of creating a magical slave if anyone can remove their chains?"

"Can you tell if there is such a trap here?"

I moved to the side of the bed and exposed Harry's wrist. It, too, was swollen. His fingers looked like plump purple sausages. I had to swallow and exhale to calm myself enough to examine the marks.

"The difficulty," I said as I studied the spell inscribed on his skin, "is that the language of spells is not always universal. The markings are merely representations of intention, powered by the will of the practitioner. Some witches will use the language of their birth, and others will include symbols or markings to express their intent for the spell. The longer the witch has practiced, the more individual her spells become."

He leaned down next to me, shoulder to shoulder, to study the fading blue marks that circled Harry's wrist like a tattooed bracelet.

"Can he have done this spell to himself?" he asked.

"Technically, yes, but why? And look at the direction of the marks. These were written from the end of the hand, not the other way."

"What can you make out?"

"These"—I pointed to a series of four symbols—"are from old Celtic spells Druids used to allow them to see through the eyes of an animal." That explained the green glow coming from Harry's face the night he was outside my home. Whoever used the spell had been watching through Harry's eyes. A shiver of fear raced down my spine as my skin tightened in disgust.

"And this one," I added, "is part of a French spell that turns the person's will back on themselves. A violent man will receive violence. Which explains the nature of his reaction. He essentially beat himself bloody. No wonder his hands are swollen."

Tony leaned away, breathing hard. "The nurses said all the bones in his hand are broken. He never landed a blow. Bloody hell."

I lifted his arm as gingerly as possible to get a look at the underside of his wrist, the part I hadn't been able to see during our encounter in the Narrows. There was the end of the spell, the tether that would unravel the whole thing if pulled. And if I tried to tug the string, it would kill Harry and probably me, too. I lay his hand back down, then took a few steps away from the bed, fetching up against the wall and squeaking in surprise.

Tony reached out and steadied me, catching my arm in one hand and bracing my back with the other. "Are you alright?"

I nodded, mouth dry, and had to swallow a few times to bring the words past the sudden tightness in my throat. "We cannot remove the spell. It will kill him, and likely whoever is unlucky enough to try and remove it. It can only be undone by the witch who cast it… or by the sunrise on Samhain."

"Samhain? The harvest festival?"

I shook my head. "It is not merely a harvest festival. In a way, it is also the last goodbye to the light before winter. Samhain is also the day this world and the spirit world pass closest to one another. It is a time of incredible power for those capable of magic. Certain castings can only be completed on Samhain because of the amount of power they require. It would be akin to using a windmill during a thunderstorm."

His blonde brows dropped low over his eyes. "So, whatever this witch is planning, it will be over the morning after the harvest celebration?"

"It may not be a witch," I warned him. "The magic used in the circle is activated by artifice, though it is a form I have never seen, and I have it on good authority it is unique."

"But, dwarves cannot do magic," he said.

"They can if the spell is activated by the power channeled through the runes, instead of the body of a witch. Or so it appears."

The inspector was a smart man. It took him only a few moments to understand the implications. He pointed to Harry's wrist. "But that spell has no artifice."

A thought struck me, making my heart pump harder. "That is his left hand, the arm most associated with the heart. Have you checked his body for other markings?"

We looked at one another for a moment, then began pulling back the blankets and moving Harry's clothing around. Sure enough, a trail of ink ran up the man's arm and ended in a circle inscribed over his heart. A circle strikingly similar to the one that activated the kidnapping spell.

"So this could have been inked by anyone who understands artificery?"

"I don't think so. At least, not yet. But if the knowledge of this circulates through the population..."

Tony Hardwicke, the hardened inspector of Scotland Yard, lost all color.

"Right now," I added, "this knowledge is incredibly rare. And whoever concocted it knows artifice, and witchcraft, and has enough money to study their history in a way that has allowed them to combine the two. In addition, I would guess this person is well-traveled, as there are several languages used in this spell and the words are all colloquial."

"And whatever they're planning," he said in a weak voice, "it will end tomorrow night?"

"As that's when the compulsion spell expires, it's as good a guess as any."

"We haven't much time."

"No, we don't." I rubbed the goosebumps on my arms and then set my jaw and looked up. "Shall we go talk with the honorable headmistress?"

Tony's eyes hardened, and his hands tightened into fists. "Let's."

Mrs. Edwards looked thinner and frailer when we found her bustling through the halls of Andrews Home for Destitute Children. Her silk blouse was wrinkled, and she held a set of keys so tightly that every tendon stood out on the back of her hand. When she saw Inspector Hardwicke, she dredged up whatever reserves she had left and forced herself to stand tall.

"Matron Edwards," I said. "May I introduce you to Inspector Hardwicke, of Scotland Yard?"

She offered him a smile masquerading as welcome, but her lips were pale. "Inspector, I am pleased to meet you. What can I do for you?"

"You can tell me whether you are selling the children in your care."

Any strength she might have had fled, and her hands began shaking.

"How dare you," she whispered. "How dare you accuse me of such a thing?"

"It was a question, Matron, not an accusation. But five orphaned children have gone missing within two miles of Andrews, and this is the only orphanage in this part of the city. It is rather suspicious. I want to know which of these children were under your care."

He held out a sheet of paper with five names written in angry, slashing letters.

She took the paper, read the names, and promptly fainted. The inspector barely caught her before she crumpled to the ground.

"Where can we take her?" he asked as he scooped her up.

"Er... her office. On the second floor."

He followed me up the stairs and deposited the woman in her chair. I was gratified to see wool blankets covering the mattresses, but somehow, it didn't seem like enough.

"Do you have smelling salts?" Tony asked.

"Do I appear to be the kind of woman who faints?"

He eyed me. "You appear to be the kind of woman uniquely outfitted to irritate me. You also appear to have packed an entire home in that carpetbag of yours."

I frowned at him, set the heavy bag on the table, and dug through the contents.

"You know," I told him conversationally, "you're supremely annoying when you're right."

That earned me the first genuine smile I had seen from the man. He looked almost boyish, and the expression compensated for some of the ravages of worry on his features. I refused to smile back but handed over the little vial. He held it away from his face, pulled the stopper out, and swiped it once beneath the woman's nose.

Mrs. Edwards jerked awake, her eyes swinging about wildly as she coughed and brushed at the offensive smell. "What on earth," she began, then realized who was in the room with her and went completely still.

Tony backed up, leaving her plenty of space so she would not feel threatened, and said, "Tell me about the children."

"I am sure I do not know what you mean."

I had been scanning her office, and a folded piece of paper caught my attention. I plucked it from the seat of the chair where it had been thoughtlessly abandoned and held it up. The headline read, "Girl Found Murdered in Hyde Park."

"These children," I said coldly.

She swallowed.

"Do you know who this girl was?" Tony asked.

"No."

I slapped the paper down on the desk in front of the woman. She flinched. I said, "Very well. Why don't I go ask the rest of the children who is missing from their number? I'm certain they know who has come and gone in the past week."

"Leave the children alone," she said, but her voice was weak.

"If you tell me what you know about the victims, I won't have to ask them."

"That is," Inspector Hardwicke said, "unless you'd like your name in the paper tomorrow. In which case, I will be happy to share the details with our local journalists. Perhaps you prefer the spotlight, Mrs. Edwards."

Her soft face crumbled into a mess of lines and lumps, complete with rivers of tears to break up the topography. The idea that everyone would know what she had done broke the woman.

"He said," she sobbed, "he said they would only be taken and held. He swore they wouldn't be harmed."

"Who?" Tony growled.

"A—a man. An elvish man. He—he said they just wanted to scare the humans, to soften us up. He promised enough money to care for the rest of the children."

"And you took that money and spent it yourself," I spat.

"Only a bit of it! I swear! I work hard here, I deserve something nice, don't I? I never would have agreed if I thought—" Her eyes strayed to the headline and she made a little gagging noise, then covered her mouth with her hand. "I never would have agreed if—"

"What was this man's name?"

"He gave no name," she insisted. "No real name. He said to call him Mr. Capstone."

"How were you supposed to contact Mr. Capstone?"

"I wasn't. He would just deposit the money for me to pick up."

"Where?"

"Here," she said. "In the laundry, when it is returned. A white bag is packed in with the sheets."

"And how do you choose which children to sell off?" I growled. "Or do you simply let the kidnappers pick which innocent lives to destroy?"

Some life came back into her face as indignation. "They said they wouldn't hurt the children. And they would only take the children old enough to work and provide for themselves, not the little ones."

"They're all little ones! All of them are defenseless children, you sick—" Tony spun and clamped a hand over my mouth.

"I know," he said softly. "I know. But this doesn't help. We'll find them."

His eyes were soft and understanding. He wasn't any less angry than I, just better at controlling it. I pulled in a deep breath through my nose and nodded. He let me go. But when he turned back around, Mrs. Edwards was pointing a gun at his chest.

Her hands shook, making the barrel waver between Tony and me. "This wasn't supposed to happen," she said, tears streaming down her cheeks. Then she turned the pistol toward her temple and fired.

The report was so loud my ears rang. Her body crumpled onto the chair, limp. Blood and other viscera splattered the opposite wall. I turned and vomited.

"Son of a bitch," Tony said. His voice sounded tired.

---

It took several hours to wait for more officers, to clean up the mess, to give my statement, and process what happened. A woman was dead. There were no spells inked upon her. She was simply a tired, greedy woman who took a bribe that made her life easier with no thought for those under her care.

She hadn't given us nearly enough information, and now we could learn nothing else, except a deal had been struck with an elven man—Mr. Capstone—who only wanted to scare the humans.

When all was said and done, Tony and I sat outside on the narrow stairs, shivering in the biting wind, but not moving.

Tony cleared his throat in an effort to sound businesslike. "Where does this leave us? We only have till Samhain, and we still don't know who was behind this."

"Mr. Capstone is the only lead we have," I agreed, "and I may have a way to find out who he is. But I've got to go to a ball, first."

"A ball?"

I sighed. "Yes. I am waiting for a list of dwarves who have enough money, resources, and connections to have created this new artifice. And tonight, Mama is throwing a ball with some of the most influential members of the aristocracy. If I can connect who is willing to sell powerful magic for political gain to who is looking to buy it, I may have our man."

Tony looked down at his hands, considering. We didn't have many more options, and no other clues to follow.

"I guess we're going to a ball, then," he said.

"We?"

He ignored the incredulity in my voice. "I'll want to see your exchanges firsthand," he said. "I may notice something you do not. And two of us working is better than one."

He was right, whether I wanted to deny it or not, so I said, "We only have one problem, then, inspector."

"And what is that?"

"You," I told him seriously, "have absolutely nothing to wear."

# 14

# *Dancing and Diatribes*

## GWEN

As soon as I arrived home, Mr. Yates handed me Delilah's letter. It was short and direct, a simple list of names of the artificers who had enough resources to do the research and experimentation necessary to alter artificery to allow it to power a spell.

Of all the artificers in London, she believed only three possessed the skill. I puzzled over the names as Charlotte helped me stuff myself into the new dress Mama purchased for me, and curl my hair into something resembling a fashionable style. As Charlotte worked, I fiddled with the list, considering how I could best make use of this knowledge when I joined the ball downstairs.

As if worrying about the children, and whatever would happen to them on Samhain, wasn't enough, my stomach tangled itself in knots every time I thought about walking down the stairs to endure haughty expressions, sidelong glances, and whispers.

I avoided gatherings like this for years, even fleeing the country to distance myself from this very situation. Now here I was, preparing to attend a bloody ball.

On top of everything, I had warned Mr. Yates to expect Inspector Hardwicke, but I had not warned Mama, and I wasn't looking forward to explaining myself. My first move, I decided as I descended the stairs, was to find a glass of champagne. Several glasses.

Once I convinced myself not to throw up, I descended the stairs to the sound of merrymaking. Laughter punctuated the gentle hum of conversation and mixed with the mouth-watering scent of the refreshments Monsieur had the kitchen staff working on since the previous evening. It promised to be a successful soiree for Mama, but whether the inspector and I would walk away with the information we needed remained to be seen. At least I had a place to start with Delilah's list fresh in my mind.

I could avoid it no longer. It was time to feed the wolves.

The hallway shrank before me and I wobbled on the bottom step, clutching the banister with both hands. I looked in on Sally and Sam when I'd returned home from Scotland Yard, and envied them now, snug in their beds with a long night of sleep ahead of them. Perhaps I should check on them before joining the festivities. I was stalling, and I knew it, but moving forward was impossible.

"There you are, darling," Mama said, appearing in the hall as if by magic. She looked every inch a duchess, with her blonde hair piled atop her head and pearls woven through the thick waves with silk ribbon. The deep blue beaded gown she wore made her pale skin glow. She smiled and took my hands to hold me at arm's length.

"I am so glad I remembered your size," she cooed. "Just look at you. You look as if you stepped out of a fairy story."

Her pleasure was so apparent that I couldn't help but feel a little smug about my appearance. She had surprised me with the gown, which she'd apparently ordered weeks before she came to town, and finished it without any fittings. It was, unfortunately, a traditional gown, which meant Charlotte had to help me into and out of it, but the gold and cream dress was covered in lace and embroidered with gold sequins in a delicate floral pattern that made me look like a princess.

I had to admit it was a stunning creation. The deep scoop of neckline showed just enough décolletage to be interesting, and the beaded sleeves tinkled when I moved my arms. The train might be a bit of a problem for maneuvering around a ballroom, but it was so gorgeously ornate, with alternating layers of lace and beaded designs, it would be worth the trouble.

"Thank you, Mama. It's beautiful."

"So are you, dear heart." Then she leaned in close and whispered in a conspiratorial tone, "Don't sneak any sweets to the children before you go into the ball. I already smuggled them treats hours ago, and Mrs. Chapman will have both our heads for spoiling them if she catches us."

"I was, in fact, contemplating doing just that," I admitted.

She turned me back down the hall toward the ballroom and dragged me along, arm-in-arm. "I thought you might. No fear, my love. Climbing back onto the horse after being thrown is always scariest the first time, but there's nothing to fear. You are not the same untried girl you were years ago."

If she only knew how true that was. But some wounds weren't easy or quick to heal. I let myself be carried along by the tide of Mama's certainty until we stood in the doorway of the ballroom. The festivities were, in fact, spread through several rooms in the house. Mama set aside rooms for cards, dancing, refreshments, and supper, but it was early and most of the guests had already gathered for the first few dances while spirits were high.

Dwarven lamps and chandeliers lit the room with an even, warm light without heating the room as regular lamps or candles would. The double doors to the balconies were already open to mitigate the heat of so many bodies. And a good thing, too. Humans, elves, and dwarves crowded the room until it was just full enough without being uncomfortable.

Gold, jewels, lace, velvet, diamonds, yards of silk, and gallons of perfume turned the space into a kaleidoscope of wealth. People chatted in groups around the edges of the room and watched the dancing as the musicians began to play.

"Breathe, darling," Mama whispered.

I sucked in a breath, nearly passing out with the relief of air, and reminded myself I had done far more dangerous and frightening things than spend the evening surrounded by the cream of the British aristocracy. I would settle into the strength I had earned, and wear it like armor.

Since I was feeling brave, I told Mama, "You remember the—the tragedy last night?"

Her smile faded. "Of course. Poor James is still sedated. It is all anyone is talking about, that and the other kidnappings."

"Indeed. Well, Inspector Hardwicke of Scotland Yard will be here tonight to observe."

"What? Why on earth would they observe our guests?"

"They think there may be some politicians involved. It is a convoluted tale and will by no means interrupt or distract from the festivities."

She frowned at the gathering dancers, then said, "Well, if he believes it may help them track down whoever hurt that poor girl, then, of course, he is welcome, but I cannot imagine anyone here being involved in such an affair."

I reassured her as much as I was able before the dancing began.

As the hostess, Mama led the first dance on the arm of the highest-ranking man in attendance, and I wandered to the edge of the room to reconnoiter the space and decide where to start. I needed someone with knowledge of politics and the connections to guess who might arrange secret deals with whom. It would have to be someone who either had sympathy for the cause of equality, or who needed knowledge of the magic.

I spotted Lord Kensington across the room, smiling and chatting with a pretty, red-headed girl. He might introduce me to other members of parliament, but I doubted it. Upon whom else could I impose? I decided to take a tour of the room and listen.

"Heard she was mutilated in the most dreadful manner," someone's voice said, only to be cut off by another voice saying, "Lottie, really, you should not talk of such things! It is so disturbing and I want to have fun tonight."

Other guests spoke of the growing number of kidnappings, of who was certain to be engaged by spring, and whose horse had taken the prize in the last race. But Mama was right, the topic discussed more than any other was the kidnappings, and no wonder.

I began my second circuit of the room as the first dance ended. The gentlemen returned their partners to their chaperones or guided them off for refreshments, and I realized that one of the names on Delilah's list, the Honorable Mr. Stackhouse, stood to one side of the room with a group of men and elves. No doubt they'd head off for cards once it was proper to abandon the women.

I made my way across the room, listening hard.

My hearing was rather acute, a gift I'd always found to be a mixed blessing because it allowed me to hear things I would not have otherwise heard, and also to hear things I wished I had not. I prayed this time the results would be in my favor.

"They most certainly will," one gentleman, a tall fellow with hollow cheeks and dark eyes said. "You wait and see. If they don't catch the kidnappers within two weeks, I'll eat my hat."

"Are the Artificers looking into it, Stackey?" another asked.

The dwarven man had shaved his whiskers to expose a spectacular cleft chin, but even more impressive was the red mustache that hung almost down to his belt. He had braided each side with jewels and baubles and oiled the hair till it shined in the lamplight.

"You had better believe we are," he said in a voice that sounded like it echoed out of a cave. "Those children have gone missing too close to home, and the Artificers wish to make it clear we had nothing to do with it."

A third man raised a set of barely-there eyebrows in surprise. "Surely no one has suggested such a thing?"

"Not in so many words," Mr. Stackhouse grumbled. "But some have implied that the proximity to the Row is suspicious, what with the demonstrations expanding beyond our small clubs. They feel the growing strength of the Artificer's and Artisan's Guilds is threatening, instead of reassuring. This is exactly why we need reform."

My ears pricked up, and I turned as if to examine a painting, thinking *I'm not suspicious at all.*

"For my part, I would not be at all surprised if this was a bid from the electric companies to throw suspicion on the validity of our movement. They cannot get a bigger market share so long as electricity remains so much more unstable than artificery. And their chief officers are humans. Until all of us are on equal footing, there will always be suspicion and we will always be helpless to stop it. Particularly if there is something for them to gain."

I caught myself before slapping my forehead in embarrassment. How had I not guessed? If humans felt threatened by the movement for equal representation, there was a good chance at least some of them would blame these kidnappings on the dwarves or elves to stoke distrust. It was precisely the sort of disgusting tactic politicians mastered. The three races had lived together for hundreds of years, but only a fool would believe there was anything like true equality.

How could there be, without equal representation in the legislature and aristocracy? Elves and dwarves owned land and property, but the crown only granted hereditary titles and privileges, which included the passing of estates, to humans. Operating the most powerful guilds in Europe gave them the money to buy or bribe politicians, but only for the most successful, and that was not the same as holding the titles and positions themselves.

An act like this would sew distrust and suspicion, making the fight for equal representation harder. Then, of course, there was the mysterious Mr. Capstone. Mrs. Edwards had said he was an elf. Why would he be involved in turning public opinion against his own people?

I was so caught up in suppositions I almost didn't hear the next thing Mr. Stackhouse said.

"Of course, that will change, once the legislation passes. We've made some rather exciting advancements that should provide all the leverage we need to convince our mutual friend to sponsor the bill."

I almost choked on my champagne.

"Shhh," the tall man said, casting wary eyes around the room. "Watch your tongue, Stackey. The situation is too precarious to expose in a place like this."

Mr. Stackhouse rumbled his assent, and the conversation devolved into more mundane topics. I needed more information. If I finagled an introduction, and perhaps a dance, I may learn more. But first, I needed to find Inspector Hardwicke and identify the men so he could investigate them, as well.

I found Mama, instead. Or, I should say, she found me. It was time to make the rounds and she would not take no for an answer. She dragged me from group to group making introductions, and the experience was worse than I expected.

People who remembered the infamous engagement watched me with morbid curiosity, wondering if I would make a scene at some point during the night. Those I'd known in my past life as a hopeful debutant smirked at me with barely disguised incivility.

Once my back was turned, several people even mentioned, quite loudly, that they only agreed to attend the ball either because they were fond of Mama—scared of her, more likely—or they hoped to witness something scandalous.

But I expected those responses. I smiled and pretended they didn't bother me. The ones that hurt the most, that wormed their way beneath my armor, were the kind words and pitying glances. As we walked between groups of Mama's acquaintances, I searched the crowd for a set of broad shoulders and blonde hair, but the inspector either had not arrived or he blended in far better than I expected.

Mr. Stackhouse had not yet left the room, so I endeavored to keep one eye on him, an exercise which was also a good distraction. At least, until Mama introduced me to Lady MacBride.

"And this is your lovely daughter, och, how pleased I am to meet you, my dear. Such a brave soul to be out in public, I must commend you. I know it's been years but such trauma does leave its mark, does it not?"

It wasn't so much the empathy in her rheumy eyes or the kind solicitude in her light brogue, but that she would not allow a subject change and chattered away as my heart beat like a drum in my ears.

"Of course, when I lost my Amelia I didn't leave the house for a year, but we had lived a good, full life together by then, and there was not a better wife in all the country. She gave me years of happiness. It must have been a different story for you, what with your sister being a twin and so young at the time."

Someone in the group must have seen either my panicked expression or Mama's pale face because they tried to rein the old lady in by changing the discussion. But she was either happily ensconced in morbidity or oblivious because she missed every hint.

"Helena, I'm sure neither of these ladies wants to relive such an experience," one woman said, her eyes flicking back and forth between Mama and me.

"Nor would I!" Lady MacBride said with some enthusiasm as she patted my hand. "Such a sad state of affairs it was. How long was it before they found you, my dear? For I believe I heard it was three days but surely you did not survive in the forest so long on your own? Such a brave soul you are, and here all grown up and at a ball. You must be so proud of her, Your Grace, so proud—"

Mama cut in, said she was very proud, then excused us and dragged me away. My feet refused to move but I stumbled after her, much to the pleasure of several guests who appeared to be getting just the scene they hoped for.

But I could not bring myself to care. I saw the empty dirt where Lia had stood moments before, smiling, with her hair falling all around her and a crown of flowers on her head. I felt the cold pillow where her head had once lay while we whispered secrets in the dark. I heard her laughter and tasted salty tears on my lips.

"Gigi, don't cry," she would say, and kiss my cheek. She had always been braver than me. If I had disappeared, she would have found me. She never would have stopped looking.

A sharp sting on the back of my arm brought me falling back into my body and I gasped as the world tilted back into place. Mama's worried eyes were there, grounding me.

"Did you pinch me?" I asked. My voice sounded dazed, even to my ears.

She sighed in relief. We were in the card room. No one had ventured here yet. Mama must have dragged me in to give me a moment to regain my composure.

"Yes, I did. You..." She swallowed. "For a moment, I thought I had lost you again."

I pressed both hands against my cheeks, but no moisture leaked through my gloves. At least I had not cried. "I'm still here, Mama."

As soon as she was certain I was truly okay, anger replaced the worry in her eyes. "I cannot believe that old bird would be so crass. Won't she be surprised to find salt in her tea instead of sugar?"

"Mama," I laughed, "you can't!"

"Oh, I most certainly can."

Humor filled the hole in my stomach. I said, "Shall I fetch the salt?"

She smiled, and I smiled back.

"Are you ready to go back, or do you need a moment? You don't have to stay if you aren't ready, but"—she looked over her shoulder—"I hate to let those vultures see you in distress. They will think they've caused it, and I'll be damned if I let them think they can affect my daughter that way. I was so certain things would be different since so much time has passed."

I would not wallow in pity or memories and I refused to let Mama do the same. And anyway, I had a mission to accomplish.

So I looked her in the eye and said, "I'm fine, Mama. Promise."
I had to be.

We re-entered the ballroom just as a foxtrot began. The room erupted in excited chatter as couples populated the dance floor. My eyes flew across the room, cataloging and discarding faces. Mr. Stackhouse was still there, though with a different group, but no inspector. Where was the damned man?

"Why Lady Gwen," purred a deep voice from my right. "You do clean up rather well."

I turned.

A tall, dark-haired man stood alone in a pool of shadows beyond the open balcony doors. Like the rest of the men in the room, he wore a black suit. It fitted him like a second skin, clinging to the line of shoulder and thigh like a lover. Unlike the rest of the guests, his shirt, vest, and tie were also black, a bit of shadow in human form. His face was obscured by the dim light, but his voice sent goosebumps shivering down my spine.

I straightened my shoulders. "Excuse me, sir. Are we acquainted that you address me so familiar?"

"Not nearly as well as I would like us to be," he said and stepped into the light with the powerful, svelte elegance of a hunting cat.

He was as handsome as his voice suggested, with a long, straight nose, lips that were expressive and finely carved rather than full, and dark eyes that burned from beneath heavy brows tilted upward in the center. The entire effect was one of aristocratic, sardonic amusement, but failed to mask an intimidating intensity.

He moved with the easy, confident grace of a fighter. My instincts screamed this was a dangerous man. I fought the desire either to step away from him or to step closer. And I refused to back down.

Instead, I held my ground and raised my chin. "I'm sorry to disappoint you, then."

He smiled, a slow curl of the lips and tilt of the head that made my fists clench in reflex. "Oh, you could never disappoint me."

"I'm quite certain I can. In fact, I intend to do so right now."

I turned away on unsteady feet only to feel a hand on my shoulder that spun me around just as the first notes of the waltz began. One hand on the center of my back pulled me hard against his chest and the other turned us into a graceful spin.

"What do you think you're doing?" I demanded.

Instead of the scolding tone I had intended, my voice was breathy and uneven. Feeling the length of him pressed against the front of my body made it harder to maintain any coherent train of thought.

"Isn't it obvious, dear girl? I'm dancing with you."

"You did not ask me, and I never accepted."

"I know," he said with mock sadness. "You never would have said yes, so I intervened to save you from yourself."

I managed a scornful laugh. "Save me? I'm quite capable of handling myself, sir, so if you will release me—"

"I'm only trying to help you, my lady," he said *my lady* like it was a term of endearment and tightened his grip on my waist. "People will talk if you don't dance at least once."

"People already talk, and I have no desire to add fuel to the fire. Let me go. I have more important things to do tonight than entertain an arrogant stranger."

"But doesn't every unmarried woman dream of sharing a stimulating conversation with a handsome stranger?"

"Find me a handsome stranger and I'll tell you."

"Lady Gwen," he scolded, "you wound me to the heart."

"You must have a heart, first, sir, and I have my doubts."

"If I have no heart, it's only because you've stolen it." He smiled a knee-wobbling smile and spun us again, his fingers splayed wide across my back, keeping me pulled tight against his chest. He leaned in, my heart stopped, and he whispered against my ear, "Be on your guard, lady. Things are not as simple as they seem and there is more at stake than you can dream. The gate will open at the standing stones. Do not go alone."

The music stopped and so did we. The stranger let me go only reluctantly, his fingers trailing across my back and down to my waist. He stepped back and bowed over my hand, kissing my knuckles. A bolt of heat shot up my arm though his lips only touched the silk of my glove. Then he winked at me, turned, and left. Half of the room stared as he passed through the crowd and disappeared, and the other half stared at me.

I stood for the space of a long breath, shock locking me in place just long enough for Inspector Hardwicke to stalk toward me from the door, his expression disapproving. Had he only just arrived?

I swallowed and hurried off the dance floor and toward the balcony, hoping he would follow. And hoping I would have enough time to steady myself before he joined me. My hands were still clenched into fists to stop them from shaking.

"Lady St. James?"

I plastered what I hoped was a welcoming smile on my face, turned, and said, "Inspector. We meet again."

"Who was that?"

So much for polite trivialities. "I don't know."

"But you were dancing with him."

"It wasn't my idea, I assure you."

"Do you mean to tell me he forced you into an embrace?"

"Well, in a manner of speaking—" I began, but his eyes narrowed dangerously, and he turned as if to follow. I could not allow that. Too many important things were happening and god's breath, I would never live it down.

I put a hand on his forearm and said, "I have learned something."

He turned back and looked down at my hand.

I removed it, then plowed on, "Do you see the dwarven man with the long red mustache?"

After a glare at me, he turned his attention toward the ballroom. "Yes."

"His name is Mr. Stackhouse. He is one of the few dwarves in the Artificer's Guild who has the resources to create or discover the"—I dropped my voice—"the magic we've seen at work. I overheard him speaking to the men he is leaving with, saying they made exciting advancements that would convince an acquaintance to sponsor a bill in the commons. No," I said before he asked. "They did not name the man. What kept you, by the way?"

His lips thinned to a line, and the muscle in his jaw flexed. A look of sick helplessness flashed in his eyes, and a sinking feeling made me dizzy as I guessed what caused it.

"No," I breathed.

He nodded once.

"Who?"

He cleared his throat. "One of the boys."

The balcony felt like it would tip to the side as frustrated helplessness washed over me. How could someone hurt a child? And why? My already clenched fists tightened in fury, and a spike of pain shot up my arm as something sharp jabbed my palm.

I loosened my fingers and looked down. A pendant necklace on a silver chain sat on my palm. Where had it... the stranger. He must have left it in my hand when he kissed my knuckles. I held it up to the light and my mouth dropped open. It was the triquetra.

I grabbed the inspector's arm and dragged him after me. He grunted, began to object, then remained silent as I pulled him through the ballroom, down the hall, and into the foyer where we might reasonably expect some privacy.

People meandered about, moving from the card room to the refreshments and back to the ballroom. They stared at us with pleasantly scandalized expressions, but I ignored them and stopped beneath a lamp to display the necklace open on my palm.

"Look at this," I ordered.

He did, but not before raising a brow at me.

"This is a triquetra enclosed by a circle," I told him. "It is a common symbol in this part of the world, with several meanings, but it was drawn at the center of the kidnapping spell—"

"I saw it," he interrupted.

"Quite. But it was also inked on a letter inviting me to the building on Tromwell, the one you discovered me at this morning.

The women there knew I'd been investigating the kidnappings and offered to help."

"You didn't tell me about that." His brows lowered in disapproval, but I pretended not to notice and turned the necklace over to examine the back.

"Where did you get this?" he asked.

"I think the stranger pressed it into my hand while we were dancing. I didn't notice because these gloves are thick and I was angry," I said absently.

"You are not acquainted with the man? Did he say anything to you about the necklace?"

"No, and no, but he said something about... things are not as simple as they seem, and there being more at stake than I knew. He also said, 'the gate will open at the standing stones'."

He poked the arc with one blunt finger. "Are those initials?"

I tipped the necklace to catch the light and read, "C.M."

"Who is C.M.?"

"I don't know," I muttered, staring hard at the necklace.

C.M. Who did I know with those initials? They stuck in the roof of my mouth but I couldn't pry them out. My mind flew, trying to place anyone I'd heard of with those initials. Mr. Capstone? That didn't quite fit.

Then there was the triquetra, a symbol of the power of three, the maiden, mother, and crone; the body, soul, and spirit; the water, earth, and sky. All of those triune aspects were used in the practice of magic and spirituality.

"Lady St. James."

The symbol had been employed both in the circle and the letter from the Triumphant Sisterhood. *Tri,* meaning three, but this symbol was bounded by a circle. Containment? Continuity? Eternity? Was the Sisterhood more involved than they'd led me to believe?

"Lady St. James."

If the dwarves were selling magic to the humans for political gain, how were the elves tied in? Mr. Capstone was supposedly procuring children who were being kidnapped using the symbol, but the only kidnappers anyone witnessed were human. There was *something* there.

"Gwenevere!"

My spine stiffened, and I looked up. Mr. Yates, Inspector Hardwicke, and Percy Bywater the hatter stood staring at me. I grasped the threads of my thoughts, trying to pull them back together but they fluttered away like spider silk in a breeze. I was so close!

"Dammit," I growled. "What?"

Percy clasped both hands together and said, "May I have a word? In private?"

I tightened my fingers around the necklace, ready to ask him to meet with me some other time, but his eyes were so wide and panicked that I hesitated. Why was my favorite hat maker here so late? Tony was consulting Mr. Yates, presumably about the dark stranger, so speaking to Percy for a moment couldn't hurt.

"I'm sorry," I said and motioned to a spot a few feet away where we'd have at least a moderate expectation of speaking privately. "Please."

Percy fidgeted with his hands, rubbing and clasping them as he prepared himself to say whatever was making him so uncomfortable.

"Percy," I said. "Are you quite well?"

He choked out what could only charitably be called a laugh. "No. I am not. But I had to speak with you. I am sorry, Gwen."

"Sorry? For what? Coming so late? This ball will drag on till three o'clock in the morning or later. No need to be sorry."

"No." He met my eyes and there was deep sadness and fear in his lovely face. "I lied to you. And I regret it. Very deeply. If I would have said something perhaps... but no. There's no point in that, now. I must tell you before anyone else gets hurt."

Little shockwaves of fear prickled along my neck and forearms. "Percy, what do you mean?"

He took a deep breath, eyes averted as if he didn't want to look at me; as if he were ashamed. "When I saw your notes this morning, and the markings you recorded, I told you I was simply shocked. That wasn't true. I recognized the symbols."

"What? How?"

"Elves live a long time. Longer than humans and dwarves. Your kind wouldn't remember but we do. We do."

"Remember what?"

"Those symbols. They're fae, Gwen. Real faerie magic."

The floor dropped, my knees turned to water, and the world went dark.

# 15

# The Trouble with Little Brothers

## SALLY

The little brat had run away again.

Sally pulled her woolen coat tighter around her shoulders and hurried down the dark street. Monsieur had given her leftovers after supper, and the napkin-wrapped bundles stuffed into her pockets bounced against her legs as she strode, carried along by fear and anger. Why would he run away now when they were safe, warm, and well-fed?

She had been happy to climb the narrow stairs to her snug room after supper, happy to think that before long Lady Gwen would teach her to read so she could choose books from the library. Happy to daydream of the opportunities opening up for Sam when he got older. She lay on her bed imagining her future and listening to the bumps and thumps of movement on the floors below.

When the musicians started warming up, Sally crept to Sam's room to ask if he wanted to sneak downstairs to listen. She was certain he'd never heard music like that before. They would lean against the banister and close their eyes, letting the music drag them away.

But Sam wasn't in his room. And now, instead of laying in her warm bed or listening to music, she was trudging across town in the dark through a filmy fog that stuck to her face and hair, to search for her ungrateful brother.

She'd already been walking for more than an hour. He had better hope she found him where she'd expected to, because if she had to search all night, she wouldn't wait for Lady Gwen to fire them. She'd just kick Sam out on his ungrateful little arse. Of course, she knew she'd never do such a thing but the angry thoughts helped keep her motivated, warm, and, more importantly, warded off the panic. What was he thinking, running away when there were kidnappers and murders?

She stopped herself before thinking about that. They had overheard Mr. Yates and Mrs. Chapman talking about it. The idea of something happening to her little brother made Sally walk faster. She would drag him home, tie him to the bloody bed by his shoelaces, and sit on him. Then she would sing annoying songs and poke his forehead until he went mad.

Sally comforted herself with thoughts of retribution until she reached their old home and stood at the door, alone. There was no drunken laughter, no rumble of wheels or echo of footsteps to disturb the still air. The kidnappings and murders had scared the whole city, but eastsiders knew better than anyone the dangers that prowled the streets at night. They were safely inside. As she and Sam should have been.

A shiver of unease made her bound up the stairs two at a time. The door to the small flat was open, and a dark figure stood in the center of the room, silhouetted by the small window. Moonlight glinted off the blade of a small knife.

"Sam!" she cried. "You blithering idiot, what do you think you're doing?"

He folded the knife down into its handle with a little click and turned toward the window. "I just had to make sure," he said.

"If you keep running away like this, we're going to get fired."

"So? We made do before."

"Only because we stole other people's money, money they worked hard for."

"Dad worked hard, too, and look where that got him."

She refused to let the destroyed hope in his voice erase her anger. He had to learn that their father was not coming back. "He lost his fortune because he was a selfish fool."

"And how do you know?" he snarled. "You never cared. You didn't even look for him when he left. You hated him, and everybody knew it. He probably left to get away from you!"

Sally clenched her fists. She'd never been tempted to hit her brother, but when he defended that man it was almost impossible not to explode. For years, she let Sam keep his illusions because she did not have the heart to tell her brother who their father really was.

If Sam thought their father drank in grief after being swindled by his partner, then he could still believe the man had loved them, he had merely been broken by losing his fortune. That fiction was better than knowing the truth: he simply did not care about them, not enough to stop drinking or to stay. It hurt in ways Sam did not deserve.

But if he kept believing the lie, he would never stop searching and hoping, and never stop putting himself in danger. So she unbuttoned her coat and pulled down the neck of her dress as she walked toward her brother.

"Do you see this?" she said, pulling the fabric down until a pale circle of lumpy scar tissue below her collarbone showed silver in the moonlight.

He eyed her suspiciously. "What is it?"

"Father gave me this one night when he didn't have any money left for drink. I took it to buy bread because we hadn't eaten in two days. He put his cigar out on my chest to punish me."

"You shouldn't have taken his money," Sam said, but his angry tone didn't match the sick look on his face.

"And this?" She pulled her arm out of the jacket and unbuttoned the cuff to expose a long, jagged scar on her forearm. "I got this one when he pushed me down the stairs for trying to stop him from beating our mother."

"Stop it."

"He beat her so hard one night that she died, Sam. And then he left us. I don't know if he couldn't live with his guilt or he was just too tired to keep trying, but he left us. I had to find someone to help me with Mama's body. You remember?"

"That's not what happened!" Sam shouted, tears streaming down his face. "She was yelling at him, and he couldn't help it.

He was scared 'cause she was sick. She shouldn't have made him so mad. He put on his coat and said, 'I'll be back, Sammy-boy.' He never meant to stay away."

"She was sick because we didn't have any medicine to help with her chest. He drank all our money away."

"No, he didn't."

"Yes. He did."

Sam screamed then. It was a broken sound wrenched from the bottom of his soul. He turned and kicked the table. It wobbled. He kicked it again and again until the repairs gave way and it crumpled to the floor like a squashed bug. He tore at the mattress with his knife, toppled the little dresser, and kicked and punched and screamed until all the strength went out of him and he collapsed in a sobbing heap.

He pushed her away at first, but his protests grew weaker until he finally turned and wrapped his arms around her stomach. She cradled him like a broken doll as he cried. When he was very little and scraped his knee, or was bullied by another boy, he would run to Sally and bury his face in her stomach to cry.

But these were not the innocent tears of a child, and Sally couldn't soothe or tease them away. So she cried, too, and held him until the tears were wrung out of them both. Then they shared the food she'd stuffed in her pockets, eating in silence amidst the wreckage of their past.

Sally cleared her throat and buttoned up her jacket. "Let's go home, Sam."

"That place isn't home," he said, wiping his nose on the back of his arm.

"But it could be."

He didn't argue, only took her hand as she hauled him to his feet. When she closed the door, she knew it was the last time either of them would ever see the place. A cold, lonely pain shot through her chest, leaving emptiness behind it. The emptiness hurt, but it left space for hope to grow.

They walked away from the building, left the Narrows and the mud and the dark, empty windows, and began the long walk back to the west end and the new life they would build for themselves there.

"What will you do with your first pay?" she asked Sam, hoping to distract him with more pleasant thoughts.

He didn't answer. When she looked down at him, his eyes looked far away in the moonlight. He only said, "Do you hear that?"

She turned her head, trying to listen, but heard nothing. Sam pulled her down the street, his pace increasing and excitement coloring his voice as he said, "It's him! It's got to be him!"

"What are you talking about?"

He stopped, dragged her around a corner, and said, "There he is!" and started running.

Time slowed as Sally realized what was happening. She saw Sam's outline in the shadow, his stubby legs pumping as he ran right toward the pale circle marked on the ground.

She shouted, "Sammy, no! Come back!" and sprinted after him.

She felt it, now. It was the draw of home, of love; a promise of safety floated on the air in a siren-sweet song impossible to ignore. But the draw couldn't touch her, not as it did before, because she knew what it meant: Sam was in danger.

She caught him by the arm just before he reached the circle chalked on the ground. She tightened her grip and dug her heels in to stop his forward momentum, pulling them both backward and away from the magic. He turned on her in a fury, pummeling her with his feet and fists and screaming, but she weathered his attack and held on.

Suddenly his weight was lifted away, and the man stood there in the shadows, holding a struggling Sam off the ground by the back of his coat.

"What's all this, then? Two instead of one? Wait..." The man narrowed his eyes at Sally. "Haven't I seen you before?"

Sally pushed herself to her feet, her heart thundering in her ears, watching as Sam reached for the circle and cried. She had to save him. There was nothing else to be done, and no time to think. So Sally attacked the man.

She was nearly as tall as Lady Gwen in her heels, and years of running the streets had taught her the price of not fighting back. She threw herself at the man with every dirty trick she'd learned from her father, using her elbows, her knees, even her forehead, and her teeth.

As she fought she screamed, "Sammy, run! *Run!*"

The man had to let go of Sam to fend her off, and she managed to avoid a few looping blows. When he finally connected, her cheek exploded with pain and she spun dizzily to the ground, ears ringing. Vague, angry voices floated somewhere above her, shoes scuffled on the cobbles, and a knife blade snicked open. Grunting, thumps, and then the heavy thud of a body falling limp to the ground. Someone hauled her up, but everything spun and shapes were only dark blobs of weak light against the night.

A voice said, "Little prick," and she heard nothing else.

---

It was a long time before Sally came fully back to consciousness. She had fuzzy impressions of floating, of horses, of smelly blankets, and then, finally, warmth. A body was pressed up against her back and another to her front, warm and loose-jointed with sleep.

They rocked gently back and forth in the dark, but faint light leaked in from a series of cracks. She squeezed her eyes shut and tried to remember what had happened, but the creaking of wheels and the steady clop of hooves dragged her down into sleep.

The second time she woke, Sally jerked to a sitting position gasping.

"Sammy?" she gasped, turning the other bodies enough to see their faces.

"Sally?"

She spun, ignoring the grunts and moans from the other sleepers, and saw a head of long blonde hair. "Virginia?"

A little sob escaped the other girl's lips and she stifled it with both hands. All around them the others were waking, pushing themselves into sitting positions and rubbing their eyes. There were five of them, still wearing the clothes they'd been kidnapped in. Blankets and pillows lay strewn about the floor, and two casks of water wobbled in the corner, but there was nowhere to relieve themselves.

"How did we get in here?" Sally asked.

"I don't know," Virginia wiped her eyes with her hands. "Last thing I remember, we were all in the stone room and Will brought our dinner."

"Will?"

"He's the one what keeps us here," the other girl said. Her brown hair was matted, and she smelled as if she hadn't bathed in a long time.

"Where are they taking us?" a smaller boy asked. Sally guessed he must have been about Sam's age.

"What's your name?" she asked him.

"Angus," he sniffed.

"I don't know, Angus. But we're going to find a way out."

"When they took Mary," Virginia said in a small voice, "she never come back."

Dread settled on Sally like a blanket, cold and heavy, but at least Sam was not in the closed carriage. It reminded her of the old coaches the bobbies used to transport criminals, but the small windows had been boarded over. If Sam wasn't here, that meant he'd either gotten free or... she couldn't think about the other option.

"Let's find a way out of here," she said.

Sally freed herself from the tangle of limbs and pressed her hands against the wood, sliding her fingers along every seam and crack, searching for any weakness to exploit. When she found none, she started pounding, pushing, and kicking at the door frame.

"Help!" she screamed "We're hostages! They kidnapped us! Please, help! Help!"

The other children took up her cries, and soon they had the carriage rocking back and forth so hard she thought they might tip it over.

"Come on," she encouraged, throwing herself against the wall. "Push!"

The wagon rocked to a stop, the metallic sound of clinking signaled chains being unlocked, and the door swung open. Blinded by the sunlight, she saw only a silhouette, but shaded her eyes until the form resolved itself into the man who had tried to kidnap Sam last night.

With a cry, the bigger boy—Sally hadn't gotten his name—leaped for the open door. The man caught him by the front of his shirt and punched him in the stomach. He doubled up in pain, not even able to gasp for air. The man dropped him to the dusty ground.

"You'll keep quiet and still back here, or every one of you will get the same treatment, see?"

"Don't hurt him, Will," the dark-haired girl pleaded. "Please."

Will's face went red, he pulled the boy up from the ground and slapped him viciously across the face.

"Is that what you want?" Will demanded, shaking the boy who sucked air like a flopping fish. "You'll shut up or he'll take every slap meant for you, hear me? I was ordered to bring you alive. There were no orders about what shape you had to be in, so it's no trouble to me if I need to beat every one of you senseless, first."

The boy was making weak, pitiful sobbing noises and blood dripped from his nose onto the dark blankets where Will dropped him. Virginia bit her lip. The other girl shied away from the door, and Angus curled into a little ball on the floor, whimpering to himself.

Seeing the children cower brought back every feeling of helplessness Sally had ever felt as a child, looking up into the angry, hopeless face of her father.

"You're a big strong man, aren't you?" Sally spat. "You aren't fit for any job a real man would do so you have to hurt small children!"

After a moment of shocked silence, Will lunged up inside the coach. His hand shot out like a striking snake and he grabbed Sally by the collar of her coat, pulling her close enough to smell the onion and stale beer on his breath.

"If you don't keep your bleedin' mouth shut, I'll show you just how much of a man I am with both fists. You hear me, girl?"

That was the only threat that might have cowed her. But they were five and there was only one of him. And if the other girl had never come back, then wasn't any chance worth taking? Besides, Sally had survived many beatings.

She pushed her hands against his chest and whispered, "No. Please, don't. We'll be quiet."

She dropped her head and let her shoulders sag, as if in acquiescence, just long enough to let him think she had given up. When his hand loosened on her shirt, she fisted her own hands in his coat and jerked her knee up.

He hadn't been expecting the blow, and it caught him solidly between the legs. A high-pitched wheezing sound escaped his lips as he doubled over. But that wasn't good enough. He needed to stay down long enough for them all to run, so she lifted her leg and brought the heel of her foot down on his toes with all the force of her body.

There was a crunching noise, a cry of pain, and Sally tackled him, bowling them both over and out of the coach. He hit the ground beneath her with a woof of expelled air as her weight landed on him. Everything went fuzzy for a moment, but she pulled herself up to sit on his chest and screamed to the other children, "Run!"

They piled out of the boarded-up coach and took off, little puffs of dust flying from their feet. Beneath her, Will was still blurry-eyed from the fall, so she climbed off him, picked up her skirts, and ran to catch up. Now and then she looked over her shoulder, but no carriage or horse followed them. The boy who had been punched began to lag, so she locked elbows with him and pulled, forcing him to keep up.

When they had run more than a mile with no sign of the man, she allowed the children to slow to a walk. They stumbled along, panting and sweating, as Sally surveyed the landscape. Where were they? They needed to find help. She herded them off the dirt road to rest in the grass and climbed as high as she dared into the closest tree.

They were on a country road surrounded by open fields with small copses of trees dotting the rolling landscape. The hills were just tall enough to hide any nearby buildings, and no water ran close enough to hear. There were only two directions, north, and south, and north was the only choice that didn't lead to a kidnapper. She shinnied down the trunk, scraping her shin on the bark, and took a moment to fix her clothes.

Every one of them was scared, but she knew something about how to deal with frightened children. As long as she looked and sounded like she knew what she was doing, they would listen. So she took a deep breath, forced her hands to relax, and prepared to marshal the children. But the thud of horse hooves and the creak of wagon wheels echoed up the path.

"Get farther from the road," Sally urged them in a low voice, shepherding them into the tall grass, and forcing them to lay prone while the sounds grew nearer. She lay on her stomach and pressed herself flat as the cold dew that still clung to the grass seeped through her coat. Virginia reached out and took her hand, gripping it with surprising strength. In the distance to the south, a man driving a coach appeared. He was hunched over and had one hand pressed to his ribs. His bald head caught the sunlight. Will. He would surely spot them as soon as he got close enough.

"Don't move," she breathed, hoping the children would obey her.

Just then, a bay horse appeared coming over the hill to the north, and behind it, a closed coach pulled by a pair of horses. It was a woman dressed in fine clothes, riding astride as a man might, in a split skirt that showed high black boots. This woman might be their only hope.

"Run for help," Sally said and sprung to her feet. The rest of the children followed suit and sprinted toward the woman.

"Help us!" the smaller boy cried. "My lady, please help! We were kidnapped."

"We escaped."

"Help!"

The woman pulled her horse to a stop, showing a flash of fine leather gloves, and looked down at them with surprise written on her fine features. "You were kidnapped?"

"Yes, my lady," Virginia said. "We need your help, please. He's right there on the road!"

The woman held up her hands and said, "Children, children, please. Calm down and speak one at a time. You," she turned her eyes to Sally. "What is your name?"

"Sally, ma'am."

"Sally," the woman said. "Is this true, you were kidnapped?"

"Yes, ma'am. We were taken from town and only managed to escape. The man is right there, coming toward us!"

The coach pulled to a stop next to the woman, and she exchanged a glance with the driver. "Harris, it appears these poor children have been the victims of a kidnapping. We must sort all this out."

The man's eyes widened. "Of course, my lady. What would you have me do?"

"The children said their kidnapper is the man driving the coach toward us. Please take up the coach gun and hand it to me, just in case."

"Yes, ma'am," he replied, and stood to retrieve the weapon.

The woman removed her riding gloves one at a time, and Sally wanted to beg her to hurry. Will was getting closer and she removed each finger as if she had all the time in the world. Sally pulled the children behind her, prepared to tell them to spread out and run through the field.

Then she noticed the lady's hands, and they were not the hands of a relatively young aristocrat; they were gnarled and bent, with age spots, strange callouses, and prominent purple veins. But she took the proffered weapon with plenty of dexterity and raised it at the approaching driver.

A deep sense of unease made Sally's scalp prickle. She rubbed sweaty palms against her skirt and backed toward the grass at the edge of the road, pushing the other children behind her. Will pulled up, and the woman said, "That will be close enough."

Will pulled back the reins and winced, pressing one hand harder against his ribs. Satisfaction dulled the edges of her dread, and Sally hoped she'd broken a few of his ribs when she landed on him. With any luck, the woman would shoot the bastard.

"How did these children get away from you?" the woman asked. Her cultured voice sounded exasperated.

"It was the big one," he jerked his chin at Sally. "The bitch bowled me over. I think she broke my ribs."

"What is he talking about my lady?" Harris asked. The man's fists were balled at his sides as he glared at Will.

The woman sighed and said, "I am so sorry, Harris. I cannot tell you how sorry."

Then she turned the coach gun on her driver and pulled the trigger. Harris cried out and fell from the driver's seat with his hands in the air.

Sally was moving before Harris' body hit the ground. "Run!" she called to the other children, pushing them in front of her into the grass at the side of the road.

"Stop," the woman commanded.

Sally's legs locked up as if she'd run into wet cement. She tumbled in the grass, rolled over twice, and lay on her side facing the road. The sound of a hammer being cocked was loud, even amongst the heaving, panting, and crying of the other children.

"Go and fetch them, William," the lady said. "And if you fail me now, I will shoot you in the head and finish this myself."

Will grunted as he climbed down from the carriage and limped toward the children. They had to get away! Sally tried to push herself to her feet, tried to kick backward and away from him, but her legs were locked in place and wouldn't obey her.

Sweat trickled down the sides of her face to soak her collar, but she could not put more space between herself and the sullen face of Will the Kidnapper. He picked up the children, one at a time, grunting and panting as he carried them to the coach and tossed them into the back. At last, he approached Sally. There was a warped, feral smile on his face when he bent over and hauled her up into his arms.

He squeezed. "I'm gonna make you pay, you little bitch. And the mistress don't need to know how. So you'll keep your mouth shut unless you want me to start cutting pieces off your friends one at a time."

She shook her head back and forth, tears rolling from the corners of her eyes. There was no way to stop him and no way to get back to Sam. Bile rose in the back of her throat.

"No, William," the woman's voice cut through Sally's horror like a hot knife. "Bring that one to my coach. I will need a driver to replace Harris and she looks strong enough.

Will squeezed her again, making her ribs creak as he carried her toward the lady's carriage. He dropped her on the ground near the hooves of the horses and turned to stalk back to the other coach.

The lady said, "Please stand up, girl."

As if by magic, life flooded back into Sally's legs. They tingled painfully, but she could move them. Wild hope surged in her, but the woman said, "Do not run. I can stop you with a word, and if I have to drag you back, I will not be pleased. Just climb to the driver's seat and take the reins, please."

Sally flexed her cold fingers and pushed herself to stand. When she looked up, the barrel of the gun was pointed squarely at her face. The woman's eyes were not as cold as her voice. In fact, her strange hands shook, and her eyes were filled with unshed tears. A growth, nothing so benign as a mole or freckle, marred the side of her face, leaving Sally wondering if it had always been there, or only just appeared.

"Climb up," she ordered.

Sally did. The barrel of the gun never wavered.

The woman laid the weapon across her lap and began pulling her gloves on again, hiding the twisted fingers beneath the supple leather. She picked the gun back up and said, "Drive. And please believe me, girl: I do not wish to harm any of you, but I will kill you if you do not do as you are told. I have sacrificed too much to stop now."

Unlike the blustery fury of Will or even her father, this woman's cold determination frightened Sally to the marrow of her bones. Because, unlike Will or her father, she had already proved her willingness to do lethal violence.

And unlike Lady Gwen, Sally was certain this woman was a witch.

# 16

## *Discoveries*

### GWEN

The sun broke through the leafy canopy in golden pillars, creating a colonnade that turned the forest into a sanctuary. Pollen floated in a spring breeze, dancing in and out of the light like pixies.

We ran across the moss-soft ground in our bare feet, adorned with wildflowers and staffs we'd fashioned from the branches of fallen trees. Lia was faster than me, but not as nimble. We dodged in and out of the trees, leaping roots and tumbling streams alike.

"Come on, Gigi," Lia called over her shoulder. "Catch me up!"

My feet flew across the earth, kicking up clumps of dark soil until we broke through the forest canopy and into the flower-filled clearing. The earth was bright with pale spring growth, scattered with new flowers and warming in the sun. Lia caught my arm, and we spun, laughing, looking up at the sky till we were too dizzy to stand, drunk with freedom.

*As we lay with the sun warm on our faces, Lia turned to me. "Do you think we can convince Mama to give us a grand tour?"*

*This, again?* "Why are you in such a hurry to escape to the continent?" *I asked and raised my arms to the magical landscape.* "What could you want more than this?"

*Lia sat up and brushed the grass out of her long hair.* "I want the world, Gigi. I want to see the pyramids and the Great Wall and the Obelisk of Taryn. I want to learn to speak a hundred languages and find lost treasure and fall in love. I can't do that here."

*I thought of Thomas, the handsome stable boy, and felt a little shiver of pleasure as I remembered his dimpled smile.* "Who says you have to travel to find love? And what do you want with marriage, anyway? You've seen Mama and Papa. It hasn't worked out too well for them."

*She snorted.* "They're not in love. But"—*she sat up and smiled a conspiratorial smile*—"I have caught Mama reading old letters. She got all calf-eyed and smiled to herself and I am certain she was in love, at least once. I want to know what makes her face go all soft."

"I still don't understand why you have to leave Wainwright to do it."

"I'm not talking about only me, silly. I can't go without you."

"But I'm happy here."

*She shoved my shoulder.* "Why? Still waiting for your faerie prince to walk out of the forest?"

"Oh shut up, that was ages ago."

"It was not."

"I am never telling you another secret, Lia."

She grinned. "Oh yes, you will. And I will tell you all of mine, and we will explore the world and have love affairs and disappoint Mama terribly. And then we'll grow old and be a couple of old biddies together, always whispering of our adventures."

I folded my hands behind my head as the clouds sailed by on an ocean of perfect blue. We talked of our plans, of what we'd do when we were finally out in society, and how we would take rakish lovers and have torrid affairs and learn magic and become famous. But the sun dropped low, and a chill entered the spring air, and the hairs on my arms finally stood up to warn me of the approaching sunset.

"We had better get back," I said, dusting off my knees and fetching my discarded staff. "Mama will send Guillaume after us if we don't hurry."

"We should lay an ambush for him," Lia said, "and string him up and carry him home like a hunting trophy on safari."

"We could never pack him. He's the heaviest of all the hounds."

"But it would be fun to try."

The forest was cooler, the ground pulled the warmth from my bare feet as we walked, and the lowering sun left room for the shadows to climb out of their hiding places. Pixies rolled themselves up in leaves or hid in the closing petals of flowers, robbing the forest of their light. Dusk was a dangerous time, a time of change, where the sun gave up her throne but the moon hadn't yet taken control, and anything might happen.

"We should hurry," I said, shivering, and increased my speed to a quick trot, but Lia grabbed my arm, pulling us both to a stop.

"Gigi, look!"

*I followed her pointed finger. Amanita mushrooms stood proudly in a perfect faerie circle as if preparing for a dance, their little caps tilted at jaunty angles. Lia skipped to it, examining the phenomenon with a charmed smile.*

"Don't get so close to it," I warned, rubbing at my arms to bring some warmth back. "Faerie circles aren't safe."

*She rolled her eyes.* "You read too many books, Gigi. Besides, isn't this how you're supposed to find your faerie prince?"

"It is not," *I said, stiffly.* "They're supposed to come to you. If you get taken by the fae, they can hold you hostage. You might never get back. It's completely different."

*She smiled a wicked smile and lifted a leg to step over the line of mushrooms.* "Let's find out, shall we?"

*All the muscles in my body went rigid with fright.* "No! Lia this isn't the time to tease me. Please don't step in there, it's not safe."

*She grinned and jumped, landing in the center of the circle with both feet. I closed my eyes so tightly it hurt, but she only laughed at me.*

"Open your eyes you coward, I'm fine. Look."

*When I opened my eyes, she stood there with a cheeky grin on her lovely face and waggled her fingers at me.* "See? It's fine. Want to come in?"

*I tucked both hands behind my back.* "I would rather you come out."

"Oh, stop worrying so much and have a bit of fun. Besides, you know I would never go anywhere without you."

"Lia, please."

She made that face, the one letting me know I was ruining all her fun, but then froze as if an invisible hand had reached out and grabbed her shoulder. A chill spread through the air and my stomach dropped so hard it felt like falling out of a tree. Lia opened her mouth, but no sound came out. One moment she was standing there, looking at me with eyes so wide the whites shown all around them, and the next she was simply gone.

She was gone.

The universe fell apart. I couldn't feel her anymore, couldn't feel her in the place she'd always been before, somewhere in my chest. I broke the mushrooms apart with my staff, I dug in the ground, and I screamed her name until my throat ached.

When the huntsmen found me, feverish and nearly dead, I tried to tell them that the faeries had stolen my sister, but they didn't believe me. Everyone thought her kidnapped or run away. They talked on and on about my ordeal, and they never let me go outside. So, as soon as no one was paying attention, I snuck out of the house and lost myself in the woods screaming her name.

Guillaume always found me, sniffing me out and then laying by my side and howling until they picked me up and carried me home, cold and starved. But no matter how I searched, in the forest or in books about faerie lore, I never found my twin sister.

Faeries had stolen her.

---

The acrid burn of smelling salts made my body convulse so hard my bones hurt. I jerked upward, eyes flying open to. Mr. Yates,

Inspector Hardwicke, Mama, and Percy gathered round me in the study, their faces drawn tight in lines of worry.

I pushed myself backward and turned away from the scent, coughing. They had carried me into the study and laid me on the same chaise we had used as a bed for Sally the night I found her.

"She's okay," Mama said, relieved, pressing her gloved hand to my cheek.

"I am okay, Mama. A little too much excitement, nothing to worry over." I gave her a smile in the hope she would believe me and go back to the party before I interrogated Percy. The encounter with Lady MacBride had been enough of an emotional shock for Mama. Learning her remaining daughter was deeply involved in a dangerous investigation would only make things worse.

"Are you certain, my dear? I know it has been a difficult night for you. Though I saw you dancing with that handsome stranger. How he was admitted without being on the guest list I do not know, but I cannot say I regret it. Just watching the fellow move was a pleasure, and the two of you together were truly something to see. You have not danced in ages."

I decided to ignore the comment about the stranger—that deserved its own investigation—and touch on the first part of her comment. "Indeed, I am rather tired. If you don't mind, I will relax here for a bit. But do not leave your guests, Mama. They will wonder where you've got to. And Percy will be here with me. And the intrepid inspector. Have you been introduced?"

"We have not."

"Inspector Hardwicke, this is Her Grace, the Duchess of Wainwright. Mama, this is Inspector Hardwicke of Scotland Yard."

There was bowing and polite niceties but Mama continued to glance back and forth between the three of us, clearly uncomfortable leaving me alone with two men. Mrs. Chapman appeared, carrying a tray of tea, and some of the tension left her. No one would find Mrs. Chapman an unsuitable chaperone.

"Very well," Mama finally acquiesced. "But I will come to check on you, before long."

We watched the duchess leave, floating elegantly away, and everyone breathed a collective sigh of relief. Mrs. Chapman handed me a fragrant cup that had already been treated with honey and cream.

I took a warming sip then turned to my friend and said, "Percy?"

The foot of the chaise sank under Percy's weight as he sat next to my legs, his shoulders slumped. "I'm sorry, Gwen, I didn't know the answer would affect you so. Are you certain you are well?"

"Don't apologize," I ordered. "Explain."

He gave the inspector a quick glance from the corner of his up-tilted eyes, then raised a brow at me. I nodded to let him know it was okay to speak in front of the inspector. After all, we were committed now.

Percy looked down at his clasped hands and said, "You already know most of it from your studies. The fae are not some fairy tale, not pretty little pixies with wings, but truly powerful beings who once lived amongst us. Taller than humans, fairer than the elves, stronger than the dwarves."

Inspector Hardwicke snorted, but I gave him a quelling glare and told Percy, "Yes, I know this. Please get to the point."

"The elves have long memories as well as long lives. My great-grandmother was still alive when the fae were banished to the Sunset Lands. She told the stories to my grandmother, and I heard some of them when I was young. She spoke of the war, and of the rebel faeries who joined with humans and taught them magic. But humans cannot wield it long enough to win a war; it warps their minds and bodies until it kills them. What the fae gave humans was ritual magic that requires no will to channel it."

"But those circles used modified runes."

"No." He shook his head. "They are symbols of magic, the original source of many of the runes artificers use today. The runes of today are streamlined and more efficient. The symbols you found command a wilder, more powerful magic. That is not suitable for safe, predictable artificery, so the dwarves modified them. They perfected them for artifice until settling on the runes of today."

"Why not keep the more powerful magic?" Tony asked.

"Imagine buying one of those new motor vehicles and never knowing when it might try to take off and fly on you."

"That certainly presents an amusing picture," I said. "But this magic has either been hidden or forgotten for years, because there is no record of it; not in the histories or in dwarven lore. Why would it resurface now?"

Percy raised frightened eyes to my face. "That is the question, isn't it? It's why I was afraid to tell you when I recognized the symbols. When they were exiled, the three races agreed to destroy all that was left of the fae; their cities and strongholds, their books and magics. It should not still exist and yet..."

He let the thought hang in the air. Someone had resurrected faerie magic. Where had they found it? And why employ it now? "Is it possible that someone kept the knowledge? Preserved some trace of what humans learned from the fae?"

"I do not know. Perhaps if my people kept written records instead of oral histories." He shrugged. "But from what my grandmother told me, the destruction was thorough. The war brought the three races to near extinction, and no one wanted any chance of rekindling the fire."

"And yet," I said, "there will always be those who hesitate when asked to give up power. Surely there was someone who desired that power enough to hide it. Are any elves still alive who could have known enough of this magic to reproduce it? Who may have preserved and used or sold it?"

Percy shook his head. "I doubt it very much, but I cannot deny the possibility."

"This isn't pertinent. What we need to know right now is who benefits from the use of it," Inspector Hardwicke said. "Where it came from is of no importance for the present. We need to know who is using it and where they've taken the victims."

"I only know this," Percy said. "The fae have never given away knowledge that does not benefit them. Even the rebels who joined the humans believed they would benefit from the decision. Altruism is not in their nature."

I remembered my sister standing in the faerie ring and closed my eyes against the pain. Ophelia hadn't simply disappeared because the fae were a myth. She had either run away or been kidnapped, and I had invented the story of her disappearance in my grief to explain the pain.

At least, that was what the experts Mama hired told me repeatedly as they tried to "fix" me. I studied everything I could learn about faeries, magic, the occult, and anything else that might prove to me I had not created the story to comfort myself. And yet, hundreds of people went missing every year with no explanation, never to be found.

So, what if I was right? What if my sister's disappearance was proof the fae still reached through to mortal lands in the right circumstances? And here we were on the eve of Samhain when the veil would be thinnest.

"I know the fae were exiled but... is it possible for them to come back? To breach the wall separating us from the Sunset Lands?"

Percy gave an elegant shrug. "Who's to say? After a thousand years, it has never happened."

"For the moment, let's assume it is possible. Why would the fae give mortals access to this ritual magic again, when it thwarted them the last time?"

"I cannot even pretend to guess," Percy said. "But if it were to happen, you can be certain the results would be something the fae desire."

"This gets us no closer to the answer we need," the inspector snapped. "These conjectures are interesting but unimportant. I will say it again: who is using the magic and where are they hiding the victims?"

I opened my left hand. The necklace was still in my palm, the triquetra glowing softly in the lamplight. "I think I know who we can ask."

Percy begged leave to go, and he was so ashen-faced that I could not ask him to stay. He had already given me more than I had dreamed of, more than I ever dared to hope: a link to the lost children, and maybe, someday, to Lia. I walked him to the door, arm in arm.

"I am sorry, my friend," he said when we stood on the landing. "I should have told you right away but"—he raised his hands and shook his head—"I was afraid. The fae and the elves have a history and that old fear is pressed into us by the stories we learn. Perhaps if I had told you—"

"You told me now," I reassured him, but he only smiled weakly.

His driver pulled up, and Percy gave my hand a quick kiss before climbing into the carriage. They disappeared into the night, and I wondered if the Triumphant Sisterhood would have something to say about this symbol, why they had used it on the letter they sent me, and who C.M. was.

The breeze picked up, pushing walls of fog into rolling banks that revealed, then concealed whole city blocks. It whistled through the bare branches and between buildings, almost like a voice. Except... I turned my head, straining. There was a voice. A familiar voice.

The fog rolled back just long enough to reveal a small form running toward me, then it disappeared as the word *lady* was carried to me by the breeze. I picked up my skirt and started running. Sam plowed into me, panting, and wrapped his arms around my waist.

His little body was covered in sweat and he panted in great ripping gasps.

"Samuel, what are you doing out here? You are supposed to be in bed. Are you okay? What happened?"

He took a few big swallows of air to slow his breathing, and panted, "Sally—gone. He took—her. Took her!"

My heart let go of my ribcage and did a freefall into my stomach. "What do you mean he took Sally?"

"It's—my fault," he sobbed, and then the boy collapsed into hysterical crying.

Tony appeared a second later, lifted Sam into his arms, and carried the boy into the house. He swallowed two cups of Mrs. Chapman's tea and sat shivering by the fire with a throw blanket wrapped around his shoulders. His teeth made an audible clicking noise as he tried to explain.

"I just had to check," he said, "t-to be s-sure. He m-might come back. I thought Sa-sally... Sally..." He sobbed and clutched the blanket closer. "I thought Sally was asleep. But she followed m-me. And then we started w-walking b-back and—" The rest of the story followed, and every word was a knife in the stomach.

Brave, sweet Sally was gone. They had kidnapped her. Sam tried to fight the man, but the kidnapper had taken his knife away and struck him so that he hit the ground, only waking once they disappeared. Then he'd run back here.

I took his shoulders in my hands and knelt, waiting until Sam looked me in the eye. "I am going to find Sally," I promised him. "I will get her back."

He gave me a stoic nod, then his little face broke, and he threw himself into my arms with a wail. "It's my fault," he said again.

But it wasn't his fault. It was mine. I had promised the boy we'd take out an ad in the paper to let his father know where he was. And I had been so busy I'd forgotten my promise. So he felt the need to check on his own, and now Sally was gone. And it was my fault.

I looked up at the inspector over the top of Sam's head, and his expression mirrored how I felt. As if he had failed somehow, failed again. But behind that, and deeper, was resolve. We were going to find these children. We had to. And before Samhain was over.

Mrs. Chapman brought Sam up to bed after the inspector had gently wheedled as much information out of him as the boy could bear. The story mimicked everything we already knew about the power of the circle and the men that hid in wait for their prey to appear.

"Let us break these events down," Inspector Hardwicke said. "We need to find the common thread."

So, we began piecing together all of our information, both of us pacing as we spoke.

We knew an elf had contacted and paid Mrs. Edwards to kidnap the children from her orphanage and, according to her, the intent was to scare the humans. This may or may not be in relation to the impending legislation the dwarves and elves hoped to introduce to the House of Commons.

The kidnappers were using old magic to draw the children to them, faerie magic unseen for hundreds of years. But we didn't know why or who had unearthed it.

And the men kidnapping the children were under a kind of compulsion spell set to end the morning after Samhain, and that was not faerie magic but of the human variety.

And two of the seven kidnapped children had been murdered.

A symbol in the magic circle was also being used by a group calling themselves the Triumphant Sisterhood, who had somehow found out what I was doing and requested to give aid.

And now a stranger left me with a necklace bearing the symbol inscribed with C.M. and the words, *things are not as simple as they seem* and *there is more at stake than you can dream. The gate will open at the standing stones. Do not go alone.*

Who was he, where did the necklace come from, and why had he given it to me?

I had more questions than answers.

"C.M. may be our only connection," the inspector said, at last.

"I would not mind asking the Triumphant Sisterhood a few more questions," I said. "But using a similar symbol does not guarantee C.M. is connected to them."

"Can you think of another way to guess the initials? Because as far as I can tell, this is the best lead we have to follow."

We stopped pacing as we met in the center of the room, staring at one another's faces as if the answer might lie hidden somewhere behind our eyes.

"How are you, darling?" Mama said from the doorway. "We are moving on to supper soon, if you are hungry."

I raised a brow at the inspector, but he only shook his head, turned, and continued pacing. Mama eyed the man, then reached up to touch my face. "How are you feeling? The guests have been asking after you."

I winced. "I'm sure they have."

Just one more rumor for the gossip mill. They would all carry the interesting story of my premature departure and the dance with the stranger to the rest of the social events they attended—

"Mama," I said, excitement bubbling up in my chest as a thought struck, "do you have the guest list for the ball?"

She lowered her brows. "Of course. But why do you need it?"

"Forgive me, Your Grace," the inspector said. "I am the one who needs it. Might that be possible?"

"Of course," she said slowly, eyeing us in turn. "Let me fetch it."

A few minutes later she returned with a neatly printed list of guests, with little marks for who had RSVP'd and who had cried off. The inspector and I huddled over the paper, tracing the names until my eye caught on a name and my breath stopped.

"Mama, why did Lady Monmouth not join us tonight?"

Her head tilted to the side. "I believe her daughter's condition has not improved. Why do you ask?"

I held up the necklace. "I found this, and I wondered if it might not belong to Lady Monmouth. Her name is Cassandra, is it not?"

"It is, yes. And I have seen her wear a silver chain occasionally, but it is usually tucked beneath her collar."

The inspector and I locked eyes. He considered my face for a moment, then nodded.

"Mama," I said, "I must go with the inspector. We believe this necklace was stolen and may be connected to the recent kidnappings. I have been helping the inspector on this case, and time may be running out to find the children. We just learned"—I stumbled over the words as Mama's face darkened with fear and anger—"Sa—Sally has also been kidnapped this evening. And I have to find her."

The building fury drained from her face, leaving it pale for a heartbreaking instant. Everything I had been struggling with for days, the memories, the fears, came crashing down on her, too. But she was as strong as steel.

Her back straightened, her chin raised, and she said, "You go and find our Sally. Inspector"—she turned to Tony—"you will protect my daughter with your life. Am I understood?"

He swallowed. "Yes, Your Grace."

Then she turned all the force of her will back on me, and I shrank beneath it. "We will talk about this, Gwenevere."

"Yes, ma'am."

Then she looked back and forth between us and threw her hands in the air. "Well? What are you waiting for? Go and find those children!"

# 17

## *Secret Doors*

## GWEN

"I cannot," Inspector Hardwicke told me for the fifth time.

"But—"

"What should I tell them? I suspect a member of the aristocracy is using magic to kidnap children?"

I clenched my fists. "Well, you don't have to say it like that."

"There is no way to make any member of the police force believe me. Not unless they've seen the magic at work, as I have. We need solid evidence of a connection between Lady Monmouth and the kidnappings first, and we do not have time to establish one."

"Fine. Then we can go to her townhouse and—"

"For the last time, we cannot sneak into the home of a private citizen at three o'clock in the morning. I will bend the rules because this case is outside the average jurisdiction but we do not have enough proof to justify breaking and entering. We would likely be shot or have dogs sicced on us."

I kicked the leg of the chair in frustration. "I don't want to break into anything. I just can't stay here and do nothing while Sally's trail grows cold."

He took my hands, pried my fingers open, and held them between his larger hands. The gesture was unexpected and strangely comforting, and some warmth seeped back into my cold fingers. "Waiting till morning is the smartest move we can currently make. I know you want to find the girl. I do, too. But if we go running about in the dark, we will be at a disadvantage. They will turn us away and they will have every right to do so. In the morning, they will have no excuse not to speak to me."

I pulled my hands out of his, strode over to the desk, leaned my fists against the table, and let my head hang limp on my shoulders. "How am I supposed to wait?"

"Profitably."

"What do you mean by that?"

He walked across the room and took my umbrella from the stand near the door, then pulled the blade from the shaft. "You have more tools, do you not? If you cannot or will not sleep, then prepare. But, if you can sleep"—he slid the blade back into the umbrella—"do so. The children will need you sharp and functioning at your best. What can you do for them if you are so tired you fall apart?"

I didn't want to agree with him, I wanted to be hunting, but I could not escape the logic. If we knocked on Lady Monmouth's door at three o'clock in the morning, the butler would refuse to wake his mistress for anything less than an emergency, and only if he answered the door.

The suspicion of a lost necklace certainly would not rate as an emergency. We might lie about something else, but I didn't know enough of Lady Monmouth to come up with anything convincing. Short of setting something on fire, there was nothing to do for at least four hours. That setting something on fire did not sound like a bad idea was a good indicator of my emotional state.

A guest bedroom was made up for the inspector, and I only flopped into my own bed once I had prepared every conceivable tool I possessed. I turned the dial on the little brass alarm clock to wake me at six o'clock and flopped onto the bed without removing so much as a hairpin. Aristotle peeked down at me from the corner bedpost and flapped his wings irritably.

"I know, my friend. Me, too. But the damned inspector is right."

I slept little, and what sleep I managed to steal was filled with dreams of Sally running through the woods, crying. I only saw her blonde hair flash through the trees, but I never caught up.

I met the inspector on the street at a quarter-to-seven the next morning, wearing my warmest walking skirt and jacket. He still wore his tuxedo, which I had not had time to appreciate, but was now covered by a dark greatcoat that hung down to his knees.

"Well, you look rather dashing, inspector. In a dark and sinister way." I thought he might smile at that, but he only raised a quizzical brow at my umbrella, carpet bag, and the raven on my shoulder.

"Better prepared than sorry," I said brightly, though my chest was still tight with worry and the nausea would not subside.

"Why are you bringing a raven?"

"Aristotle decided to join us. He wouldn't accept polite refusal."

He gave the bird a sidelong glance from narrowed brown eyes but said, "Where is the coach?"

"It's not coming."

"What do you mean?"

"We won't be taking the coach. There isn't enough time for it."

Just then James appeared, coming round the corner into the square and the inspector gave a huff of disbelief. "We'll be traveling in this? Where did it come from?"

I smiled. "It was in the shop. We will move much faster now."

He groaned, and my smile widened.

James pulled the little auto to a stop and climbed out, handing me a pair of driving gloves and goggles. I thanked him, climbed into the driver's seat, and pulled my scarf up over the top of my hat to protect my neck and face from the wind. The car sagged under the inspector's weight, and he muttered, "I can't believe I'm letting a woman drive me round in a piece of shoddy machinery."

"It is not shoddy. If you want to know, it is a very complex piece with several unique features I hope to employ one day."

His deep, disturbed sigh was highly gratifying. I reached for the shifter to put the vehicle into drive when a shout made both of us swivel in our seats.

"Wait!" Sam bolted down the stairs away from Mrs. Chapman, who was hampered by her skirt and limp.

"Samuel Dawes," I said in my very best imitation of Mama. "Exactly what do you think you are doing?"

"I'm coming with you," he panted.

"No, my lad, you are not."

"She's my sister!"

"Yes, and do you think she would thank me for putting you in danger, too?"

His face screwed up in lines of determination. "She's in danger because of me. You have to let me help."

"Sam—"

"If you make me stay I'll run away. I'll follow you, anyway."

"Not if you are locked in your room."

His chin trembled and the pulse at the base of his throat beat wildly, but it was the pleading in his brown eyes that stopped me. "Please don't lock me in, my lady. Don't. I can't stay here while you look for Sally. I have to help. I'm small and I'm fast and I can get into places where people can't see me. I can help. Please."

"He's not as young as he appears," Inspector Hardwicke murmured. "Children like him never are. And he won't be able to forgive himself if he doesn't try."

Sam must have seen the softening in my expression because he leaped onto the small back bench seat of the little car without a word and settled in, pulling his coat and scarf tight. I squeezed the steering wheel till the wood squeaked in protest, then took a deep breath and tried to calm myself. Aristotle hopped from my shoulder and took shelter out of the wind next to the boy.

I was about to hunt down kidnappers with a twelve-year-old pickpocket, a raven, and a police officer who didn't quite trust me. What could possibly go wrong?

"Hang on tight," I said through my teeth, pushed the shifter into drive, and took off at a less-than-safe speed down the street. Horses, carriages, buggies, and wagons were the primary mode of transportation, but autos had begun to appear on the streets of New London with increasing regularity. Most were nothing more than buggy boxes with wheels and engines, but as they did with most things, the dwarves had made vast improvements to the simple design.

I may regularly ridicule the excesses of my class, but there was something to be said about the ability to commission tools as helpful as my auto. It was full of cubby holes and secret compartments in which to store interesting things, and hopefully a few surprises as well.

I appreciated it, particularly as we wove between wagons and carriages with ease even James could not have matched. I found myself grateful for the thick wool coat and scarf, as the morning was particularly chill and the wind made my cheeks burn as we motored toward Lady Monmouth's townhouse.

It was a rather imposing edifice, several stories high and dark grey with gargoyles and buttresses that made the place feel less like a home and more like a temple.

I twisted to look at Sam. "You are to stay here. Do you understand me? If we need you—" I said before he interrupted, "I will fetch you. But in the meantime, you must wait, or I will take you home and chain you to the bed."

His lips compressed into a thin line, but he nodded. I would take what I could get.

The inspector and I approached the house and knocked. There was no answer. We exchanged a worried glance.

"The servant's entrance?" he suggested.

We rounded the building and took the stairs down to the lower door the servants used to enter and exit the house without being spotted. That, too, was locked and quiet. I gave the inspector a quick, speculative glance, then pulled a small satchel of tools from one of my skirt pockets and held the leather-wrapped bundle up for him to see.

"What is that?"

I unwrapped the leather to reveal a set of slim metal rods and hooks. His expression darkened. "Lady St. James," he said, stiffly. "Are you suggesting breaking and entering?"

"I am."

"I cannot allow it."

I blew a frustrated breath through my nose and said, "Inspector, I highly value your dedication to the law but we are not trying to steal from the woman. We are trying to find out whether she is tied to a series of kidnappings and two murders. No one answered either door. What is the likelihood that the woman and her servants have vacated the townhouse just as the worst weather of the year is about to set in?"

I think he would have turned me down even then if it had not been for the blood-curdling scream. The door muffled the noise, but it was very clearly a feminine scream of pain and horror. Every muscle in my body tensed in reaction, and the inspector's jaw set. He looked at my tools, looked at the door, then reared back and kicked the door just inside the handle.

The wood splintered. He kicked again and the wood around the locks broke free. Gun in hand, he eased into the house. I replaced the lock picks and pulled the blade free of the umbrella, then followed him into the dark.

The downstairs hallway was completely silent, as was the butler's pantry and kitchen, where the fire had been banked. No sign of a screaming woman. I followed the inspector up the stairs, moving so slowly that my leg muscles burned. He was surprisingly quiet for a big man.

A woman lay on the upstairs landing near the front door with her back against the wall and a thick trickle of blood oozing from her nose. Her eyes were wide and unfocused, but not vacant.

"Ma'am," the inspector said, kneeling next to her. "What happened? Are you alright?"

She whimpered and her head shook, not in a negative but as if she had a tremor, or she was trying to respond but some force kept her head still. Her lips moved as if making an "m" sound but no noise came out.

"Shhhh," I said, "calm down, miss. Breathe. Nothing will happen to you while we are here."

The woman, a maid by her dress, closed her eyes and pulled a slow breath in through her nose. Then she opened her mouth to speak and immediately started shaking.

"C-c-c-" she stuttered, her brows drawn together so tightly they touched. "C-cla-cla."

Inspector Hardwicke tried to calm her but the shaking got worse, her entire body convulsing as the capillaries on her cheeks burst, leaving little purple lines blooming beneath her skin. I grabbed her arm and there, beneath the sleeve, was the compulsion spell.

"Dammit," I growled, laying the woman's head in my lap so it would stop banging against the wall. "Hush, it's okay. Don't hurt yourself."

"Cla-cla—" She grunted as her body rose from the floor. "Claire! Claire!"

The breaking started. Muffled, meaty pops sounded in a staccato rhythm as her bones shifted beneath her skin.

"Claire!" she screamed, "Monmo... estay..."

With a final, sharp crack, the woman's head jerked at an unnatural angle and her body went limp. It fell back to the floor with a heavy thump. Blood ran from her ears and the corners of her eyes. My stomach roiled as I pushed myself backward and away from the broken body. Harry had stopped trying to tell us anything, and he was still alive. This woman had not given up, despite incredible physical pain. And the spell had killed her.

"Bloody fucking hell," the inspector growled as he scowled down at the body and the blue ink that made her exposed wrist look bruised. He pressed two fingers to her neck and swore again. Then he looked at me. His expression softened, and he pulled me into his arms.

I didn't realize I was shaking until he pressed me against him. Something about her death had been different. Perhaps it was how hard she fought to tell us whatever it was she had been trying to say. Claire, monmo, estay... whatever that meant.

He didn't try to tell me everything would be okay, just gave me the comfort of human touch for a few moments while the worst of the shaking slowly subsided. I leaned back and took a deep breath. "I'm okay, Inspector. Thank you."

He looked down at me for a long moment, eyes soft, and said, "Call me Tony."

"Then you must call me Gwen."

"Oh, I couldn't—"

"Tony," I interrupted, "shut up."

The shadow of a smile crossed his face.

We returned to the poor woman's body but found no other clues about who she was or what she wanted to tell us.

"Should we move her? It seems wrong to leave her on the floor like this."

Tony frowned. "We can't. I will have to explain how we found her, and if we move the body, it will contaminate the clues. We can check the rest of the house, instead."

I nodded, but it was difficult to leave her broken body bleeding slowly on the floor.

The rest of the house was quiet and empty, full of the signs of regular daily life. Upstairs the rooms were much as I expected until I opened a particular bedroom.

Stuffed animals sat neatly in chairs, a perfect tea set in miniature on the table, piles of fanciful watercolor paintings on the desk, and a tray of medicine on the nightstand near the bed. This was Lady Monmouth's daughter's room. I traced my fingers across the back of the armchair next to the bed and wondered how many nights Lady Monmouth sat there, watching over her daughter.

I had a sudden, vivid memory of Mama sleeping in a chair next to my bed after they had found me starving in the woods. Her skin had been pale, her eye sockets purple, her cheeks hollow. She had looked so fragile it was painful to remember, even many years later.

There was a little book with a red leather cover next to the bed. I picked it up and opened the cover. Inside it read, "This diary contains the secret thoughts and observations of Claire Elizabeth Marie Monmouth." She drew flowers and butterflies around the introduction, turning it into a little piece of art.

Claire.

The maid had been trying to tell us something about Lady Monmouth's daughter. I returned the book to its place and hurried off to find Lady Monmouth's room, only to run bodily into Tony standing in the hallway with his hands pressed flush against the wood paneling.

"I felt something," he said as he examined the wall. "A draft of air."

I squeezed in next to him and ran my own hands along the wall. The panel was cold to the touch, as if there were an open space behind it where cold air stole the heat, but the panel next to it was nearly room temperature.

"A hidden door," I breathed.

"Where is the switch?"

In a sudden flash of intuition, I pulled the necklace from my pocket and began running it over the wood in a pattern that would cover the entire surface. As I got close to eye level, the necklace stuck to the wall and hung there. A magnet? When I moved the necklace something behind the wall clicked, and a seam appeared in the wood. I pressed, and the door swung silently inward.

Tony pulled his gun out, and I followed him once again into the dark, heart racing. The passage opened to a small room with wood-paneled walls and tables set all along two corners. It was too dark to see anything else because the room had no windows. Tony pulled a match from his jacket and dragged it across the bottom of his shoe.

There were jars, cans, and crockery full of all manner of things, none of them labeled. Herbs hung drying from the ceiling, bowls with various substances sat on the table, and in the center of the room, a magic circle had been painted in white. There were no spells in it, but if anyone performed magic in this room, the circle would contain it.

"Oh my," I breathed, taking it all in. "Lady Monmouth is a witch. But how? I have seen the woman, she bears no sign of it! She still has the blush of youth about her, there is nothing bent or crooked. How could she practice magic and hide it?"

"Perhaps she has not been practicing long?"

"No, this collection would have taken many years to acquire."

"How long has Claire been sick?"

"Not long, I believe. And the Monmouths have lived primarily in town for years, according to my mother."

"Primarily in town?" Tony interrupted. "They have a country estate?"

"I believe so. Monmouth esta—that's what she was trying to tell us!"

"What?"

I grabbed his sleeve in excitement. "The maid! She said Claire, monmo, estay. Claire, Monmouth Estate. Lady Monmouth has taken her daughter to the country. But why would the maid be spellbound and punished for..."

Everything came crashing down on me at once. The words came out in a shocked monotone as I realized what was about to happen. "Lady Monmouth is using a spell to keep her daughter alive, and she is powering it with the lives of other children. God's breath, how did I not realize this?"

I remembered the look in her eye as we spoke of motherhood, the way all life drained from her face when Yates delivered the note. She was desperate.

"She's taken Claire to Monmouth Estate to complete the spell. The first girl was murdered the night Lady Monmouth left dinner early because Claire took a turn for the worst. Another murder, and another kidnapping. She created the spell to draw children of a similar age, and thus minimize the loss of power in transferring life force. And she used a compulsion spell on her minions to stop them from exposing her. They kidnapped five children for her, one for each point of the pentagram. Pythagoras believed it represented health and some cultures also—but how does Mr. Capstone come into play? And the necklace? Well, that—"

"Gwen."

"Sorry," I said, taking a steadying breath and pulling my mind back on track. "She'll place the children at the points inside the circle and, if my guess is right, funnel their life force back into her daughter. The only place she can do that with any privacy and control will be her estate. And her connection to power will be greatest on Samhain."

Tony grabbed my shoulders and forced me to look at his face. He shook me and said, "Are you certain of this? Gwen! Are you certain?"

"As certain as I can be. It fits almost every clue except Mr. Capstone. And perhaps she hired him?"

He stared at me for a long moment, then said, "How far is Monmouth Estate?"

"Somewhere near fifty miles, in Kent. I've never been there, so we will need directions at some point."

"Then we must leave now."

"What about the maid?"

He paused, troubled. "We must save who we can, when we can. But we won't leave her. We will see that she's properly cared for when we return."

That would have to be good enough. I followed Tony back through the empty house, passed the body of the brave woman who had tried to protect a young girl, and to the auto where Sam and Aristotle huddled beneath a blanket in the back seat.

Sam popped his head out of the blanket and looked at us with glowing expectation. Watching his hope die when Sally did not join us almost broke my heart. I climbed into the car and rested my hand on his shoulder. "Don't worry, Sam. We think we know where she's been taken."

He bit his lips together but nodded. I started the auto and headed out of London and southeast, to Kent. We bumped along through town until the buildings began to spread out, being slowly replaced by grass and trees dressed in fall colors. The verge grew up along the edges of the road, and provided something of a windbreak, though we didn't benefit much in the open front seat.

The steady rock and rumble of the engine soon lolled Sam to sleep, but Tony and I sat silent and chilled. He watched the landscape with an intent, hungry expression, as if expecting a meal to pop out round the next corner. His nose had been broken at some point in the past, which made the bluff, honest lines of his face strangely more intriguing.

"Why did you become a police officer?"

He blinked, startled out of whatever thoughts he had been entertaining, and looked down at his hands. A little silver franc sat on his palm, the engraving worn and softened from much handling. "That is a direct question."

"Must we truly fall back on propriety even now... Tony?"

By his expression, I guessed he already regretted giving me permission to address him by his given name, but he sighed and pocketed the coin. "Will you forever be throwing me off my guard?"

"I have no intention—"

"Lies. You enjoy making me uncomfortable."

I hesitated for a moment, then sighed and admitted, "I cannot help myself. You're just so stodgy."

"I am not stodgy."

"You're uncomfortable riding in this auto with me, are you not?"

There was a long pause before he finally admitted, "Yes."

"Why?"

"Because you have no chaperone. It is improper."

I laughed at him. I couldn't help myself. "Stodgy. As if I am not an adult who can decide what situations are safe for my own honor."

"It isn't you, Lady Gwen, it's what other people will believe of you, and how they might treat you because of it. I dislike the idea of contributing to poor opinions of you."

"That is rich, my dear fellow, considering your opinion of me is not so favorable."

At least he had the grace to look ashamed. "I admit I was too hasty in judging your character simply by the circumstances in which you found yourself. But you must also admit any thinking person would have found them suspicious."

"I do admit it. It is an unfortunate aspect of my nature that I have no ability to avoid compromising situations."

"Such as being seen alone with me in an auto driving off into the country?"

"We are not alone."

He looked back over his shoulder. Sam slept beneath his blanket with Aristotle nestled comfortably close, his beak tucked beneath his wing. "We might as well be, at least to spectators."

"No woman's virtue would be safer than with you, I am sure of it."

His face flushed, and I laughed. "I am sorry. If you want me to stop teasing you, there is a simple solution."

"And what is that?"

"Answer my question."

He rolled his eyes and leaned against the backrest, shoulders slumped. "Fine. I will answer your question if you answer mine."

"Damn. I have a feeling I don't want to tell you the answer to whatever it is you are going to ask me, but I agree."

For a while Tony looked down at his hands, clenching and unclenching his fists. When he spoke, his voice was soft and low, and I had to strain to hear it over the engine and wind.

"My father was attacked by bandits on his way back from a business trip to France when I was ten years old. They didn't only rob him but beat him senseless. His brain never healed properly from the trauma. He couldn't remember how to pack his pipe anymore, much less run a business. I remember sitting by his feet and tucking the tobacco into the chamber for him. He acted as if I were performing magic."

"It must have been difficult to see your father reduced so."

He gave a jerky nod. "My mother began taking in washing and selling embroidery to supplement what savings we had left. It was the blisters on her hands that did it, I think. I promised myself I would do everything in my power to keep families like mine from suffering because of lawlessness."

"I am sorry your family endured so much."

He shrugged. "Others have suffered more. My older brothers had enough money to buy commissions in the Army and Navy, so they, at least, had a promise of a better life."

"And you?"

He frowned, then the expression cleared. "My uncle felt it his responsibility to provide for my education." He said the words with a mixture of gratitude and regret. That was a sentiment I understood too well. I felt it every time I looked at my mother and remembered the least worthy of her daughters had survived to adulthood.

Ophelia had been something special, full of vibrant life and courage, like a bonfire on a summer evening. People had been drawn to her warmth. I was a careful, cautious thing, always thinking, always worried, with about as much heat as a firefly. But Mama had fought for my life as if it were something worth saving, night after night when I snuck out or refused to eat. She'd fought for me every day since. It was her goodness, not my merit that had kept her loving me. I had done little enough to deserve it.

I wondered if Tony felt the same about his mother's sacrifice. How could one ever earn such love?

"Your mother must have been grateful to your uncle."

He rubbed a hand across his jaw. "I think she was ashamed to accept his help."

"Too proud?"

He smiled, and it transformed his face into something younger, more open. He almost looked charming. "You have no idea."

"But not too proud to care for her boys."

"No. Never that."

"We were lucky to have such mothers, were we not?"

His lips pressed together, and he looked at me from the corner of his eyes. "I know I was. Your mother... Well, to be frank, the woman is intimidating."

"Truly," I laughed. "I will never understand how someone so small can carry around so much authority."

"And now it is my turn to ask a question."

"Bollocks. I hoped you had forgotten."

He grinned, clearly satisfied to have the upper hand. "No such luck. A personal question deserves a personal question. Why are you intent on compromising your reputation?"

I blinked. The damned man had asked a question I had not been expecting. It took me a moment to decide how to answer. "I don't have any reputation to save, Inspector."

"What happened to Tony?"

I gave him a narrow look. "Refrain from pointing out my discomfort, sir, if you will."

He allowed me some silence as the countryside passed, shades of green and gold seen through breaks in the hedge, bright sunlight on the grass that warmed everything before the impending clouds cast the landscape in shadow. I was just beginning to earn this man's trust, and maybe a bit of his respect, and the idea of casting it all aside and having him look at me the way everyone else did... Well, I didn't like the idea.

But I had made a bargain. And if he looked at me with disdain, then it would be no different from most of my life. At least I was used to it.

Before I could talk myself out of it, I said, "I ruined my reputation when I was eighteen. Before that, I was simply an oddity, a spectacle. The wild girl whose sister was killed in the woods. Or kidnapped, depending on which story one heard. No one actively disliked me, at least. And I was the heiress to the Duchy of Wainwright, which carried its own fascination for my peers. So, while I wasn't exactly on equal footing with them, they still desired my company.

"I had not been much in society, and I remember thinking myself popular, feeling little surges of joy and belonging when I received invitations or was asked to dance, or the other young debutantes would gather around me to talk. It never occurred to me I was a spectacle, not a friend. People wanted to say they had spoken with me, not that they were intimates of mine. I maintained those illusions just long enough to get myself engaged to a suitable young man, ruin the engagement, destroy his sitting room in a pique, and storm out of his home during a dinner party. You can imagine the reaction of my interested peers."

"I can also imagine the reaction of your formidable mother."

"Oh no, you cannot. But it was spectacular, on all counts. In any case"—I waved my hand, dismissing the ordeal—"I left for the continent. I traveled and had adventures and took lovers, and learned the rules of polite society we are so bent on upholding do not exist in other places; that being a good person does not hinge on the inflexible beliefs I was raised around. People live happy, good lives who are not bound by the rules of the British aristocracy. And now that I have returned... I find it difficult to abide by them simply for the comfort of others, particularly when it was their inflexible, short-sighted codes that pushed me out of my home."

He watched me for a long time. At least, for what felt like a long time. I kept my eyes on the road, realizing I had shared more than was sensible, but if those things would push him to think badly of me, then I may as well get it out of the way now.

"You took lovers?"

I snorted. "After everything I explained, that is what you think most important?"

"No," he said, slowly, "but—I would not expect a lady to share such things. It is rather a private matter, and... and I know what such knowledge might cost you, in the wrong hands."

Perhaps he did. Perhaps he knew people would no longer be willing to associate even with Mama if I were to be included in her social circle. They would not attend dinner parties I was invited to. I would no longer be merely unpopular but interesting; I would be a pariah. And perhaps some part of me hoped for that outcome. At least then it would stop hurting so much when I was rejected.

"Stop!" Tony barked, and the snap of command in his voice made me smash my foot down on the brake, throwing Sam off his seat with a yowl and making Aristotle leap into flight, croaking at me in reproach.

There, at the side of the road where the verge opened up onto a vista of rolling hills, lay a corpse in a pool of blood.

# 18

## *Trapped*

## GWEN

We leaped out of the front seat and hurried to the body. The man had been shot. Blood congealed in a pool beneath him where the dirt had not soaked it up. Tony bent to check for any signs of life, but I knew without touching him that he was dead.

Whatever leaves the body when someone dies had already fled. It was like the difference between the feeling of entering a house someone lives in, and entering an abandoned building. No one was home, and the structure was empty.

I turned to catch Sam before he got close enough to ogle the corpse and pushed him back to the other side of the road. There were enough sad sights in his memory. Aristotle was not to be contained, however, and he hopped around inspecting the body, occasionally leaping up and away when Tony batted a hand at him.

I climbed back into the driver's seat to wait for the report. Tony would know what to look for. From that perspective, I saw down the road and off into the grass, and something caught my eye. I squinted, then leaped down for the second time in as many minutes.

"Sally has been here!" I shouted.

Tony and Sam joined me as I crouched on the road and examined the mess of footprints, hoofprints, and wheel tracks.

"See this print," I pointed to the boot print with a distinctive X carved into the sole. "That is Sally."

"How do you know it's hers?" Sam asked in awe.

"Look at the bottom of your boot."

He leaned and picked up his foot, twisting to see the sole of his boot.

"Wait," he said, then peered at the ground and compared the print to the other marks of varying sizes. "Why do we have X's on our shoes?"

"Because I put them there to track you."

Sam's eyes widened. I expected him to get angry, but he said, "Brilliant! You could find someone anywhere so long as they don't take off their shoes!"

"Provided the roads aren't paved," I muttered, continuing to read the prints. "They were in the grass, here look at all the crushed bits."

There were at least three bodies lying in the grass at some point, perhaps more depending on how closely they lay together. I studied the edge of the road.

Tony said, "Look, here are more! They walked this way from the southeast."

"So they were walking in a group, it looks like five children by the sizes of their shoes. And then they hid in the grass. Sally emerges from the grass, but the other four sets of prints do not. Instead, there is a man's shoe back and forth to this set of wagon tracks that turned about and headed southeast again."

"They tried to escape," Tony said, awe coloring his voice.

"Possibly. And we know they were all here and alive no more than two hours ago."

"How do you know the time?" Sam demanded, his eyes bright.

"The edges of the prints," Tony said, offering me a wink.

We hurried back into the auto and followed the tracks southeast. I stopped again where the tracks turned in a circle and read what I could from the muddled mess.

"Our Sally," I said, impressed. "She had the man on the ground, crouching over him. Look here"—I pointed to the other prints—"that's when the children got out and ran. She's fighting."

Yes, they had been caught, but we were on the right trail, and Sally was fighting. We were going to find them. We climbed back into the auto, feeling hopeful, and resumed our journey.

Tony told me the dead body had no spells inked onto his skin, so his relationship to the affair was harder to read, but I had a feeling his death was another Lady Monmouth would have to answer for.

We did not have time to bury him or search out local authorities. We would have to care for his body on our way back, as well as the maid who had died with Claire's name on her lips. I promised myself I would find their families when this was over.

A couple of farmers gave us directions because the wheel tracks crossed too many times with other travelers to be read clearly, but less than an hour later Monmouth Manor rose above the horizon in stately arrogance, half a mile or so off the road.

The area around it was cultivated, with forests behind and rolling hills dotted with hedges that fenced in Monmouth land. A few lonely trees stood sentinel, bare branches looking like hands raised in supplication to a dark, lowering sky.

I stopped the auto at the end of the long drive and considered the edifice before us. The children might be anywhere on the grounds, and we didn't have a clue where to look. It was already late afternoon, and whatever was going to happen would likely happen within a few hours. Spells were strongest when the world was full of the energy of change.

"Alright," Tony said. "It is time for the both of you to listen to me and listen well. We don't know what we're walking into, but we know these people are both willing and able to do violence. If you find something dangerous, tell me. If you aren't sure what to do, run. Protect yourself first, or there will be no one left to help the children. Understand?"

Sam said, "Yes, sir," in a small voice. I only rolled my eyes.

"Let us not announce ourselves by driving up to the house," Tony continued. "We walk from here, split up and search the grounds thoroughly, and only approach the house once we're sure the children are inside it."

I gave Tony a pointed look. "Split up? Are you certain that's the best option?"

"With limited time and only the three of us, it's the only option. If we find something, meet back here and I'll decide what to do.

I don't want anyone stumbling into any magic circles or other nonsense I cannot fight or predict."

"I don't like letting Sam do this," I said.

"I can help!" the boy insisted, balling his fists. "I'm smaller and quieter than you, and no one will see me. And if you leave me here I'll go, anyway. If you tie me up, I'll chew through the ropes. I'll scream. I don't care what you say."

"He can do this," Tony said. "And he deserves the right to try."

My teeth ground together as I considered what trouble the boy might get into, but Tony was right. We hadn't much time, and there were five innocent lives depending on us. Maybe more.

"Very well," I said, "but Aristotle is going with you. And you are not to do anything on your own. You hear me, Samuel?"

"Yes, ma'am."

Then I turned to Aristotle, who sat on Sam's shoulder, and gave him a serious look. "Stay with Sam. Protect him. Sound the alarm if he gets in trouble."

Aristotle croaked and hopped to the boy's opposite shoulder.

I opened the carpetbag and began packing the pockets of my skirts with tools that might come in handy, then pulled out a small pocket knife. "Sam, hold out your hand."

I placed the knife on his open palm. "Just until we get yours back," I told him. His eyes gleamed, and the knife disappeared into his trouser pocket.

"Do you have anything else in your arsenal, my lady?" Tony asked with a wry twist of his mouth.

"Wouldn't you like to know?"

"Are we ready then? Let's be off. Sam will take the back of the house, and Gwen the right side. I'll take the left. Let us meet back here in an hour."

And just like that, we set off.

Similar to Wainwright, Monmouth Estate was peppered with outbuildings dotting the landscape near the main house. A stable, a coach house, the groundskeeper's cottage, the barn, the kennels, and other smaller buildings.

I crept toward the house through the long grass and in the shadow of the stable. It was tall enough that one would have to be watching from the third-floor window to see me, so I was relatively safe from view. Any grand country house was always busy simply because of the upkeep required to keep the home clean and functioning. There should have been gardeners, groundskeepers, stablemen, and many other domestic workers performing their usual duties.

But no one moved about the place. It was as silent as the townhouse had been, which made all the hairs on my body stand at attention. Wind was picking up leaves and howling as it pushed them across the countryside, trailing a row of angry clouds behind. The atmosphere was almost apocalyptic. But at least the wind would cover whatever small noises I made.

I inched around the stable, listening hard; nothing but swishing tails, contented chomping, and the bored shifting of weight as horses got comfortable in their stalls. No boots thumping on the wood floor, no spitting or humming or even heavy breathing of a man at work. After a quick look around to make sure no one was watching, I slipped inside. Nothing.

Phaetons and buggies sat alone and unused in the coach house. Nothing of note anywhere I looked but wind and approaching darkness and a feeling in the air that made my skin prickle in apprehension. I always felt that otherworldly chill on Samhain, as if anything could happen. But no sign of the children. After an hour passed, I crept the half mile back toward the auto, parked in the cover of the hedgerow near the road. Tony appeared minutes later, his face set in grim lines. We leaned against the wheel and waited for Sam.

"Any luck?" I asked, though I already knew the answer.

"Nothing."

"We're going to have to sneak into the house."

"You'll be doing no such thing. No, raise your hands, Inspector," a voice ordered, and a man with a familiar face stepped out from behind the auto with a rifle raised to his shoulder.

"You," I snarled.

"And you'll keep your hands up where I can see them, lady. Or I'll put a bullet in your head. No, one better," he said with a satisfied smile. "Either of you misbehaves, I'll put a bullet in the other one."

"Where are the children?"

"I don't know what you're on about. Now"—he pointed the gun at my head—"you're going to take that gun out real slow like, and toss it toward me. Move slow, bobby. If you spook me, I might shoot the lady, here."

Tony kept one arm in the air and reached with agonizing slowness into his coat. He pulled the gun out with two fingers and tossed it on the ground.

"Now, turn around real slow and walk to the house."

I opened my mouth but Tony gave me a quelling look, and I bit back the retort.

"We'll cooperate," he told the man, "no need for violence."

"I'll be the judge of that. Walk."

The man who had kidnapped Virginia began herding us toward the manor. He stayed far enough behind that trying to jump him was out of the question. I prayed Sam had seen us and was smart enough to stay well away.

When we got close to the house, the kidnapper said, "Open the door, Inspector. And if you try anything funny, I'll add an extra hole to the woman."

Tony opened the door, and I begrudgingly entered Monmouth. It was warm inside, and quiet save for the sound of labored breathing.

"Don't patronize me you prick," the kidnapper said from outside the door. "I ain't stupid enough to put you behind me. Go inside and keep your hands up."

As he walked us down the hallway, I thought of everything I had in my pockets—and a few other hidden tools in more interesting places—and felt a sudden glee that men were stupid enough not to suspect women capable of violence. He had removed Tony's weapon, but I still had several. I just needed a chance to use them.

But my plans fizzled when we entered a large room that must have been a banqueting hall in the past and now served as a kind of living room. It boasted a hearth big enough for five tall men to stand in, rows of bookshelves, and several seating arrangements. Near the hearth, close enough to the fire to stay warm, Lady Monmouth sat in a leather chair. Next to her, a young girl lay on a bed with a pale blue coverlet draped across her thin frame.

"Lady Gwen," Cassandra Monmouth said. "Welcome to my home."

Her voice was worn, her eyes tired, but she offered us something like a warm smile. "I would offer you a seat, but I must have William check you for weapons, first, I'm afraid. William, if you would be so kind? Oh, and please do not move. I am tired, and I have no wish to harm either of you."

Then she gestured with her hand, and every muscle in my body locked painfully. William the Kidnapper made certain we could not move and began searching us. He pulled two more guns from Tony's jacket and boot, and then stood in front of me.

He eyed me with a sneer and began with my ankles. Despite my inability to move, I felt every touch of his cold, calloused hands as he felt his way up my legs, then from my wrists to my waist, a lascivious grin on his face.

Finally, he began patting my skirt. He found pocket after pocket, pulling out my iron letter opener, the satchel of herbs, and several other tools he would have no way to recognize. He jerked his hand out of one pocket and looked at his fingers.

"What the hell is this?" He sniffed. "Salt?"

"Lady Gwen is clever," Cassandra said. "She came prepared. I am sorry your preparations will not serve you. I have a different purpose for you."

When William finally finished, he grunted and scooped everything into a burlap sack.

"Keep the guns," she told him, "burn the rest."

He smiled at me when he tossed the bag into the fire. There went my last chance to protect myself and Tony. So much for my brilliant plans.

"Now that it is safe," she waved a hand again and blood flowed back into my muscles in a rush, making me dizzy. "Please take a seat. And remember, I do not intend to hurt you. Do not force me to it. I have had enough of death."

Tony and I sat in chairs facing Lady Monmouth and her daughter, whose labored breathing was a constant background noise.

"Where are the children, lady?" Tony said. His voice was hard, cutting.

"They are here. But they are not your concern. You have done a brave and noble thing, but I cannot allow you to take them from me. I need them."

"Cassandra," I said, trying to keep my voice as understanding as I could manage despite my anger and fear. "You cannot do this. These children are innocent of any wrong, they deserve to live."

"So, you have discovered my plan." She nodded to herself. "I thought you were smart enough. I'm glad to see I am still a good judge of character. That is why I accepted your mother's invitation, after all. And you are right, of course. The children are innocent. That is exactly why I need them. And they do deserve to live." Her face hardened then, her eyes reflecting the fire like burning coals. "But so does my daughter."

"You would buy her life with the lives of these others? How can you do such a monstrous thing? You are not an evil woman, I would swear it."

Her smile was sad. "Love may make monsters of us all, lady. And yes, I will kill them. I would kill a hundred children so Claire might live. A thousand."

Tony growled, but I noticed, for the first time, Cassandra's hands. She had worn gloves at the dinner party but her skin was bare now, and her hands were bent, almost skeletal, covered in deep wrinkles and age spots and what looked like tree bark in places. She had long, elegant fingers at the party. They were now crooked and arthritic, with large knuckles and fragile skin.

"The magic will kill you," I whispered.

She raised her hands, turning them in the firelight. They did not look like human hands. "I know."

"How have you hidden it?"

"That is none of your concern. But our time grows short, and I want to tell you why you are here." She leaned forward and her tired eyes fixed on my face. They were pleading, intense, and hard to look away from. "I believe you are a good woman, Lady Gwen. I know your mother, and she is a good woman as well. When Claire is healed by the magic, I will be dead. My family disowned me when I married Lord Monmouth, and he drank himself to death, so Claire will have no one. No one but you. I have made you her guardian"—she gestured to a stack of papers on the table between us—"and the arbiter of her inheritance in the sum of twenty-thousand pounds. There are other stipulations, but I'm sure you will become acquainted with those."

I felt like someone had just struck me with a hammer. Every thought seized up, and I found myself stuttering, "How? How can you do this? You don't know me, and neither does she. And these children—"

"I am speaking of my child," she snapped, her eyes straying to the bed where the girl lay, struggling to breathe, her eyes closed. "My child. My baby. And she is going to live."

Then she turned her gaze on Tony. "I did not anticipate your presence, inspector, but I am glad you are here. You can testify to the veracity of all these claims in court."

"Is this the legacy you want to leave your daughter?" he asked, his voice soft, "To know that her mother was a murderer, and she is only alive because other people had to die?"

She closed her eyes. "At least she will live to have those concerns. And she will know how desperately she was loved. There is nothing more to be said. William, please tie our guests. The staff will return in the morning to find you here and release you. I am sorry, but you will be uncomfortable until then."

She regarded us as William the kidnapper tied our hands and feet to the arms and legs of the wooden chairs. The stench of the burning herbs and other tools I had brought filled the room with a bitter odor.

When he was finished tying the knots, she said, "Has the circle been drawn to my exact specifications?"

"It has, my lady. I broke several sod cutters to do it."

"Good. You have been most helpful, William. I will release you soon, and you shall have the reward you were promised. For now, help me carry Claire to the table, and then go back for the rest of the children. We must begin the ritual."

They prepared to lift the mattress the girl lay on and I blurted, "Cassandra. Where did you learn this magic?"

She raised a brow, lifted the dying girl, and said, "What can that matter to you?"

They carried the girl toward the door as I shouted, "Don't do this! Please! Cassandra, please!"

But they were gone and my pleas only echoed back until they faded to nothing.

"Dammit," I snarled, and jerked my arms and feet against the bonds. "Rheumy, pustulated, carrion-fed, son-of-a—"

"Gwen."

"Bow-legged goat and a three-faced—"

"Gwen!"

I stopped jerking at the bonds and blinked back the tears that were making it hard to see. "What?"

"Calm down."

"I can't! Weren't you here for any of that? This is—I don't—understand..."

The tears did fall, then, and I didn't bother to try and blink them back.

"We can still stop this. We have to get out of these bonds. You're smart enough to figure a way out of this. Think!"

I took a shuddering breath and tried to calm my pounding heart, to push away the vision of Claire's pale, sunken face, of the love and determination in her mother's expression, of Sally and Virginia and the other children being led to their deaths.

Of the sacrifice Cassandra was about to make.

I closed my eyes and felt my body, beginning in my chest. I followed my heartbeat down my arms to the bonds there. Tight, and well tied. Down into my stomach, hollow with hunger. Through my thighs, calves, and into my ankles where they pressed painfully against the wood. There would be no wriggling out of these bonds. So I pictured the chair, the grain of the wood, the joints, and the glue and nails.

"We might break the chairs," I said, my voice sounding slow and lazy. "But it will take some force."

Tony took that as a directive and started jerking his full (and considerable) weight from side to side, twisting his torso to try to turn the chair. It squeaked and groaned under the abuse until they both tipped over and crashed to the floor. His head bounced off the rug and he lay on his side, breathing hard.

"I can't tell if this is worse," he panted, "or better."

"At least you have a comfortable rug for your head."

"There is that."

We sat in silence for a long time, as the sun dropped below the horizon and darkness crept into the hall. The fire began to die, and the room to darken. Tony continued to struggle against his bonds, tearing the skin off his wrists, but it was useless. I wracked my brain until I had exhausted every option and my head felt full of cotton.

"I can't get us out," I said.

My voice sounded small and broken and I didn't care. What was the use of maintaining my dignity when I had utterly failed? All of my carefully prepared tools and all of our desperate plans had unraveled. Sweet, brave Sally was being prepared for sacrifice and I was sitting in a warm living room. I jerked my arms against the bonds, twisted them, wrenched my shoulders, and strained every muscle in my upper body, feeling blood trickle from my wrists to my fingertips. And it was still no use.

I let my head fall back against the chair and cried, "I can't get us out!"

"I can."

I turned my head so fast it hurt. Sam stood in the doorway, his face pink with excitement, one hand stuffed into the pocket of his pants.

"Sam! I was so worried. You're okay?"

"Yep!" he said, and then held the pocket knife I'd given him triumphantly in the air.

"Come on then, boy, no time to lose," Tony said, and Sam jogged across the room.

"Did you find anything?" I asked as he sawed away at the ropes.

"I found something," Sam said, but his lip trembled as he tried to master himself. "There was a coach hidden in the rose bushes behind the house. There were blankets inside and—and blood on the wood by the door."

Tony and I exchanged a look, but Sam wasn't done.

"I—I—"

"It's okay Sam," I said. "You don't have to—"

"I lost Aristotle!" he cried, and buried his face in his hands.

My heart gave a painful lurch. "You didn't lose him, my darling," I assured the boy, though there was a wrenching sensation in my chest. "Aristotle belongs to himself. If he left, it was because he chose to. Don't you fret. We have work to do, remember?"

He wiped savagely at his eyes, nodded, sniffed, and resumed cutting. "I went back to the auto, but you weren't there, so I waited under the blanket. Aristotle flew off, and it had been a long time, so I followed him. That's when I saw the man who kidnapped Sally. He was carrying a boy over his shoulder and heading out into the field. So I started looking for you."

"And you found us," I said, dabbing the blood from my wrists with the sleeve of my jacket as Sam started work on Tony's bonds.

"How'd you fall over?" he asked the big man.

Tony raised his head to give me a half-amused, half-exasperated look. "Your mistress had an idea."

"Ooh," Sam said, wisely.

"And I've got another one," I said. "Let's go stop Lady Monmouth and save those children."

"I can get behind that. How will we do it?"

"We must break the spell and damage the circle. But—" I hesitated and looked at Tony and Sam. Breaking the circle would release the magic, draining what had been gathered in a single, explosive burst that may catch all of us in a dangerously powerful vortex of energy.

But if it was only broken on one side, perhaps I could control the direction of the blast.

"But what?"

"We're going to need weapons," I said, and prayed we wouldn't be too late.

# 19

## *Inside the Circle*

## GWEN

The moon peeked out from behind racing clouds only rarely, leaving us little light to navigate by, but that did not affect Sam. He led us across the fields away from the house, creeping like a shadow over the dimly lit landscape. We stumbled upon a dirt path pointing in the right general direction and followed it for nearly fifteen minutes before we saw the light.

A bonfire roared behind a copse of trees in a natural depression in the landscape, protected from view but giving us enough light to see by. We eased down the hillside, our progress painfully slow, as our breath made puffs of ghostly vapor that caught the intermittent moonlight before drifting away. My fingers stung with cold.

We crept closer, using bushes and boulders as cover, until we saw the site of the ritual clearly. My stomach twisted itself into a knot, and I took a few deep breaths to come to terms with the scene.

They had cleared the land in a perfect circle nearly twenty feet in diameter, cutting the shape into the soil. The line was clean and filled with something white: salt or chalk? In the exact center lay Claire, her body exposed on a stone surface the shape of a coffin lid. At one end of the circle, Cassandra stood, nude, with her hands held in front of her in supplication.

Directly opposite her, on the other side of the circle, stood a massive doorway built of two standing stone doorposts with another laid across the top as a lintel. It was ancient, covered in moss, and connected both sides of the circle in a clean line. The children lay on matching stones at five equidistant points around the inside of the circle. Their clothes were rumpled and dirty, and they lay as still as if their lives had already been taken.

But the ritual hadn't begun yet. We still had time.

Symbols had been cut in the sod along the inside of the circle, filled with the same white substance as the outer circle, and connected by a web of straight lines, glowing in the moonlight. It was a different pattern than the spell used to kidnap the children, but used many of the same symbols Percy claimed were fae magic.

This circle did not rely on the runes to power the spell. That meant trouble. I could not fudge the circle and release the magic from the outside, the way Delilah had when testing the circle in her workshop. Which meant we had to get inside the circle before she released enough power to seal it.

"We have to get down there," I whispered urgently to Tony. "If she seals the circle, we won't be able to get through!"

"What do we do?"

"Break the circle before she channels enough power to seal it, stop the ritual by any means necessary."

We stood from our hiding spot and rushed down the last stretch of hillside as Cassandra's voice filled the air with sonorous chanting in a language I'd never heard. It was smooth and musical, filled with sibilance and rolling r's that made the air vibrate.

The circle began to glow.

I broke into a dead run across the uneven ground, hiking my skirts up and shouting, "Hurry!"

Tony sprinted off ahead of me, his legs unencumbered by skirts, and closed the distance fast. The air above the circle began to bend and warp like heat waves above a fire. He was going to make it. He had to make it. My feet dug into the turf, making up the distance between us as I sprinted headlong at the shimmering wall.

A blue-green wave, something like an aurora, undulated along the line, beginning with Cassandra and spreading fast. It slid along both sides of the circle and met at the standing stone doorway. Then the circle flashed white and lit up like a beacon, shooting into the sky and hitting the low-lying clouds. Tony burst into the clearing and leaped. He hit the circle head-on and flattened against a shimmering wall of power.

The circle flashed and rippled, like Tony had been a stone falling into a still pond. The ripples spread from the impact, then settled back down to immobility, but Tony crumpled to the grass, his limbs bent at wrong angles.

I skidded to a stop next to his body and fell to my knees with Sam close on my heels. Tony was breathing, his pulse strong. I reached out and touched the wall of power with one finger. A shockwave of something like electricity shot up my arm. I screamed and fell back in pain. He had hit that power with his full body. It was a miracle he wasn't dead. I slapped his cheek and his eyelids fluttered.

"Tony? Can you hear me?"

A gunshot cracked, punctuating Cassandra's chanting with the promise of death. I flinched, pulling Sam against my body and searching the surrounding darkness. Where had it come from? The copse of trees was at our back, and that made the most sense as a hiding place.

I grabbed Sam and hustled him behind the closest boulder I could find, putting the boulder between us and the trees. I didn't have time to pull Tony after us, but I had to keep Sam safe, first.

"Stay low," I breathed close to his ear as I searched the landscape for the shooter. I saw a small red flash, then heard the crack of thunder, and a spray of shards exploded across the surface of the rock. The fragments cut my cheek, and I dropped back down behind the boulder as warm blood dripped down the side of my face.

"My lady?" Sam's voice was small and scared.

"It's okay, Sam," I said, hoping he didn't notice the tremor in my voice. "It's nothing. Listen to me: I must get to the inspector and pull him to safety, and you must stay here."

The gun rang out again, and a clump of dirt exploded near the edge of the boulder. Sam squeaked and threw his arms up to cover his head. Knowing the few seconds between shots would be my best chance, I picked up my skirts and ran. Little tufts of grass grew in uneven clumps that had me stumbling as I sprinted, finally landing on Tony with my full body weight. He groaned and tried to twist away, but I pushed myself off of him, grabbed the fabric of his coat at the shoulders, and pulled with all the strength in my legs. He was heavy and my muscles were still weak from the circle.

A bullet may tear into my back at any time.

"Help me," I grunted. "Come on, Tony."

His heels scrabbled against the turf but not with enough strength to help. He was just too heavy to move.

"Drop him."

I froze. William the Kidnapper walked into the firelight from around the boulder, holding Sam by the collar, one of Tony's guns jammed against the boy's back. The shifting light from the magic circle threw his features into lurid relief, casting grotesque shadows across his face as he smiled.

I let go of Tony, breathing hard, and stared in horror at the boy. "Don't hurt him. Please."

"Step away from the inspector."

I swallowed, missing my umbrella terribly, but took a cautious step away at an angle that would put me between Tony and the gunman.

"Good girl. Now," he said, "I'd like to see what I got such a good feel of earlier. Take off your jacket."

A thrill of fear and disgust made me shudder as my stomach soured. My jaw clenched, but I didn't move.

Fury tightened his features, and he shook Sam by the collar. "Now!"

I unbuttoned the jacket with shaking fingers, trying to keep my eyes on his face so he would not look at Sam, and pulled the jacket off slowly. The October wind caught my shirt and pressed it against my body, cutting through the fabric and hitting me with pins and needles, making my whole body shake. I shifted my stance, as if moving to keep warm, and readied my feet.

"Good," he grunted, the tip of the gun drooping as he focused on me, "now the rest. Can't have you hiding any weapons in all that cloth, can we?"

Sam spun with shocking speed and drove the tip of the knife I'd given him up under the man's breastbone. It wasn't long enough to do serious damage, especially with the boy's minimal strength and the thickness of the kidnapper's jacket, but it gave me the chance to bolt across the intervening distance and throw myself at the man.

I caught his gun arm and bore him backward as he screamed in pain. We crashed to the ground in a tangle and I landed hard on the hilt of the knife, which jammed it deeper as it scraped against my corset. Thank god for corsets. I lifted his arm in both hands and slammed it against the ground hard enough to fling the gun into the darkness.

He grabbed the back of my head with his free hand, fingers snarled in my hair, and wrenched me off him, rolling to cover my body and press me down into the cold earth.

"You bitch!" he growled, panting in pain, and slapped me. My cheek exploded with buzzing pain and I bucked, trying to get my legs beneath me to use the leverage of my hips and unseat him. But my skirt tangled around my legs and I couldn't gain purchase. Killing me now wouldn't take much effort, even with the wound Sam and I had given him. He tightened his fist in my hair, pulling out clumps, and leaned close to my face.

"I'm going to make you beg," he hissed, and spit dripped from his mouth onto my cheek.

"Leave her alone!" Sam threw himself at the man's back but Will batted him away by a backhanded blow. He tripped over his feet and landed on his back in the grass with a cry. I screamed and twisted with all the force in my body, but Will the Kidnapper sat too high on my torso and crushed my rib cage beneath his hips, pushing all the leftover air from my lungs.

"I'm going to enjoy watching you die," he growled, his rank breath bathing my face in a wash of moist heat.

"Would you do it from a bit farther back," I wheezed. "Your breath is horrid."

His mouth twisted in fury and he slapped me again, then curled his fingers around my throat and squeezed. I had been trained for this, and I tried not to panic, but my training had mostly been in britches and with the skirts tangled around my legs I couldn't get the leverage I needed to create room beneath my body. He was leaning back at the full distance of his long arms, out of reach for striking. My vision began to go black, fading at the edges.

Then he was gone. I dragged in a deep breath, coughed at the scratching pain, and blinked in surprise. Sam knelt next to me and helped me sit up. His eyes were wide, and a bruise was already beginning to purple his cheek.

"Are you okay, my lady?"

I pulled him against my side, holding him close for a moment, and saw Tony locked in a boxer's grapple, straining against Will for control. He was wounded, but Tony had been electrocuted by the magic; he wouldn't have much stamina. I wobbled to my feet, caught my breath, and searched for a hand-sized stone to use as a club. Sam was faster. He snatched up a rock and threw it with surprising aim. It whizzed through the air and hit Will in the side of the head. The man grunted and pulled Tony in a half-circle, putting his body between us.

"Go for the legs," I told Sam, and picked up a rock the size of an apple.

Tony twisted his shoulders, freed one arm, and sank an uppercut into Will's stomach, right atop the wound. The man squealed, jerking back, and Sam let another rock fly, this one hitting him squarely in the face.

I circled round the pair with my rock at the ready.

Will gave up on grappling, dropped his head, and rushed Tony like a charging bull. Tony caught the tackle in the stomach, wrapped his arms around Will's chest, and fell back a couple of feet, dropping his hips and splaying his feet wide for balance. There was my opportunity.

I darted in and swung the rock down on his head with all my strength. His body went limp, and Tony let him fall to the ground. His shoulders heaved as he stared down at the body. After a few more ragged breaths, his knees buckled, and he collapsed.

I crouched near him and put one hand on his shoulder. "Are you alright?"

He looked up at me, his eyes still dazed, and said, "Are you?"

I only managed a nod as I stared at the circle. The symbols were lighting up with pale green light, one at a time as Cassandra chanted. Her body had already changed. She no longer looked like a fit woman in her late thirties. As the magic coursed through her,

her back cracked and hunched forward. Her breasts sagged, and unnatural growths began appearing on her skin as it loosened its hold on her muscles and hung in flaps from her bones. Cassandra was not aging, but deforming, being drained and warped by the magic. It would course through her, pulling from her resources until nothing was left but an empty, twisted husk.

And if she didn't stop? There would be nothing left of her but dust. The magic pulsed and swirled, sending out a shockwave of power. The color had drained from the cheeks of the children lying around the edges of the circle. Their skin took on a waxy sheen, and their hair hung in lank strands around their faces. Their life force was being stolen and funneled away.

They were dying.

"I have to stop this," I muttered.

But I was at a loss for how. There was no way past the circle. The wind picked up again and blew my hair into my face. I pushed the curling strands back with more force than necessary and touched... my hat. I was still wearing my hat. It was crooked and dangling after the kidnapper had grabbed me by the hair. The hat pin bent, but it held.

I jerked the pin out and ripped the hat off.

Tony said, "What are you doing?"

"I can get in there," I said, shaking the hat to unfold it.

"No, you can't." He pushed himself to his feet, wobbled, and grabbed my shoulders. "I'm twice your size and weight and that power nearly killed me."

"But I have something you don't have," I said, and held the jacket up triumphantly.

"A coat?"

"A very special coat. That circle is full of energy, something like electricity."

"Sure as hell felt like it."

"This jacket was woven with very fine metallic threads and artifice. It should act something like a Faraday cage."

"A what?"

"Don't you know anything about physics, Inspector? If it works like I hope it will," I said as I pulled on the jacket and started pushing the buttons through, "it should channel the energy of the circle around me, like a stone in a river. I won't actually break the circle, because the circle will think I'm part of it."

"It will think?"

"More or less."

"But... what about your legs, your face?"

"I'll probably be burned," I said, "but I have to try. Look."

The symbols near the end third of the circle lit with green light, and little traceries began undulating in the air around the stone door, as if strands of energy were weaving together to form a portal. I buttoned the jacket and pulled up the collar. It wasn't much more protection, but I would take whatever I could get. I turned, faced Tony and said, "Wish me luck."

His eyes flashed with some emotion, something too fast for me to recognize, but he said, "Be careful, Gwen."

I gave him a cheeky smile and turned toward the circle. My heart thundered in my ears and my knees wobbled, but Sally lay across the circle, her face ashen as life energy was siphoned out of her. I had to get inside and stop the ritual, and I had to do it now.

I reached beneath the jacket, stuffed my fingers into the bottom of my corset, and pulled out the gift the Triumphant Sisterhood had given me to help rescue the children: a quartz necklace. I pulled the collar of the coat up, slid on the necklace, and tucked my head into the fabric like a turtle. After a deep breath, I balled my fist inside the jacket sleeve to protect my hand, and reached out toward the shifting wall of deadly energy.

# 20

## *Say Goodbye*

### GWEN

It felt like sticking my hand in an oven. The energy crackled over the jacket, popping and snapping with little blue flashes of power, but I gritted my teeth and pushed my arm through. It actually worked. Tendrils of smoke rose from the organic fibers. I would need to hurry, or I might avoid the magical energy only to catch fire. I held my breath and pushed my shoulder through, then leaned in, torso first.

My face immediately flushed with heat and pain but the necklace caught the energy and warped it, protecting my face by channeling it through the crystals. I wrapped my arms over my head and kept pushing.

The heat and pain only subsided enough to be bearable. But then power washed over my legs like boiling water, and I screamed, toppling sideways. As soon as my torso had passed fully through the circle and there was nothing left of my makeshift Faraday cage, it shot me out of the energy field with enough force that I flew a good five feet and landed hard against a boulder, then curled on my right side. All the air rushed from my lungs, and I blinked dizzily.

Directly opposite me, the second to last symbols in the circle lit up, sending their own threads of power toward the stone door. They wove together and flashed with luminescent tendrils of light that puffed away into smoke, leaving a door inside the frame of stone.

A picture began to form behind the door woven of light. It came slowly into focus, like adjusting the rings on a telescope. A woman stood on the opposite side of the magic portal wearing a green dress, her long blonde hair falling in tumbled waves to her hips. Her arms were thrown open, mirroring the pose Cassandra still held, but her face was serene, proud, and commanding.

And familiar.

I forgot to breathe. Everything faded away; the clearing, the children, the sonorous chanting, the chilly night air, all of it. My chest squeezed so hard that a little whine escaped my lips. If I had been standing, my knees would have given out.

Lia.

My sister stood in the doorway, regal and proud and... alive. Her familiar features had lost their girlish softness and instead had a striking angularity, as if she were carved of marble.

*She was alive.*

I panted, pulling in sharp little whining breaths, the only air my constricted chest would allow. Tears ran down my face unchecked. Lia was alive. She was alive. And she was on the other side of the door.

Something clicked in my mind. The last symbols began to fill with power. The picture became clearer... and Lia was not the only person in the door. Behind her were a score of people so beautiful the sight of them made my stomach hurt. They were tall and elegant, with proud eyes and features so symmetrical they couldn't be real. Their skin was smooth and luminous as if lit with an inner light.

Faeries. Not just faeries, but *Áes Sídhe*.

They were waiting on the other side of the door, one that became more real with every second. Once the final symbols glowed, the children would be dead and the door would open.

An inhuman scream shocked me enough to turn away from the vision of my sister. A piece of the night broke away and shot through the sky directly toward Cassandra's face.

Aristotle.

He crashed into her, his beak and claws flashing in the firelight. He pecked and scratched, distracting Cassandra from the ritual as she tried to fight him off. The Symbol lost power.

I had to save the children. But... if I did nothing, if I allowed the ritual to continue, the door would open, and with it... Lia. My sister.

*My sister.*

She was so close. I could hold her, hear her voice again. A potential future flashed across my mind, and I saw us laughing together, sitting in the sunshine over a picnic, holding each other's hands, and sipping wine by the fire during Yule.

And more than that, I would have a safe place, again. Someone to tell my secrets to, who loved me and all my imperfections because we were part of one another. The hole where Lia had been would be filled. And Claire would live. She didn't have to suffer anymore. She could leave her bed, live her life, and fall in love.

But at what price?

The girl lay on the stone with color in her cheeks and a chest that didn't struggle to rise. She was healing, and the other children were dying. Sally, Virginia, and the rest were fading away. Claire blinked, her eyes darted around in confusion, and she pushed herself up to sit. Her hair fell across her shoulders and a healthy pink flush spread across her cheeks. She was so young.

If I broke this circle, I condemned her to death. If I broke the circle, I was saying goodbye to my sister, to the piece of my heart I had been longing for since losing her so many years ago. I would lose a future I wanted so much my hands shook.

But if this spell opened a door to the Sunset Lands, it wasn't by accident. Every history of the Fae Wars told the same story: in a bid for power and control, faeries turned on mortals. The resulting war lasted years, killing so many and destroying so much that it ushered in a dark age. And now they waited behind a thin veil, waiting to come back to mortal lands.

Lia stood at the door like a goddess. I memorized her features, then turned and ran toward Cassandra, my heart breaking with every step. The witch grabbed Aristotle by the wings and flung him away with a wrenching cry. He hit one of the large stones and something cracked. My friend fell to the ground and didn't move.

Blood dripped down the witch's face and onto her sunken chest. Her limbs were twisted, her spine bent, and what was left of her lustrous hair hung limp and thin on a spotted scalp. Channeling the magic had broken her body, but her voice remained. She saw me for the first time, and panic twisted her features.

"Cassandra, stop!" I cried. "Please don't do this!"

She pointed a finger at me, prepared to lock up my limbs with the same spell she had used earlier. If she caught me now, everyone in this circle would die. Claire might live, but if the fae came through, would they leave any of us alive?

A voice, soft and sweet, said, "Mama?"

One simple word stopped everything. Cassandra gasped, her eyes flying to her daughter, and I reached into my pocket, fingers curling around the object I saved from the fireplace. As mother and daughter regarded one another, I shifted my posture.

"Mama is that... is that you? What is happening? What happened to you, what is this?"

Claire touched her chest, and her eyes roamed around the circle, slowly widening with realization and horror. She turned back to her mother, eyes luminous with tears. "Oh, Mama. What have you done?"

"I'm saving you, my love." Cassandra's voice was thick with emotion, but her eyes were resolute. She began to chant again, and the last symbol glowed. Claire looked at me, saw what I held, and tears spilled onto her cheeks. She knew what I was going to do and knew what I was asking her. Lips trembling, lashes studded with glowing tears, she nodded.

I cast a desperate glance at the portal. I needed to see her face one last time before I destroyed any chance we had of seeing one another again. Lia was there—looking at me. Her eyes were no longer proud but wide with shock. Her mouth hung open, and her chest heaved. I watched as her lips formed the word *Gigi*.

My face crumbled, tears streamed down my cheeks, everything I was fell apart under the weight of saying goodbye to my other half, my twin, my heart... but I spun and threw the cast iron letter opener with a hollow cry dragged from the pit in my chest.

It sailed through the air and hit the witch in the face with enough force to take her off her feet. Did I kill the woman or break the circle? The energy rebounded like a rubber band, snapping back toward the broken symbol. Time slowed. I turned and dove for the circle, digging my burning hands into the earth near the edge, and tore a furrow out of the grass.

The fae door disintegrated as if a thread were pulled from the weave and the rest of the garment unraveled. My sister's stricken face lost focus and faded until there was only darkness between the stones. The energy rushed back toward the broken part of the spell—toward me.

I jerked the jacket over my head and lunged forward with a scream, breaking fully through the circle just as the power hit the broken symbol and erupted.

Everything went white. The river of power caught me and dragged me along with a speeding current, but one of crackling heat instead of cold. My skirt went up in flames, I smelled burning hair, and then everything went dark but my memories of Lia's face.

I floated in an uneasy daze for a while, hearing the echoes of cries, of running water, flapping wings, and wind moaning across the plain.

"It's out," a voice panted, "it's out. I think it's okay."

"Gwen?"

I coughed, and it burned. The heat had singed my throat and lungs. Breathing hurt.

"How can I help you?" I croaked.

"How you can joke now"—strong arms reached under my back and lifted me into a sitting position—"I will never know. Are you okay?"

I blinked, flexed my fingers, then tried to move my legs and sucked a long breath in through my teeth. They moved, but it hurt. A lot. I looked down at myself. My skirt was burned away, and my drawers were singed black at the edges. My calves were bright red, and blisters had already formed on the exposed skin.

"It's hard to say," I muttered, plucking at what was left of the tattered pieces of my skirt. Then I remembered the smell of burning hair and asked, "Do I... do I have any hair left?"

Tony knelt by my side and touched my face. "You've only lost a bit at the tips."

It was stupid for something so vain to make me feel emotional, but a sob escaped and I put a hand over my mouth to stifle it. Tony pulled me against his body and held me while I cried, whispering little meaningless noises of comfort. After a few moments, I was at least marginally in control of myself and prepared to deal with the repercussions of what I had done.

"Your necklace is ruined, though," he said, lifting the chain of crystals with one finger; they were burned and cracked.

"What a shame."

"How are you?"

"I'm okay," I said.

He examined my eyes a moment, his face very close to mine. Then he leaned in and pressed his lips to my cheek at the corner of my mouth. A little burst of warmth spread across my skin, and he gave me a gentle smile.

"You will be," he said.

I blinked, then said, "Help me to stand?"

Tony levered me to my feet and held me until I stood on my own, but he didn't let go of my arm. The children huddled in a group around Claire's body, holding one another. Sally sat at the head of the little group, her arms around Sam. Her eyes were red, and exhaustion lined her face, but she caught my eye and smiled. It was a small smile, but it was the most beautiful thing I had seen in a long, long time.

"Aristotle? Did he—" I choked, thinking of the brave little bird who had thrown himself at the witch. "Is he—"

"He's hurt, but I think he'll be okay. See?"

Sam might have been in Sally's arms, but he held Aristotle on his lap, slowly stroking the bird's back. Aristotle seemed happy enough to stay there.

I limped toward the children and levered myself down, with Tony's help, to sit beside Claire. The signs of health were gone. Her slender body was hollow and wasted, her cheeks sallow, her hair limp. I touched her cheek and found it cold, but still wet with the tears she shed for her mother and for herself. My own eyes filled. She had been good, and brave. She had deserved to live, and I had killed her as surely as if I had pulled a trigger.

I forced myself to ask, "Lady Monmouth?"

Tony's mouth turned down in an unhappy line. "Dead. The release of all that energy was... rather spectacular. She screamed, and when we finally reached you, she was gone. There isn't much left of her body."

I turned to look over my shoulder at the spot I had broken in the circle. A long, deep furrow was scorched into the earth for more than thirty yards, and only a pale green spot of healthy grass was left, vaguely human-shaped, where I had lay as the power poured over me.

It shouldn't have worked. Given what I knew of magic, none of it should have worked. But it was hard to focus on why when my legs burned and throbbed incessantly. Even so, I would rather take the pain than see what was left of the mother who had sacrificed everything—her body, her life, her very humanity—to save her child.

The children gathered round me while Tony dug a grave to bury what was left of Cassandra Monmouth. It didn't take long. And no one even bothered about William the Kidnapper.

I lay my head on Sally's shoulder and she petted my hair while we waited. I was exhausted, my body hurt, and the empty spot in my chest throbbed with each heartbeat. Since Lia had been taken, I had been half a person, building up a false identity for myself and pretending to be someone who could handle being alone when I was born to be one half of a whole.

Every now and then the false identity would fail, and I would be forced to rely on something else to cope with the pain. I had failed to find a way to Lia so many times that I finally consigned myself to a life alone. Except she was alive, she was somewhere real. Had I saved her, she would have come back and been my sister again, filled up the empty parts of me with her laughter and mischief.

And instead, I had consigned the both of us to be alone. Again.

Tony and the children bore Claire's body back to Monmouth using Tony's coat as a litter. They lay her in her own bed. It seemed fitting. Hauling my injured carcass back to the manor was an experience not worth recalling.

We fed the children with scrounged food from the pantry, then gathered, at last, to sleep in the same room in which they had kept us hostage. They huddled together in the warmth of a freshly stoked fire, snoring quietly, safe and alive. And I had killed two women to do it.

And lost my sister.

Tony searched until he found a liquor cabinet and poured me a generous amount of brandy. I swallowed it in two gulps and held the empty glass out for more. Once the room was spinning nicely, we cleaned my legs. Or, I should say, Tony cleaned my legs, and I screamed into a pillow as he washed the dirt off, carefully dried the burns, and wrapped them gently in clean cloth stolen from the linen closet. I tried to focus on the physical pain, and not think about Claire, Cassandra, and my sister, who was alive but out of my reach.

After propping my legs up on a footstool, Tony sat in an armchair across from me, his handsome face sagging with exhaustion and grief. "We can't tell people the truth about what happened here, can we?"

"About magic rituals and witches?" I asked, and knocked back another shot of brandy. "They would never believe us. Maybe people in the country would, where a few wise women still practice openly, but in New London? That would be an uphill battle."

"This changes things, doesn't it?"

"Worse than you know."

He cocked his head. "What do you mean?"

I hesitated, wondering how much farther I could bring him into this. He had almost died tonight when he'd run into the circle. He had a career that mattered to him. But I thought, maybe, the two of us had begun to forge a friendship. He was a good man, and he cared about people enough to put himself in danger. He would want to know.

I took a deep breath and said, with only moderate slurring of consonants, "The fae are trying to come back."

His face went blank. He now knew what magic was capable of, and had been there when Percy explained the history of faerie magic, so he appreciated the gravity of that statement.

He only said, "Explain."

"There was a door at the head of the circle in the standing stones. Every symbol contri—contributed some of its light to the door. They were on the other side. Waiting. The greatest mystery of this affair has been the originashun–origin–of this magic." I stifled a hiccup and scowled at him. "I am not drunk, sir, don't look at me like that. It is highly unlikely for even an experienced practitioner to have discovered it. Magic is difficult enough on its own without mastering artificery and manipulating it to this degree. Faeries must have contacted Cassandra, somehow. They gave her the spells to save her daughter, spells that also allowed them a portal back to the mortal world."

"And she was so desperate to save her daughter, she would have agreed to anything."

"It is not a certainty or even a complete theory, but it is the only thing that makes sense." I did hiccup that time, but Tony ignored it. He really was a kind, handsome man.

"How did they get through to give her the magic?"

I yawned. "I don't know. But Percy was right. That was not human magic, and the fae were there, waiting on the other side of the door, dressed for battle."

Except for my sister, who looked like a conquering queen in her green dress.

"This isn't over, then."

Tony and I looked at one another, contemplating everything that had happened. "No. If they tried once, it means they want to get back. I cannot see why they would not try again."

He took a deep breath, sighed, and leaned his head against the back of the chair. "What do we do?"

"I'm not sure, yet. But I think I know where to go to get some answers."

"I'm coming with you."

I smiled. It was weak and felt out of place on my face. "I would be delighted, Inspector."

# 21

# *The Aftermath*

# GWEN

It took two weeks for my legs to heal enough to walk any distance without the rub of my skirts causing so much pain that I had to be medicated. They were swollen and blistered in several places, and I avoided looking at them as much as possible. There would be scars, and I didn't want to see them blossoming on my skin.

Mama had been standing on the stoop when we returned, having received the message we sent ahead. Tony carried me up the stairs while she followed with her hands clutching her skirt and her lips pinched together until they were white with strain. He stopped at the threshold and I threw my arms around Mama with a sob, letting her warmth and the steady, sure force of her love wrap around me like a blanket.

She took over my care when Tony delivered me and proceeded to scold and bully and run the house like a wartime general on a rampage.

I didn't complain once. Not aloud, anyway.

One night I woke from a nightmare to find her curled in a chair by my bed, a heavy blanket across her lap, her head resting on folded arms. Tears filled my eyes as I thought of Cassandra and Claire. I reached out and took her hand, just to feel the warmth of her skin. Her eyes fluttered open, and she clasped my hand in both of hers.

"You are alright, my love. I'm here," she said.

I wanted to tell her about Lia, then. She deserved to know her child was alive, but how could I give her hope when there was nothing to be done? Lia was still gone, and Mama had grieved and accepted it years ago. Telling her now would rip open old wounds that would never heal, because no matter how much we missed her, Lia still couldn't come home.

There would be the constant worry of where she was, if she was well or suffering, if she was happy or in pain, and the knowledge that you would never know the answers. I was going to have to live with that, and it wasn't fair to ask Mama to live with it, too.

So I said nothing and took her hand, promising myself to be a better daughter to the woman who loved me so deeply. I fell asleep with her hand warm in mine, knowing she was there and I was safe. At least for now.

Aristotle lost a few of his flight feathers and had some bumps and bruises that he exaggerated for sympathy. He was given to limping around and dragging his wing dramatically, which resulted in many treats from Monsieur. I even caught Mrs. Chapman sneaking him a few bites when she thought no one would see her. The feathery little fiend was a hero, as far as I was concerned, and he deserved some extra treats, even if he lied to get them.

Sam stopped running away, and Mr. Yates began sending him on errands outside the house. We all agreed that keeping the boy locked indoors was a mistake, and he brought exuberant life into the house no one realized had been missing. Sally spent her evenings in my room with a chalkboard in her hand. She was a quick study, and the excitement in her eyes as she began reading was the only thing that kept me in bed long enough to heal properly.

I was sitting in the study with three books open on the desk before me when Tony called, at last. Mama could not fawn over him enough, and even though I had promised myself I would stop resenting her attention, I was ready for her to go back to Wainwright. Not telling her about Lia was getting harder every day, and I slept less as I dove into books about fae mythology. I would not tell Mama about her daughter until I found a way to get my sister back.

Tony looked down at my books and raised a questioning eyebrow. I hadn't seen him since he deposited me at home, and he looked well-rested, his cheeks full again. If he had a bit of a haunted look in the back of his eyes, well... so did we all.

"How are the children?" I asked.

I decided to dispense with formality between us because it always threw him off. If the 'Lady St. James' honorific appeared in his vocabulary again, I might snap.

He blinked at me, threw an embarrassed glance at Mama who widened her eyes at my lack of a proper formal greeting, and said, "Ah, they are well. The orphanage took your advice and propositioned Mrs. Maisie. Turns out her last name is Grant. She agreed to leave the laundry and manage the orphanage, instead. After an introduction, the sponsors agreed to take her on. She's running that place like a proper school." He turned to Mama. "And she told me to thank you for the donation, Your Grace."

"I am pleased to have been of assistance," Mama said.

Tony turned back to me and asked, "Are you ready?"

I closed my books, picked up the new umbrella Delilah had made me, and said, "As ready as I can be. Shall we?"

The building on Tromwell Lane was just as large and silent as it had been the last time I visited. But I was not alone this time. Tony and I strode into the building with no effort at disguise, clacking our heels on the marble floor for effect. Patricia appeared again at the top of the stairs in her black dress.

"Lady St. James, Inspector Hardwicke, you are welcome," she said. "Please follow me."

The door opened silently, and this time the room was empty save for Madame Matilda, who stood in the center of the space with her hands folded in front of her.

"I have been expecting you. Please come in. May I offer you any refreshments?"

I didn't answer, but Tony said, "No, thank you, Madame."

She dismissed Patricia and gestured to three chairs at a round table. We sat. Before speaking, I pulled the amber necklace out of the neck of my dress. Madame Matilda looked at it and gave me a small nod of respect. So she *had* recognized the purpose of the pendant. One point for me.

"You must have questions," she began. "Please ask. I will answer what I can."

I folded my hands on the table in front of myself, looked her in the eye, and said, "Why did you lie to me?"

"At no point in our conversation did I speak an untruth."

"You told me you wished to help in my investigation. Not that you wished me to destroy a threat to your coven."

A dark eyebrow rose. "We did wish to help. That was the truth. I did not volunteer more information than you requested."

I snorted. It was easy to see how this conversation would progress. "How have you hidden your coven?"

She tilted her head and her eyes took on a faraway expression as if she were waiting for information. A moment later she nodded and said, "You, and most people like you, suffer from misinformation, but it is a helpful lie, and allows us to practice in safety because it leads you to mistake the nature of witchcraft. You believe human bodies are not capable of wielding magic without damage. That is because the power was never meant to be wielded on a large scale by one witch. And those who attempt such feats bear the scars of it on their bodies, proof they chased power for selfish purposes.

"To create our workings, we spread the magic between us. When the effect of channeling is divided, it takes a lesser toll. But we must be of one will and one mind, in perfect unison and agreement, for the working to be successful. That is difficult. Incredibly difficult. Which is why covens such as ours are rare. The lure of power is too much for some to ignore. But used properly, we can accomplish great feats without damage."

She held up her bare arms, arms smooth and brown, with only natural markings like scars, wrinkles, and freckles, as proof.

"And Lady Monmouth was not in agreement?"

"Cassandra wanted to save her daughter's life."

"And you didn't?" Tony asked.

"Of course we did, Inspector. But a working of such magnitude…" She shook her head, shoulders slumping. "It would have damaged every member of the coven if it were even possible. Healing the body of systemic illness is wildly complex. Healing a cut or a broken bone is simply a case of encouraging the body to speed up the natural healing process, and giving it the energy to do so. But teaching the body to recognize a part of itself as an illness is another matter entirely. We all agreed to do research, but that was not enough for her. She began workings on her own, dangerous workings that may have exposed all of us."

"So you cast her out."

"We had no choice. Please, believe me. The Sisterhood does more good in New London than you will ever know. We could not risk being exposed."

"And so you sicced me on your onetime sister to free your coven from the whole affair."

"It appeared to be the best option, as you were already involved and clearly quite capable. That was the reason for our interview. If we had not believed you clever enough, we would never have given you the information you needed to find her." Her apologetic smile made a hot flush creep up my cheeks.

Tony leaned forward and said, "She almost died, Madame. And now she carries the guilt of responsibility for two deaths that would not have been on her hands if you had taken responsibility for your own failure."

Matilda sat up straight, her shoulders settled, chin raised. She was as regal as a queen and might have given Mama a run for her money in the authority department. But Madame Matilda's regality was cool and unaffected, whereas Mama's was warm. It made the woman feel like she was not quite human.

But her voice sounded convincing enough when she said, "I am sorry, Lady St. James. You will never know how much. We all grieve the loss of our sister, deeply. If there had been any other option, we would have taken it."

"Instead, you ignored a desperate woman while she summoned the fae to learn magic to save her daughter's life because you were unreliable," I said.

The woman's face went slack with surprise. Point two for me. She had not suspected what Cassandra was doing, only that it was dark magic. "She what? You must be mistaken."

"Do you still believe me as clever and capable as you professed? Do you think I would give you this information if I was uncertain of it?"

"But, she would never—it is forbidden!"

"Oh," I said in a deadly quiet voice, "she would. She did. At least four innocent people are dead because of the lengths to which Cassandra Monmouth was willing to go for the love of her daughter. And she knew the act would kill her. Do you think being forbidden made any difference to her?"

While Madame Matilda grappled with that thought, I ran over what she had inadvertently revealed. Somewhere, the witches kept knowledge for summoning faeries, knowledge Cassandra had access to. That had only been a guess but having Matilda confirm it changed the entire landscape of possibilities. If humans still had ways to contact fae despite their exile, then perhaps fae had ways of contacting humans. Perhaps there was still a way to get to Lia.

"If summoning faeries is forbidden, how was Lady Monmouth able to do it?" Tony asked.

Matilda swallowed, and that far-away look slid over her eyes once more. A moment later she said, "I can not tell you the answer to that question."

Tony's expression hardened. "Please believe me, Madame, the only reason I am here now with Lady St. James and not twenty police officers is that I respected her request to hear you out before making any decisions. You are already breaking the law by living and practicing here. If your coven is a danger to the people of New London, I will not allow it to stand."

"And please believe me, Inspector, and with all due respect... you could not stop us. You have no proof, other than the accusations of a woman who has already been discredited by her peers. And the women of the Triumphant Sisterhood are more powerful than you can imagine, in more than simply magic."

"Except that you could not save a dying child or her mother."

They stared at one another across the table, eyes locked. I expected to see sparks flying in no time, so I stood up and brushed off my skirt.

"Everyone failed," I said. "And people have died for it. If Cassandra summoned fae, then other witches can. That is a danger for both of us. I need to know enough about the logistics to protect people from the repercussions of another such act. And if you begin to doubt my ability to connect the dots"—I pulled the silver necklace out of my pocket and let the symbol drop to the end of the chain—"remember that I am very good at finding things that are lost. I also always hedge my bets. Whatever information I share with you is only a small piece of what I know or am planning. Do not underestimate me."

"Lady St. James," Madame Matilda said in icy tones, "please take your own advice. It is only by our goodwill that you are not dead, and that you leave this building with your life and mind intact. Amnesia is not uncommon, and the inspector is in a very dangerous line of work. We would prefer to work with you, not against you, but you must understand that we will take steps to protect ourselves."

"Of course. And so will I. Which is why there are three copies of a letter kept at three separate locations around the city that will be delivered to Scotland Yard, Parliament, and The Times if anything suspicious or untoward happens to befall the inspector or me. You see, I have a very good memory. The first thing I did upon leaving you after our last meeting was draw likenesses of every woman in this room. I also had unfettered access to Lady Monmouth's laboratory while searching for her, and I learned several interesting things. So, as you can imagine, the letter contains some quite damning information. We certainly would not want that information to fall into unfriendly hands, would we?

"I encourage you to view things from my perspective. And consider sharing your information with me. I will wait for an answer. But I will not wait long. Inspector? I believe I'd like to go home."

Tony stood up, offered me an arm, and we left Matilda sitting at the table alone.

"Is all that true," Tony whispered on our way down the stairs. "You have letters with evidence waiting to be sent?"

"No. But she doesn't know that. Given how secretive she and her sisters are, I don't believe that is a chance she will take."

"Clever. But you might have just made a dangerous enemy," Tony said as he handed me into the coach.

"I hope I've just made a valuable ally."

"You make allies by threatening people? That is a novel approach."

"No, I let her know I would not be manipulated, and that we were on the same side. I just did it through a show of strength rather than one of supplication. That makes me a valuable ally instead of a weak patsy."

"Speaking of allies," he said, leaning on the door frame. "I do hope you will consider me one. I will admit I was mistaken about you, and beg your forgiveness. I was not prepared to protect people from magic, but you were, and you did. If it happens again, I will need the advice of someone who knows more than I do."

"Well, that shouldn't be hard."

He frowned at me, but I grinned, unrepentant.

"I need someone I can trust, Gwen. Someone who will help me keep the people of New London safe."

That had been hard-earned. "You can count on me, then, Inspector."

He smiled, closed the door, and banged on the side.

---

James pulled us to a stop just outside the front door of the Iron Rose. We had passed several officers who were keeping a close watch on the meetings and demonstrations growing across the city. They brandished nightsticks and grumpy expressions with equal facility as the tone of the demonstrations became more pointed and activist. They were equal citizens under the law and they already carried all the same responsibilities. Now they deserved the benefits. In fact, it was far too long in coming.

The protests and meetings were still peaceful, but if their grievances were not taken seriously, the League for Equal Rights would be throwing bricks through windows alongside the suffragettes. I made a mental note to keep a few bricks handy.

I hesitated outside the door for a long moment, gathering the courage to ask my friend to do something dangerous. If it worked, it could make Delilah the most sought-after Artificer in the city. Perhaps in all of Europe. If it didn't work, I might kill us both or unleash something catastrophic on the citizens of New London.

After a deep breath, I breezed through the door, ignoring the lingering soreness in my legs, and called, "Delilah my darling! Where are you?"

A curly head popped out from around the side of a forge. Her face was red and sweat-soaked, and she glowered at me.

"Don't stop on my account," I told her as I pulled off my gloves. "I will keep until you've finished."

She pulled a glowing hot piece of metal from the forge, carried it to an anvil using long metal tongs, and proceeded to beat the metal into compliance. When she was done, she pushed the metal back into the coals, brushed her hands on her leather apron, and wiped her face with a white rag she pulled from her pocket. "What do you want?"

"Lovely to see you too. I'm well, thanks for asking."

She scowled at me. "I have commissions, Gwen, and no time for chatter. What do you need?"

"A smile of welcome from my friend wouldn't be amiss. I did almost die, you know."

She pulled the hammer from her pocket and brandished it at me, letting me know I was about to almost die again.

"Alright," I said, both hands in the air, "no need for violence. I, too, have a commission for you. A few, actually."

She raised an eyebrow. "Go on."

"I've learned a bit more about the magic we discovered. It isn't artifice, D. At least, not in the way we think of it. It's faerie magic."

She nearly dropped the hammer. "But those are runes," she insisted, "just altered."

"Not exactly. They are the precursor to many of the runes we use. We were right that they were related to artificery, but we had the relationship backward. The way I understand it, these were part of the magic the fae traitors taught to humans during the wars.

But the magic wasn't reliable enough to empower everyday items for stable, predictable artificery, so the dwarves altered, simplified, and codified it. But that process removed the runes ability to channel magic, and can only focus natural forces like electromagnetic fields, or heat. What you and I re-discovered is that the early fae runes can be used to power magic if the sequence is right. No channeler needed."

Her gaze flitted back and forth as she thought through all the implications of that before landing on me and narrowing suspiciously. "If I'm willing to accept that, it means someone else out there has access to fae magic instead of just altered artificery."

"Yes."

"It doesn't change our situation much. It's still highly dangerous information, and we still don't know who has access to it."

"Well, we know that at least three of the people who had access to it are dead."

"Tell me why that's my business?"

"Because if you don't develop the knowledge, someone else will. Someone who may not have your scruples."

Her lips thinned into an unhappy line. "That's true enough."

"You haven't used it yet, have you?"

"Of course, I haven't! Who do you take me for?"

"What would you say to a wealthy benefactor? Someone who can fund your research in exchange for a few new toys?"

"I'd say you're out of your slagging mind."

"Maybe," I conceded. "But I do have a lot of money."

"This might put me in trouble with the Artificer's Guild. They aren't happy about my success already, imagine what they would say if I began flaunting brand new technology they didn't discover?"

"You would be rich enough not to care what they think."

Delilah loved making money. Not because she was greedy; the woman led a relatively simple life, but because the money represented her success. It was proof that she was good—more than good—at her craft and that she deserved to be included in the ranks of expert Artificers. Her resistance was fading.

She leaned over the table between us and pointed the hammer at me. "It wouldn't be safe. I'd have to cut down on the commissions I take, and you'd have to be willing to test the gadgets. I also reserve the right to use the discoveries in new inventions."

I folded my arms. "Only if we both agree they are safe and won't release this knowledge to the public."

"It's going to cost you, Lady St. James."

"I knew that already."

Delilah spit in her broad palm and held it out to me.

I watched the gob of spit slide across her hand and said, "Delilah, that is disgusting. Let's just write up a contract, shall we?"

That earned me another glare, but I ignored it as I pulled a set of blueprints out of my bag and unrolled them on the table. "Now, here are some ideas I've had."

After leaving Delilah to examine the schematics, I stopped at my lawyer's office to ask him to draw up the contract, and sign a few papers to fund a few new projects and... charities.

It turned out Cassandra had not been lying. She made me Claire's legal guardian and the arbiter of her estate. When Claire died, control of the estate had legally transferred to me. The title and estate of Monmouth itself would, of course, revert to the crown, to be doled out later when someone pleased the reigning monarch. But I now owned several small properties and the liquid assets that were meant to have been Claire's dowry.

I looked down at the papers I had just signed. Claire should have been alive to enjoy these, but I hoped my decision would honor her memory and the selflessness she had shown in the last few moments of her life.

Sam and Sally would never have to worry about their futures again, and the other children who had been kidnapped would all have safe places to live. They could go to school and make lives for themselves that did not include hard labor in factories. It was a very small piece of good amidst the tragedy, but it was good worth holding on to. I tucked the papers into my bag and lost myself in thought.

We had survived, at least most of us had, and we deserved a bit of hope and happiness. But there were still too many unanswered questions to let me rest easy. Who was Mr. Capstone? If he wasn't tied to Cassandra, what was he planning and why had he contracted to kidnap children from the orphanage?

Who was the stranger at the ball who had given me Cassandra's necklace? How had he gotten it, how did he know I needed it, and why had he given it to me?

And more than that, sitting at the back of my mind with an ice pick planted in my brain, was the knowledge that Lia was alive. The knowledge wouldn't let me rest. It was a constant pain that would not abate or lessen.

She was on the other side of whatever kept the mortal world and the Sunset Lands apart, and apparently, it wasn't an insurmountable barrier. The question was, how could I reach across without endangering everyone on my side of the line?

When I got home, I locked myself in the study and pulled the bottle from the secret drawer in my desk. It only took a couple of swallows, but euphoria hit and softened all the sharp edges of my thoughts until they rattled around in my brain without cutting it to bloody shreds.

A croaking sound made me raise my head to see Aristotle on his perch. He hopped to the windowsill, down to the floor, and walked across the room with stately grace. He may have exaggerated his injuries, but he still didn't trust his wings enough to fly. When he got to the desk, he tilted his head and waited to be picked up.

"Well, of course, Your Majesty," I said, lifting him to the desktop as lassitude stole over me.

He strutted around, picking at my books and papers, then stopped, tilted his head at me, and said, "Save the girl?"

Cassandra, Claire, the girl and boy who had been murdered. I hadn't saved them.

Sally, Virginia, and the rest? They were safe, at least mostly.

And Lia?

I folded my right arm on the books and lay my head on my elbow, running my fingers over the soft feathers on the raven's back and thinking about everything I would need to learn and do, and all the risks I would have to be willing to take.

"Yes, my friend," I said at last. "We're going to save the girl."

## THE END

*To read the exclusive epilogue from Sally's point of view, go to **nicoleyork.com/sallysepilogue***
Keep reading for Chapter One of Moonstruck; Book Two of The Gwen St. James Affair

# Chapter One of *Moonstruck*

## SAM

Sam never wanted to pick a pocket so much as he did while watching the visitors of the New London Zoo crowd together, staring in oblivious rapture at the sleeping baby unicorn. He could have stuffed his hands into their pockets while blowing a kazoo and they never would have noticed.

To make matters worse, the late spring day was warm and balmy, and half the men had unbuttoned their jackets and waistcoats to take advantage of any stray breeze. The flash of fine watch chains, rings, cufflinks, and jeweled brooches caught his eye no matter which way he turned. Little coin purses dangled from wrists and the bulge of wallets screamed at him from vest and trouser pockets.

He could clean this place out before anyone realized what was missing, and now that he owned fine clothes, he would blend in. No one would look at him twice as he made off with their possessions.

Sam folded his arms and tucked his hands safely into his armpits.

It was useless to imagine dipping his fingers into the waistcoat of some careless mark and walking away with a shiny new timepiece. He wasn't a thief, anymore; he was the ward of Lady Gwenevere St. James, and all the fine things he used to lust after were now part of his daily life.

He and his sister were respectable now, and they could do things only wealthy people did: like buy sweets at a bakery, or stand around with other wealthy people watching a baby unicorn sleep. Neither of them needed to steal. He leaned on the rail and told himself he was glad about that.

Lady Gwen joined him, her umbrella and hat combining to cast as much shade as a small tree. She used a full black umbrella instead of the white lacy parasols the other ladies used. Unlike the rest of the crowd, Lady Gwen had no desire to display her rank and wealth with jewelry. Whatever money she carried was tucked away in places Sam couldn't guess at. The last time she paid for something, the money had been under her hat. Hard to pickpocket a lady's hair.

"Why the long sigh?" she asked.

He thought over how much to say. This was the first time he'd ever visited the zoo without having to hide from security, and he was nearly thirteen years old. Instead of dodging guards and scaling trees, laughing under his breath as his clever hiding spots went overlooked by the confused bobbies on his trail, they strolled from exhibit to exhibit without a care in the world.

"I...thought the unicorns would be more exciting," he said. "All they do is lay around and sleep. I don't understand why everyone was so keen to see them, they don't look like nothin' but skinny horses."

"Don't look like *anything,*" Lady Gwen corrected with a smile. "Do try to avoid double negatives before mid-day, my dear, they make my teeth ache."

Sally leaned far over the fence to peer at the little white animal and said in a dreamy voice, "I don't know how you can say that, Sammy. They're perfectly magical. Look how small the foal is with its pink nose and bit of horn poking out of its hair."

Sam frowned at his sister, then at the animal. It was smaller than a horse, with spindly legs more like a goat, and a little downy tuft of a beard on its chin. Its neck was a bit longer and it had feathery hair around its cloven hooves, but so did some horses.

He said, "Can we go see the lions, instead? Or at least something with claws and teeth?"

Lady Gwen considered him for a moment, her dark eyes sparkling with laughter, but her voice was solemn when she asked, "Sally, why are there so few unicorns in captivity?"

"Because unicorns are both clever and elusive," Sally said as if reciting a passage from a book. "Their white fur takes on the hue of the light reflected by their surroundings, and they're as nimble as a goat, so they can climb trees and sheer cliffs to get away from their pursuers. And if a unicorn is cornered, it can strike with its hooves and horn."

"And how many men have unicorns killed?" Lady Gwen asked.

"Twice as many as lions for every human encounter."

"Why?"

"Because men *expect* lions to be dangerous."

Lady Gwen gave him an affectionate pat on the shoulder. "There's a lesson in there somewhere, Samuel."

So, the Unicorn was more interesting than he thought, but the beast still just lay in the shade, panting, with its legs curled up to the side.

"Can we at least see a manticore or something?" he asked.

"Manticores are only a myth, I'm afraid. If they are real, we've never seen one. There are none in this zoo, in any case. However," –Lady Gwen pulled a watch out of some pocket so well concealed Sam hadn't even seen it– "we can watch the crocodiles. Inspector Hardwicke will meet us there, shortly."

Sally sighed one of those girl sighs full of secret wishes. She thought nobody noticed, but every time the Inspector visited Lady Gwen, Sally's cheeks turned pink.

He kept the knowledge to himself, and his hands in his pockets, as they walked along the paved path toward the crocodile pit. A welcome breeze lifted the sweaty hair off his forehead but carried with it the sticky-sweet scent of caramel apples mixed with the ripe stench of animal dung and a distant humming sound, like angry bees.

Lady Gwen raised her parasol as if she'd had a grand idea. "While we're walking, let's make good use of our time. Sally, what are the medicinal uses of Monkshood?"

Sally rattled off an answer filled with words that sounded like a foreign language, so he ignored them. Ever since they moved into Lady Gwen's townhouse, his sister had been on a mission to learn everything about everything. She spent hours curled up in a chair in the study, reading obscure books by the steady light of Dwarven

Lamps. Lady Gwen seemed to think it was a good idea, so they talked about useless facts whenever Sally's tutor wasn't teaching her how to be a lady.

*Girls.* Couldn't they just enjoy a few quiet moments to think?

Sam had a tutor, too, but he was learning to read and speak like a gentleman, not memorize rubbish about plants. The speaking part was harder than the reading. He would always sound like he was from the Narrows, but as long as he had money, who cared how he sounded?

"Did you get any of that, Samuel?"

He hesitated for only a moment before answering Lady Gwen. "You can use it for fevers, gout and," —what was the word?— "rheumatism."

Lady Gwen blinked at him. "So you can. Well, *you* cannot, don't get it into your head to muck about with any. Just touching the plant could kill you. But those are a few of its traditional uses, in any case. Well done."

"If it's so dangerous, why are we learning about it?"

She stopped walking and bent to look him in the eye. "Of all the things to learn in the world, what do you suppose we should know most about: the innocuous things, or the things that can do us harm?"

He thought that over as they approached the crocodile pit, wondering if he should learn about crocodiles, too, since they were dangerous. Inspector Hardwicke waited there, almost a head taller than the people around him and twice as wide. His hair was a few shades lighter than Sally's dark blonde, and he had the jaw of a boxer. The man also had big, capable hands that needed wide pockets.

Sam smiled and flexed his smaller, nimble fingers.

The inspector must have heard them coming because he turned, bowed his head, and smiled at Lady Gwen for just a moment too long. That gave Sam the chance to slip away from her side and blend into the crowd around the viewing platform.

"Lady St.James," the inspector said, using her formal address the way he only did in public, then bobbed his head at Sally. "Miss Dawes."

Sally blushed. She was such a ninny. The man barely even glanced at her, what did she have to blush for?

"Good morning, Inspector," Lady Gwen said, stepping close enough for a handshake.

Sam edged around a woman and her children to slip up on the inspector from the right side. The man was right-handed, so when he reached out to shake Lady Gwen's hand it pulled the fabric of the coat away from his body. Sam slipped his fingers into the exposed pocket.

Nothing. The Inspector was learning.

Sam backed up, hurried around the edge of the crowd, waited a moment as if he'd lagged behind, then ran in from the opposite direction, waving and shouting, "Tony!" before tripping and plowing into Sally's back.

She squealed and tumbled forward into the Inspector and the three of them slammed together with an *oof*, arms flailing as they steadied themselves. Sam slid his hands over all the usual spots but felt no wallet or watch or bulge that indicated valuables.

The inspector righted himself, straightened the two of them, and asked, "Are you all right?"

Sally blushed again, this time as red as the roses Mrs. Chapman put on the table in the foyer, and mumbled something about being fine.

"Samuel," Lady Gwen sighed. "That was clumsy. A little subtlety goes a long way."

The inspector narrowed his eyes, then widened them as realization set in. He patted a spot on the outside of his jacket with his right hand before checking the more obvious places Sam already searched.

Gotcha.

"Not this time, scamp," the inspector said, satisfied his possessions were safe.

"You're getting better, I guess."

"Maybe next time."

The Inspector was a good cop and an honest man. He'd never win at this game. Sam hid his amusement behind a mask of disappointment and said with a shrug, "I suppose so."

"Shall we have a look at our reptilian friends?" Lady Gwen asked.

The four of them made their way around the crowd of spectators to an open spot along the fence. A steep embankment lay on the opposite side of the wrought iron, leading down to a pond where the dozing crocodiles sunned themselves or floated lazily through the green scum on top of the water, leaving brownish trails behind them.

A few of the onlookers leaned far out and pointed as one of the crocodiles sank beneath the surface, which was a precarious place to balance with so much danger beneath. What would happen if one of them fell in? After a scream and a great splash, the crocodiles would sink and turn to swim toward the unlucky victim as they struggled to climb the muddy bank. Some people would toss jackets down the slope while the braver citizens held hands to form a human bridge.

But crocodiles were faster than they looked, and when one or two climbed the bank and opened their toothy mouths--

"What news?" Lady Gwen asked the inspector.

Sam pulled his attention away from the daydream and focused on listening while his eyes roamed over the scaly predators.

"We've been watching the building and every delivery for months. There is no sign the mysterious Mr. Capstone has been communicating or paying anyone from the orphanages by hiding bribes in the laundry deliveries," the Inspector said. He sounded tired as he took off his hat and ran his hand through his hair.

Lady Gwen said, "Then either Mrs. Edwards was lying about the bribes, or Mr. Capstone has reneged on their arrangement."

"I doubt whether he had agreements with the other orphanages since no more children have gone missing under *suspicious* circumstances."

Suspicious was the inspector's code word for magic. Sam shivered despite the heat. He remembered what magic felt like the first time he'd encountered it, so many months ago. It felt like *home*. It was a mother's arms reaching out with the promise of love and safety, only to drag him down a narrow alley at night where the only person waiting for him was a kidnapper.

No orphan who ever dreamed of being rescued by their long-lost family could resist the pull of *that* magic.

Luckily for Sam, his sister had been with him. Sally fought for him like an angry badger, but she was no match for a full-grown man. Sam had tried to save her but got a knock on the head for his trouble, and spent the rest of the night running back to the townhouse on Grosvenor Square with tears streaming down his face, looking for help.

Lady Gwen and the Inspector tracked the kidnapper, saved Sally, and stopped the witch responsible for the kidnappings before she sacrificed the orphan children to save her sick daughter. If there had been no more kidnappings, maybe it really was over. Maybe he could sleep without nightmares, or without waking to the sound of Sally's muffled crying through the wall that separated their rooms.

"I am glad to hear it," Lady Gwen said. "Though, it makes catching him much more difficult."

"Assuming he is a real person."

Lady Gwen made a very un-lady-like sound.

"I know you don't want to admit it," The inspector said, keeping his voice low enough to blend with the hum of the crowd, "but we must consider whether Mrs. Edwards lied to cover her involvement. It is possible the witch worked directly with Mrs. Edwards to arrange the kidnappings. Mr. Capstone may not exist, at all."

"Do you believe that?"

He sighed and rubbed the back of his neck with one hand. "No. I don't. But we must consider all possibilities. It's been months with no proof for our trouble. If I don't find something convincing soon, my superiors are going to recall the men I've been using."

"I know how much you've fought for this investigation. Don't lose heart. There is one strong piece of her testimony in favor of Mr. Capstone being a real person: the particulars Mrs. Edwards provided. If we assume she was lying, she chose to fabricate details strangely unrelated to the truth. Why make Mr. Capstone a Dwarf who wanted to kidnap the orphans to scare humans?"

"Why, indeed."

"And scaring the humans had nothing to do with Lady Monmouth's plan to save Clai—her daughter." Lady Gwen's voice caught on the girl's name and Sam flinched. He had held Claire's hand as she died, her skin slowly growing cold once the spell keeping her alive vanished. She'd only been a year or two older than him. Of course, sacrificing other children to save Claire had been wrong. But in a strange way, Sam envied Claire such a mother. If their father had loved him and Sally half as much, perhaps he wouldn't have abandoned them.

The wind picked up again, dragging away the stale mud and pondwater scent of the crocodile pond and bringing with it...voices? What sounded earlier like the faraway buzzing of bees matured into the ruckus of rhythmic shouting.

The conversation behind him paused.

Lady Gwen tilted her head to listen. "Another demonstration?"

"A big one," the Inspector said. "Had to go several blocks out of my way to avoid them, but it was peaceful."

"That brings us to my point," Lady Gwen said in a voice Sam had to strain to hear. "I think this Mr. Capstone business is more likely tied to the impending legislation for equality. He is the only piece of the puzzle that doesn't fit into Lady Monmouth's plan to save her daughter through sacrificial magic. She used compulsion spells to control everyone she worked with, but Mrs. Edwards had no spells upon her when we questioned her at the orphanage."

"The bit about scaring the humans is suggestive, I'll grant you. But it would only make Parliament less likely to approve the bill."

"I never suggested which side of the affair he was on. If he is working for equality, he may be misguided in believing humans would acquiesce through fear. But if he is trying to suppress the bill because he does not want elves and dwarves to be granted hereditary titles alongside humans, then perhaps he seeks to discredit them."

"True, enough. But we can speak of it another time." The Inspector's voice carried a tone that said he meant something other than what he'd said, but Sam wasn't sure what. When he spoke again, his voice was lower and harder to hear. "You still plan to go through with this?"

Through with what? It didn't sound as if the Inspector liked the idea of Lady Gwen doing whatever it was. Sam began weaving through the crowd, casually shifting his weight and leaning as if he were only looking for an opportunity to view the exhibit from a better angle.

"You know what we saw that night," Lady Gwen replied in the same tone of voice she used when teaching Sam something he wasn't interested in learning. "Just because the Fae have done nothing overt since Samhain" —she said something Sam couldn't make out above the growing noise of the protests outside— "and unless we know how she gained access to that magic, there will be nothing to stop them. And if Mr. Capstone is still active, I will not risk anything happening to Sally. She's already been touched by magic, and magic leaves traces."

Sam's stomach tightened into a fist.

"We will learn nothing if you work yourself until you cannot function. Don't think I do not see it on your face."

"That," her voice was crisp and detached, "is not your concern, Inspector."

He ignored her switch to a formal address and stepped closer, raising his hands as if he would hold Lady Gwen's, but stopped. "You are taking too many chances, Gwen. I don't—"

Inspector Hardwicke didn't have a chance to finish his thought, because the protesters had drawn closer, and the next shout of, "Polity for equality! Polity for equality!" was loud enough to make everyone turn. Vibrations from hundreds of feet made the ground tremble.

"What's a polity?" Sam asked.

The Inspector spun, surprised to find Sam standing behind him. Sam smiled and held up the inspector's badge and wallet. The man's jaw tightened, and Sam dropped the pilfered items onto his palm, still grinning. Tony wouldn't ask how Sam had known where the items were, and Sam wouldn't offer the information. That was part of the game.

"Better luck next time, guv."

The inspector stuffed his valuables back into his pockets with thin lips and a grim expression. "I thought I had you."

"I guess you need more practice, after all."

A loud crash sounded outside the walls of the zoo, followed by a single scream. That scream was joined by another, then another, growing like a snowball, picking up shouts of indignation and ending in a sustained howl from the crowd of protestors.

"That doesn't sound promising," Lady Gwen said.

"It does not," the Inspector agreed.

Behind them, the crowd of Zoogoers shifted and muttered. The atmosphere of the place changed. Like dropping ink in water, the sense of discomfort, of fear, billowed out in invisible tendrils infecting everything it reached. Sam's whole body tensed, muscles primed to move, to flee, to hide.

Sally met his eyes, the same knowledge on her face. The lessons taught by life on the streets were carved beneath the skin, down in their very bones.

"We should go," Lady Gwen and the Inspector said at the same time.

"This way," the Inspector said, and ushered them down the path leading away from the front of the Zoo. A gust of wind dragged all the tree limbs toward the fleeing crowd, and Sam's heartbeat sped up at the acrid burn of smoke in his nostrils. Something in the city was on fire. The ground continued to shake.

Zoo visitors who weren't hurrying toward the exit were frozen, staring wide-eyed at the walls. Even people without the finely honed senses of street urchins felt the sense of impending danger.

"Come on," the Inspector ordered in his most officious voice. "Don't just stand there, move along! That's right, Ma'am, this way, please."

As their party gathered more frightened visitors, Sam's desire to flee grew so strong that the only thing keeping him moving in an orderly fashion was Sally's hand clamped painfully on his own. She was still bigger than him, still stronger, and just as scared, but so were the other visitors. They bumped one another, muttered in frightened voices every time a scream rose from outside the walls, and several people tried to part from the group, thinking they would be safer on their own. Sam wasn't sure they were wrong.

"Keep calm," the Inspector called to them over the rising shouts, cries, and crashes in the city. "Everything will be fine. We're going to the opposite side of the zoo, where we can exit safely. Sir, stay with the group please, thank you."

A siren wailed nearby, the sound soaring above the racket of shouting, and several ladies gave little cries of distress. Sam was surprised to find that, even in his fear, he had room for disgust. Fire should have been less terrifying to people who lived in stone houses. And sirens were only used by the Metropolitan Fire Brigade that served the West End and downtown, equipped with all the latest artificery to keep rich people—and their money—safe. In the Narrows, the fire brigade consisted of what buckets, axes, and wet blankets the inhabitants managed to gather. If they were lucky, the older wagons would show up before the fire spread and too many people died of smoke inhalation.

Lady Gwen turned and said over her shoulder in a low voice, "Stay close to me."

Sam knew that tone of voice. Sally tightened her grip and he squeezed back.

The smoke thickened, and the group huddled together like frightened sheep being driven before the storm, Inspector Hardwicke as the sheepdog snapping at their heels.

A horse screamed and the entire group flinched and froze. The shouting and screaming from outside the walls reached a crescendo, followed by a crash that made Sam jump, and the wall not ten feet in front of them crumbled inward in a cloud of dust and madness. For a heartbeat, everything moved in slow motion. The fancy new fire engine followed the tumbling brick as it toppled sideways through the broken wall and onto the path, dragging with it the screaming team of horses. A ton of wood and metal crashed to the ground, the siren stopped and the reservoir broke, sending a wave of shin-deep water rushing toward them hard enough to pull Sam and everyone around him off their feet.

He lost grip of Sally's hand and rolled, then hit the iron fence post separating the path from the smaller exhibits. He grabbed the rail to steady himself, then pulled himself upright. The shiny brass horn of the siren, etched with runes to amplify sound, lay in a muddy puddle at his feet.

A crowd of people swarmed through the break in the wall, some holding signs, some wearing the frantic expression of hunted animals, and others with the bright gleam of destruction in their eyes. They ran in every direction, leaping over the sopping bodies of the other visitors who had been dragged to the ground.

"Sally!" He yelled, but the crowd caught him up, and he could do nothing but get dragged along in the press of running bodies, even as he heard Lady Gwen scream his name.

Instinct took over.

He turned with the tide and ran as fast as his sturdy legs could carry him, trying to separate himself from the crowd, searching for the first opportunity to break away into someplace dark and hidden. But they pressed in on one another like a living wall, and when one person fell, the rest trampled them in their haste to flee. Sam squeezed between two men, avoided getting kicked, and pushed himself toward the edge of the crowd near the fence. Someone stepped on his foot, he stumbled, grabbed a sleeve to steady himself, was jerked off his feet, and hit the path hard enough to knock the wind from his lungs.

Someone stepped on his leg and he cried out, curling in on himself and trying to roll away but stomping feet hit the ground everywhere. If he didn't move, he would be crushed. A hand curled around his wrist and pulled. Sam tried to help, scrabbling at the stone even as someone kicked him hard in the ribs trying to leap over him.

He hit the ground again, this time on his side, but kept rolling and panting, sobs of pain breaking through with every other breath. He couldn't stay on the ground. He pushed to his feet to find himself on one of the lanes that turned off the main path toward a closed exhibit. He had managed to roll beneath the barricade.

He was safe.

At least, he thought he was safe until he looked up into the face of the person who had pulled him free.

*To continue reading Moonstruck, go to https://amzn.to/4OOwVuj*

## *Also By*

## Other titles by this author include

**SERIES: The Gwen St. James Affair**

**Moonstruck**

Gwenevere St. James may be a lady, but she's never been interested in playing by the rules. Instead of ingratiating herself into high society, she spent a decade searching the world and studying the occult for a way to find her lost twin sister.

So when a coven of witches offers her a missing person's case in return for a book of spells guaranteed to locate her twin at last, Gwen cannot refuse, even if it means doing something she swore she would never do: attend a country party for the wealthy elite.

But the case is far more complicated and dangerous than she expected. Villagers whisper of ghostly riders in the night, and an unknown monster hunts the nearby forest, putting everyone in danger.

As people go missing and innocent bystanders die, Gwen must make a choice: how many lives will she risk for the thing she wants most?

## SERIES: The Ververse Chronicles

## The Founding Trilogy

### The Laws of Founding

*Legends and fairytales aren't all they're cracked up to be; especially when they're trying to kill you.*

Since losing her father, Allie Chapter has stumbled through life, using friends, books, and alcohol to numb the pain. When she wakes up in the wrong world and gets kidnapped by supernatural forces, everything changes. Allie learns she is a Walker, blessed–or cursed–with the power to travel between different versions of Earth.

Allie must rely on Ronan, her devastatingly handsome mentor, to guide her through magical worlds she's only dreamed of, and teach her the Laws that govern all Walkers–Laws she must not break at any cost.

But a failed assassination attempt turns her dream into a nightmare. The Ververse is full of danger, and whoever wants her dead may also be behind her father's accident. As she searches for answers, Allie must decide what makes breaking the Laws worthwhile: love, or revenge?

But when she learns she is a Walker, one of the rare few with the ability to travel between different versions of Earth, an entirely new problem arises: can she master her powers fast enough to figure out why someone wants her dead?

**The Founding Lie**

*The monsters we face aren't always the ones we expect.*

As the newest member of the interdimensional police force, it's Allie Chapter's responsibility to find out who is stealing magical weapons and bring them to justice before war breaks out.

She's certain the thief is Goll MacMorna, the man who still haunts her nightmares, and she intends to prove it...no matter the cost.

She will either free herself from her nightmares or discover the real monster is the one in the mirror.

**The Founding War**

*"Necessity knows no cruelty. She only makes demands, and we answer as seems best to us."*

Allie Chapter went from aimless college student to interdimensional cop in less than a year. Now she's an outlaw, hunted by both sides of an oncoming war that threatens to destroy the Eververse. As her newly discovered magic grows in strength, Allie realizes she might be the only one who can stop the war and save countless innocent lives from obliteration. But her allies have betrayed her, and powers too large to comprehend are manipulating the battlefield, hoping to use her gifts for their own purposes. With no one left to trust, Allie must rely on her wits and her conscience to make the ultimate decision: sacrifice her future–and maybe her life–for the greater good, or save the people she loves and let the Eververse fall.

# Acknowledgements

No novel happens on its own, and I have been blessed to be surrounded by amazing artists, craftspeople, and friends who both supported me and helped refine this book to make it something to be proud of. Huge thanks to the following incredible folks:

Elena Nedeleva, the cover illustrator, who brought Gwen and her world to life in a way I never thought possible.

My line editor, Abbie Lynn Smith, who organized and standardized all the mistakes of my wild writing brain so the book would actually be legible for readers.

Alpha reader, Lauren Sevier, who always encourages me and makes me feel like a way bigger author than I really am. I appreciate you so much!

Beta readers like Abbie Lynn Smith and Frank Booker, who not only catch mistakes and give feedback, but are free with their support and praise.

And finally—and most importantly—to my family. You put up with my writerly eccentricities, listen to me blather about characters, help me work through plotholes, and still manage to love me, anyway. Not only would I be a far less effective writer without you, I would be a far poorer person in every way. I love you more than anything, always.

Ingram Content Group UK Ltd.
Milton Keynes UK
UKHW010717200423
420491UK00001B/98